THE BABYLON GENE

Alex Churton is a writer and composer. He was the founder editor of *Freemasonry Today*, and is an acknowledged expert on Western Esotericism. He is the author of ten non-fiction titles on subjects such as alchemy, the Rosicrucians and Judas. This is his first novel.

THE BABYLON GENE

ALEX CHURTON

HEAD
ZEUS

First published in the UK in 2012 by Head of Zeus Ltd.

This paperback edition published in 2013 by Head of Zeus Ltd.

Copyright © Alex Churton, 2012

The moral right of Alex Churton to be identified as the author of this work has been asserted in accordance with the Copyright, Designs and Patents Act of 1988.

9 7 5 3 1 2 4 6 8

A CIP catalogue record for this book is available from the British Library.

Paperback ISBN: 9781908800473
eBook ISBN: 9781908800848

Printed and bound by CPI Group (UK) Ltd, Croydon, CR0 4YY.

Head of Zeus Ltd
Clerkenwell House
45-47 Clerkenwell Green
London, EC1R 0HT

www.headofzeus.com

Author's Note

The Babylon Gene is a work of fiction based on real events and situations of recent history. While interpretations of those events and situations are entirely the author's, the historical, scientific and theological background to the story has been thoroughly researched.

The Yezidis are a real people, the inheritors of an ancient spiritual and historical tradition. All of the Yezidi characters in the novel are fictional. The characters' involvement in military and intelligence operations is likewise fictional. A select bibliography is included at the end of the novel.

I dedicate this work to the cherished memory of my late friend, Michael Embleton, who stood by the book, and me, through thick and thin.

No eternal reward will forgive us now for wasting the dawn.

Jim Morrison, 'THE WASP (Texas Radio and the Big Beat)';
The Doors, 1971

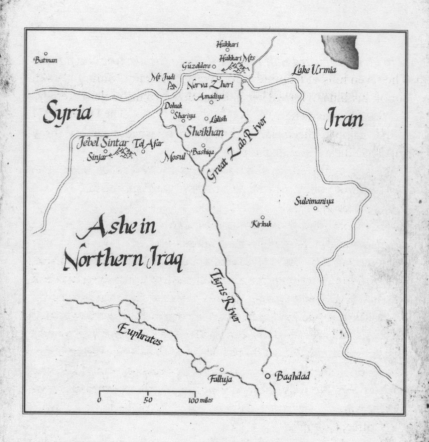

1

The seven hills of Istanbul were awash with rain. Mahmut Aslan shook his blue nylon jacket and handed it to his male secretary.

'So, Ali, what's new?'

Ali gripped the jacket tightly; rain splashed over his shiny shoes. 'Did sir enjoy his holiday?'

'Yes, sir enjoyed his holiday and is thrilled to be back. The very sight of you, Corporal Ali, fills me with optimism.'

'Optimism, sir?'

'My next holiday cannot be far away.'

Ali winced. First goal to the Colonel.

The district of Ümraniye, where Colonel Aslan had his office, was nothing to write home about, but Ali Wilmaz liked his desk job. It was a lot better than clean-up ops on the Iraqi border.

In May '93, Ali had seen thirty unarmed colleagues executed by the Kurdistan Workers Party (PKK) in Diyarbakir province, southeast Turkey. Now, in spite of more than a decade of elimination tactics – and the odd political concession – the PKK was back at war. Nobody relished a posting to the southeast; it was a dirty war.

'Coffee, Colonel?'

'Later, Ali.' Aslan looked up from the pile of reports on his desk. 'Why wasn't my coffee here when I arrived?'

'You were late, sir.'

'Then why isn't it cold on my desk?'

Ali coughed. 'You're often late, Colonel.'

'Of course I'm late! Half of Istanbul is late when it rains!'

1

'Of course, sir. The rain.'

'Of course, Ali. And Ali...'

'Sir!'

'Clean your shoes. You're not a seagull!'

Ali retreated to the makeshift reception.

Aslan slumped back in his moulded plastic chair, lifted his feet onto the desk, lit his pipe and contemplated the ghostly ripple of reflected rainfall that hovered over the portrait of the great Mustapha Kemal Atatürk opposite.

Everything Aslan did came under Atatürk's keen eye; dead for sixty-six years, the giant still watched over Turkey. Atatürk, father of the Turks – a man with a dream.

Aslan ground his teeth around the pipe stem. Should he turn on the desk light. The dim room suited his melancholy. Adding the tedious half-light of a 60 watt bulb would be sacrilegious. His lair was a temple of gloom.

What had he done to deserve this fifth-floor excuse for an office in the National Security Council's Police Liaison Department, perched high – but not high enough – above one of the dreariest quarters of Istanbul?

What had he done? Aslan had done everything: exemplary field operations, intelligence gathering, and the grin-and-bear-it arse-licking that goes with any elevation through the poisoned gateau of bureaucracy. As the interface between the government's security operations and the military-dominated National Security Council, he tried to avoid making enemies, but sometimes standing tall meant standing in someone's way. His loyalty was simple: Turkey. No party; no philosophy. Turkey was the only cause Aslan took as sacred.

At least his holidays had improved. Thailand had been a lot more entertaining for a widower than sunny, divided Cyprus.

Aslan tore off the precious few vacation days from his roll calendar to reveal the date: Wednesday 10 March 2004.

*

2

The red bulb on his nicotine-greased phone flickered into half-life with a strangled whine.

'Celalettin Celik for you, sir.'

'Put him through, Ali.'

'Colonel Aslan?'

'Yes, Celik, what is it?'

'I have a press conference in half an hour, Colonel. Any comments before I request a news blackout?'

Aslan squinted, looked up at General Atatürk for inspiration, found none, and took a sharp intake of pipe smoke. What the hell was Istanbul's police chief talking about?

'I pride myself, Celik, on knowing most of what's happening in this city, but mind-reading is not my strong suit.'

'Terrorism, Colonel. You've heard, surely?'

Aslan drank deeply from the coffee his secretary had just handed him. 'Thank you, Ali. You can go.'

'Sir, there's just—'

'Later, Ali.' Aslan returned his attention to the police chief as Ali lingered in the doorway. 'Terrorism? More than heard of it, Celik.'

'Pardon me, Colonel. I meant have you heard about last night?'

'I've just come off a late plane from Bangkok. I haven't even had time to wash.'

'Welcome home, Colonel. I'm surprised your secretary has not already acquainted you with the facts.'

'My secretary, Celik, can hardly make a decent cup of coffee.' Aslan emptied the cup and winked at the anxious Ali, indicating with his left hand that he'd best stay. 'So, what is it?'

'Bomb. Masonic Lodge in Kartal District.'

'Freemasons?' Aslan licked his forefinger and smoothed his thin, fair eyebrows.

'There are fatalities. Our boys have sealed the place off, naturally.'

Aslan thought for a second, then clenched his fist. 'Tell the press as little as possible. Don't speculate. Just the usual things:

"Highly experienced teams of experts are covering all leads." The voice of calm and reason. You do it so well.'

Aslan winked at Ali again. 'Now, Celik, you've spoken to the governor, haven't you?'

'Of course, Colonel. Late last night. He's already made a statement. Announced a full press briefing for Monday morning.'

'Man's a lunatic.' Aslan swept back his long, blonde hair and took a deep breath. 'I'll meet you at the scene in an hour.' He looked at the sheets of rain belting against the stained windows. 'Better make that an hour and a half.'

Aslan slammed the receiver into its cradle. 'Ali!'

'Sir!'

'Soap.'

2

Hemmed in by rusting Dogans and Sahins, Ali deftly manoeuvred his boss's olive BMW up the steep slipperiness of Suleiman Caddesi. The snail's pace soon slowed to a mechanical rigor mortis.

Aslan pondered the scene. A traffic jam is a perfectly democratic phenomenon, he thought. When the wheels stop moving, everyone's equal.

He cleared some condensation from the rear window. If Ümraniye was soulless, Kartal was pure carrion: grey commercial blocks stripped to the bone. The occasional swathe of faded pink-and-yellow tiling, intended to subdue the monotony, became itself monotonous: lined up above the drab shop fronts like so many rotten teeth.

Down came the rain, blurring everything.

'It's the wipers, sir.'

Aslan looked up from Ali's briefing document on the previous night's events, spread across his knees. 'Wipers, Ali? Is that what they're calling terrorists these days?'

'No, sir. These old cars. Their wipers can't deal with the rain. That's why people are always late in Istanbul.'

Aslan shook his head at Ali's perennial genius for stating the obvious. 'Was it raining last night, Ali?'

'Belting down, sir.'

'Deduction?'

'Sir?'

'Well, Corporal Ali, those guys who hit the Association of the

Grand Temple of Free and Accepted Masons of Turkey must have arrived late.'

'I don't understand, sir.'

'Most of the Freemasons had left by the time the shooting started.'

'Amateurs, sir. Hitching a ride on the al-Qaeda bandwagon.'

'Paid to think, are you, Corporal?'

'Forgive me, Colonel.'

'Not at all. You think away. Many a fool taught his teacher a lesson.'

'If you say so, sir.'

'Don't you read your Rumi?'

'Sir?'

'Our great mystic poet, Jalaluddin Rumi.'

'Not since he gave up football, sir.'

Aslan laughed. 'Your first goal of the day, Ali. Well done.'

'We're nearly there, Colonel.'

Through the rain engulfing the BMW's big windscreen, Aslan could just see lines of policemen in their soaked blue jackets directing traffic away from the site of the atrocity. A CNN Turkey News transit van was obscured behind a pack of foreign photographers, TV cameramen, producers and journalists, many of them pleading with the young policemen. The policemen nervously fingered their pistol holsters.

Behind the excited throng, exhibiting their customary patience in the face of officialdom, waited the more familiar faces of news-hacks from *Hürriyet*, *Milliyet* and *Sabah* – Turkey's mass circulation dailies.

Ali slammed on the brakes and Aslan lurched forwards, his broad forehead hitting the back of the driver's seat.

'Arsehole!' Ali tore into the driver who'd skidded close to the BMW, trying to avoid a gas cylinder truck.

'Easy, easy,' counselled Aslan to his unnerved driver. 'It's only a gas truck. You can't go thirty metres in this city without one of these crawlers climbing up your arse.'

A fist banged on the nearside window of the BMW. Aslan instinctively reached for his Beretta, holstered to his left shin, then recognised the anxious face of Celik leaning out of the adjacent Merc. 'Celik! How many atrocities do you want in twenty-four hours?' Aslan lowered his window.

'Join us in my car, Colonel. I don't want any more reporters on my back. Ever since we discussed joining the EU they think they can do what they like. We can enter from the side.'

'The EU?'

'Very amusing, Colonel.' Ali stifled a laugh as he made eye contact with Aslan in the rear-view mirror.

'Thank you, Ali. Now see to the car. And Ali—'

'Sir?'

'Stay with it till I call you.'

Ali began reversing the BMW.

'Not now, Ali! Let me get out first!'

'Can I help with the door, sir?'

'Bugger the door, Ali! I'll do it myself. Like everything else round here.' Aslan heaved his big frame out of the BMW and squeezed into the back seat of Celik's Merc.

Celik was chewing an outsize thumbnail; his bloodshot eyes avoided Aslan's stare. 'Thank you, Colonel. Make yourself comfortable.'

'You were right to call me.'

'You know I'd never do anything without informing the NSC.'

'I'm not the National Security Council, Celik. Just the liaison department. And where would you be without us, eh?'

Celik gave a half smile. It was a good job he was a flexible thinker, as the complexities of the Turkish justice system were mind-boggling. His loyalties were split between the city governor, Muammar Güler; the head of the moderately Islamic Justice and Development Party – the AKP – Recep Tayip Erdogan; and the vehemently secular army. And of course there was always the chaotic court of public opinion to answer to as well. It was a lot of pressure to bear, even for Celik's broad shoulders.

Celik buttoned up his grey British Gannex raincoat and ushered Aslan out of his car and into a side alley, away from the klaxons and the rain. He tried to think of something ingratiating to say to the roughly dressed colonel. He wanted to say how much like Turkish movie heartthrob Cüneyt Arkin Aslan looked, with his slicked-back mane and tanned, ready-for-action features, but Celik doubted the compliment would have much effect. There was something annoying about Aslan. Whatever it was, it marked him out from the usual egotists, place-men and slippery smilers who populated the government. Aslan was neither easily flattered nor easily impressed. But was it modesty – or conceit?

Celik pushed the stainless-steel bar of a fire-exit door.

'Where's the light, Chief?'

Celik fumbled for the switch. Aslan heard it click, but no light appeared. The men edged forward, touching the cold concrete walls of the service corridor. Aslan felt glass crunch beneath his shoes. 'So much for the bulb.'

'The blast, Colonel.'

'Possibly.'

As they rounded a corner, the men's breathing eased. In the darkness, they could just make out a dull, door-shaped halo. Aslan gave it a hard kick. Swinging wide, the exit bar rattling in its own echo, the steel proscenium revealed a horrible scene.

3

In the grimy light of the washed-out morning, the men's eyes slowly adjusted to the gloom. The once-tidy *meyhane* was now a mangled web of steel and Formica tables, wooden chairs, broken olive oil bottles and mineral water tumblers strewn across a swamp of stale melons, cheese, pools of raki, red wine, bottled beer, bread rolls and cutlery. About the many gaping craters in the plaster, faded photographs of Alpine scenery, portraits of Atatürk, and kitsch Kaiser Wilhelms now dangled awkwardly, their glass shelters shattered. Blood congealed on table tops beneath electric wiring weirdly suspended from cracks in the false ceiling.

'Another triumph for a cause,' muttered Aslan.

'But which cause, Colonel?'

'Not Turkey's, Celik. Not ours.'

The broken glass doors of the restaurant scraped open. Three men in white chemical-resistant suits entered the dusty dining area.

'Bomb disposal, Colonel. It's a formality. Gives the TV people something to show anxious viewers.'

'Right.' Aslan pointed to a large double door to the left of the toilets. 'And through there is the Lodge itself?'

'Yes, my respected friend. Through there is the Lodge of the Association of the Grand Temple of Free and Accepted Masons of Turkey.'

Aslan's eyebrows arched as his eyes widened. 'All part of Istanbul's rich cultural heritage, no doubt. Must we be blind-folded before entering?' Aslan tried the door handle.

'Locked, Colonel. I've spoken to the Worshipful Master—'

'The who?'

'It's what we – pardon me, *they* call the president of a Lodge. "Worshipful" just means respected. It comes from England originally.'

'And "Master" just means Master?'

'A traditional honorific, Colonel. Master of the Craft. "Craft" being their word for the brotherhood of Freemasons. Anyhow, he was anxious we would not violate the Lodge.'

'Violate it? It's not sacred, is it?'

'I suppose they would like a member to be present. A formality, nothing more.'

Aslan reached into his breast pocket and withdrew a small steel contraption, like a penknife. He plunged it quickly into the lock and played with the mechanism.

'But Colonel...'

'Relax, Celik.' Aslan pushed the doors open.

An oil generator pumped a weak current into a globe-like pearl bulb in the centre of the ceiling: a precaution against Istanbul's occasional power cuts.

Below the light, a chequered floor was arranged with richly upholstered seats, set to the left and the right like choir stalls before an altar.

'So this is Freemasonry!' exclaimed Aslan as he took in the precise arrangement of the furniture – the tall, mahogany throne positioned where you might expect to find the altar, the row of high-backed chairs behind it, and the tattered pre-war Turkish flag that hung over them.

'You've never visited a Lodge before, Colonel?'

'I confess, never. I've seen pictures of course.' Aslan strode across the chequered floor. 'Clever of them to see life as a chess game.' He sat down on the leather-cushioned throne, its gold-leaf wearing thin. 'And this is?'

'The throne of Suleiman,' replied the police chief, 'where the Worshipful Master sits. And those special seats behind you are for the Past Masters – retired Worshipful Masters.'

Aslan felt a frisson of power as he spread his palms along the elegant leather armrests of King Solomon's throne. 'Feels good, Chief. But I think I need to do some reading. So, the terrorists missed their target.'

'We can't be sure of that, Colonel.'

Celik sat himself down behind a low lectern halfway down the front row of seats. On it rested a leather-bound copy of the Koran in Turkish. 'There's something odd about last night's events.'

Aslan sat up in his throne. 'No doubt of that, Celik.'

'This was nothing like the November attacks on the British Consulate, that British-owned bank and the synagogues. They were well planned, well financed – a big operation. Trucks filled with bombs. Dozens of dead. Hundreds of wounded. Big publicity for the fundamentalist cause. It made al-Qaeda look bold and powerful. And the message was obvious to anyone who watched the news.'

Aslan sighed. 'Let's stick to last night. What happened?'

Celik spread his fingers around the volume of the Koran. 'Two men carrying automatics burst into the *meyhane* at 10.59 p.m. One set off explosives strapped to his body.'

'So we won't be interviewing him.'

'Destiny decreed only two victims.'

'The other being the waiter, right? I read that in Ali's brief.'

'Forty-seven years old. Before the bomb went off, grenades were thrown and shots were fired at the diners – about forty of them. Four were wounded. The second bomber's explosives failed to detonate properly. He lost a hand and is on the critical list with stomach wounds.'

'My heart bleeds. What kind of bombs were they carrying?'

'Pipe bombs. Fourteen of them, stuffed into hunting jackets, packed with nails and wired by batteries. Another twist—'

Aslan stood up abruptly. 'Yes?'

'They brought bottles of petrol. The survivor was carried to an ambulance screaming "Damn Israel!" Said he wanted to burn the Freemasons alive.'

'If only we had a time machine, we could send these dupes back to the Middle Ages where they'd be happy.'

'It's the paperback culture, Colonel. A kind of nostalgia.'

'Romantics with pipe bombs. Potent blend. Not my idea of a night out.'

'Love and suicide have always been close, Colonel.'

'Among young fools, perhaps. If I'd mentioned suicide to my late beloved, she'd have killed me.'

The banter quickly evaporated into silence. Aslan's eyes rose to the bulb in the ceiling. It had begun to flicker. 'Jews... Freemasons... That broadens the palette. Anyone admitted responsibility?'

'Not yet, Colonel. Not even IBDA-C.'

'IBDA-C, the Islamic Great Eastern Raiders Front... Weren't they first to claim responsibility for the November bombings?'

Celik nodded.

'And did not our dear IBDA-C use pipe bombs in the mid-nineties?'

'That was against churches and nightclubs, Colonel.' Celik shook his head. 'IBDA-C weren't up to the November bombings. Not on their own, anyway. But something like this maybe?'

Aslan stared at the throne of King Solomon. 'This is no chair for me, Celik. Suleiman had wisdom and was beloved of God.' He inhaled deeply. 'So, what do we have?'

Celik shrugged. 'The usual suspects.'

'Is this usual?'

12

4

The sinuous strings of the first movement of Debussy's *La Mer* washed about the apartment. A storm was brewing. Toby Ashe looked up from his laptop to see the gorgeous figure of a golden-tanned blonde entering with a goblet of red wine, wearing one of his own white shirts and little else. Ashe turned back to his emails.

'Can I drink this?' asked the girl in a pleasant, county accent.

'Didn't you have enough last night?'

The girl knocked it back in one. 'Ugh!'

'That would be your last cigarette.'

'I'm giving up.'

'Self-denial, Amanda? Hadn't thought of you as an ascetic.'

'A what?'

'Kind of nun.'

The girl approached and ran her fingers through the long strands of Ashe's tousled, copper-brown hair. 'A very horny nun.'

'Weren't you going?'

'Is that what you want, Toby Ashe?'

He thought for a second. 'Right now, yes.'

'Well fuck you then!' Amanda turned to the bedroom door, paused for a second, then launched the goblet at Ashe. The glass shattered on the back of his chair and fell into the sheepskin rug.

Unruffled, Ashe turned from his Mac and looked sympathetically towards Amanda.

'If you really want to throw the book at me, Amanda, why not try one of mine?'

Amanda's lively blue eyes focused on a small pile of paperbacks on the windowsill. Grabbing the first that came to hand, she hurled it hard at Ashe's head.

Ashe ducked and returned to his laptop. 'Judging from the weight and texture of your chosen missile, Amanda, I should say I've been struck by my most popular work to date, *The Generous Gene*. Pity you didn't read it first.'

Slamming the bedroom door behind her, a muffled voice emerged from within. 'I didn't come for your books!'

'Blast!' Ashe's eye alighted on a familiar email address. '*Now* what do they want?' Faced with a choice of two possible worlds, his index finger hovered on the mouse: to open or not to open. He bit his lip. There was work to be done, but there was something about Amanda's rage which turned him on.

Ashe entered the bedroom calmly, half expecting to be hit by another book. Amanda had stripped off his shirt and now lay sprawled on the crumpled bed.

'Just because your real parents didn't want you, Toby, it's no excuse to be so bloody difficult.'

'*Vicious*, Amanda? What I didn't tell you last night was that my dear adopted parents regularly informed me that I was nothing less than a miracle. A gift from above.'

'A *git* from above, more like. Typical of you to suggest you adopted them, rather than the other way round.'

'Which way round would you like it?'

'You know what I like.'

'You can keep those on.'

'Which? Knickers or stilettos?'

'Both. It's always interesting with the knickers.'

'Heightens pleasure, does it?'

'You were made for fucking, Amanda.'

'Who isn't?'

*

14

Post coitum, triste. Sex with Amanda had been exciting and Ashe wondered if dismissing her as a one-night stand had really been a good idea. But something was wrong in his life: lengthening shadows were threatening to envelop him, and poor Amanda had turned up at just the wrong moment.

For the last seven of his thirty-three years, Ashe had made the cathedral city of Lichfield, Staffordshire, his base. The first time he had set foot in this ancient market town, whose grand cathedral gave it city status, he had felt at once a kind of peace, almost a homecoming. He was not surprised to discover later that writers throughout history had described Lichfield as England's 'omphalos': a kind of primordial navel, a centre and fount for the country's soul.

Ashe's decision to quit London in May '97 had served him well, despite the scepticism of his many friends who had moved to the capital straight after graduating from Oxford and stayed there. Having left behind a successful career in TV documentaries to focus on his writing, Ashe found Lichfield's relaxed pleasures and jewel-box of characters less distracting. He devoted his prodigious energies to producing a series of books – works that combined popular science with what Ashe called 'experimental spirituality'. Thanks to two non-fiction international bestsellers, he could enjoy a pleasant lifestyle, so long as he kept his head.

The Generous Gene, his most widely appreciated book, was both a humorous refutation of popular atheism and a vindication of spiritual knowledge in a sane mind. Every age has its prophets of atheism and every age has its defenders of the spiritual life, though Ashe disdained to appear as a prophet of anything. Resolutely refusing all requests for media appearances and interviews, the man behind the bestsellers remained invisible to the general public. Ashe could have gathered a devoted following if he had wanted one; such behaviour would have attracted greater sales, but not contentment.

Ashe's problem was his *other* job. It made him feel a kind of fraud, or ghost: someone removed from life. Strolling about the cold Cathedral Close in search of clarity, Ashe passed by the sandstone tombs of forgotten medieval dignitaries, clinging for salvation to the walls of the three-spired cathedral. He knew that even if he decided to see Amanda again, an invisible wall would always separate them, like the wall that kept the lesser servants of the Church outside the warm Lady Chapel within.

For he could tell neither Amanda nor anybody else that he had been recruited for the Secret Intelligence Service while studying psychology and behavioural sciences at Oxford. A tutor's recommendation, a useful bout of 'playing soldiers' with the Oxford Training Corps, and a rugged talent for mountaineering, as well as impressive intellectual skills, had led to a secret rendezvous and subsequent invitation to join the Service shortly after graduation. Ashe liked to think it was chiefly loyalty to his country that had made him accept the burden of working for the Service, but in truth he was attracted to the idea of unknown agencies being determinative not only in science but in global power-politics as well. His superiors, nevertheless, had detected a maverick quality in Ashe which had, to date, kept him confined largely to research, presentational and advisory roles. Ashe had to slake his thirst for active adventure in foreign expeditions that served none but his own need to be relieved of discipline.

Surely now was the time to seize that holiday and head for France's Languedoc region. Caught between Amanda's attention seeking and a communication (unopened) from that Other Job, why not take this chance to accomplish the hike he had long dreamed of doing, from the medieval Cathar castles of the Corbières across the Pyrenees to Catalonia and the medieval churches of Lérida; lush vineyards, romance and *no responsibilities*.

Fired up with this new decisiveness, Ashe dashed back to his apartment, located in what had been the old Swan Hotel, across from the pool that had once been the cathedral's moat. A quick scout of the net would secure him a first-class ticket to a better state of mind.

The apartment door was open. Ashe found a note lying on his old Bang & Olufsen record deck: eloquence, scrawled with a black mascara brush.

I only seem to go for bastards, Toby Ashe, and I'm not sure about you.

The inevitable phone number. The open door was symbolic; the note, he surmised, desperate. Ashe screwed it up. He opened the CD player in his black hi-fi stack. Out with the melancholy waves of Debussy, in with the boundless, star-bound freedom of Jimi Hendrix.

Soon the flat was vibrating with the magma-swamp, earth-core bass of 'Hey Baby (New Rising Sun)'. Hendrix's angel extended her mysterious invitation to step into her world 'a while'. Long enough, presumably, to realise that she was The One: the angel of love, liberty and an elusive wisdom lost on the timid and the earth-chained.

Ashe poured himself an early tumbler of Talisker and typed his password into his Mac. Still flashing in a corner of the screen was that familiar greeting code:

OB_B5pearl.

He toyed with the mouse. What if he had already left for France when the message had arrived? He could be out of Lichfield in minutes. They'd probably never know.

OB_B5pearl.

He knew what it meant. A call from on high. An obligation. Tired of being at the beck and call of… someone, this was the fate of the man who knew something; he would never be left alone. To know is to be a marked man.

Ashe stared at the delete button. It grew and grew until it filled his mind's eye. Delete and go! Delete and freedom. The angel was calling him.

'Fuck it!' said Ashe, out loud.

OB_B5pearl.

He double-clicked. The message was stark, boringly simple:

Saturday, noon.

Ashe sat back in his upright chair. Caught again. *England expects...* He sent a blank reply, deleted the message, swigged back the malt, looked at his watch and turned off the *New Rising Sun*.

5

What the hell was that?

Ashe's Saab 9-3 convertible tore into a screeching skid and spun round 45 degrees. The figure in the lane didn't budge. Pulling himself together, Ashe lowered the window, trying to discern the ghostlike figure standing bolt upright in the lane. Wrapped head to toe in green camouflage, the figure – apparently male – stared into space, his dark eyes framed by a veil like a Tuareg warrior.

'You getting out of the road, or d'you want to commit suicide?' Ashe's voice failed on the word 'suicide'. 'Suicide' now sounded more like murder, a refusal to die alone, a willingness to kill.

A hollow voice emerged from the creased camouflage. 'The prophet has spoken.'

'Oh fuck!' A shiver shot up Ashe's spine. The man approached him. Before Ashe could depress the clutch, a mud-stained hand reached into the Saab and stuffed a crumpled piece of paper into Ashe's jacket. Then, as fast as the hand had appeared, the man was gone, dissolving into the bushes and trees that clawed at the lane's edge. Ashe spread the paper over his steering wheel. Rough letters in black charcoal conveyed the word of the green prophet:

THE TOWER OF BABEL IS REBUILT
AND MUST BE DESTROYED

Obviously a religious nut; Ashe knew all about *them*. Did this one merit attention? Maybe. The weird encounter had occurred uncomfortably close to his destination.

The committee of SIS Dept B5(b), known affectionately as ODDBALLS, met six times a year at a fine converted farmhouse in Broxbourne Woods, near Little Brickenden, Hertfordshire, close to the M10–M25 link between London and Cambridge. The house belonged to Admiral Lord Gabriel Whitmore.

Crunching gravel, Ashe approached the polished green door, framed by Doric columns. The admiral's butler opened it.

'Good morning, Dr Ashe.'

Ashe heard the grandfather clock in the hall chime midday. 'Afternoon, Reynolds. Admiral aboard?'

'No, not today sir, but the department is. May I show you to the Tower, sir?'

Reynolds, Whitmore's one-time ADC and now fiercely loyal butler, was a stocky man in his early forties with a vividly veined, ocean-washed face. He shared his employer's conceit that the house was a ship, albeit in dry dock.

Reynolds led Ashe through the echoing library to a parlour smelling of Brasso.

'You haven't seen a guy lurking round here in camouflage gear, handing out "end of the world" leaflets, have you Reynolds?'

Reynolds seemed shocked. 'We do get some strange ones, sir. Couldn't have been security staff, could it, sir? Training exercise, I mean.'

'You never see the security round here.'

Reynolds thought for a second. 'We're not all that far from the psychiatric hospital outside Hatfield. You do get the occasional, er... waif and stray.'

'Care in the community, Reynolds?'

'I'm afraid so, sir.'

'Might explain it.'

Reynolds smiled awkwardly and checked his waistcoat pocket

watch. 'I'm afraid they're waiting for you, sir.' He marched Ashe out across the neat rear garden towards the Tower.

Constructed as an observatory in simple but elegant red-brick in 1824, the Tower was King George IVs retirement gift to a favourite admiral of the fleet. Its past was colourful. Rumours persisted of house parties assembled within its cool curvature to practise white magic, and other things, in Edwardian times. An oriental dancer accompanied by a beautiful female violinist from New Zealand had performed a turn that scandalised the usually broadminded wives of the intelligence elite. It was even said that a spirit, manifesting itself before a select coterie, had accurately predicted the First World War two years before it happened. But the days when British intelligence entertained supernatural intelligences were long gone.

The genius behind ODDBALLS was Major General Maxwell Fuller-Knight KCVO. During the darkest days of the Second World War, Fuller-Knight realised that interest in ersatz occultism was a significant characteristic of both present and incipient dictators and terrorists. Not infrequently, the Oddball-type would inject cod mysticism and subjective ecstasies into their extreme political or religious views. Some Oddballs were cleverer than others. Very cunning Oddballs were not always so obviously odd. Bad magicians had always been as attractive as good ones – especially when their followers did not realise it was a form of magic they were being attracted to. Charismatic types used images and words, usually with the 'Holy Book' flavour – the ancient stock-in-trade of the magician. After the images and words came the bombs and the guns. Whatever degree of threat the Oddball's appearance posed to the peace of the world, their appearance was likely to be as regular as a winter cold, and as difficult to predict.

Fuller-Knight's insight was, like all insights of genius, so obvious that the idea of forming a group to consolidate the idea would have appeared sensible to anyone but a politician – or a potential Oddball. Fortunately for Fuller-Knight, the scheme was mooted to Winston Churchill who, initially amused, was subsequently captivated by the idea. But all that had been in the curiously enlightened days – and nights – of the Second World War. After the war, men's minds were moved strangely. ODDBALLS itself began to appear decidedly odd; the world was surely getting better.

ODDBALLS was put in mothballs.

Then, just in time for the millennium, came the smiling, butter-wouldn't-melt-in-his-mouth image of Osama bin Laden. You could have read about him in a Fuller-Knight profile of 1946 – not by name of course, but by type. Fuller-Knight had foreseen the apostle with the machine gun, the rich but humble servant who looked like a prophet and dressed with the cameras in mind.

It had been hard to relaunch B5(b). However, once it was realised the Americans were considering a similar idea, SIS chiefs finally approved the department's revival, under scrutiny. Resurrected in 2000, ODDBALLS extended the anti-fifth-columnist brief of its wartime predecessor to concentrate on locating, investigating and assessing charismatic movements and individuals whose commitments, propaganda or general direction indicated a stance of superior insight, knowledge or destiny to the rest of humankind. The method was first to assess potential security risks, and second to grade risks in order of seriousness, with recommendations for investigation or action. ODDBALLS' remit was global.

Psychological profiles were important. Did the subject assume a superior morality or consider him or herself beyond good and evil? Did the subject believe he or she was specially chosen, called or otherwise marked out by God or some other remarkable authority?

There were many Oddballs and they came in many shapes, sizes and colours.

*

Sobering shafts of clean light beamed through the six portholes that pierced the whitewashed brickwork, illuminating the ODD-BALLS committee as they sat at the round, varnished walnut table, set on the Tower's chequered floor. It was appropriate that such a gathering of minds took place in a room whose atmosphere was reminiscent of a nursery.

Each member's area of expertise was like a prized toy, be it psychology, esotericism, theology, politics and economics, code-breaking, field operations, history, science or technology. Among the dozen regular participants, Ashe alone lacked extensive service experience (undergraduate OTC activities were not taken seriously). As such, he could be regarded as somewhat suspect. His hair was a little too long; his Chelsea boots betokened a lack of discipline. His manner was at times too personal, even emotional. But Ashe carried lightly about him a natural, old-world charm that covered many a sin. Only one member found Ashe's charm as suspect as the rest of him. Under the hard eyes and stentorian tones of the committee chair, Commodore Adrian Marston, Ashe could never do right.

Marston sniffed as Ashe took his seat. 'Well, now we are *all* here, at last – don't trouble to apologise, Ashe – we may give our undivided attention to the archdeacon's summary.'

Archdeacon Aleric Loveday-Rose MC looked across to Ashe. 'Dr Ashe?'

Ashe withdrew a slim blue card file from a battered briefcase and handed it to the archdeacon with a smile. Years of army, university and missionary service in the world's most inhospitable climes had diminished neither the archdeacon's inner fire and good humour, nor his essential seriousness. He addressed the committee.

'As you are all aware, this meeting was initially scheduled for March 20th to assess progress in investigations into the November 2003 bombings targeted against British and Jewish persons, property and security in Istanbul. I regret to say, however, that on the 9th of this month, another atrocity took place, this time in Istanbul's Kartal District. In view of this, it was decided to bring the meeting forward as a matter of urgency.'

Impatient, Marston interjected. 'Urgency is right. But do we have hard evidence, Archdeacon, for links between the November bombings and this week's attack on the Istanbul Masonic Lodge?'

'Too early for definite conclusions, Commodore. Nevertheless, there appear to be links between these separate events, with national security implications.'

Marston was not satisfied. 'Can you define that interest in this instance, Archdeacon?' Marston glanced about the committee, expecting approval for his acuity.

The archdeacon patted his file. 'Certainly, Commodore. It will become obvious as I read you my updated summary on the November 2003 bombings.'

Ashe coughed.

'Excuse me, Dr Ashe. I ought to have said "*our* summary".'

'Why?' Marston was annoyed.

'Dr Ashe assisted with the draft, Commodore.'

'This isn't an awards ceremony,' huffed Marston. 'It's your *job*, Ashe. We're all doing our bit – and time is short.'

'Quite so, Commodore.' The archdeacon gave Marston a stern look, then winked discreetly at Ashe. 'The summary is as follows: On 20 November 2003, five days after the truck-bombing of two synagogues in Istanbul, suicide bombers detonated explosives-packed trucks at the British Consulate and at the HSBC bank, also in Istanbul, killing thirty and wounding four hundred. Our esteemed Consul General, Roger Short, was among the victims, I regret to say, together with a number of his consulate staff. Most of the casualties, as was the case in the earlier synagogue attacks, were Turkish Muslims. While the extreme fundamentalist group IBDA-C, also known as the Islamic Great Eastern Raiders Front, claimed responsibility, it now appears the operation was beyond their capacity. We now understand that although executed independently, the attacks received Osama bin Laden's blessing. The 20 November attack was probably timed to coincide with the meeting in London of US President George Bush and British PM Tony Blair. It was aimed at Western – and particularly British – financial interests while securing propaganda value in Europe, America, the Middle East, and Turkey itself.'

'And the culprits?' Marston jumped the gun.

'Turkish security forces have arrested seventy-four suspects. According to the MIT – Turkey's National Intelligence Organisation – the chief perpetrators formed an al-Qaeda-backed cell of Turkish militants, aided and abetted by a small number of Syrian jihadists. Regrettably, Syrian nationals involved in the attacks evaded arrest. They are now, we understand, operating secretly in Iraq, together with at least three Turkish-born "al-Qaeda warriors", as they call themselves, who were trained at camps at Kandahar and Kabul, Afghanistan. They also fled Turkey. MIT reports that the fugitives include the Syrian Hafiz Razak, a skilled forger and bomb-maker. Razak is probably associated with a new al-Qaeda cell, active in Fallujah and linked to the Ansar al-Islam network in Iraq. The presence, or alleged presence, in Iraq of men responsible for the Istanbul bombings reinforces the British and American security interest in the bombings and the pressing need to bring the perpetrators and their supporters to justice.'

Marston nodded vigorously. 'That's clear.'

'We also possess independent information concerning several other conspirators. This gives us additional opportunities to cooperate with the MIT, and with the CIA. The CIA is naturally as concerned as we are with terrorists crossing into Iraq at this time. Mutual assistance should benefit new investigations.'

Marston butted in. '*Mutual* may be right, but we must not expect cordiality.'

'That is not my experience, Commodore.'

Marston quickly looked Ashe up and down. 'Really, Ashe? And how does your experience touch this matter?'

The archdeacon came to Ashe's rescue. 'Dr Ashe will now

demonstrate how November's atrocities in Istanbul relate to this week's Masonic Lodge bombing.'

The archdeacon's tone could not disguise his pride in Toby Ashe, a pride that had taken root during the archdeacon's residency at All Souls College, Oxford. Ashe was the archdeacon's favourite secret service recruit.

'Please explain to the committee, Dr Ashe, why you think an attack on a Masonic Lodge in Turkey could be al-Qaeda-inspired?'

Ashe smoothed his hair back behind his ears and took a deep breath. 'Your expression "al-Qaeda-inspired" is a good one, Archdeacon. But I don't think we should look at this event entirely within that frame.'

'Why not?' Marston was hot for controversy.

'I'll come to that, Commodore. But first I want to focus on why a certain kind of fundamentalist would focus on Freemasonry.'

Ashe was interrupted by a commotion at the door. A tall man with gaunt, ruddy features framed by a green polo neck was shown in by an unusually respectful Reynolds.

'Ashe, I don't think you know Brigadier Charles Radclyffe.'

Ashe stood up and reached across the table to shake the wiry Brigadier's hand. To have the Director of Special Forces at an ODDBALLS meeting was unusual.

Something big was brewing.

6

Aslan squatted uncomfortably in a Bauhaus steel-framed chair. He was unimpressed by the state-of-the-art reception area and its portraits of the Turkish army's high command, interspersed with colour prints of oil refineries, vehicle assembly lines and telecommunications facilities, terrestrial and orbital.

Aslan always dreaded the regular summonses to the Foundation for the Strengthening of the Turkish Security Forces. Ankara was another world, and the Foundation was a world within a world. Aslan accepted Turkey's status quo for its broad social and political advantages, and preferred to overlook the details; it was none of his business how the army funded its activities – so long as the cheques kept coming. That the Foundation was exempt from taxes, or any democratic financial control, and that it owned considerable shares in Turkish Telecom, Goodyear, Shell and Renault, might look strange to an outsider, but it was simply logical given the overall shape of modern Turkey. The army must survive and flourish, and this he understood: that you get nothing for free in this world.

In spite of a civilian ministerial presence, Turkey's National Security Council was still dominated by the army. While a rebalancing had recently been initiated in favour of the government, the army had a great deal of Turkey under exclusive control. The Foundation for the Strengthening of the Turkish Security Forces (TSKGV) was army owned and army run. General Ahmet Koglu, Chief of Staff of the General Secretariat of the National Security

Council, had his agile fingers in this business, as he had in every politically and economically significant pie in Turkey.

Koglu had summoned Aslan to Turkey's capital, Ankara, for a briefing. This was Koglu's favourite office – far from Istanbul, the way he liked it.

The once handsome general, his chest emblazoned with medals, thrust open the large oak door. Aslan was hit by the chill of air-conditioning.

'I hope you like medals, Colonel.' Koglu smoothed the creases from his dark-blue uniform. 'I have a meeting with the American Secretary of Defence this afternoon. Unofficial visit, but appearances…' Koglu looked derisively at Aslan's nylon zip-up jacket and open-necked shirt, 'must be maintained. When did you cease wearing uniform in the Liaison Department, Colonel?'

'We've never worn it, General. We interact with civilian personnel. That's the point of the department, sir. Not to frighten the democrats!'

Koglu's eyebrows rose in a slightly bored kind of way. 'Yes… still, there's always the danger of fraternising with them.'

The general showed Aslan into a vast, beautifully carpeted office, filled with antique furniture and Ottoman Caliphate porcelain. Exquisitely framed medieval manuscripts adorned the walls.

Koglu retired behind his white marble desk, grandly constructed in a crescent-moon shape, like the crescent of the Turkish flag. Aslan sank back into a modern red sofa while Koglu rubbed his second chin and tickled his finely trimmed black moustache. He reached for a small paperback in Arabic.

'Ever read this, Colonel?' Koglu tossed it over.

Aslan caught the book in mid-air, then flicked through the book with disdain. 'Yes, sir, a long time ago. *The Protocols of the Elders of Zion*. But… don't you have a copy in Turkish?'

Koglu smiled weakly. 'I believe, Colonel, that this book has been made into a TV drama series in Cairo. And the title, by the way, is *The Protocols of the* Meetings *of the* Learned *Elders of Zion*.'

Aslan threw it back onto the general's desk. 'Hardly material for a daytime soap.'

'Nevertheless, let us take a page at random. Ah! This looks interesting:

Who and what is in a position to overthrow an invisible force? And this is precisely what our force is. Gentile Masonry blindly serves as a screen for us and our objects, but the plan of action of our force, even its very abiding-place, remains for the whole people an unknown mystery.

'This comes from Protocol No. 4. I can't help thinking, Colonel, that this little book could be central to your investigations.'

'It's bullshit, sir.'

The general tapped his fingers on the desk. 'It states here, Colonel, that these are the secret minutes of the first Zionist Congress, held in Basle in 1897. This is nothing less than a blue-print for the long-term project of Jewish world domination.'

'Very long term, I should say, sir. Israel seems to be having a job defending a territory smaller than some of our lesser-known provinces.'

The general smiled again. 'Quite so, Colonel. But I cannot help observing that the Jewish people have come a long way since 1897. In those days, Istanbul was the centre of the Ottoman Caliphate with an empire extending west and east from Bosnia to Medina. And the Jews were *dhimmis*: tolerated, but in their place; hardly even to be considered, other than for the demands of courtesy and good manners.'

Aslan couldn't help raising his eyebrows. 'Sir, *The Protocols of the Learned Elders of Zion* is a piece of shit concocted by some clever bastards in the Tsarist secret police – the Okhrana.'

'Why would they do such a thing?'

'Many Jewish intellectuals in Russia were communists, sir. They were perceived as threats to the Tsarist religious and social order. *The Protocols* were a clear attempt to play on the fears of invisible enemies – a concept familiar to you, surely, sir.'

'I wonder what you might mean by that, Colonel.'

'This was how the Tsarist order was governed, with the full backing of the Russian Orthodox Church. The leaders of the Orthodox Church have always hated Freemasonry. For them, it's a rival spiritual power. So the Russian secret police put Jews and Freemasons together and... *abracadabra*! Conspiracy!'

Koglu sat back in his chair. 'You seem very well informed in these matters, Colonel. Especially for one who, if you don't mind me saying, told my – I mean our – chief of police, that he had never entered a Masonic Lodge before last week.'

Aslan coughed as he tried to think of an answer. 'I can read, sir. I've been consulting the latest and the best research on the subject.' That sounded a bit weak.

'Good. Very good, Colonel. Then you will also agree with us, I hope, that where there is smoke, there is fire, and that all non-Turkish forces, are a threat—'

'Potential threat, General.'

'Potential threat, yes.' The general looked to the ceiling for inspiration. 'Tell me, Colonel. Was the bombing in Kartal a potential threat?'

Aslan also looked up to the plain ceiling. He felt Koglu's eyes boring into him.

'I'm sorry, was that a rhetorical question, or did the general want an answer?'

'Answer.'

'Could you repeat the question, sir?'

'Was the bombing in Kartal a potential threat?'

'No, sir.'

'Good!' Koglu smiled. He felt on top, at last. He took a deep breath, but Aslan got in first.

'I mean, yes and no, sir. The bombing was not necessarily itself a threat. It could be seen as the execution of a threat already made, or it may have been a kind of opening salvo – a threat of worse to come. Perhaps the first stage in a demand. But that was not your original question, was it, sir? You were saying that all non-Turkish forces were a threat.'

'Covert forces, Colonel! I said covert forces!'

'Ah! I didn't catch that.'

Koglu started sorting through papers on his desk in an effort to regain his composure.

'Colonel Aslan, we are concerned – as you must be – that there may be more than meets the eye to this business.'

7

Koglu picked up a thin file, then dropped it unceremoniously onto a pile of black-and-white photographs. 'I have read the chief of police's interim report and I am far from satisfied. Perhaps you can enlighten me?'

Aslan paused. 'First of all, sir, one of the perpetrators – the survivor – has confessed to murdering a Jewish dentist in Istanbul in 2003. This does suggest that the main target of the attack was Israel, rather than Freemasonry in particular.'

Koglu looked doubtful. 'I cannot see the Israelis being hurt by an attack on a Turkish Lodge. But go on.'

'Many Jewish businessmen and intellectuals belong to Turkey's five Masonic organisations – which have, I believe, some 14,000 members.'

'14,000? A significant number.'

'That depends on the significance you wish to attach to the fact... sir.'

'The bombing is significant.'

'Regarding which, General, I think we should consider the Islamic Great Eastern Raiders Front.'

'I thought we had IBDA-C either locked up or under close observation after the November bombing? Sixty-nine indictments only a fortnight ago.'

'And a lawsuit is to be filed against another twelve suspects.'

'Good! That's something to tell the press!'

'Indeed, sir. The point is that after the November bombings against British interests in Istanbul, the news agency Anadolu Ajansi received a call from a man who said those attacks were the joint work of IBDA-C and al-Qaeda.'

'We already know this, Colonel.'

'The man also said something that... well, it passed us by at the time.'

'Yes?'

'He said, "Our attacks on the centres of international Freemasonry will continue."'

'Is the Kartal Lodge a "centre of international Freemasonry"?'

'Not exactly, sir. But from the point of view of the fundamentalist conspiracy theorist, any big British or US financial or political centre could be described as a centre of international Freemasonry, because they see Freemasonry and Zionism everywhere. That's thanks to your anti-Semitic *Protocols* propaganda. According to the allegedly invisible "Elders of Zion", the conspiracy is so vast that virtually any target is legitimate.'

General Koglu started rubbing his boot heels together.

'Sir, we must work on science, not prejudice. After the bombing, the official statement of the Lodge read as follows...' Aslan extracted a small card from his wallet. '"The bombing was an attack on modern and secular Turkish society."'

'Yes, Colonel. Celik wrote that at my dictation, then gave it to the Lodge Master to use.'

'Then you agree with it?'

'It was the right thing to say at the time.'

Koglu got up, folded his arms and turned towards the large plate-glass window. He gazed out at Ankara's vast, monotonous panorama of grey, dusky blocks and conurbation. 'I wonder, Aslan, what they out there would think of this discussion.'

'Why don't you ask them?'

'Don't be impertinent, Colonel.'

He turned to face Aslan. 'If, as the Arabs have suggested, Jews and Freemasons contributed to the end of the caliphate, how can we be sure they don't now oppose the regime that succeeded it?'

'Jews and Freemasons are the *victims* of this bombing, sir, not its perpetrators! Nothing would please the extremists more than to hear this kind of conspiracy theory become a basis for policy.

If we attack ourselves, we do their work for them.'

Koglu put his hands behind his back and locked his thumbs.

'Nevertheless, Turkey must be prepared. The army must be alert to all interests that affect national security. One must cover all possibilities, without, as you say, prejudice.'

Aslan began to object but Koglu raised his right hand abruptly. 'That is why, Colonel Aslan, I am requesting your department to ask all relevant local authorities – and you can get an article into *Hürriyet* while you're about it – to assemble information on these individuals and groups.'

Koglu reached under the pile of photographs and pulled out a printed sheet. 'It's all here. Please phrase it in appropriate language. Thank you, Colonel. If there's anything I can do to make your stay in Turkey's capital a pleasant one…'

'I'm expected back in Istanbul this afternoon, General.'

'As you will.' Koglu patted Aslan on the back and led him out of his office to the reception elevator. 'We admire your loyalty to the state. You have friends here, Colonel. Don't forget that.'

Aslan entered the brushed-steel lift and pulled the sheet out of his pocket:

In view of recent events, military staff request the authorities to gather intelligence that will enable us to take effective measures against incidents that could arise. Information is required concerning ethnic minorities, including Circassians, Gypsies, Albanians, Bosnians.

Information is sought on magicians, people who practise meditation, supporters of the EU and the USA, the socially elite, members of artistic groups, children of wealthy families, foreigners living in Turkey, Satanists, Freemasons, sympathisers with white supremacists in the Ku Klux Klan, and groups that congregate on the internet.

Aslan shook his head. More 'usual suspects'? This was ridiculous.

Or was it?

8

Reynolds hovered over the table, dispensing Parma ham onto porcelain plates heaped with salad.

'Thank you, Reynolds.'

'Ma'am.'

Karla Lindars, a strikingly attractive fifty-year-old, ultra-smart in a purple corduroy miniskirt and matching jacket, glanced admiringly at Ashe. 'You know, Toby, I found your exposition fascinating, but I want to know what the mythology is that inspires all this hatred and mayhem. We all know that politics is about manipulating dreams.'

Ashe sipped his glass of fine Florentine white and pondered the question. 'The anti-Masonic myth is a contributory factor, Karla. But I wouldn't say it was a mainspring of terrorist motivation.'

'But if you're going to attack a Masonic Lodge specifically, it must be pretty important.'

Ashe thought for a few seconds. 'Yes, it's funny, isn't it?'

Marston caught the edge of the conversation. 'I don't find it at all amusing, Ashe.'

'Not funny in that way, Commodore. But sort of uncanny the way these things can come together.'

'What blasted things, Ashe?'

'Esoteric things. Let me explain. I was asked to examine a CD not so long ago. The CD was produced at a studio in London and sold from a market-stall in Brixton. Professionally produced, using English and Asian actors' voices – very much in the style of a slick documentary. The cover announced it contained a sensational revelation of how the Knights Templar secretly control world events.'

'Come on, Ashe! We've all heard this story over and over. Balls, all of it.'

'I know, Commodore. But this wasn't just *Holy Blood, Holy Grail* kind of stuff. It was fundamentalist propaganda. Sophisticated. Even sinister.'

'Sinister?'

'A sinister conspiracy, Commodore, is what it describes. And it starts, according to the propaganda on the CD, with the Crusades. According to the myth, the Crusades were not an attempt to liberate Christian holy sites following the Turkish capture of Jerusalem in 1099.'

'Really, Ashe? What were they then?'

'The Crusades were a deliberate attempt to destroy Islam itself.'

'Preposterous!'

'Yes, Commodore. *You* know that – but people hearing this story for the first time are probably hearing about the Crusades for the first time as well. According to the myth, or propaganda, the Crusaders failed, ultimately, because God was against them. It's a small step then to say that the Crusaders were... against God.'

'I presume then we can extend the Almighty's disapproval to *any troops* on Islamic territory.'

'Precisely, Brigadier. That's the inference. As the narrative goes, the Pope's own shock troops – the Knights Templar – were kicked out of Jerusalem in 1187. By 1312, even the Pope was wondering whether or not the Templars had been corrupted and so earned God's condemnation – hence their military failure. The Templars' secrecy didn't help matters. The question was, and remains: had the Templars succumbed to Satan?'

The Brigadier interjected. 'I get it. In case Westerners say that all that "Great Satan" stuff about the US is just Iranian propaganda, the militants can argue it was the *Christian Church's own view* that the Crusaders were dupes of the Devil.'

'Spot on, Brigadier. As we all know, the Templars were condemned, despite quite justified claims of innocence. As the story goes, in spite of being tried for diabolical practices, some Templars escaped to the Western Isles of Scotland. Driven underground, the Templars – according to the story – metamorphosed into yet another secret organisation.'

'I wonder who?' asked the archdeacon, with a twinkle.

'The bloody Freemasons, of course,' chipped in the Commodore.

'Not the Priory of Sion? We've all read *The Da Vinci Code*, you know!'

'Not quite, Karla! Another trump card up the militants' sleeve is that if anyone says this is just propaganda, they can point to the fact that the story of Freemasonry's Templar origins has been repeated by Freemasons themselves for over two hundred years.'

'But all that's just a load of old myth, isn't it, Toby?'

'Myths can be very powerful, Archdeacon. This one certainly is.'

'Dr Ashe is right, Commander,' agreed Brigadier Radclyffe. 'You hear this kind of thing all over the Middle East: medieval Templars fought the armies of Islam, therefore Templars were evil. Templars became Freemasons, therefore Freemasons must be evil. Modern armies are also fighting Muslims, therefore those armies must be led by Templar-Freemasons, ancient masters of secret evil. The response? Jihad. The enemy has to be an enemy of God to inspire the real jihad.'

Ashe took up from Radclyffe. 'And it gets worse. The fact that the Templars secured the Temple Mount in Jerusalem as their headquarters immediately connects them to the Palestinian–Jewish situation. A big part of the myth is the idea that the Freemasons are somehow in league with Jewish interests to establish a Masonic–Jewish temple in Jerusalem: a temple, they say, to the "false God".'

Karla Lindars shook her head. 'This is all very sad. Is there any truth at all in this myth, Toby?'

'None. But there's a problem. Freemasons have been constructing myths around their rituals for centuries. Harmless, really. They call them "traditional histories". They were meant as moral teaching lessons, not political history. They use myths and legends. Masonic descriptions of Templars, for example, emphasise chivalry, courtesy and the idea of life as a spiritual pilgrimage, not fighting specific religious conflicts! Religious conflict is something Freemasonry is expressly against. It's a nasty trick of history that the Middle Eastern situation has become so hot at precisely the same time that old Masonic myths have found their way into post-sixties sensationalist books.'

'As you say, Toby, a nasty trick.'

'I'm sorry, Karla, but history is often a legacy we'd prefer not to inherit. Take our own role in the redrawing of the Middle Eastern political map.'

'What do you mean, Toby?'

'After the withdrawal of the Turks from the region in 1918, the dividing up of newly liberated lands between British and French influence was, for many Arabs, a betrayal.'

'And the myth explains how this so-called betrayal came about?'

'Right, Archdeacon. The alleged betrayal of Arab hopes at the end of the First World War is, according to the myth, simply a prelude to the re-establishment of the state of Israel in 1948. Israel's existence is then seen as the fulfilment of a pre-arranged, anti-Islamic plan going back centuries.'

'What bloody plan?'

'Come on, Adrian! If I follow Dr Ashe correctly, the myth suggests a secret plan that *required* the destruction of the Ottoman Caliphate in Istanbul.'

Ashe was impressed. 'Thank you, Brigadier. The alleged plan required the break-up of the Turkish Empire so that the Jews could take back their ancient homeland without serious opposition.'

Ashe paused for effect. 'In short, the Devil runs Freemasonry and the Jews used Freemasonry for their own purposes. Britain, France and America have been manipulated by Satanic powers. Only militant Islam – al-Qaeda, Hamas, Hizbollah – stand up against Zionists and the US. The US, Israel, and also, apparently, the UK, allegedly want to neutralise Islam and conquer the world by supplanting Allah's rule with that of the Dajjal.'

'Dajjal?'

'The Islamic false Messiah or anti-God, Commodore. Militants learn that there's a secret god in Masonry, and this secret god is Shaitan, Arabic for Satan.'

The table went quiet.

'All right, Ashe. We get the idea. Fundamentalist militants bombed the Masonic Lodge in Istanbul because by doing so they thought they were striking a blow against Turkey's involvement with the Unites States' pro-Israeli foreign policy.'

'That's basically it, I think, Commodore. The myth provides motivation and, in this case, the target. And the justification for the cause is secret, hidden.'

'And the cause provides the terrorist with the satisfying feeling of doing it all for God.'

'Yes, Commodore.'

Marston put his hands together beneath his nose, as if in prayer. He then arched his knuckles and, somewhat out of character, bit his lip before speaking. In spite of himself, he had been gripped by Ashe's exposition. He addressed the committee. 'Well, we have our Oddball *myth*. But do we have our actual Oddball?'

Ashe withdrew an old file from his briefcase, its cover marked in red: 'RESTRICTED'.

9

Sami al-Qasr stared at the rows and rows of black chromosomes flickering on the computer screen. These bar codes of silent soldiers spoke a language al-Qasr understood. The Iraqi doctor had devoted practically the whole of his mind to the strange inner life of the cellular nucleus. Was it any wonder, he asked himself, that he was now, perhaps, a little mad?

Tired of waiting, he smacked his large hand on the white Formica desk and looked out of the plate-glass laboratory window into the car park below. His crimson Jaguar was attracting the usual admiring comments from staff enjoying a cigarette break in the sunshine. Otherwise, RIBOTech's steel-and-glass precincts were silent.

A knock at the door.

Al-Qasr breathed deeply, then twisted his thick black moustache.

'Come!'

'Excuse me, Dr al-Qasr, Nancy left instructions—'

'Instructions?'

'You like a good strong cup of coffee around this time.'

Al-Qasr looked at the clock. 'Ah! *Elevenses*. Very good. And you are?'

'Ms Normanton, sir. Temporary intern. What's "elevenses", Dr al-Qasr?'

'Old habit I picked up in Cambridge.'

'You're from Massachusetts, Doctor?'

'No, no, no, my dear. Cambridge in England.'

The pretty girl put the coffee down by his computer. 'Gee, you've come a long way!'

'Yes... in forty years. All the way to Paradise, California. Quite a journey. Full of the unexpected.' He eyed her slender hips and long, bronzed legs. 'And please, call me Sami.'

The girl giggled, caught in al-Qasr's charming smile.

'See you soon, Ms Normanton.'

'Oh. Call me Fiona. I'll be here for a while.'

'Good.'

Fiona giggled again and closed the lab door.

Al-Qasr gulped his coffee. The chromosomes were staring at him again. They didn't carry flags; they weren't fighting each other; they didn't speak different languages. They spoke the same language. They spoke the language of science. They spoke the language of nature. Maybe they spoke the language of God. No, not God. Not God.

Al-Qasr was fed up with talk of God, especially in connection with science.

Who made the DNA? That was always the question. There was only one rational answer. It was a mystery. The mystery of evolution, of biological change. Why was it a mystery? Because it was there and no one knew why. In the absence of scientific explanation, mysteries seemed irrational.

Talk of God didn't help science; it only made religious people feel better.

Al-Qasr thought about the billions of 'bases' in the genome – billions in number but still only four varieties. It was beautiful, logical, but not moral.

Every kid doing science had heard of the bases: adenine, thymine, guanine and cytosine. A, T, G and C had become the sugary apostles at the cornerstones of life. But they didn't make anyone feel better, or behave any better. There was nothing to believe in, only to accept. What had once seemed a revelation had soon settled down to become common knowledge.

And what had all these molecules of carbon, hydrogen, oxygen and nitrogen made? They had made men and women. And what did men and women want? What came naturally: power. Power over their lives, power over other lives. The will to go on, to multiply: nature's neutral imperative.

You had to have power, but you had to have limits. You had to have a State. You had to have limits. That was always the problem. You had to belong to something. Something you could see. Something you could touch. Something that had real power.

Real power for real Arabs. *Trust your own people* – that's what his father had taught him. That's why he'd joined the Ba'ath Socialist Party in Iraq all those years ago.

For thousands of years before the Prophet, the desert Arabs had been despised as nomads, outsiders. Then the Prophet Muhammad had given them a lead role in history: all they had to do was bond together, submit to the Anvil and be new-forged into a mighty sword of destiny. The world had quaked before; it would quake again. *Rebirth…* The genes from the past reborn in the present. It was a mystery. It had been a mystery ever since God's wrath at the Tower of Babel had led Him to divide the children of Noah into the many races of the world, unable to communicate, anxious to fight. It was still a mystery.

Al-Qasr reached for the worn old paperback he kept stuffed in the bottom drawer of his desk. For years, whenever he experienced doubts, he'd looked at it for inspiration: *The Ba'ath Revolution – An Unfolding Future*, printed in Baghdad in 1968. His fingers touched the grainy black-and-white image of its author, Jalal al-Qasr, a proud man: his father.

He turned to page 78 and to a quotation underlined heavily in pencil:

While the State of the future will harmonise the morality of all religions in an Arab unity, Arabs will always draw

42

inspiration from He who came to them as the Seal of the Prophets. Even in a secular Arab State, the voice of the Prophet will be on the lips of those who no longer hunger. The Party will hold the allegiance of the heart because the Ba'athist State is good for all Arabs, but the heart of many citizens will ultimately belong to Allah. The State will not compel it; it is simply natural.

Al-Qasr had added a note to the side of the passage: 'Is science the search for His will in nature?'

Jalal had wanted Sami to follow him into politics. Sami had wanted to be a scientist, above politics, pursuing reality at its core. Now it seemed the promise of the Ba'ath movement had faded, for the time being at least. What future for the Arabs now? What future for Iraq?

Shit! He would be too late! Al-Qasr pulled out the laptop from under his desk; he was sweating. His fingers flew over the keys as he followed the links to the encrypted websites that were buried in messages from his distant family in Jordan. An image exploded onto the screen: a US Humvee blown off a distant road by a mine, shot in digital video and cut into four segments, each showing the blast from a different angle.

Then, from out of the flames, in golden Arabic script, burst the slogan:

DAGGERS OF RIGHTEOUSNESS, BROTHERS
OF AL-QAEDA

10

'The point, my dear Ashe, is that if we're to take your line any further we need... well, more than inspired guesswork. How does all this anti-Masonic activity give us a departmental programme? We can't simply take on a global or semi-global prejudice, however ill informed or perverted. Our official task is to isolate the Oddball, not to redeem the world from darkness, propaganda and superstition. We leave that job to politicians.'

The archdeacon nearly coughed up his wine.

Ashe slammed his glass hard on the table. 'Well, I'm sorry, Commodore, not to have been able to name the perpetrators of the Kartal Lodge bombing today, or reveal who funded them and why.'

'Steady on, Ashe! Please, please don't get me wrong! This old file you've dug up may be important; it may not. Perhaps if you could just summarise for us what you think is significant about it, and more importantly, what you propose we should do about it?'

Ashe flicked through the pages of the old file. 'It is a very old file, I admit. In fact it's two files combined. One from the late sixties and one from the early nineties. And I'd like to thank Karla for tracing it for me at such very short notice.'

'I second that.'

'Thank you, Archdeacon. Now, the subject of the first file is one Jalal al-Qasr.'

'Never heard of him!'

'Jalal al-Qasr, Commodore, was a fanatical supporter of the Iraqi Ba'ath Party. The Party gained control of Iraq in the 1968 coup. Even fellow Ba'athists considered Jalal al-Qasr extreme on two issues. He was rabidly anti-Masonic and irrationally hostile to Israel. Not that these were issues on which he would find much essential disagreement among his associates in the Party, but it was a question of the degrees to which he was prepared to go in furthering his hostility. Jalal was instrumental in securing the death penalty for Freemasons that became statute law under Saddam until the Coalition invasion – and Jalal linked Freemasonry to Zionism at every opportunity. Even though Jalal was an unreconstructed Stalinist socialist with no fundamentalist religious convictions, he was one of the few Ba'athists to make an impression on Egyptian radical circles, out of which al-Qaeda would eventually emerge. Though secular, Jalal's politics were drenched with a quasi-mystical flavour. His political statements could be read like prayers, his rants against enemies like incantations.'

'Sounds like an Oddball, Ashe.'

The committee nodded and murmured their agreement.

'Indeed, Commodore. And someone else thought so too. Jalal al-Qasr disappeared in 1982. Israeli Mossad agents were suspected. Jalal's body has never been found. His beliefs, however, were transmitted to a cadre of followers. They've spread far and wide. Followers include his son, Sami, a remarkable scientist. This Sami al-Qasr, the subject of the second file, worked at Cambridge with Sir Moses Beerbohm until quitting Britain abruptly, and mysteriously, in 1983.'

There was a knock at the door. Marston looked at his watch. 'That'll be Reynolds. Excuse me, Ashe, some members have taxis and trains to catch. Enter, Reynolds.'

'Taxis, sir. I'll fetch hats and coats.'

Ashe's mobile rang. Someone tutted; mobile phones were absolutely forbidden at ODDBALLS meetings.

'Dr Ashe!'

Ashe blushed and quickly exited the Tower, relieved to be in the open air again.

A voice crackled on his mobile. Ashe pressed it closer to his ear. 'I'm sorry, I can't hear you.' The crackling got worse. 'Who is speaking? Who? *Who*?'

Ashe walked away from the Tower onto the freshly cut lawn, hoping to improve the signal.

11

He raised his pounding, aching head from the wet lawn. The dampness was blood: his own, dripping down the blades of grass. Ashe's head was heavy, echoing with a strange wind, like waking in the blank afternoon after a bad dream. There was a stabbing in his eyes and a wall of noise in his ears. He was shaking, unable to focus, like a child in pain, whimpering, sick. He started to vomit onto the lawn.

Smoke and dust filled the air. In the distance: the screech of an alarm system. An old brick fell from Ashe's back as he tried to get up, still vomiting, coughing, bleeding. He fell backwards, closing his eyes again, nauseous, dizzy. He rolled over and coughed up rancid remains of lunch mixed with bile and wine; his throat stung. He opened his leaden eyes and caught a beam of sunlight as it stole through the brick dust and billowing fragments of cement.

There was something in his hand. A mobile. The line was dead. Ashe passed out – somewhere to forget the pain and the sickness. It wasn't happening. It wasn't him. It must be something else… someone else. The sun again. Gone.

S

Remember the Snake
And know
The Serpent has the power
From the root of the tree
To the Tower
From the scorpion to the flower

Thousands of miles away, in a mountainous valley in northern Iraq, a man the local Kurds called 'the Kochek' awoke from a dream.

Seated on the pale, dusty grass in the shade of an olive grove, the wise old man scratched his long, grey, matted beard, gently wiped his folded eyes, adjusted his large turban and carefully rose to his feet. As he brushed some fallen leaves from the white woollen *meyzar* pulled tight around his shoulders, his sharp eye caught the sun, beginning to set over the mountain to the north. He kissed the fingertips of his right hand and drew them to his forehead. Then he crossed his arms over his chest and bowed to the sun three times.

The Kochek removed his shoes, then bent to kiss the threshold of the *mazar* in front of him. The *mazar* had no door; it did not need one. He entered the shrine, poured olive oil from an old petrol tin into a brass standard lamp, and placed four wicks into the grooves around the top of the lamp.

A tiny flame floated above a pool of oil in a window recess. Taking a taper from beside the flame, the Kochek ignited it and brought its light to the standard lamp. Concentrating, he brought the fragile flame to the dry wicks. A beautiful golden glow lit the heart of the little shrine. A soft wind chanted quietly down the blessed valley.

The elderly Kochek touched his fingertips to his lips and his forehead once more, then stepped gingerly back over the threshold. In the distance he heard the echo of a rifle shot bouncing from rock to rock in the south. The Kochek smiled. He was thinking of Sarsaleh, the imminent Spring Festival, wondering how many would come to him this year with their dreams. The past years had been hard, but they had been harder in the greater past. He was alive; that was good. But martyrdom put you in good company: alongside the ancestors, buried under stones, watching.

His loving eye surveyed the yellow rock-roses, the gladioli, the buttercups, the red and yellow *Adonis*, the hyacinths, all crying for life and straining to break through the gleaming pebbles and grass of the mountains. His eyes penetrated the greening hills to the north, south, east and west, now touched with a fiery light. And he thought of the four wicks, the cross, the flames of the sun, bringing new light and life to good and bad alike and blessings for those who knew.

He had been with the angel and the angel had warned him, as he had warned his ancestors.

12

Mati Fless drew the hired BMW Cabriolet to a halt on the hard shoulder's crisp new tarmac. It was good to see California again. Fless turned the radio off and breathed in the creamy, fresh air wafting in from the snow-capped Sierra Nevada to the east. He cast his eye across Lake Oroville. The clear blue waters glittered like a tray of gems.

When he'd received instructions to fly to San Francisco, Fless had expected some squalid assignment in a back-lot in Haight-Ashbury or the dank corridors of a government housing project in Daly City. That was the usual environment for his kind of work. But Fless was headed for Paradise, 100 miles north of Sacramento.

Fless caught his image in the side mirror. He hated mirrors. He hated to see himself. Without an image he was invisible, just an idea, the point of somebody's will. His olive eyes seemed darker than usual, his face longer than usual, his short black hair less plenteous. He was thirty-four and he'd started thinking. Not just asking questions and settling for attractive answers, but really thinking. Deep stuff. He wouldn't last much longer in the job.

It had taken three years to get a transfer from Shin Bet's anti-subversion department to the Israeli Mossad's foreign operations branch. God, how Fless hated spying on his own people. Yes, some of the guys in the ultra-nationalist Kach were nutters – but spending days staking out student families in the hills of Samaria in the West Bank had got him right down.

Fless hadn't joined the security service to watch organic farmers, ceramicists, sculptors, theatrical types, musicians, embroiderers, stained-glass artists and candle-makers. Of course, the idealistic self-help groups were a nursery for the Bat Ayin underground, a West Bank settler group. There'd been some bad things. Fless himself had foiled a plan to detonate a cart filled with explosives next to a school in the Arab neighbourhood of At-Tur in Jerusalem. The zealot Israeli militant mentality left him cold.

The final straw for Fless had been the uncovering of a secret Kach plan to blow up the al-Aqsa mosque on the Temple Mount and replace it with an altar to be used for animal sacrifices. The whole thing gave him crazy dreams. It wasn't even something he could talk about. He couldn't drink it off his mind either. As far as Fless was concerned, the problem in the East was too much religion and not enough reality. It always had been.

But California: wow! Every kind of nutcase – but not a bomb in sight. The sun, the fir trees, the dazzle of sky on the windscreen, the roar of the engine. Fless felt intoxicated as he wound his way round the lakeside and up into the mountains towards Paradise.

The car sped up the hairpin track, higher and higher. Then Fless slammed on the brakes and reversed the car. To his left, a small sign: 'KISMET', the professor's house.

Fless continued up the track until he reached a lay-by shadowed by great pines. Taking a case from the boot, he darted into the forest. He caught his black jeans on a barbed-wire fence concealed by ferns. Maybe the fence was wired to an alarm. Listening hard, Fless backed off, following the fence down the hillside.

Ten miles away in Chico, Fless's team waited on his call.

Through a clearing, he caught his first sight of the house, an early seventies split-level job. Fless crouched on the ground for an hour. He checked the contents of his case: a hypodermic gun and a phial of something the doctor didn't order – humanely brief and fast dispersing.

Fless heard a crack behind him.

An Alsatian leapt at his neck, biting and tearing through his jersey. A blur of teeth strained for the jugular. Pulled to the ground, hard against the barbed wire, Fless rolled over with the animal as it gnawed and salivated as the scuffle intensified. Fless kept his chin down and forced his right hand against the Alsatian's beating chest, down towards his waist. Once he'd got leverage, the job was soon done.

The blade severed the dog's neck. A high-pitched bark was abruptly silenced by Fless's adept twist of the knife. The dog's legs beat helplessly in the undergrowth as its lifeblood seeped into the scattered sunlight.

'Fucking dogs!'

Fless heard a car in the distance and then a click. He felt sick. A gun barrel pushed hard into the nape of his neck.

'One move, son, and you're as dead as that dog.'

13

Aslan stormed into his office and slapped down a wet copy of *Hürriyet* in front of Ali.

'See that?'

'The official communiqué is on your desk, sir.'

'Why bother when it's all over the newspapers?'

'Might be different, sir.'

'Is it different, Ali? I presume you've read it.'

'Not really, sir.'

'Not really you haven't read it, or not really it might be different?'

'The odd word; nothing of substance.'

'See what it says here in *Hürriyet*? Did you read it?'

'I read the story in *Sabah*, sir. It all comes from the same place.'

'Well, Ali, in case there is any difference, let me read this to you.'

Ali's tired eyes looked heavenwards and blinked. Aslan carried on regardless.

'"Istanbul's governor, Muammar Güler, said that a new group with plans for further atrocities was behind the attack on the Masonic Lodge in Kartal District. He assured the public that eighteen suspects are currently in custody and have confessed to planning and preparing…" Get that, Ali? "Planning *and* preparing", what the hell's the difference? Suggests they're trying to pile up charges. Ah, look… it gets better. "We know they received

53

political and military training in camps in Afghanistan and Pakistan, but police have so far found no links between them and al-Qaeda. The governor added that 'It does not have links to currently known organisations. We are investigating whether it has links to al-Qaeda.'" Are we currently investigating links with al-Qaeda, Ali?'

'I don't know, sir. Are we?'

'If the governor says we are, Ali.'

'Then of course we are, sir. There was a bit more in *Sabah*, sir.'

'A bit more what?'

'A few more details that do not appear in the official communiqué on your desk, sir.'

'What is it?'

'Not much.'

'Not much is all we've got. Let's hear it.'

'Only, sir, that Celalettin Celik considered the attack to be the work of amateurs.'

'Since it's difficult to make a profession out of suicide bombing, he's on safe ground there. Is he suggesting blowing oneself to smithereens is a kind of hobby?'

Ali swallowed a laugh.

'And why the hell didn't Celik tell me he'd ended his so-called news blackout?'

'There's something else, sir.'

'Well?'

'The London-based Arabic newspaper *al-Quds al-Arabi* reported receiving a statement from the al-Qaeda linked group *Jund al-Quds*, Soldiers of Jerusalem, claiming responsibility.'

Aslan paused, weighing up the value of the statement. 'London, you say?'

'Yes, sir. According to *Sabah*.'

'Why's there always someone in London who knows more than we do?'

'It's been called the terrorists' international café, sir.'

'Really? More like a review bar, Ali. In the interests of what the British call fairness, every arsehole gets a hearing in London. Which reminds me…'

Aslan pulled up his plastic chair and grabbed the communiqué.

'What's this?'

'I think it's a codicil, sir.'

'Have you read it?'

Ali bit his lip.

'All right, Ali. You may now retire to your Mac and begin composing your resignation.'

'Sir! Please!'

'Only joking, Ali. It's only right my secretary should be better informed than I am. I might have to lose my memory one of these days.'

'Thank you, sir.' Ali saluted and turned on his heels.

Aslan speed-read the communiqué, then turned to the codicil. He squinted as a shock blast of sunlight punched its way from behind a cloud and burst through the wet air into the office. Aslan shielded his eyes and struggled to come to terms with what he was reading.

'Sons of bitches! Two-faced bastards! Ali! Come back in here, *now*!'

14

'I don't like torture, son. So be kind to me. Don't make me do it.'

'That's not torture. That's execution.'

'I don't think so, son. 110 volts won't kill you. Of course, if I pour this here jug of water over y'all, that could be real bad. But keep talkin', son.'

The American had tied Fless's hands with exposed live flex and plugged the end into a mains socket beneath a shelf of garden tools. Behind the American, aluminium steps led up to the three-car garage at the side of al-Qasr's house.

Fless looked around the utility basement – anything to give him an edge or an idea.

'So wha'd'ya think, son? Feel like talkin'?'

Fless shook his head.

'Sorry to hear that, 'cause the way I see it, either *a)* you came to spy on Professor al-Qasr, *b)* you came to abduct Professor al-Qasr, or *c)* you came to kill Professor al-Qasr.'

The American agent hauled his meaty thighs off the toolbox he was squatting on.

'Nice here, ain't it, son? Bet you wished you lived here. Swell place. Swell view. Folks real friendly round here too. Not like Israel, huh?'

The agent reached into his suit pocket and pulled out Fless's passport. 'I see here you're in your early thirties. Good time to be alive. Shame to die here for something no one will ever know about.'

Fless shrugged his shoulders. 'We all have a job to do.'

'What are you, *Suicide*? I'll never understand why you fellas don't keep us informed of your fun and games. I guess y'all think we're dumb. Come on, son, give me something!'

'You're not gonna hurt me. Your boss will want to speak to me first.'

'Just you keep those knees tight like a belle at the ball. Good boy!'

The American, agitated, looked up to the ground floor of the garage.

Fless stared quizzically at the tuber-faced American agent. The guy wasn't for real.

'Do it, officer. Give yourself a guilt trip.'

Agent Buckley looked at his watch. 'Excuse me a second, son... *Don't you go changin' now.*'

He laughed to himself and dialled a number on his cellphone. The signal was weak. Buckley stepped backwards up the metal stairs.

15

Ashe had come out of his coma during the early hours. As his mind finally merged with his surroundings, the strange dream about a blonde girl dancing naked with a man covered in green leaves faded. The bare room now had the unpleasant edge of reality about it. Outside it was grey.

Two SIS officers in smart blue suits entered the dim ward of Aldershot Military Hospital. They whispered to each other, then approached his bed.

'Dr Ashe, can you talk?'

'Depends on the subject.'

'I'm Giles Bagot. This is Tony Colquitt.'

'Weren't you Major Bagot the last time we met? And you were—'

'A lieutenant, yes, Toby. It's all civil-service style now.'

'Even for you... Giles?'

'We've been asked to supervise in Commodore Marston's absence.'

'Absence?'

'Lost a leg. Above the knee. Intensive care, not far from here.'

'I'm very sorry.'

Bagot smiled weakly. 'I'm afraid you must prepare yourself for a shock.'

'Shocks are for the unprepared.'

'Mrs Lindars is a friend of yours?'

Ashe's heart sank. 'Is she...?'

'Oh no! She's OK.'

'Thank God for that!'

Bagot smiled. 'Shaken, of course. Surgery on her right ear. Residual neck and back pain. Otherwise, fine.'

'And the archdeacon? He's an old friend too.'

Bagot looked down at the polished floor. 'The er... I'm sorry to say, the old boy didn't make it. Dreadfully sorry.'

Tears welled up in Ashe's throbbing eyes.

'You OK, Ashe?'

'It's this pain in my eyes – one in particular.'

'It's concussion. How's your memory?'

'A bit peculiar. I remember being at the meeting... vaguely. And I remember going outside, until... But nothing else about the day at all. How I got there, the previous day... nothing.' Ashe shook his head. 'I remember Brigadier Radclyffe turning up. That was a surprise. Is he all right?'

'Not a scratch. When the Tower blew up, he was in the house bog. Just in time.'

'Merciful relief.'

Stone-faced, Colquitt withdrew a checklist from his briefcase. 'We have some questions.'

Ashe nodded.

'Have you any ideas at all about the explosion? Special recollections? Who might be responsible?'

'God knows. Presumably a bomb.'

'Forensics are still combing the site. We're investigating the security aspect. If the location was known to our enemies, then what else did they know? Who's the leak?'

'I presume the taxi drivers are vetted.'

'Of course.'

Ashe was desperate to lighten the atmosphere. 'You don't think the butler did it, do you, Tony?'

'Reynolds? Well, it's funny you say that, isn't it, Giles?'

'Not really, Tony. The er... butler's whereabouts are a mystery.'

Ashe's sore face cracked into a pained laugh. 'The butler!'

'May have been involved, yes. Not that it adds up. According to survivors, without Reynolds, they'd have burned to death.'

'*Survivors*, Giles? How many?'

'That's what's puzzling. Thanks to Reynolds, we've only one funeral. He'd have been up for a medal if he hadn't scarpered. Now he's a suspect. But then... you yourself were not in the Tower at the time of the explosion...'

'I got a call. Remember *that* vividly. Very embarrassing.'

'Contrary to committee rules, I believe. Who spoke to you?'

'Don't know.'

'You don't know?'

'The sound was breaking up.'

'Breaking up?'

'Yes, Giles, breaking up. Could've been anyone, couldn't it? Except I presume you've already swiped my mobile?'

Colquitt withdrew it from his briefcase and handed it to Bagot. Bagot handed the mobile to Ashe.

'Appears your last call came from someone based in Staffordshire. A woman, name of... Amanda Dyott.'

Ashe laughed, painfully. 'So dear Amanda saved the bastard's life!' He shook his head. 'And I thought she wanted to kill me!'

Colquitt and Bagot looked confused. 'Are you related to this woman, Ashe?'

'Not if I can help it, Giles. She's a girl I know.'

'Know?'

'Bit of a limpet.'

Colquitt whispered something to Bagot, then turned to Ashe.

'Evidently, Toby, somebody wanted you alive.'

'I hope my wanting to be alive is not held against me.'

'But that's a problem, isn't it? Your uncanny survival.'

'Not exactly unharmed though, Giles, am I? The question, surely, is why anybody would want me – and everybody else – dead?'

'Apart from your Ms Dyott, you mean. There's the question of motive. Your phone call was certainly a lucky coincidence.'

Ashe felt the pressure beneath Bagot and Colquitt's emollient tones. 'Are you suggesting I pre-arranged the call so I could get out of harm's way?'

'We'd be foolish not to consider it. However, at this moment, you definitely look more the victim than the perpetrator.'

'Thank you very much.'

'By the way, Ashe, it's been decided that B5(b) will no longer concern itself with investigations into the Kartal Lodge bombing.'

Ashe couldn't believe his ears.

'No official encouragement for such activities, is there Tony?'

'No, Giles. Not in the light of reassurances from the Turkish Embassy. The ambassador has personally assured the PM that there is no British security interest to consider; they have the guilty people. It's an internal matter. We must focus our attention on this new atrocity here at home in the light of current evidence.'

'What "evidence"?'

'We're simply conveying to you the official position.'

'Am I to draw my own conclusions?'

'You are to act in conformity with official expectation. The PM is most concerned, above all, that we focus our intelligence efforts on Iraq, where it's most needed.'

'Still, Toby, every cloud, eh?'

'I see no silver lining, Giles.'

'We've been authorised to inform you of your appointment as acting chair of the B5(b) Advisory Committee.'

'Shouldn't that be "acting bed"? Anyhow, aren't I on your suspect list?'

'Yes, that surprised us too. But then, we don't make the policies. Just cogs in the great wheel. Like you. Now, there are a number of new security clearances to settle, and we shall need your signature on declarations in conformity with the Official Secrets Act and subsequent amendments, codicils, internal arrangements and so on.'

'I'm not even a serving officer.'

'It's the direction things are going in, as you know. We're all civil servants now.'

'Expenses?'

'There are additional expense allowances. Travel; secretarial; research.'

'As chair, I can choose areas for investigation, can I not?'

'Subject to general agreement.'

'And which general would that be?'

Colquitt rose to his feet and fumbled inside his briefcase. He handed Ashe a file. 'You don't have to sign at once. Forty-eight hours would be acceptable.'

As Ashe began to read the secrets priority status on the brown cover, his mobile rang. Bagot immediately grabbed it off the bed covers.

'Yes? No, this is not Dr Ashe. Who is speaking please?'

Ashe lurched forwards and snatched the phone. 'Ashe speaking. Who is that? Right. Call back in ten minutes.'

'That was a foreign voice, Ashe. I must ask you—'

'Until I know more about the caller, Tony, that information is reserved for the acting chair.'

'Not exactly, Ashe. In fact, not at all. Your activities are subject to scrutiny, until we get to the bottom of the Tower bombing. May we expect your unreserved cooperation?'

Ashe looked Bagot and Colquitt hard in the eyes. 'Be assured, I shall devote all my resources to getting hold of whoever killed my dear friend – and who very nearly killed me.'

16

Agent Beck studied the coffee machine outside the deputy director's office. It wasn't a hot drink that interested him. He'd drunk plenty at the five o'clock briefing with the CIA director and the thirty-nine other senior officers from the Intelligence and Operations directorates. Beck knew that the CIA's Counter Terrorism Center was still grappling with the intelligence adjustments that followed 9/11, but surely this was an over-correction: there were more directors at Langley than on *Gone with the Wind*, and Beck was just one of fifteen FBI agents who'd been transferred to headquarters to aid communication between home and abroad.

Beck eyed the coloured lights on the coffee machine; they looked suspicious. What were they wired up to? Who had made the machine? Who serviced it? How often were the contents checked for contamination? Where were the suppliers based? Who was responsible for transporting the contents? What level of clearance was required for coffee machine technicians? Who checked their movements on entering DST?

Asking questions about the obvious came naturally to the mind of a CTC agent. But maybe he needed a break. The stress was getting to him. Or was it just the constant policy changes?

A female voice with a classy southern drawl suddenly filled the dark anteroom. 'Agent Beck. Please enter my office now.'

A light whine was emitted from the steel door to his right. Beck pressed the green safety button. The door slid smoothly across. He entered a spacious, sunlit office, filled with fragrant flowers. A formal-looking lady looked over her horn-rimmed specs at the handsome man entering her office.

'Do sit down, Sherman, please.'

Leanne Gresham, deputy director of the Directorate of Science and Technology, finished signing some papers, sipped some coffee from a porcelain teacup, cleared some space in front of her, then brought her hands together over the altar of rectitude that was her desk.

'Well, Sherman?'

'Ma'am, we have information of use to you and your department.'

Gresham nodded.

'Ma'am, CTC is in receipt of a communication concerning one of your colleagues.'

'The origin of the communication, Agent Beck?'

'Classified, Deputy Director.'

Leanne Gresham removed her specs and stood up. Beck was impressed by her size: nearly six feet, with an athletic frame. 'I had thought, Sherman, that we had all entered a new era of communication. If you want help from us, then I—'

'Forgive me, Deputy Director, but this information is to help you. The source is classified because I've not been empowered to divulge it. However, if you want to contact my department and—'

'I know how to contact your department.' Gresham looked at her watch. 'I was hoping to enjoy supper with my husband.'

'Lucky man.'

'Oh! Do you think so?'

Beck smiled. Gresham glimpsed the crack in the facade.

'Now, never mind all that. What's your information, Sherman?'

'Ma'am, you have a colleague employed on government work at RIBOTech's facility at Paradise, California. An internationally renowned biochemist.'

'Several names spring to mind.' Gresham put her fountain pen to her lips and licked the top. 'Do you know anything about Paradise, Sherman? Ultra secret. But there are several men and women there who match your description.'

'This man is an Iraqi by birth.'

'Professor Sami al-Qasr has been working for the Good Guys since—'

'1992.'

'Quite so. What could our Sami have done to interest the CTC?'

'SIGINT has received a message. Concerning your professor.'

'Signals Intelligence receives some 2,500 cables a day. What makes this one stand out?' She looked at her watch again.

'It's all in this file.' Beck pulled out a slim dossier and placed it gently on Gresham's desk. 'But if I may summarise, the communication came from Baghdad.'

'Which tells us nothing.'

'The communication refers to a British air raid on one of Saddam Hussein's high-security facilities near Basra in 1992. He gives some details. They suggest insider knowledge.'

'Why do you keep saying "he"?'

Beck laughed but clipped it short. 'You have a point, Deputy Director. To be frank, we do not know the gender of the sender.'

Gresham stifled a giggle.

Beck smiled. 'The message says that the raid explains why al-Qasr's usefulness to the US has been...'

'Has been...?

'Has been less than we might have expected before his defection from Saddam's regime.'

Gresham's eyes widened. 'OK.'

'*Has* his work been disappointing, ma'am?'

'Complex question. His theoretical work has been first class. What else does the message say?'

'The message is emphatic that al-Qasr has relations with Ansar al-Sunna.'

'That's no joke.'

'Ansar al-Sunna has been getting stronger over recent months. We thought we had them on the run.'

'And you haven't?'

'Events move fast in Iraq, ma'am.'

'Anything else?'

'The message ends with a plea for the US and the world to protect the Yezidi people of northern Iraq and the Transcaucasus. Apparently, they have much to fear from Professor Sami al-Qasr.'

'The who?'

'The Yezidi people, ma'am. Natives of Kurdistan. Most live in the Kurdish Autonomous Region, near northern Iraq's border with Turkey. There's a note on the subject in the file. Frankly, it makes little sense to us.'

'Desperate lobbying, maybe. Maybe connected with the status of the Kurds of northern Iraq. A plea for attention.'

'Maybe. It's the reference to Ansar al-Sunna that makes further investigation imperative. They're the guys fuelling the insurgency.'

Gresham folded her arms and walked over to the window overlooking the complex of concrete and glass. 'I gotta say, I am surprised.'

'I'm sorry?'

'We have two security programmes in place around Professor al-Qasr already.'

'Two?'

'Yeah, and both seem pretty contradictory.'

Beck sat back in his chair.

'You see, Sherman, when Sami first came over from Iraq, after debriefing, security checks and so on, it was decided his work would be permanently shadowed by one of our experts in the microbiology field. He's kind of an understudy, except that Sami doesn't know he exists – as such. The shadow used to operate out of the Office of Research and Development. He's now based in our Office of Advanced Technologies and Programs.'

'Opened in 2001.'

'Good. You've done your homework. I hope it leaves time for fun.'

'Thank you, ma'am.'

'It was necessary for security reasons, but also because these genius researchers tend to sit on some of their discoveries longer than needs be.'

'You're spying on him.'

'On his work; not on him personally.'

'OK.'

'Secondly, he comes under our personal security cover program.'

'Personal security cover? Is he in danger?'

'Well, Sherman. Some guys are in danger. And some guys are in love. What's *your* problem?'

17

Dawn was just breaking, and the misty Sacramento Valley still shimmered with the streaks and splashes of last night's neon.

Al-Qasr pulled his black Toyota pickup into the dusty drive of Kismet to see the three-car garage door wide open. There were skid-traces by the house. Where was Buckley? Where was the dog? His sixth sense in overdrive, al-Qasr wrenched the pickup into reverse, skidded backwards into a wooden out-house – smashing its sides – and sped back up his drive towards the mountain road to Paradise.

At the shaded entrance, a Cadillac screeched out in front of him. An arm shot through the open window and took aim. Al-Qasr reversed again. A bullet grazed his windscreen, ricocheting into the darkness. The pickup hit a big BMW.

Figures ran towards him, waving handguns. Al-Qasr shoved the pickup into first, ducked below the windscreen, rammed his foot down and hurtled straight for the Cadillac blocking the drive entrance. One of the men, hit by the steel bumper, tumbled awkwardly into the bushes; the other dived out of the way.

Al-Qasr smashed into the BMW, sweeping it to the other side of the track. Inside, Mati Fless gripped the wheel, trying to keep control of the vehicle. Turning on an angle, it slipped into a ditch by the entrance.

Al-Qasr turned down the hill. A shot rang out behind him, pierced the rear window and thumped into the passenger seat headrest. Al-Qasr slammed his foot down and roared off down the hairpin bends.

Fless wanted to give chase, but was called over to his wounded comrade.

'That bastard's got nine lives, I swear it.'

At the bottom of the hill, al-Qasr pulled into a side-track and sped a hundred metres towards an old barn he'd bought for the day he knew would come. The Toyota rolled into position. Extinguishing the headlights, al-Qasr jumped out. Breathing heavily, he reached for a switch; a dim bulb flickered into life. He then pulled a tarpaulin over the pickup, turned the light off and crawled under the chassis. Feeling for a rope latch, he raised a wooden hatch. Sami al-Qasr slipped from sight like a desert hare.

18

London's little-known Hemlock Club could be addictive. Tucked away in Masons' Yard, off Duke Street, St James's, members were expected to distinguish themselves through activities the club's famous 'Rule 49' described as 'notorious and heretical'. The Rule had provided mirth for many generations of Hemlockians.

Members took wry delight in listening to archbishops publicly questioning key tenets of their faith, lawyers probing the validity of the Law, scientists suggesting Newton might be in error, and politicians declaring that democracy might not have been the sole destiny of the species. The risk of public disapprobation, condemnation or even a brief hiatus in an otherwise stainless career was regarded as a small price to pay for admission.

The doorman, dressed entirely in moleskin, nodded to Ashe then coolly appraised the stranger. Like a hangman assessing his latest client, he approached the towering Turk and inspected his neck. He then reached beneath his desk and brought out a mahogany tray bearing a selection of fine ties that had once been the property of late members. 'Perhaps sir would favour a more modern tie, to match his coat?'

Aslan assented, taking a black leather Slim Jim. It went well with his blue shirt and black Italian leather jacket. Ashe nodded his approval.

'The name "Hemlock", Dr Ashe – is it from the legend of Socrates' death? The great philosopher forced to take the poison for telling the truth?'

'Socrates has always been regarded as the true founder of the club, although the deeds of foundation – like so much that is true – lie buried beneath the rubble of time.'

'Ah! The "rubble of time". I fear we shall be seeing more of that.'

'Do you place your faith in forensics, Colonel?'

'I place faith in this.' Aslan touched his nose.

Ashe laughed politely and guided the Turkish colonel through dark corridors to the walnut-panelled restaurant. A bottle of 1998 vintage Pommery stood erect at the centre of their table. Klimt, the waiter, darted forwards to open it, his grey, greasy locks swaying over his bony shoulders.

'Why did you ring me, Colonel? How did you get my number?'

'Hardly a challenge, Dr Ashe. A NATO contact told me about the attack on your meeting. I had a hunch. The two events could be linked.'

'Two events?'

'The Lodge bombing in Istanbul.'

'Long way from Hertfordshire, Colonel.'

'Our enemies have long arms. And I confess, my assistant, Ali, in addition to being a semi-competent secretary is also a computer specialist. Generously he sacrificed his free weekend to penetrate your security wall. Ali isolated your personal interest in the Kartal Masonic attack. It gave him an opportunity to show off his English.'

While miffed, Ashe could see the funny side of the impertinence. He instinctively liked Aslan. 'I shall look forward to returning the favour.'

As the rich red Cabardès flowed and the French onion soup gave way to rack of lamb followed by coffee ice cream, Ashe discussed with Aslan the mythology of Jewish–Masonic conspiracy and its place in Islamic extremism. Aslan's views were enlightening.

By the time brandy was served, the colonel was ready to show his cards.

'Frankly, Dr Ashe, I don't enjoy your freedom of

71

investigation. I've been told investigations into the Lodge bombing must cease. I've been informed that the case is closed.'

'And is it?'

Aslan sighed deeply. 'It is always possible my superiors did not like the direction I was taking.'

'Which was?'

'An independent direction.'

'I see.' Ashe felt kinship with the colonel's predicament, but could say nothing.

'You see, Dr Ashe, in Istanbul, one cannot always see eye to eye with the revered chief of police.'

'May his name be blessed.'

Aslan smiled. 'And there are other voices… from on high.'

Ashe summoned Klimt to refill the colonel's glass. 'Thank you, Klimt.' He turned to Aslan. '*Other voices*, you say?'

The colonel nodded.

'And your hands are tied.'

Aslan grunted. 'But not my feet! Perhaps you can be my hands for a while.'

'I, Colonel?'

'How could I not think of you, Tobbi Ashe, after all you did when your consulate was hit in my city. You made quite an impression.'

'Thank you, Colonel. It was an interesting experience. But I don't see how we can help this time. The Kartal Lodge bombing is not a priority.'

'Officially?' Aslan gulped his brandy. Ashe said nothing.

Aslan thought deeply, burying his teeth into his fist. 'Would you consider pursuing a line without official encouragement, Dr Ashe?'

Ashe savoured the idea as Aslan narrowed his eyes and pointed a finger at him. 'I could offer … guidance.'

'I'd need something more concrete. Evidence of a link between the Lodge bombing and the attack on our department, for example.'

'I see.'

'By the way, who is your "friend" in NATO?'

Aslan laughed. 'I prefer to keep my friends...' He looked at Ashe directly. 'And to protect them.'

The table was silent. Aslan realised the Englishman needed more.

'Dr Ashe, as you know, Turkey today is a most complex phenomenon. What if I said to you that the Lodge bombing was not necessarily the work of extreme Islamists? Or shall we say, not the work of extremists alone.'

Aslan felt a tug on his line; Ashe had taken the hook. 'You see, Tobbi, Freemasonry is viewed with great suspicion by a faction of ultra-nationalists in my country. There are those who find *The Protocols of the Elders of Zion* stimulating. They see Jewish conspiracies everywhere. Freemasons, Jews – it's all the same to them. They see...' Aslan sighed, '... problems.'

Ashe thought hard. 'OK. What I need is the guest list. It should be on the summons to the meeting the night the Lodge was bombed. And there may have been guests not mentioned on the summons.'

'I'll see what can be done, Tobbi. No guarantees.'

'I don't need them. Your word is—'

'Best left unsaid, Dr Ashe.'

19

Giessen, Germany

It was a filthy day. Black clouds had swept down from northern Germany and plastered the Hessen region. Giessen under a cloud is a very flat place.

The elderly man patted his brown mac dry as the taxi from Marburg disappeared round a corner in a yellow streak of drizzle. The younger, taller man shook his suit trousers and wiped the mud from his conservative black shoes. He smiled at the older man. The glint in his eye suggested things could be worse. The old man's blue eyes shone back. The young man gathered up a small suitcase. It clanked as he raised it; the old man frowned.

'I know. I shall wrap it up again as soon as I can.'

'It's never good to rush.'

'It's never good to have to rush.'

The old man looked sad for a moment.

They turned into a wide, wet boulevard. On the left was a grey sports centre with an outdoor basketball park, pocked with puddles. To the right, lines of flat, uniform barracks: a NATO army base. The men hurried across the boulevard. Rain splashed over their green canvas fishing hats.

At the corner, opposite the base entrance to the base, a policeman sat in his green-and-white BMW, reporting in to his station. Through a side mirror, he observed two foreigners approaching.

The old man's long, unkempt beard reminded him of a picture he'd seen of Bhagwan Shree Rajneesh, the late sharp-eyed guru

74

with the limousine collection. The Bhagwan had been banned from entering Germany lest he influence youthful minds with his orange robes and cultish philosophy, so the policeman never knew whether the guru was a good thing or a bad thing. But he knew he was foreign.

He rubbed his forefinger and thumb, eyeing the men as they approached. No, the man was not Indian. Perhaps Italian... Spanish? Maybe an Arab.

The younger man discreetly tapped his elder's arm, alerting him to the police car. Seizing the moment, he hurried to the car and rapped on the window. People did not normally approach German policemen for directions.

He cleared the raindrops from his little moustache and in flawless German asked the policeman the way to the hospital, explaining he was a specialist and that his brother worked at Giessen's *Krankenhaus*.

'Looking for a job?'

'There is a great need for specialists.'

'Who's your friend?'

'My father. Visiting from Turkey.'

Ah! That was it! The man at the window was a *Gastarbeiter*, an immigrant worker, from Turkey. The policeman was not used to seeing Turks in suits, but now Turkey was negotiating to join the EU, he knew he'd have to get used to it. In the back of his mind was a recent pep talk on how policemen should deal with Turks experiencing racist abuse.

'I would take you to the hospital, Herr Doktor, but my orders are to stay here. Security.'

'I understand, Officer.'

'You're very close to the hospital. Turn left down Lessingstrasse at the end of the boulevard, then left again into Am Dünkelsloh. Hospital's behind the sports hall.'

'Thank you, Officer. Good day.'

'Good day, Herr Doctor.'

The policeman watched the two men walk stoically on

through the downpour. He squinted, wriggled his nose, and thought for a few seconds. 'Hey, you! Hold it!'

Seizing his companion's thin arm, the young man turned. 'Sir?'

'Come back here!'

The man splashed his way back through the puddles as the policeman got out of the car and opened the rear door. The young man caught sight of the pistol by the policeman's side, then stared into the hollow of the back seat as if it were the mouth of hell. The policeman bent inside, his back vulnerable. The young man looked to his friend. The old man shook his head.

The policeman lifted an umbrella off the floor and handed it over with a smile. 'My wife's spare. She won't miss it.'

Grappling with the tartan umbrella, the men hurried on, soon lost in the greyness.

20

Mosul, northern Iraq

'What do you think, Saddiq – buttercups around the door?'

'In Bashiqa: all right. But not here in Mosul, Qoteh. Time's not right.'

Disappointed but accepting, Qoteh gathered the flowers off the kitchen table and patted them into a wicker basket. She looked around their little shop, at the piles of Turkish and British beer cans, bottles of Greek wine and cases of American cigarettes. Her husband was right. Mosul was a war zone, a powder keg, a city of hope and a den of despair.

'If we cannot have the flowers, Saddiq, it can't be safe for Rozeh to stay here any longer.'

'She likes the school, Qoteh. She's doing well. The Americans have been kind – with books and tapes. It's a blessing.'

Qoteh took off her green silk scarf and wiped her hands and brow. She looked at herself in the little mirror below the battery-powered clock: a Marlboro promotion. The lines were pronounced about her bright blue eyes: trenches of experience. Her hardened lips were not as full as they had once been, but her daughter made her proud. She was twice as beautiful.

It had been a blessed marriage, even though they hadn't been able to have children of their own. Saddiq was a hard worker, a good learner and a pious man – despite his gambling. At least he won more than he lost, and would never bet more than he could afford. Rozeh never wanted for anything. Except, of course, what they all wanted: *peace*.

'I couldn't sleep last night, Saddiq.'

Saddiq had gone upstairs and was trying to shave. 'What was that?'

'I need some sleep.'

'We all do.' He cut himself.

Saddiq thought of the previous night's bloodshed. American planes attacked the south of the city after a suicide bomber exploded a petrol truck near a new US base, close to the airport. Saddiq hoped the bombs had hit their targets. He hoped that Khuda, the Almighty, had saved the good and brought the bad men to their end.

Over the past week, the city seemed to have been falling apart. Insurgents from the south had joined up with the radical Sunni militia Ansar al-Sunna, looting police stations of weapons and equipment. Both the Kurdistan Democratic Party and the Patriotic Union of Kurdistan seemed powerless to halt the mayhem. Without the Americans, things would probably be worse – but they never seemed to be there when the danger came.

It was a bad time, but Saddiq knew in his heart that the wicked would not prosper forever. Things had to improve some day; they just had to, so long as the Alliance did not turn their backs on the northern zone. But there was no denying it: the safe area had been safer before the invasion.

Saddiq put on his spotless white shirt and pulled up his brown cotton trousers. The question was whether to open the shop. The family needed the money; they hoped to get out – perhaps to relatives in Germany, or even to Britain, where life was good.

He looked out of the upstairs bedroom window across the bridge to the suburb of Faisaliya on the other side of the River Tigris. The state school there had both Christian and Muslim teachers, so Rozeh might get to see different sides of the truth – or she might just end up being confused. He would have preferred that she'd stayed in the country with her own people, but there was no future there. She wanted to be a doctor – something his mother could have hardly even dreamt of. Imagine, his only daughter a *doctor*! The world was changing. Rozeh knew English and could make a living in the world.

He looked at his watch. Four o'clock. She should be crossing the bridge soon, with her friend Fatima, whose father ran the old officers' club next door. And the boys whose parents worked at the law courts a couple of blocks away would protect them.

Qoteh entered the bedroom. 'Can you see her?'

'She will be home soon.'

'I know. But can you see her?'

'Please, Qoteh, we must trust in God.'

'Are there troops on the bridge?'

'Yes. They are there.'

'I never went to school, Saddiq. It was forbidden. Why did we let Rozeh go to school with the outsiders?'

'We listened to the Kochek.'

'Tell me again what he said.'

Saddiq put his warm arms around his wife. 'He said he had a vision of Rozeh. She was helping the sick. Many were dying. The world was black, but Rozeh was light. People did as she told them, men and women. She was smiling; happy in her work.'

'Are you sure your brother wasn't just trying to be nice to her?'

'Ask him.'

'He's not here. I'm asking you.'

'My old brother has never told a lie. If he says he saw Rozeh; then that is what he saw. He says she came from a special place.'

'But maybe that was in a different life; maybe her next life.'

'Maybe. Who knows these things? We must trust in God.'

'Your brother, he is a Kochek; he's supposed to know.'

Saddiq laughed. 'If he knew all that, we could take him to the airbase in the south and get the Americans to pay him 100 dollars for every piece of information. God reveals to him what we need to know; not what we want to know.'

'He's a good man. I believe him, Saddiq. He is good.'

Saddiq kissed his wife. 'God is good. Let's go downstairs. Let's open the shop for a few hours. Somebody out there needs drink and cigarettes.'

No sooner had Saddiq unbolted the front door and pulled up the shutters than a small crowd of Kurds and Assyrians gathered at the door, clutching orders from the battered clubs and bars that lined the street between the bridge and the pumping station in the west. Those who did not drink craved cigarettes – Turkish, American, British, anything.

Saddiq smiled at Qoteh through his thick black moustache and opened the cash register. Below the register was a 9 mm Browning pistol. It had cost him a lot, but that was two years ago. Now he could pick one up in the *suq* for next to nothing.

By 5.45, there was still no sign of Rozeh. Qoteh was anxious, finding it hard to concentrate on the currency transactions presented to her by eager buyers: dollars, dinars, Turkish lira.

She kept looking over to Saddiq, who was busy piling up cans of beer, cases of wine and cartons of cigarettes. Saddiq smiled and nodded gracefully. Qoteh put the radio on. They liked to listen to the US Forces network, even though they understood little of the language. But they knew their daughter would understand it, and, somehow, they were listening for her too.

Qoteh kept thinking of the joy that would be Rozeh's, so soon, at the Sarsaleh, on Wednesday in Bashiqa. *Bashiqa*: the best Spring Festival of them all! Qoteh would pull out her mother's old trunk so that Rozeh could appear on Thursday in the *debka*, the dance that brought souls alive in the eyes of all who danced and all who watched. The musicians would beat the huge tambourines that shook the earth and ruffled the feathers of the highest birds, and the hills would ring to the melodious cries of the flute.

Just thinking about the *debka* and her beautiful, sweet daughter, Qoteh could feel in her fingers, not the dry dullness of hard currency, but the soft, purple cotton of Rozeh's long chemise; she could picture the rainbow colours of her red baggy trousers, yellow waistcoat and orange jacket, with the woollen *meyzar* knotted over her right shoulder.

Qoteh would open her box of gold filigree earrings with their precious stones, the bracelets that her great-great-great-great-grandmother had worn when the English archaeologist Layard had come to excavate Nineveh across the river. Then, to set it off, the great wide belt with its huge silver buckle and silver pin – the belt she had worn on her wedding day.

A shot. An American M16. Qoteh looked to Saddiq. It came from the bridge. An explosion. Machine-gun fire.

21

'The shop is closing! The shop is closing!' Qoteh handed a journalist back his cash. 'I'm sorry, we must close.'

The US Humvee outside the shop was revving impatiently as Saddiq loaded the last crate of wine onto its trailer. As it pulled sharply away towards the bridge, several crates tumbled off the back and smashed to the ground. Loitering children picked up the broken bottles and, laughing, poured what was left of the wine into tins and buckets.

Qoteh pulled down the shutters and a bullet ricocheted off the metal. Saddiq rushed inside. He reached for the padlock by the cash register. More bullets thudded into the plasterwork outside. A child screamed.

'Don't lock the front, Saddiq! Rozeh may need to—'

'We must, Qoteh! If we see her, I will open it. I have a gun.'

Qoteh began reciting a prayer she'd heard from the midwife when her cousin's child was born. The midwife had repeated it over and over again as the birth reached its crisis point.

> *O Khatun Fakhra, help her!*
> *O Khidr Elias, help her!*
> *O Sheykh Matti, help her!*

Another explosion; more shots. Qoteh screamed. A hole had appeared at the side of the bridge; twisted steel bled from the concrete.

Qoteh looked to Saddiq. 'Tell me, husband, tell me they won't let the children cross the bridge. They will keep them at the school. Tell me, that is why she is late! They are keeping them safe at the school.'

'Yes, Qoteh. I know she is safe.'

'Tell me the angel is with her!'

'He is with us, Qoteh. He is with us.'

The street between the shop and the once great River Tigris was empty now; the children had fled with their spoils.

A gun battle on the bridge. Shouts. Bullets. Cries.

'That's her! She's come round the back.'

'But… you have not seen her cross the bridge. Saddiq! Your gun, help her!'

More banging on the back door.

'Rozeh, is that you? Is that you?'

The kicking on the door stopped. Saddiq stopped still in the shop, paralysed. More bullets outside. He was sweating; the air was angry. He reached for the gun beneath the cash register. It was there. Good. It was loaded.

'Get out of here! Go! Go! I will call the police!'

'They won't come! They won't help you! They're on the bridge! Devil worshippers! Devil worshippers! Evil! Evil! Devils! Devils! Satans! Satans! We kill you! We kill you! We kill you all! Death to the infidel!'

Qoteh was standing at the foot of the stairs, steeling herself.

'We can go, Qoteh! We have time.'

'We cannot. Rozeh!'

'Evil! Evil! Drinkers! Drunks! Corrupters of the faithful! Collaborators! Transgressors! Dogs! Devils! Devils! Devils!'

The chanting increased. The kicking on the steel door increased, echoing coldly around the shop.

'We must wait for Rozeh. This is her home. We must be here for her. What if she comes back and we are gone?'

Qoteh started screaming at the mob. 'Who are you? We know you! Yes, we know you. We know your fathers and mothers and

83

grandmothers. They know us. You know we are not evil. You know we love God. We love God.'

'Blasphemers! You Yezidis are Blasphemers! Kill the liars! Kill the devils! You bring temptation to the faithful! You ignore the Law! God smiles on the killers of the pagan Yezidi!'

'We are not pagans! We love God! We are all human beings! Like you! Leave us! Go in peace! Do God's will!'

The shop went quiet.

'Unlock the shutters, Saddiq.'

'And let them in at the front?'

'If they get in, we can at least—'

'No, we stay. We fight. If God wills, we will win.'

More explosions on the bridge; rapid fire; police alarms; the heat.

The couple heard an object roll against the metal door. A stone? Pray it be a stone.

'Get down!'

The door flew into the shop smashing through a stack of beer cans. In rushed a gang of desert Arabs, teenagers, some in black headbands emblazoned with lines from the Koran, carrying knives and machetes.

> O *Khatun Fakhra, help us!*
> O *Khidr Elias, help us!*
> O *Sheykh Matti, help us!*

Saddiq stood up. 'In the Name of God, leave this house!'

A Fedayeen, his face hidden under the trademark black woollen turban of the paramilitaries loyal to Saddam Hussein, emerged from the group. 'Polluters of the Sacred City! In the name of all the Fedayeen martyrs and all who defend the faith from the Crusaders, servants of Satan and the power of evil, you are condemned to die!'

The man gestured for the others to back off. He then took out a grenade from beneath his shirt and pulled the pin. Without a thought, Saddiq shot him between the eyes. The grenade dropped and the Fedayeen fell quickly on top of it.

'Get out! Get out!' cried one of the intruders.

The blast hurled Saddiq into the shutters as the shop's ceiling collapsed.

By seven o'clock, the bridge was quiet. American reinforcements had arrived from the south and re-established the roadblock. The skirmish did not make the news – because it wasn't news. Things like this happened all the time. At eight o'clock, teachers led a group of schoolchildren over the bridge. The boys played war games and the girls played pop music on their Walkmans.

As the line got closer to the other side, as the teachers were body-searched by the soldiers, as the moon vanished behind a huge cloud of burnt oil, as the dogs barked and life in Mosul went on, Rozeh saw her home. Only, it was not home any more.

Outside the battered shutters, buckled as if blasted by a huge fist and pulled up a few feet above a pool of deep, dark blood, was a row of bodies and body parts. These were not parts like you would buy to mend a car. These were parts that could never make a whole. They weren't people and the people were no longer in the parts. Mute, cold, pale, signifying nothing but an absence of something that had woken up that morning, dreamed of better times to come, had lunch, had… life.

Rozeh, her thick black hair framing a face wet with tears, was suddenly an orphan, a daughter of the war. The boys who a few hours earlier had scraped as much booty as they could off the road were back to see what might be left in the shop. One of them came up to Rozeh, who was staring at the blankets, wondering which of the shapes beneath was her mother or father.

'Can I give you a drink, lady?'

'No.'

'Is that your mother?'

'I don't know.'

'Maybe she'll wake up, or come out of Paradise to see you.'
Rozeh cried. The police took her away.

At the shelled-out station near the old imperial post office, the police asked her a few questions, but she had no answers. She only had a question:

'Why won't they leave us alone?'

22

Outskirts of Hamburg, Germany

Inside the Audi, the atmosphere was tense. The old man couldn't sleep; the younger man was shaken. The driver, eyes darting from catseye to headlight, was nervous. He'd taken several wrong turnings before getting on to the E22 autobahn at Lübeck, north-east of the port of Hamburg. Soon the bleak city lights and industrial outskirts of Hamburg itself filled the windscreen: not a welcoming sight.

Turning sharply off the ring-road in Wandsbek, they headed uncertainly down the wide Wandsbeker Marktstrasse towards the Altstadt and the city centre. The road was clear and the pavements were empty. As they passed the old Lutheran church in the Jacobs-Park, dimly lit by an orange spotlight, the driver looked nervously to the rear-view mirror.

'*Polizei.*'

'Continue.'

The younger man turned to look back. The green-and-white BMW was gaining ground fast. By the time they'd reached the junction at the Mühlendamm, it was tailgating the Audi. Hands sweating, the driver saw two policemen, one taking their registration number, the other making a radio call. He rubbed the back of his neck. His knees felt stiff. He bit his lip and gripped the steering wheel as if it were the last link with life.

His nerve broke. The car squealed to a stop outside the Marienkrankenhaus hospital. Unable to brake in time, the police skidded into the Audi's rear. The passengers lurched forwards,

87

the old man's nose smashing into the driver's seat, spurting blood over his grey moustache.

'What are you doing, you fool!' The younger man gripped the driver's shoulder.

While the policemen were recovering from the shock, the Audi driver hammered into reverse and ground the police car into a lamp-post. Its right bumper wrenched into the wheel cavity; the car was crippled.

The Audi driver cut his lights, revved the engine and stormed into first. He U-turned up the one-way Mühlendamm and headed north, dodging startled traffic up Schürbeker Strasse to the busy junction with Mundsburger Damm.

'Stop! This is insane! What are you doing?' The younger man pulled a silk handkerchief from his breast pocket and thrust it under the nose of the old man. The old man said nothing.

Deaf to all entreaties, the driver slammed his foot down; he had no work permit. Deportation was unthinkable.

Racing south down Mundsburger Damm, they were soon in sight of the glittering Aussenalster Lake. Ignoring a red light, the driver screeched into Buchtstrasse's narrow funnel and skidded to a halt outside a department store.

'I get new plates.'

Hurling himself out amid the howling of sirens, he dashed round to the boot of the car.

The old man looked at his friend. While the driver tried frantically to screw the plates to the back of the Audi, the men flung open the back doors and disappeared into the shadows. The younger man pointed. 'This way! Do you have the case?'

The old man nodded.

The driver shot up from behind the open boot. 'Hey! What about my money? It's a long way from Giessen!'

The men were nearly at the end of the street. 'You'll get your reward! God be with you!'

They rounded the corner into Sechslingspforte.

'Just keep walking. How's your nose?'

'Not broken, but I...' The old man started coughing. 'No... no... It's all right. I'm not sick. It's just that... Do you know the saying from the Christian Bible?' He stopped, inviting the younger man to look around at the display lights in the shop windows; the neon glitter high above the hotels and fashionable stores; the fairy-lit floating restaurants on the lake; the yellow street lights, and the beams of passing cars. 'See! There is light everywhere, but we walk in the cold shadows.'

'Is that it?'

'No! It says: "The birds have their nests; the fox has his lair. But the son of man has nowhere to lay his head."'

23

The 2.8 roaring litres of turbocharged V6 Saab 9-3 churned up the gravel outside Peover Hall, a handsome Tudor brick stately home in mid-Cheshire. Ashe stepped out of the Rosso Bologna open convertible to admiring glances from women in black miniskirts, large hats and veils. Admiral Lord Whitmore was not so impressed. Recently returned from France with Lady Nancy, he was not yet re-accustomed to the throb and tension of British life.

Lady Nancy, a radiant seventy-five, stepped nimbly over the gravel to greet Ashe. 'So nice to see you, Toby. Such a pity about the circumstances.'

'Yes. A terrible thing.'

'Save the jaw-jaw, Ashe, we're walking in procession. Get in line, man.'

Ignoring her husband, Lady Nancy took Ashe's arm as over a hundred mourners formed themselves into a quiet line that edged its way towards St Lawrence's Church, Over Peover, one of Cheshire's fine old chapels, set peacefully in the wooded grounds around Peover Hall.

Soon Ashe found himself nudging a marble sarcophagus. Sir Philip Mainwaring lay recumbent, his armoured hands raised in prayer as they had been since his entombment in 1652.

It had been Loveday-Rose's special wish to be buried at Peover. One of the late archdeacon's hobbies had been Cheshire history. The chapel of St Lawrence had always seemed to concentrate that interest in his rich imagination. Loveday-Rose cared about England's future because he had loved its past. Ashe had imbibed much of the same philosophy; it had been a powerful bond between them.

The service began with a platitudinous address from a Bunter-faced 'team' vicar. Ashe started to yawn. A nudge in the ribs from Lady Nancy returned him to the end of the vicar's vacuous vale-diction. 'And now Toby is going to say a few words about his old friend.'

Relief flowed like a wave over the congregation as Ashe got up and made his way past the unctuous vicar to the Jacobean wooden pulpit.

He steadied himself. 'A great man has passed from us.' Ashe paused, staring into the lake of distinguished faces melting before his eyes. Emotion was getting the better of him.

'The silver chain has snapped; the golden bowl is broken. Archdeacon Aleric Loveday-Rose, Military Cross, was the kind of man the Church of England cannot replace. The vitality of the Victorian age provided the mettle of his upbringing, and the fire and fury of wars and revolutions informed his adulthood. Aleric was truly a match for his times.

'How was it possible for this man, who had witnessed the twentieth century's carnage at first hand, to say to me that, at the end of this terrible century, Truth, Beauty and Love had survived intact?

'He could say it because *he* had survived intact; his integrity still shining.

'Aleric, my dear friend, you have crossed the bridge – and you are home. And I do not think its light and its furnishings will be strange to you.

'Farewell, my friend.'

A few members of the congregation began spontaneously to clap, gently and tentatively. But as Ashe's final words echoed from the stone floor to the vaulted roof, and as the stained glass cast beams of many colours across the nave, the applause became a swell.

Ashe left the pulpit and returned briskly to his seat. Admiral Whitmore nodded in sage approval; Lady Nancy gripped Ashe's hand while clearing tears from her rouged cheeks. 'Thank you, Toby.'

The reception on the neat lawns of Peover Hall was a stylish upper-class affair.

Admiral Lord Whitmore, his weathered jowls deeply tanned, approached Ashe. 'That was a damn fine address, Ashe. Though I'm never quite sure if you're serious – and, dammit, I never see you shooting! You don't hunt, and whenever the subject of sport comes up, you disappear.'

'It's a dull boy that doesn't like sport, Lord Whitmore.'

'There you go again! Are you trying to tell me you're dull?'

'That's enough, Gabriel,' interjected Lady Nancy. 'Toby has all the right values – that's what counts, isn't it, Toby?'

'I hope so.'

'You see, Gabriel, you just have to face the fact that there are different kinds of clever people – and some are a bit cleverer than you.'

'Tosh! Clever is one thing; useful is another. Ideas need to be applied. I bloody well hope you find who smashed up my Tower! And bring that damned butler of mine to the bar of justice!'

Ashe's mobile emitted a gentle tone. He made a swift apology and took refuge beneath the boughs of an ancient cedar.

'Colonel! Where are you?'

'Hamburg. Visiting relatives in St Pauli. Listen... Is this a secure line?'

'Yes, but I haven't much time.'

'I have that list for you. I'm posting it from here. There will be no cover note and no source references.'

'Understood.'

'This call never happened. I can do no more for you. Good luck!'

The line went dead.

Ashe felt a tap on his shoulder.

'Hello!'

'Hello. You must be…'

'I'm the archdeacon's niece.'

'Melissa!'

'You remember!'

'What are you doing now?'

'Publishing.'

'Lucky publishing.'

'Lucky me.'

Melissa was attractive. A fountain of deep brown wavy hair cascaded around her rosy face, framing her bright eyes and aquiline nose. She was wearing Ashe's favourite kind of dress: cotton, with a plunging neckline, buttoned at the front.

'You know, Uncle was a very good judge of character. He liked you a lot.'

From the corner of his eye, Ashe saw two men in dark suits and black ties. Surely not…? Giles Bagot and Tony Colquitt approached like beagles on a scent.

Ashe put his arm around Melissa and began to walk round the back of the cedar towards a nest of rhododendrons.

'I say, Ashe! Ashe!'

Ashe tried to ignore them. Melissa looked at him with compassionate eyes. 'Go on, you'd better talk to them. We can catch up later.' She squeezed Ashe's hand and headed off, her full bottom swaying sexily in her breezy dress.

'Glad to see you've recovered, Dr Ashe. Perhaps you'll feel more communicative today.'

'Small talk over, Giles?'

'That's bloody charming, Ashe.'

'You want to know who phoned me. And I can't tell you.'

'What are you up to, Ashe?'

'I can't tell you the name. It was a Turkish journalist. Anonymous source. Said he had a contact in NATO. Said he'd

93

heard about the explosion at the Tower and believed it was linked to something in Istanbul.'

'Nothing else?'

'Zero.'

Bagot sighed. 'Why didn't you get more out of him?'

'Told him I couldn't go further without proof of ID.'

'Good. Proper procedure.'

'That's it. Now, if you'll excuse me.'

Ashe headed back to the reception. The wine was beginning to flow. He caught Melissa's eye. 'Are you staying with your family tonight, Melissa?'

24

Sherman Beck hurried through the angular maze of the CTC's operations coordinating area. He had just three minutes to make a meeting with his director on the seventh floor. If he didn't make it, Beck risked his work being buried beneath piles of new leads. Take a week off for a bad cold and you might come back to a different war.

Computers peeped, phones bleeped, and every wall seemed steeped in TV sets: al-Jazeera, CNN, military command centres. It made the Fox newsroom look parochial.

Beck jumped into the elevator. His director shared the seventh floor with the Director of Central Intelligence. This was politically useful for Lee Kellner, who made the most of it. A former sub-editor for the *Washington Post*, fifty-five-year-old Kellner regarded his ability to sift relevant from irrelevant stories as second to none. 'Proven in Commerce' was his motto, and it was stuck to his door – as were the entrails of those who crossed him, or so he bragged.

'You got five minutes max.'

'Just five?'

'Give or take your balls. D'ya wanna make the President's Threat Matrix Report?'

'Dr Sami al-Qasr, sir. Having met with Leanne Gresham, I feel—'

'*Feel*, Beck?'

'Think, sir.'

Kellner nodded.

'I think the communication regarding Professor al-Qasr at Paradise, California, sir, requires immediate action.'

'Reason?'

'D'you recall the Gitana, Daley, Rikanik and Kelly investigations?'

'David Kelly? The British guy. Worked for the Rockingham Cell and UNSCOM.'

'Yes, sir. Biological weapons specialist. Committed suicide July 2003.'

'Alleged suicide. Big scandal in Britain. Remind me about the other guys.'

'Your investigation explored relations between Kelly and the US bio-defence industry. Looked for a link with the mysterious deaths of Francisco Gitana, Greg Daley and Boris Rikanik.'

'And there wasn't one, was there?'

'File's still open, sir. Regarding Gitana, Daley and Rikanik. Gitana and Daley were both involved in DNA sequencing.'

'Refresh.'

'Weaponised pathogens, sir. In theory, it's possible to create a weapon that targets only certain races.'

'You got me. Keep talking.'

'In November 2001, Gitana was found unconscious in a Miami parking lot, after receiving a late call. Inquest said natural causes, but his family claimed four men attacked him. A few weeks later, Daley washed up 300 miles downstream from a Mississippi bridge on which his car was found with the lights on and the keys in the ignition. He'd just left a Memphis banquet for fellow researchers.'

'Mississippi. It's coming back now. And Rikanik?'

'Found dead, 16 November 2001, in his bed. Only ten days after meeting Daley in Boston to discuss DNA sequencing. Colleagues said he was in good health. Rikanik is the Russian who fled to Britain from the Soviet Union in 1989. He brought us Russian plans to use cruise missiles to spread smallpox and plague.'

'Such charm!'

'Said they got the idea from us, sir.'

'Of course. What didn't they steal from us? Fucking plague, that's what!'

'The Russian plans ended with the fall of the old regime. Rikanik warned MI6 debriefers the weapons could be used by terror groups, with missiles from China or North Korea. I personally believe Kelly was one of the debriefers, sir, and that he also helped Rikanik establish a laboratory for his company, Omicron Biotech, at the UK's defence research establishment at Porton Down. Among other things, they were working on the diagnostic and therapeutic treatment of anthrax.'

'Useful. Go on.'

'Rikanik was a senior advisor in the establishment of RIBOTech at Paradise, California.'

'Interesting. Suspicious death?'

'Rikanik's death was only announced a month after the event by Timothy Randall, an ex-MI6 officer – Randall is also a specialist in DNA sequencing – currently living in Virginia. The autopsy was apparently undertaken by MI6. Details were not given at the inquest.'

'No surprises, Beck. What's all this got to do with Sami al-Qasr?' Kellner looked at his watch. 'And your time is running out.'

'He works at RIBOTech, sir. In January 2002, Professor al-Qasr contacted Leanne Gresham at the Directorate of Science and Technology. He demanded special protection.'

'From whom?'

'From the Israelis, sir.'

25

Ashe lay in bed, watching the rain beat the ivy against his bedroom window. He'd woken feeling guilty. Somehow, his casual relations with Amanda and the explosion in Hertfordshire had become fused. Had the blow to his head been some kind of punishment? The idea was absurd, but he couldn't quite get rid of it.

Was his memory playing tricks? He could remember the row with Amanda but little else until the meeting at the Tower. Something had happened in between; he was sure of it.

Now there was Melissa. What was her part in all of this? They'd kissed; they'd watched the sun set over the Cheshire Plain. She'd wanted more. He'd wanted more, but something held him back. Was it guilt, or something else?

A parcel tumbled onto the hall carpet.

Ashe tore open the jiffy bag to find a bundle of printed papers: a list with some explanatory notes.

Aslan had been true to his word: a list of names. Two columns:

1: Lodge Members.   2: Guests.

Ashe sat, naked and cross-legged on his sheepskin rug, sipping a glass of champagne as he worked his way carefully down the list.

There had been many guests at the Kartal Lodge on that fateful March night in Istanbul: several Jewish businessmen, some police officials, a few visitors from Sweden and Germany, a Turkish Buddhist, someone called Baba Sheykh, and, most interestingly to Ashe, a number of Kurdish politicians based in

Istanbul. These Aslan had underlined in red, adding some supplementary printed notes on an appended sheet. The names were:

Hatip Semdin
Sabri Gunay
Resit Yazar
Ali Yildiz

The supplementary notes, evidently compiled by someone in Aslan's team who wrote excellent English, were instructive. Colonel Aslan had decided to give Ashe a basic lesson in Turkish politics.

In the early 1980s, a minority of Turkish Kurds, mostly in southeastern Turkey, began campaigning for recognition as a distinct culture, demanding the right to use their own language and enjoy their own literature and traditions. The Turkish Constitution did not recognise anything but Turkish identity within its boundaries. Even the use of the Kurdish language – Kurmanji – was forbidden.

A small minority of Kurds agitated for self-government. These agitators, and persons sympathetic to them, were accused of imperilling national unity and Turkish identity. Acts of terrorism began. Atrocities on both sides escalated quickly; many innocent people suffered.

By the mid-nineties over 30,000 people had died in the conflict; hundreds of villages had been forcibly evacuated. Hundreds of thousands of Kurds had been resettled to other parts of Turkey. Many suffered hard times.

Until 1991, Kurds operated within the national parties, particularly the Social Democratic People's Party, the SHP. The SHP was sympathetic to full Kurdish equality. After the '91 elections, a number of Kurdish deputies formed their own party, the Labour Party (HEP).

Ashe checked the guest-list names and saw that two of those deputies – Resit Yazar and Ali Yildiz – had been invited to the Masonic Lodge that night.

In April '93 the HEP was declared illegal, but by then the deputies had already formed a new pro-Kurdish party: the Demokrasi Partisi. The Democracy Party was also banned in 1994. It was succeeded by the Halkin Demokrasi Partisi, or HADEP.

HADEP is widely recognised as the moderate voice of Kurdish aspirations in Turkey, in contrast to the illegal pro-Kurdish party that supports armed resistance and acts of terror. That illegal party is the Kurdish Workers Party, or PKK.

The PKK revoked a ceasefire declaration in 2003. The Turkish government estimates that there are currently between 4,500 and 5,000 PKK guerrillas across the Turkish border in the 'safe zone' or autonomous Kurdish Region of northern Iraq. In effect, they have been protected both by the UN and by US firepower since the first Gulf War.

Iraqi Kurds do not favour the PKK's methods, because the PKK threaten the Iraqi Kurds' own position, compromising their own desires for independence. As a result of the PKK's presence, Turkish troops crossed the border into Iraq with very different objectives to those of American troops in the region.

The Americans wish to secure broad Iraqi Kurdish support for a democratic settlement in Iraq. The Turkish premier, Erdogan, has accused the United States of double standards in its definition of its war against terror, because the USA gave no encouragement to the annihilation of PKK guerrillas in northern Iraq. The Turkish government perceives little effective difference between the PKK and al-Qaeda, since al-Qaeda is prepared to exploit the PKK cause as a means of destabilising Turkey's secular Constitution.

Aslan had added another note, but already Ashe felt like he was poking about in a hornets' nest.

Last week, Turkish police raided the office of the legal Kurdish nationalist party, HADEP, in Istanbul. Twenty-four arrests were made – some as a result of the raid, others after protest marches for Kurdish rights. Among those arrested were Hatip Semdin and Sabri Gunay – both of them visitors to the Lodge on the night of the bombing.

What could Ashe conclude from this information? Who had most to gain from the deaths of Semdin, Gunay, Yazar and Yildiz? Islamic radical terrorists, or Turkey's military and security interests? It was unkind of Aslan to leave his new friend with this dilemma. The issue was complicated even further by the new question. Who had most to gain from blowing up a British intelligence advisory committee investigating threats to British interests in Istanbul?

There were other questions: what were four Kurdish politicians doing at a Masonic Lodge in Istanbul in the first place? However much the Lodge prided itself on representing a modern, secular, even progressive Turkey, a country open to the world, it was absurd to think a Turkish Lodge would promote Kurdish rights, even indirectly. Urban, secular-minded Turks frequently associated Kurdish rights with a reactionary, rural, fundamentalist Muslim culture. For many 'Westernised' Turks, the Muslim traditionalist demand that Islamic girls wear the headscarf epitomised the issue of encroaching backwardness.

Aslan's last note – almost valedictory in its plainness – was a simple fact, but ambiguous in its implications:

Resit Yazar and Ali Yildiz are currently in Iraq, sought
by Turkish agents for observational purposes.

No further information is available.

Aslan was clearly urging Ashe to see a link between the Kartal
Lodge bombing and the atrocity at the Tower. But where was the
link? Aslan pointed to Iraq; the clue rested with Yildiz and Yazar.

The conclusion seemed inescapable. Ashe should go to Iraq.
Find them. See what they were doing – and what they knew. Had
not even the PM recommended that ODDBALLS concentrate its
energies on Iraq? Nothing could be simpler.

Nothing could be more dangerous.

Go to Iraq? The whole wide world was aware of the perils in
Iraq: a country split open like the belly of a stricken dragon,
fought over by any number of interests.

Ashe knew whom he should contact. His hand stopped by the
phone. Just hold on, Ashe. Think. *Think*. What would Loveday-
Rose have advised? Thinking of the archdeacon made him think
of Melissa.

Melissa. Another life; another promise. *Melissa*... The good
life; friends, family, invitations above the fireplace, the bosom of
society; cosiness, children, holidays, breezing into country pubs,
gazing into each other's eyes, growing old comfortably.

Bollocks.

The voice of the archdeacon came into his head. 'You must
face what you fear.'

Faith. It was a risk.

Ashe found himself dialling an old number.

26

Dogs were barking; the old cobblestones were wet with urine and early morning drizzle.

'Shit!'

'Dog shit. It's everywhere round here.'

The old man wiped his shoe against the kerb. The bar opposite was still open. It was called 'Babylon'.

'Want to go in?'

The younger man looked around Hein-Köllisch-Platz. They had entered the heart of St Pauli, close to Hamburg's red-light district and the famous haunts of the early, so-called 'savage', Beatles. The Beatles had been tamed, but Hamburg, thankfully, still had a few rough edges.

The old man spotted a bench beneath a tree and sat down. The younger man felt his friend's need for a hot drink and a bed. There was another corner bar opposite. Within its cosy shadows, two young Kurds drank coffee, smoked and discussed football.

'I'm looking for the Kurdish Centre.'

The youths stubbed their cigarettes out. 'You alone?'

'I've a friend outside. He's not well.'

They nodded to the barman. The barman whisked up a cappuccino and grabbed a chocolate croissant.

The old man had passed out. The Kurds tried to wake him. A ship's horn echoed up from the docks at the bottom of the steep cobblestoned hill.

The old man was coughing.

'Drink this. Speak Kurmanji. Where you from? Turkey? Iraq?'

'My case. Where is it?'

103

'By your feet.'

'Thank God.'

'Need a doctor?'

'Coffee's good.'

The old man nibbled at the croissant while the Kurds addressed his friend. 'The Community Centre's round the corner in Silbersackstrasse. If nobody's up, we'll find a way in.'

'Have you a blanket?'

The barman nodded. 'Anyone after you?'

'It's been… pretty bad.'

The old man gripped his friend's hand. 'No… It's been *interesting*.'

Half an hour later, Hamburg's streets were washed in dismal dawn light. As the men shuffled into Silbersackstrasse, they passed a newsagent's window covered with posters in German, Turkish and Kurdish. Next door, a handpainted sign in rainbow-coloured letters announced that they had reached the St Pauli Kurdish Community Centre. Its spartan café served as an informal advice centre for newly arrived immigrants and asylum seekers. An emergency dormitory occupied the top floor. The light was on inside.

The younger man tried the reinforced metal door. Three youths in leather jackets were seated round a table in the grim reception; they did not look Kurdish. As the new arrivals entered, the youths disappeared round the back.

'Hey!' cried the younger man. 'I thought they told you we were coming!'

No answer.

'Please! A bed for my friend! What's the matter with you? Please!'

There was scuffling round the front. The youths who'd rushed to the back emerged on the front pavement. Shadows darkened the front door. A car drew up outside. A door slammed. Some words in Turkish.

The front door was kicked open. The younger man looked up. '*You!*'

27

It was raining hard. Ali entered the Community Centre and slammed the front door. He slung his black mac over a worn Formica-topped table and looked at the two men sitting on chairs in the corner. The old one was wrapped in a blanket, apparently asleep; the other, dressed in a suit, was sitting back, relaxed, one ankle resting on his knee.

'Recognise these characters, Ali?'

'No, sir.'

'Got the file?'

'Yes, sir.' Ali handed Aslan an oversized ring-file with a blue plastic cover.

'Don't give it to me! See if you can identify these men.'

Ali sat down at the table and began leafing through the inch-square photos of all politicians and their aides closely connected with Kurdish rights.

'Ali!'

'Sir?'

'This man here thinks he knows me.'

'Forgive me sir, why don't you just ask them who they are?'

'Brilliant, Ali, as ever. And you think I haven't done so already?'

'Their reply?'

'No reply. But fear not, soldier, there will be.'

Aslan addressed the man at the table. 'I've been misinformed. You are not Yildiz and Yazar.' He waited to see if they reacted. 'Yildiz and Yazar, I presume, are still in Iraq.'

The two men still did not react.

'So, I suppose you've never heard of them.'

Aslan looked closely at the men. There was something familiar about their faces.

'You have no residence permits.'

'Forgive me, sir,' said the younger man. 'I wonder what the German authorities would make of your own unofficial visit. Or is this typical of Turkish security methods?'

Aslan nodded to the guard. The guard slapped the man about the face.

'Wish to repeat the question?'

The younger man said nothing.

'Please don't give up talking to us. I really am interested in all that you have to say. What do you think I want to hear? Speak.'

The younger man said nothing. Aslan nodded. Another slap in the face.

'I didn't think you were the complaining type. In any case, who would listen? You could be Turkish citizens; you could be from Iraq. Our friend who works here doesn't know. He did tell us two mystery guests were expected last night, and you're about as mysterious as any I've seen for a while. Frankly, my friends, I've no interest in your lives. But *you*...' He pointed to the younger man. 'You know who I am.'

The man shook his head.

'Yes, I think you do. Here we both are in a strange city – presuming it is strange to you – and yet here we are in this one rotten little room, and you indicate you know me. In fact, you couldn't stop yourself from telling me you knew me! And now, all of a sudden, you're bashful. Why would you know who I am? Are you a drug dealer? Many pushers wear smart suits. A bomber?'

'I... think I was mistaken, sir. You looked like someone. The man I was thinking about. He would have recognised me too.'

'You should have been an actor, my friend. Except actors try to make their performance credible. And I don't believe a word you're saying. Why? Because I look into your intelligent eyes, and I can see that you don't believe a word you're saying. I don't think you're a man who likes playing parts. I don't even think you lie habitually. Unlike my colleagues behind you. Look at their eyes. They betray nothing. They could lie through their teeth on an order from me. You'd never know. But you... tell me now, who did you think I was?'

'I think there are many Kurds who would mistake you for another man.'

'Which man?'

'You can't be him.'

'Who can't I be? Tell me! Who can't I be? Tell me, my friend, who am I not? In your opinion. In the bad light. In Hamburg. This morning. Who am I like?'

'I... thought you resembled a colonel in the Turkish Special Forces.'

'A colonel?'

'Yes... Aslan. Mahmut Aslan.'

Aslan bit his lip, hard.

'Hear that, Ali? My fame has preceded me.'

'Interesting, sir.'

'Ali, the old man has a suitcase between his legs. Care to open it?'

The old man awoke, with a start.

'You, old man! Who are you?'

'I'm... I'm...'

'Go on, man! Ali, take the case.'

'Sir.'

'Who are you?'

'I am a Kurd.'

'It's heavy, sir.'

'Just put it on the table. I know you're a Kurd – or, at least, you might be. You might be from Afghanistan, for all I know. Perhaps the Americans are looking—'

The old man tried to seize the case from Ali's grip.

'Important to you, old man, is it? The case? Is it important? What's your name?'

107

'Don't tell him!'

Aslan nodded to the guard, who slapped the younger man hard.

'It's rattling, sir. Some kind of mechanism inside.'

'Özdagan! Take the case to the car. Give it the onceover for booby traps.'

'Sir.'

There was a knock on the door to the back room. 'What is it?'

'How long you going to be in there? Why have you locked the door? We have a family coming in soon. Please!'

'Patience. This is a security issue. Nobody leaves and nobody comes in without my order. Now return to your TV. Unless you want trouble.'

The man behind the door disappeared.

'What is in the case, old man?'

'Say nothing.'

The guard slapped the younger man again.

'Did I tell you to do that, Bas?'

'Sorry, sir.'

'Don't say sorry to me, Bas. Apologise to the gentleman here.'

'Sir?'

'Never mind. Forgive my enthusiastic colleague. He wants to get on in the service. He's just learning to follow orders without thought or conscience.'

The old man looked desperate. He turned to his younger friend. 'They will see!'

'Oh yes, old man. We shall see. We shall see everything. Now *you*. You know who I am. How do you know?'

The younger man's bright eyes surveyed the hunk of man standing before him. He looked into his eyes without fear. 'Aslan. Turkish for "lion". Lions have teeth, claws...'

'Cut the bullshit. You didn't meet me in a zoo. Where was it?'

'Do you remember these places, Colonel: Diyarbakir, Bitlis, Silvan, Batman, Hoshap? You were well known in those places. Redwan, Midyat, Van, Zakho—'

'Enough! That was fifteen years ago.'

'What's he saying, sir?'

'I think he's trying to incriminate himself, Ali. All areas where the PKK operated in the nineties. We may have found ourselves a terrorist. Stroke of luck perhaps.'

'I'm not PKK.'

'He says he's not, sir.'

'Yes, I heard.' Aslan noted the sincerity on the man's face. He also recognised that no terrorist suspect would have been so open about knowing him, or about revealing where he had encountered him. But the suspect did not have to know that.

'I'm sorry. You turn up in Hamburg – a known hangout for terrorists – with no papers, and no ID. You say you know me, a security officer. That must be a million to one chance! You demonstrate familiarity with some of the trouble spots of our southeastern provinces. And you ask me to take your word that you're not a dangerous terrorist setting up a new cell in Germany. My friend, you're either extraordinarily bold, or absurdly stupid. Or perhaps you are a suicidal maniac utterly careless for your personal safety. A fanatic! Why are you in Hamburg?'

'You would not understand.'

'Try me.'

'You ask how I know you in those places. That is easy to answer. I am a doctor.'

'Doctor?'

'Medical doctor. Some of your Special Police victims were my patients.'

'Bas, leave the room!'

'Sir?'

'Leave the room! Help Özdogan with the case. Go on! Get out!'

'Sir!'

28

Aslan sat down at the table. 'Can you prove to me you're a doctor?'

'Why don't you break your leg? I could set it for you. Or even your neck.'

'So you don't like me. So what?'

'Do you want to be liked?'

'Lions are proud. Tread carefully.'

'Have you been treading carefully, Colonel? Where your men went, they rounded up suspects. And being a suspect means you live in a village where someone says a terrorist has visited. And what is a collaborator? Someone who speaks Kurdish. You tortured people for information. You murdered innocent people. I soaked up their blood and heard their last words. I often heard your name – Aslan. Aslan was an authority, an order – an excuse.'

'Many stories were told about me. Propaganda, most of it. PKK lies.'

'Most of it?'

'I'm not proud of everything I had to do. I did my duty. You did yours. Sometimes innocent people and guilty people look the same. Look at you two! One looks like a tramp, the other, an accountant. What am I to make of that? Are you innocent illegals, or guilty illegals? Guilty or innocent, you're in the wrong place at the wrong time. Why? Because I'm here, and you won't say anything. That was always the problem!'

'Problem, Colonel?'

'They never speak!'

'They're frightened, Colonel.'

'Yes, yes! They're always fucking frightened! If people stood up to the terrorists, we could finish the job quickly, without all the mess.'

'Is that what you call it?'

'Every combat zone is a mess, Doctor. Chechnya, Kosovo... Their problems have been bleeding the countries white for years. We didn't want that in Turkey. We wanted to sort it out quickly and get on with the future. Better than a long, slow drip of perpetual misery. We wanted to sort it out!'

'The old way.'

'If you like. The way we know best. It worked before.'

'And is it sorted out?'

'Mistakes were made. Mistakes were made... in the past. It's over.'

Aslan got up and started pacing the narrow room. 'There's something about you, Doctor. Something strange. Why don't you tell me about yourself, then all this trouble can go away. Give me something.'

'Give something to Colonel Aslan, who took everything from my—'

'Your what?'

'My patients, Colonel.'

'Your Turkish is good. Better than my Kurdish. Not born in Turkey, were you?'

The doctor said nothing.

Özdogan opened the front door.

'Who gave you permission to enter? Get out!'

Özdogan slammed the door and stood outside with Bas in the rain.

Ali looked up at Aslan. Suddenly, he did not recognise his boss. 'Sir?'

'Ali?'

'Nothing, sir.'

'Memories hard, are they Colonel?'

111

Aslan slapped the doctor hard across his face. Blood poured from his nose, but his eyes did not leave those of his attacker.

'Damn it! I need some fresh air.' Aslan nearly wrenched the door off its hinges, then took a deep breath. The two security men were soaked to the skin.

'Why aren't you in the car?'

'Waiting for your orders, sir.'

'My... why is everyone always waiting for orders? Why not just do them?'

'You told us to—'

'I know what I said! Come in! What's in the case? Is it safe?'

'Nothing came up on the screen, sir. I'd say it's clean.'

'Of course it's safe.' Aslan snatched it from Özdogan and threw it onto the table.

The old man was startled. 'Please! Please! It's sacred!'

'Sacred? What's the old man talking about?'

'Some old junk, sir.'

'Let's have a look at it then!'

Özdogan opened the suitcase wide above the table and let the contents fall clanging onto the surface. Aslan's eyebrows rose as he surveyed the scattered contents.

There were three bronze pieces. One had a large circular base with two spheres above it, and a screw thread. The second had a smaller base and was crowned with three spheres of decreasing size. Aslan picked up the third piece. Its graceful, sinuous shape resembled a cock or a dove. Its tail curved round flamboyantly at the back; its beak was long and arched downwards.

Its meaning suddenly dawned on Aslan. He dropped the piece on the table as if it were red hot.

'Close your book, Ali.'

'Why, sir?'

'Don't ask *why*! I'm sick of people forever asking why. Ask *them*!' He pointed to the two men. 'Ask *them* why!' The two men shrugged their shoulders.

'Ali! Photograph them for the records. Özdogan! Bas! Back to the car. These men have nothing to do with our mission. The old man is an antiques dealer and the young man is clearly his son, protecting him. It's a matter for German immigration.

'Our apologies, gentlemen. A case of mistaken identity.'

29

Standing at the front hatch of the RAF Hercules, fingers shaking, Ashe gripped his blue canvas bag. Baghdad International Airport felt like a vast oven. A blanket of heat penetrated his beige cotton clothes, welding them damply to his skin.

'Come on, mate. Only ten minutes left to unload!'

Ashe was hurried down the ladder to the scorching tarmac. The muscular corporal jogged to the rear of the aircraft to supervise the scheduled roll-off of replacement vehicles and parts.

Ashe wiped his brow and dropped his bag, half expecting it to fry like an egg on the shimmering runway. If the Pope had kissed this turf, he'd have left his lips behind.

From the direction of the distant control tower and its nearby lookout posts, a Land Rover Defender 110 sped towards him. Ashe thought longingly of the green fields of RAF Brize Norton. He could be back there just in time for pub-closing. All he had to do was turn round and climb back up.

Too late. The Land Rover drew up smartly to the side of the cockpit. Out stepped a good-looking, enthusiastic young officer. Smiling, he extended a huge right hand.

'Welcome to Baghdad International! How do you feel?'

'Good to see you again, Simon. Bloody good.'

'Toby, I'm afraid you'll have to sit in the back of the Snatch.'

'Snatch?'

'This is an in-and-out vehicle.'

'What?' The noise from the Hercules was deafening.

'IN AND OUT! Snatch!'

'Check!'

Ashe climbed into the rear seat. In front of him was an American private, face obscured by helmet and shades, gripping an M4 carbine: small but lethal enough to incapacitate anyone within 600 metres.

'You're not in uniform, Simon.'

'Officially, I'm off duty. But pass me my helmet will you? There's one for passengers on the right. Put the body armour on as well. Straps are self-explanatory.'

As he buckled the helmet strapping around his face, the reality of the situation struck Ashe. 'Are we likely to make it through the international zone in one piece?'

Major Richmond put the Snatch into first and sped off towards the roadblock at the airport perimeter. 'Look in the back!'

'What?'

'Rear of the vehicle. Take a look.'

Through the narrow window behind the back seat sat two US marines. One of them cuddled the hard butt of a massive Browning .50 calibre heavy machine gun, mounted to the rear. The other clutched an M16A2. They both kept a keen eye on everything around them.

'Quite a deterrent!'

'Unfortunately, Toby, deterrents attract the mad.'

'You're sure putting me at my ease, Simon.'

'You'll be all right. But this is Baghdad, Toby, and no one forced you to come. Keep your eyes peeled and learn from what you see – and what you don't. We were lucky to get support this morning. Incident at the UN Food Programme.'

'Incident?'

'Suicide bomber. Seems to be a never-ending supply of them.'

'Home grown?'

'Some. Many slip over the Syrian border. It's an open wound.'

Ashe had already been briefed on Major Simon Richmond's position in Baghdad. At the request of US military intelligence, he had been seconded to Baghdad from his Basra posting with the 1st Battalion, the Royal Regiment of Fusiliers. Having made an impression on senior American staff, Richmond was clearly a rising star.

As the Snatch sped along the corridor between the leafy suburbs of Baghdad and the Green Zone at the city's centre, Ashe studied Richmond, noting the confident tilt of his jaw, and his steady blue-eyed gaze. Ashe had known him since Richmond was a shy teenager – a likeable, open-faced youth eager to follow his father into the army. Judging by the speed and authority with which he now received and relayed messages via the radio mike attached to his helmet, he had taken to officer training like a duck to water. Seeing him in his element like this, Ashe experienced a pride normally reserved for fathers.

Ashe studied the rows of shell-damaged but still attractive sandy-coloured hotels, offices, residences and shops that lined the four-lane motorway into the historic metropolis. Many of the newer structures had been the work of British construction teams, most of whom had enjoyed a decent life in Baghdad before the first Gulf War.

By and large, the Brits were not unpopular in Iraq – out of uniform, anyhow. Iraqi hospitality was legendary, and Ashe recalled a saying that some attributed to the Prophet Muhammad: 'When you entertain a stranger, you are entertaining God.'

'OK, Toby, you see over there? That's the al-Kindi Gate – one of the three entrances to the secure area.'

'The Green Zone.'

'You've got the River Tigris on either side, and the US, UK and Australian embassies inside it.'

Ashe looked out of the bulletproof windows. Blackhawk helicopters buzzed about the perimeter. 'Are those snipers on the walls?'

'Yeah, they're watching every possible point of entry. It's like a sleep session for them, before they head back out there themselves.'

M1 Abrams tanks were as common as taxis in Trafalgar Square. Humvees and Bradley combat vehicles filled the gaps and lined the road to the entrance. Queues of Iraqi civilian workers shuffled up to the checkpoint, one by one, towards the body searches. Any one of them could bring instant death to dozens of men, women and children.

'Ten thousand work there every day, Toby.'

'That's a lot of body searches.'

'We've trained the Iraqis to do the job.'

'What are they like to work with?'

'They do the job, but there are problems.'

'Yeah? Like what?'

'They're cowed by authority. I'll give you an example. An Iraqi guard is approached by someone looking like an officer. The guard asks for ID, which he is obliged to do. The officer screams at the guard, "I'm your superior!", or something like that. The guard lets the man through. When we ask later, "Did you let a man dressed as an officer through without showing ID?", he says "No". We ask again. He says, "I always ask for ID. Those are my orders." Different way of life.

'People lie as a matter of course, because pride, for men, is more important than telling the truth. Truth is for religion. Truth comes with authority: something you must do or must believe. In ordinary life, truth costs money; it could cost you your livelihood, or your life – or the lives of your family, which is everything.

'In Iraq, the truth is always veiled. They never believe official pronouncements. They want to see the body. If you ask a question, people will tend to give the answer they think you want to hear. Telling lies is almost a way of being polite – preserving your pride as well as theirs. If you ask the way to somewhere and they don't know the answer, they'll give you the wrong route just to appear helpful and so they don't lose face. You get used to it.'

'Tricky.'

'No one asked us to come!'

Ashe took in the barricades and concrete blast walls ringing the priority offices.

117

'You'll be wanting the UK Embassy.'

'Check. And a drink. I'm parched.'

'Toby, I'm sorry. Here!'

Richmond handed Ashe a large bottle of Vittel mineral water from under his seat. 'It's a bit warm – I meant to give it to you at the airport.'

Ashe took as big a swig as he could and passed the bottle to the American private.

'Thank you, sir.'

The Snatch drew up at the embassy checkpoint. The American soldiers smiled but still looked distinctly stiff and nervous. The Snatch was waved through.

'Right, Toby. If you still want that bed at the Coalition HQ, I'll pick you up if you can call me before five. Give me your mobile. I'll type my number in… That's it. You can keep the body armour, but I need the helmet back in the car. I'll do what I can, but I should tell you, I'm under orders most of the time.'

Ashe removed the helmet and shook hands with Richmond. The major waved the marines off to rejoin their unit. 'See you 'round, fellas. Keep your heads down.'

'We will, sir.'

Ashe entered the reception of the pockmarked embassy. To the right of the reception desk, a gunner from the 1st Battalion, the Irish Guards, adjusted the optical sight of his formidable FN Minimi light machine gun. Concrete and sandbags provided cover.

'I have an appointment with the ambassador.'

'Papers please, Mr…?'

'Ashe, Toby Ashe. Schedule B operation.'

The British staff receptionist, a Hindu with a Derbyshire accent, carefully perused Ashe's papers and checked them on his computer. He then telephoned the ambassador's office. The receptionist appeared somewhat doubtful as he looked Ashe up and down. He nodded at his interlocutor, then put the phone down abruptly.

'I'm afraid, Mr Ashe, the ambassador is on a shopping expedition.'

'Shopping expedition?'

'If you would like to wait, there's also a compound cafeteria, sir. Here's your pass. Please wear it at all times. No exceptions, sir.'

'How long?'

'Maybe one hour. Maybe two.'

'I'll try the cafeteria.'

'It's very nice, sir.'

It was heartening to know there was something nice in Baghdad. After having his bag scoured by security, Ashe was directed towards a small quadrangle at the centre of the compound. Olive trees and date palms offered a luscious shade to the few dozen staff enjoying an early lunch and a beer. An Iraqi barman in a bright white shirt and black tie stood proudly behind the rolled stainless-steel bar. Ashe bought a bottle of Löwenbräu in pounds sterling and began to relax a little, despite the leaden weight of body armour suspended over his breastbone, back and crotch. He did not feel like taking it off.

He took a seat by a small enamelled fountain. What had once been a refreshing torrent was now a thirst-inducing trickle, but the wetness caught the sun, and the splashing sounds were welcome enough.

My God, Ashe thought to himself, *what have I done?* He reached inside his canvas bag for a notebook and began confiding his thoughts to paper. The important thing is—

'Toby Ashe! What the fuck are you doing here?'

'Mick! I was just asking myself that very question.'

30

Michael Curzon QC was an unusual choice for UK ambassador to Iraq. He was not a career diplomat but a barrister destined to sit in judgement at the High Court. Widely known for his intense intellectual skills – and extraordinary cynicism – he was also politically conservative. This made him an unlikely candidate for such a key position in the British government's Iraqi operational equations. Nevertheless, he spoke fluent Arabic, got on well with senior civil service personnel, and had made a great impression on certain notable US industrialists in his capacity as a commercial barrister.

A commercial background was considered a significant component for one who, it was supposed, would have to wrestle with major issues of contract and tender. 'A tall, cool customer with his finger on the pulse' was how the US ambassador to the Court of St James described him.

Curzon had a great knowledge of US mores and sensitivities and had, much to his surprise, impressed the PM. Perhaps it had something to do with the case he had assisted Cherie Blair with during the previous year. Curzon was also popular with a number of senior British military personnel, having been called upon to assist in various procurement debacles that had reached the High Court over the past years.

All in all, his was the kind of appointment that could only have been made when the government felt itself under extreme pressure, even crisis, when pure competence and fresh thinking were deemed more important than political positioning. War would always erect an invisible barrier between the PM and his party; the man at the top had entered the real world – and there was no way back.

Ashe himself was not surprised. He'd known Curzon as a postgraduate at Brasenose College, Oxford. Each had eyed the other's career and lifestyle choices with interest and, on occasion, a little envy. Their friendship was strong, though distant, and not a little mysterious to the friends of both.

'Congratulations, Mick.'

'Sshh! No one calls me Mick around here.'

Curzon took a seat and smiled at his old pal. 'Toby, I'd love to socialise, but you couldn't have come at a worse time. I'll be back in London, hopefully, for a week's leave some time in the summer. We can meet up then.'

'Bloomsbury seems a long way from here.'

'Don't remind me. I'd far rather be downing a few pints with you in the Plough in Museum Street.'

'I understand, Michael. I wasn't expecting a reception party. But just tell me briefly, what's it like?'

Curzon whispered, 'Fucking awful. Let me give you an example of the insanity here. This morning, I had arrangements to meet the Australian ambassador. So, the tosspot decides, "Wouldn't it be nice to go on a shopping expedition?" So I say, "Maybe when things are a bit quieter". "No," he says, he'd told colleagues that Baghdad was not as bad as the newspapers made out. Wanted a taste of life outside the Green Zone.'

'Or death, presumably.'

'You get the picture. Anyhow, imagine this. We're walking round the *suq* wearing suits and body armour – looking like pricks – surrounded by bodyguards and Special Forces and he's putting his fucking shopping into three LAVs.'

'LAVs?'

'Armoured cars. Meanwhile, he's got a photographer – I don't know if it was his idea or not – taking snapshots and video for the evening news in Sydney or something. Or maybe for when he decides he wants to be premier of Australia. So I'm looking round nervously trying to appear in control – he's carrying on like he hasn't a fucking care in the world – and there's this bloody great explosion. Everyone stops dead still – and he's still negotiating over a bunch of flowers.

'The guy from US special forces tells me his presence is urgently required elsewhere, and could I inform the Aussie ambassador he's got better things to do than fill the ambassador's grandchildren's Christmas stocking? So I have to bundle the tosspot into the armoured car and all the while he's complaining he hasn't finished his shopping, and what will his daughter say, and why is everyone panicking, and—'

'The explosion?'

'I'm getting to that. I've just had a report. Two insurgents were doing their duty for the sake of whatever the fuck they think they're doing it for. They'd dropped off a suicide bomber near the UN Food Programme.'

'My escort told me about that one.'

'Yeah, well, what he didn't tell you was that these two charlies in the Toyota pickup then made their way round to the al-Rashid.'

'Al...?'

'Used to be a big tourist hotel. It's Coalition now. Anyway, they've got a rocket launcher welded to the back of the pickup truck. And what do they do? They stand right behind the bloody rockets to video themselves and the rockets doing this great service. I ask you Toby – stand directly behind the rocket launcher! Anyhow, we've got the video of their jolly japes. They're not looking too pleased with themselves now. We'd show it on the evening news but a) it would probably only encourage others, and b) it's probably against their fucking human rights!'

Curzon looked at his watch. 'Right, you'll be wanting to see the SIS desk head.'

'Crayke.'

'Yes, Crayke. Strange fellow, but impressive in his way. Oh, and by the way, welcome to Baghdad!'

Curzon led Ashe back into the compound's main building and down a long, cool, busy corridor. At its end was a door marked 'Authorised Personnel Only', in English and Arabic. Curzon took out a bunch of passkeys, punched a number onto a keypad, pressed his thumb onto a small screen and played with the lock.

The door opened onto a rough set of concrete steps. As everywhere in the embassy, CCTV cameras tracked every move.

'Watch your step, Toby. No compensation allowed. The insurance people regard everything that happens here as an act of God. Very convenient. It gets narrower at the top.'

Three flights up, the men came to another exterior door.

'Ambassador's Department. Please pronounce your name clearly.'

'Curzon here. One guest.'

'Please insert your five-digit code.'

Curzon typed in three digits.

'What happened to the other two, Mick?'

'There are no other two. It's a security trip.'

The door opened onto a red-carpeted corridor.

'You never know who's going to turn up. Actually, it's so the blood doesn't show. Only kidding. My suite is next to Crayke's current office. Follow me.'

At the end of the corridor was a thick metal door; to its right, an open-plan office. Sitting outside the suite were two plainclothes security men of distinctly Anglo-Saxon appearance, carrying Uzi machine guns.

'Papers please, sir.'

Ah, *Essex*, thought Ashe. The Thames estuary blends uneasily with the Tigris.

'Recommendation of the ambassador insufficient, eh?'

The security men had heard it all before. 'Papers, sir.' One of them scanned Ashe's papers with a small magnifying glass he placed over his eye, while the second man frisked him. 'Leave your bag here, sir, unless you require a particular item.'

Curzon put his hand on Ashe's shoulder. 'Gotta go, Toby. Maybe see you later – if not, the Plough. Don't let the goons get you down.'

'How about the Hemlock?'

'You must be joking. Bunch of nutters.'

31

The dour-faced security staff completed their check and radioed in. 'A Dr Ashe for Desk. Right. Wait a second, Dr Ashe.'

The blast-proof door eased open. Behind it stood a sharp-eyed Iraqi woman.

'I am Mrs Aziz, Mr Crayke's assistant. Do come in.'

Crayke's windowless office was divided into two. Electric fans operated from the ceiling and from every corner, but failed to dissipate the body odour.

Ashe heard a voice from behind the door into the inner sanctum of the SIS desk head, Baghdad.

'Enter now, Dr Ashe.' Mrs Aziz smiled and opened the connecting door.

Attired in a short-sleeved cotton shirt and khaki shorts, Crayke sat in a wicker armchair in a corner behind the door. His grey hair, what remained of it, was cut regimentally short about the exaggerated, bony dome of his head. His voice was deep, but slightly thin and gravelly – a result of throat-cancer surgery and a continued penchant for the occasional cheroot or pipe.

'Good, Ashe. Come in. Welcome to the Armpit. Nice to meet you at last.'

'At last?'

'I've had my eye on you for quite some time.' As if reading his mind, Crayke added. 'And I am not referring to our friends Colquitt and Bagot.'

'That's a relief.'

'And that is the sole relief you are likely to get here. No

matter. You write interesting books, Ashe. Not all of them, of course. But one in particular struck me some years ago. It was about magical signs, cryptography and the origins of modern science. Some of it very good indeed.'

'*The Golden Thread*. It didn't sell.'

'Too deep for the herd, I dare say. Such books may not sell, but we should be poorer without them. Nevertheless, I was not altogether convinced by some of your arguments. You'll find understanding the esoteric a great deal easier if you first banish from your mind the concepts of God and spirits.'

'Rather defeats the object, doesn't it?'

'Better, I think, than being defeated *by* the object.'

Ashe was in the presence of a mind: one with voltage. Baghdad suddenly looked a brighter place. Crayke pulled himself out of the creaking wicker chair and offered his long, leathery hand. 'Ranald Crayke. But do call me "sir". I don't want you to get into the habit of using my name.'

'Yes, sir.'

'I'll call you Ashe, because I can't get used to all this first name nonsense. God knows, even my wife calls me Crayke. Right. Sit down.'

Crayke seated himself behind his packed desk and spread his bat-like hands across its red leather top. 'Seeing as I'm known to the security staff here as "Desk", I thought I'd better have a pretty good one. Comes from Saddam's palace, not far from here. Used to belong to the Ottoman governor of Baghdad back in the old days. Good to be in touch with history. Gives a man perspective.'

'I feel the same, sir.'

'I know you do. I knew your friend, the late archdeacon, very well. I am so sorry we have lost him. Gives me a certain personal interest in your current activities.'

'Revenge, sir?'

'Justice. It's a politer word. Richmond tells me you need a source handler.' Crayke lit a fat Burmese cheroot. 'Smoke?'

'No thanks, sir. Gave up years ago.'

Crayke puffed a deep brown-and-grey cloud into the room.

'Good man, Major Richmond. Still, the DIA have got him for the time being.'

He inhaled his cheroot. 'You want to find out what's happened to these Turkish chaps.'

'Kurdish actually.'

'Citizens of Turkey. Resit Yazar and Ali Yildiz.'

'Yes, sir. Find them. Talk to them. If necessary, bring them in.'

'You're not a cowboy, Ashe! You sound like President Bush!'

'Excuse me, sir.'

'Look, I have studied your preliminary request for official assistance. As far as I can see, your sole basis for linking terrorism in Istanbul to the Tower atrocity is a contact you enjoy with Turkish security forces – which you won't name, for "operational reasons".'

'That's right, sir.'

'I can tell you, Ashe, that it was only my personal intervention that secured approval of your request for resources. Predictably, objections were raised that your plans were an indulgence, a private holiday.'

'I can think of better destinations, sir.'

Crayke laughed amid a geyser of rising phlegm. 'Care to let me in on your little secret? Who is your Turkish contact?'

'Colonel Mahmut Aslan, sir.'

Crayke stubbed out his cheroot. A smile emerged on his face and his eyes widened, as if gaining inspiration from a higher sphere. 'Right. Zappa's your man. Of course, he's also the US Defense Intelligence Agency's man. You'll have to tolerate some interference from them. I can't spare you one of my own.'

'I'm not sure I'd like to share this with the Americans at this stage, sir.'

'This is Baghdad, Ashe. Here we share everything – even our underwear if needs be. Mutual trust is vital in conflict zones. Do you have any objective reason why DIA involvement might prejudice your investigation? Think carefully, Ashe.'

'Not at the moment, sir.'

'Do you expect to?'

'Too early to say, sir.'

'I'm afraid that's insufficient. If you want a source handler, Zappa's the only available man with the requisite knowledge. The DIA will be prepared to keep this from the Turks, if I request it.'

'Can you trust them to keep it from the Turks, sir? It's most important to this operation that they know nothing. Nothing at all.'

'I shall make that clear. By the way, Ashe, forgive me for asking, but is there an esoteric angle to your enquiries?'

'Not that I'm aware of, sir.'

'Hmm...' Crayke lit another cheroot, inhaled deeply and exhaled a pillar of foul-smelling smoke.

'When we are deeply engaged in something, Ashe, the cloud we create about us bears all the signs of the inner man. There must be something in this investigation that has made you willing to risk your life here in Iraq.'

'I was nearly killed in England, sir.'

'I doubt if that's your reason. Esoteric concepts are an eternal key to thought, a persistent dimension. But they bear the imprint of the knowledge of the times in which they are expressed.'

'Could that be, sir, why genuine traditions were not meant to be written down?'

'All writing is, in a sense, a betrayal, Ashe. Try and remember this as you proceed.'

The door opened abruptly. Mrs Aziz stood in the doorway with a cup of strong coffee for Crayke.

'Thank you, Mrs Aziz. Do call Major Richmond. If you can reach him before five, Mr Ashe will have a bed for the night. I'm sure he needs one. Right, Mr Ashe?'

32

'Seems you were right about the Israelis, Beck.'

Beck nodded slowly; he didn't want to jump to conclusions.

Lee Kellner had met Beck off the plane at Chicago O'Hare Airport and driven him to an old FBI detention and interrogation centre on the city's outskirts, now shared with the CIA.

Constructed to cool off some of Chicago's most notorious gangsters in the twenties, the second-rate Art Deco block had seen through every colourful and colourless phase of America's extraordinary history of crime. Now surrounded by derelict land, its old pink walls had recently been whitewashed in a sprucing-up initiative funded by the Department for Homeland Security.

Homeland Security was muscling in on many aspects of cherished Bureau and Agency autonomy, causing the security services some discomfort. The threat of terrorism diminished the good humour that might have greased the inevitable changes. The media had them all in the dock.

Was Mati Fless a Homeland Security case, an internal criminal matter for the Bureau, or an aspect of Agency overseas ops? The answer was to bang him up in the Wrigley-St Francis facility and see whether the suspect himself offered any clues.

Kellner pushed open the steel door of Interrogation Chamber No. 1. Two agents stood to attention.

Beck was surprised to see Fless dressed in an orange prison boiler suit, shackled at the feet. Having read a detailed report on Fless's capture, such precautions seemed excessive.

'You guys wanna get some air.'

'Thank you, sir.'

'You deserve it.' Kellner stared at Fless. 'Don't get up, Mr Fless.'

'I wasn't going to.'

'I'd like you to meet Agent Beck. I think you two have a lot in common. Had Beck been faster off the mark, it might have been him you killed, and not Agent Buckley.'

'I did not kill your Agent Buckley.'

'You didn't?'

'No. He killed himself.'

Kellner looked at Beck and raised his eyebrows.

Beck looked back at Kellner. 'Anything yet from the Israeli Embassy, sir, on Agent Matthias Fless?'

Fless perked up.

'Embassy denies all knowledge of the operation, but admits Fless has on occasion been employed in a freelance capacity by the security services. The usual bullshit.'

'What about our own internal Mossad contacts, sir?'

'They say they're investigating the matter and ask us to keep them informed.'

'Fairly safe to conclude this was a Mossad operation, sir.'

Kellner looked to Fless, who was smiling. 'Used to be in Shin Bet, didn't you, Mati?'

'Yeah.'

'Interesting work?'

'Mr Kellner, I did not kill your man. You know as well as I do that surveillance operations often go wrong. I had no idea al-Qasr was protected by an agent.'

'What happened to Buckley?'

'He was torturing me.'

'Torturing?'

'Tied me up to the mains.'

'Unorthodox, wouldn't you say, Agent Beck?'

'Fless's story's been confirmed, sir. Exposed mains wires located at the scene.'

Kellner's eyes did not shift from Fless's. He continued speaking to Beck. 'Could've been planted.'

'It's a bit baroque, sir.'

'What?'

'Baroque. A bit intricate.'

'These Mossad boys can be very smart, Beck. So, Fless, who did kill Buckley?'

'He shot himself.'

'Oh please!'

'Stupid, I know. My team—'

'His team, as he puts it... I'd say four henchmen – where *do* you find these guys, Fless? His team, Agent Beck, is sitting next door.'

'Doing what, sir?'

'Awaiting deportation.'

Beck looked surprised.

'Executive orders, before you ask.'

'My team arrived, Mr Kellner. They saw your agent. Buckley was on the metal stairs trying to phone *his* team – or should I say henchmen? Buckley turned to see my men, tried to reach for his automatic while putting the cellphone down. He dropped the phone. My men saw me – saw what he'd done to me. He fumbled with his gun in his shoulder holster and shot himself. I can only presume it was not deliberate.'

'Very amusing, Fless.'

'I gotta say, Mr Buckley did not seem quite "all there" that afternoon. I think he'd been drinking. I think your forensic people will bear this out.'

Kellner whispered to Beck, 'They do.' He turned again to Fless. 'Whatever you say, Mr Fless, a court of law may see things differently.'

'Sure. I understand. You want me to cooperate. What do you want to know?'

'Agent Beck, I believe you have some questions for Mr Fless.'

'Mr Fless, what do you know concerning the deaths of Gitana, Daley, Rikanik – and the British man, Kelly?'

'The last one I've heard of. Who are the others?'

'You've never heard of Gitana, Daley or Rikanik?'

'That's what I said.'

'Will you take a lie detector on that?'

'Sure.'

Beck consulted his file. He pulled out a large black-and-white photograph and placed it on the table in front of Fless. 'Do you recognise this man, Mr Fless?'

Fless laughed.

'Do you recognise this man?'

'My double! At last! Do you know the story about the man who killed his double – only to find he had killed himself?'

Lee Kellner stifled a laugh. He was privately concerned that Fless might run rings around the Bureau man with a foot in the Agency door. 'This man, Fless, is you.'

'There's a resemblance.'

Kellner was annoyed. 'It's not a fucking resemblance, Fless. This is you. And you know we know it is.'

'If I knew what you knew, would you know what I know?'

Kellner sighed. 'Just tell him, Sherman. Jeez! We're s'posed to be on the same fuckin' side!' Kellner shook his head.

Fless addressed Beck. 'So you think it's me.'

'What do you know of the deaths of five Russian microbiologists. October 2001?'

'Refresh my overworked memory, Agent Beck.'

'October 2001. A commercial flight from Israel to Novosibirsk in Siberia. Blown up over the Black Sea by a Ukrainian surface-to-air-missile.'

'Yes. It was all over the news. Everyone was killed.'

'Novosibirsk, Mr Fless. Home to a research institute; the scientific capital of Siberia.'

'That a fact?'

'It has fifty facilities and thirteen universities.'

'Even so, I'd prefer to study elsewhere. Are you suggesting I killed these five microbiologists? What do you think? I just ring up the Ukrainian military and "Hey! I'd like you to blow up a civilian plane"?'

'A Mossad team was sent to investigate.'

'Naturally.'

'The report has never been published.'

'Of course not. And who says there was a report?'

'This photograph, Mr Fless, has a date on the back.'

Fless turned it over. 'What do you know! October 2001. You're a magician!'

'It's not only the date, Mr Fless. It's the place. Do you recognise it?'

Fless gave Beck a doe-eyed look.

'Let me refresh your memory. This photograph was taken at the Institute for Biological Research. One of the most secret places in Israel.'

'Not any more, apparently. But do tell me more.'

'The visible parts of the facility are in the Tel Aviv suburb of Ness Ziona.'

Kellner studied Fless's eyes; they gave nothing away.

'Most of the institute's twelve acres of facilities, Mr Fless, are underground. Laboratories are reached only via airlocks.'

'Are you sure you should be telling me all this? As an Israeli citizen, I should be innocent of such knowledge.'

'David Kelly was connected to the Institute.'

'What does that mean?'

'About the time you were photographed there.'

'Was I photographed there?'

Beck sat back in his chair and drew breath. 'Does the name Dedi Zucker mean anything to you?'

'Of course, Agent Beck. Anyone with an interest in politics in Israel – which I suppose is everyone – has heard of Dedi Zucker.'

'Zucker caused a storm in the Knesset. Claimed the Institute was trying to create an ethnic bioweapon.'

'A what?'

'A weapon that could specifically target Arabs by the manipulation of DNA sequencing.'

Fless laughed. 'Beware of the Israeli lunatic fringe, Agent Beck. Many of my compatriots have a kind of epic, biblical, even apocalyptic feeling for current affairs. They would not be surprised if scientists could make the Red Sea part again for Moses and the children! These kinds of conspiracy claims get made all the time. I know plenty of people who think God Himself is going to acquire real estate on the Temple Mount in Jerusalem and rule the world like a sultan! It's all bullshit.'

Beck looked to his notes again as Kellner mopped his brow with a handkerchief.

'Why were you involved in the surveillance, as you put it, of Professor al-Qasr, one of this nation's most respected scientists?'

'At last! At last, a realistic question. You say, "one of this nation's most respected scientists". Is that an honorary citation? Or is that a fact?'

Beck turned to Kellner. Kellner's eyes motioned to the door. He stood up. 'OK, Mati, we're going outside to consult for a few minutes. You take a break and clear your thoughts.'

'Sure. Take your time.'

33

Fiona Normanton unbuttoned al-Qasr's denim shirt. She rubbed her soft fingertips over the rough hairs of his chest, kissed his neck and lay back on the cream duvet. 'Do you like me?'

Al-Qasr smiled, admiring the rich blue woollen beach top she was wearing with its bright orange stars and yellow moons. 'I've always loved brunettes.'

'I got highlights!'

'So I see.' Al-Qasr picked at the deep blue wool that rested on her tiny navel. 'Did you make this?'

Fiona laughed. 'No, silly. I got it in Reno. There's a great wool shop there.'

'Hard to believe. Expensive?'

'Do you like expensive things?'

'Yeah. I think I'd miss them if they were taken away.' He looked out to the lake through the glass doors.

All morning al-Qasr had been at Fiona's apartment at Oroville while the FBI engaged in a second forensic sweep of his house up at Paradise. While Bureau agents took the place apart, the couple had swum in Fiona's little pool overlooking the lake and talked a lot about life in California.

Fiona took al-Qasr's large warm hand and placed it on her thigh. He fingered the edge of her sky-blue cotton panties and tickled her gently.

'Mmm... Don't stop.'

He slid his hand round under the cotton and stroked her smooth round hips and bottom. She pulled him closer, nudging his moustache with her little nose. She opened her lips and they kissed. His hand moved over the soft, round mound of Fiona's stomach.

'Shall I take this off?'

'No, I like it. It suits you.'

'OK.'

Al-Qasr lifted the cosy wool over her breasts.

'Hey! Do you know what?'

'Yeah. I'm boring, I'm middle-aged and I'm... just a little crazy about you.'

'Oh, you don't have to say that! Hey, Sami. If you lick my tits, I'm told the nipples come up like sombreros!'

Al-Qasr laughed again. Fiona Normanton was a lot of fun.

'Go on! Try it.'

'OK.'

'See what I mean?'

'Fuck! You're right, Fiona! They do.'

'Don't stop, Sami. I feel the flame of fornication rising through my body.'

Fiona suddenly sat up and pulled her panties down. 'Go on!'

'What?'

'You know! Lick me, silly! Now.'

Soon Fiona was breathing heavily; she moaned his name.

'Hey, hey!'

'What's the matter, Sami? Don't I turn you on?'

'No, no. It's just...'

'Are you having a problem... you know, getting it—'

'No, it's not that. I guess I don't feel like rushing.'

'Oh! Oh, I see. Sorry, Sami.'

'No, it's my fault.'

'I got an idea. You just lie back a second.'

Fiona slipped his buff-coloured chinos down his long, olive legs.

'God, Sami! You look ready enough for me!'

'OK, but...'

'Look, I'll lie here for a minute and you just lie back and think about whatever you want to think about. OK?'

Fiona positioned herself on the duvet and slid her right hand down as she spread her long legs. Al-Qasr moved on to his side and kissed her shoulder.

'Fiona?'

'Mmm?'

'What's it been like in the office the past few days?'

'Mmm... Hot.'

'Apart from that.'

'I guess we missed you.'

'I had things to do.'

'Really, like what?'

'Oh just things... You know.'

Fiona let out a deep groan. 'Kiss me, Sami.'

'Did... did anyone come into my laboratory?'

''Course not. God! No one gets past me!'

'You sure? No one's been messing with my computer? My files?'

'Oh Sami!' Fiona started to shiver. 'No, baby. All your secrets are safe.'

34

'OK, Fless, you got something on al-Qasr? Let's hear it.'

Fless took a deep breath. 'Your CTC received a communication from a doctor in Iraq. About al-Qasr.'

Beck whispered in Kellner's ear. 'How the hell does he know?'

'Which communication would this be?'

'The same one you received, Mr Kellner. We intercepted it.'

'Fucking Mossad again! Won't you ever trust us?'

'Of course we trust you. We trust you to screw up.'

'Time will tell, Fless.' Kellner looked at the shackles round Fless's feet. 'Looks to me like everyone's screwing up. So, let's concentrate on the enemy. And Fless...'

'Yes?'

'Just can the adolescent, jerk-off shit!'

That stung. It wasn't the first time Fless had been accused of being an arsehole.

'How do we know you didn't concoct the whole damn thing in the first place? For all we know, this began as an Israeli plot to make us suspect al-Qasr.'

'You didn't reply to the message. That gave my mission its urgency. Then you interrupted us.'

'An action for which I offer no apologies. Tell me, Mr Fless, did you understand the reference to the British air raid of 1992, and why al-Qasr might have been less useful to our scientific effort than he first appeared?'

'Yeah, well, we hoped you might reveal something, something to throw light on this question. All we observed was that al-Qasr defected to the USA shortly after the British raid. One thing I *can* tell you…'

'Shoot.'

'The message accused al-Qasr of links with Ansar al-Sunna. I can positively confirm this.'

'Positively?'

'Absolute certainty. Absolute certainty, Mr Kellner. No question. But you will have your own methods. No doubt your people are going through al-Qasr's things right now, so confirmation will come soon enough. Let me repeat: under your very noses, your famous scientist has been in regular two-way communication with the forces of Ansar al-Sunna in northern Iraq. And not only in Iraq.'

'Where else?'

'Europe.'

Kellner looked at Beck. Beck sucked in his lower lip.

'Surely, gentlemen, that information is worth my freedom?'

Kellner got out of his chair. 'Excuse us a minute, Mati.'

Fless smiled indulgently and looked at the stationary fan blades above. 'I need some air.'

'Sorry, sir. Security. Had a suicide try to cut his—'

'OK, Beck, spare us the details. Hear that, Fless? It's for your own good.' Kellner drew his finger across his throat.

In the corridor outside, Beck and Kellner whispered frantically to one another.

'OK, Sherman, don't shove it down my neck. I know we've lost valuable time. It's true. But it's not too late.'

'Do we bring al-Qasr in, sir?'

Kellner looked at the tranquil Fless through the one-way plate set in the door.

'Fless could be useful to us.'

'But shall I bring al-Qasr in, sir?'

'No, Beck. You sit tight. I got our Iraqi scientist very closely covered.'

139

'But Buckley's dead!'

'Buckley was working for al-Qasr. That's how it was set up. His own little protector. But when I first heard about this business, I put an undercover agent right inside the hornet's nest.'

'You didn't tell me, sir.'

'And you know what?'

'Sir?'

'This agent ain't workin' for Leanne Gresham. This agent's workin' for *me*.'

35

Constructed for emergencies only, al-Qasr's underground hide-away was hellishly cramped. Below the battery-powered lamp bracketed to the hardboard panel, al-Qasr squinted at his laptop, sweat dripping onto his keyboard.

Fiona hadn't fooled him. He'd suspected an Agency honey-trap from the start. It had taken him all morning, and all of his wiles, to distract her long enough to link his laptop to her hard drive: a state-of-the-art metaphor from which al-Qasr derived private satisfaction. He'd long realised his so-called colleague Bob Lowenfeld's interest wasn't simply academic. Experience of Lowenfeld's duplicity had given al-Qasr the scent. Having accessed Bob's computer data and codes, Fiona's system would be a breeze to crack. Al-Qasr smiled at the prospect of 'listening in' to internal CIA traffic and observing their inevitable pursuit of him. It would not be long now; his hour was almost upon him.

Al-Qasr stopped dead. A CCTV system monitoring his lab flickered into life. Al-Qasr slammed the laptop closed and focused on the monitor. *Bob Lowenfeld!* Lowenfeld was extracting additional drives from al-Qasr's computer and imaging system.

'Motherfucker!'

Al-Qasr skidded his Jag by the entrance to RIBOTech's car park. He didn't want to be seen from his lab window. He reversed, parked beneath a cluster of tall pines, and walked round in the dappled light to the rear trade entrance. He knocked on the cafeteria's kitchen window.

'Sorry, Jolene, think I left something in the cafeteria over lunch.'

'Oh, I didn't see you.'

'I'm the invisible man.'

'You look all right to me, honey!'

Smiling, the cook returned to her washing up, while al-Qasr strode through the dining hall to the back stairs. The first-floor reception was empty: normal for a Saturday afternoon. The only thing that mattered was to extract his latest files before Lowenfeld found them. Distracted by Fiona, he'd been stupid.

His office door was open.

Fiona.

She turned in shock. 'Professor! I er...'

Al-Qasr smiled. 'What a nice surprise. Can't you get enough of old Sami?'

36

After two nights in Coalition Camp Montezuma with the 82nd Airborne, Ashe was transported back south, to Baghdad's Green Zone. Richmond had swung Ashe basic quarters in the Defense Intelligence Agency HQ, close to the Assassins' Gate entrance to the Green Zone. The drawback was that the HQ was mostly underground. While relatively cool compared to the stifling streets outside, being so close to bomb-damaged sewerage pipes, it could also get mighty smelly.

Ashe observed Richmond's daily operations, mostly high-risk sorties against suspected insurgents and hunts for arms caches. Street-by-street battles, interrogations, area reconnaissance, rescue missions – these were the order of the day, and they all took their toll on the nerves. Ashe was learning to adjust to the cruder conversation of those around him, and to their much coarser humour.

Alongside the thrill of action and reaction ran the perennial downside of casualties, treachery, false leads, frustration with equipment and with the number – as well as quality – of men available, not to mention the often depressing news from home.

The war had become a political football to competing parties in Britain, the US and elsewhere. Supercilious opposition was widespread throughout Europe. Morale was on a knife's edge, but the desire to fulfil the mission and install a democratic government in Iraq in less than a year kept the forces going. This was a worthy objective for those wishing to be seen as fighting the good fight. As a visiting colonel put it to Ashe one night over a game of poker, 'Hell, son! If some bastard tried to steal our democracy back home, wouldn't y'all expect a bloody battle?'

This was the sort of question that did not invite a response, and Ashe chose to listen rather than assert his own observations of the situation. Buttoning his lip, however, made his secretion in the bowels of Baghdad a kind of prison, but he would just have to wait; experienced source handlers could not be summoned from the air at will.

Ashe was sitting in the DIA canteen reading the *New York Times* one afternoon when a sweating Richmond marched in. Smiling, he tossed his helmet onto Ashe's table.

Ashe studied Richmond's bloodshot eyes. 'How'd it go, Major?'

'Tough one, Toby. Can I get you a fresh beer?'

Richmond showed his chit card to the Kuwaiti steward; he didn't carry loose change into combat. The major turned to Ashe. 'Someone I want you to meet.'

Through the double doors burst a big man in an Hawaiian shirt, with a gut that tumbled over his shorts like a snowdrift over a precipice. His broad forehead was dripping wet.

Ashe got up from the steel table. 'Vincent Zappa, I presume.'

'Vinny. It's Vinny.'

'Vinny, hi – I'm Toby Ashe.'

'Very pleased to meet you at last, Toby. Simon here's told me a lot about you.'

'Beer, Vinny?'

'Sure, Major. Large one. And a bourbon chaser. Christ, Toby! Hell of a day out!'

'Tell me about it?'

'Sure, I'll tell ya. Yours truly was escorting a subject back to the Green Zone, OK? Major was out in front. I had two guys in a Humvee behind. I got the suspect cuffed next to me. Terrified. Next thing, a landmine's detonated under the wheels of the guys in front. The suspect leans back, kicks the driver in the back of the neck, head butts ol' Zappa here, somehow gets out the car while it's skidding up the sidewalk and rolls to the side of the street. Our car rams into the side of a house. The guy gets picked up by insurgents. There's AK-47 fire from all sides. The driver's hit. I'm down on the floor of the car. The Humvee team's under heavy fire. Major's outta the Snatch in no time, throws a grenade – hits some bastards on the roof. Our team strafes the windows – there's more fire coming straight outta there. Air's filled with stone and concrete and Lord knows what else. The guys inside the house start chanting some Arabic stuff. Then the damn house blows up. Booby-trapped. Our guys behind are showered in shit – and then, before you could say "the Alamo", the street's empty. We got one dead, one severely wounded and we lost our suspect. But hear this, Toby, your guy Richmond. Jeez! What a fuckin' hero.'

Zappa sank the bourbon in one, then demolished the beer. 'My shout, Major.'

Ashe noticed Richmond looking pensive, his face taut, his eyes red. 'Did you get that, Simon? You're the hero of the hour.'

'Mission was a failure, Toby. And the casualties... The driver was a lovely guy.'

'Sure, I'll drink to that.' Zappa was ready for another trip to the bar. 'Don't take it so bad, Major. You did all a man could.'

'Give me five minutes, Vinny. I'll think of something.'

'But we don't get that extra five damn minutes, do we, Major? That's the whole damn thing. You can't be ready for everything. Progress is treading in dog shit and avoiding it in future. Now drink that fuckin' beer, Richmond; that's an order!'

Richmond raised his eyes from the floor and gave a rueful smile.

'Come on, my man! We'll make the motherfuckers pay, next time round. Just thank the Lord we got a next time. And by the way, Limey...'

'Yes?'

'Thanks for saving my life.'

'It was nothing.'

'Maybe to you, boy. But to me – hell! – it's all I got!'

Richmond smiled again, nodded and drank deep. 'All right, chaps. You get to know one another. I'd better go and write the report – and the letters home.'

Zappa got up and shook Richmond's hand firmly. 'Thanks again, buddy.'

'You just look after my friend here.'

'You bet, Major.'

Richmond grinned unconvincingly and sloped off.

'Sometimes you Brits can be so damn cool. And other times, so fuckin' sensitive.'

'We feel the same about you.'

'You do?'

'Yeah.'

'Well, how about that! I gotta tell ya, Toby. I didn't have all that much respect for you English guys before this war began, but I sure as hell do now. Goddamn! Between us, we're gonna have to save this whole chicken-shit world!'

'Do you think the world's ready for that, Vinny?'

'There ya go again, asking questions. You think too much, my man! If you'd been out there today, you'd soon see, Toby, that in this life you got two squares to stand on. Black or white. And if you get caught jumping from one to the other in an unbalanced way, you'll get your balls blown off!'

'Very Masonic way of looking at it.'

'Sure, I'm a Freemason. You?'

'Lapsed.'

'Don't give Uncle Vinny that "lapsed" shit! Once a Brother, always a Brother!'

'Have you read the request from Desk, Vinny?'

'Wha'd'ya mean "read"? Desk don't do paper, Toby.'

'Right.'

'Hell, son. You should know better, after all I heard about you. Damn hell, I heard you were some kind of a magician or something.'

'Not quite.'

'Not quite. You Brits! Here's to ya!'

Zappa had located another bourbon. 'Right, Toby, shoot!'

'The issue is whether or not you have a source, or may obtain a source who can put me in touch with—'

'Yeah, yeah. Those Kurdish guys. OK. I've just come back from Kirkuk in the north. And neither the Kurdistan Democratic Party, nor the Patriotic Union of Kurdistan is a hundred per cent sympathetic to Kurdish agitators within Turkey. I refer to the PKK.'

'As far as I know, neither of the guys I'm looking for are extremists. They might even be Freemasons – in Istanbul.'

Zappa raised his eyebrows and paused for a few seconds.

'Be that as it may, my man. I don't know what they expect to achieve by speaking to Massoud Barzani or Jalal Talabani. You say Turkish agents are tracking your guys in Iraq. If Barzani or Talabani got wind of that, they'd stay outta sight.'

'Officially, perhaps. But as I said, these deputies are probably moderates. Or appear to be.'

'OK, Toby. But you can be sure Turkish intelligence suspects they've got some relationship with the PKK. Why else would two Turkish Kurds come to northern Iraq?'

'Maybe they've come for protection, simply to avoid arrest. The point is, we don't know. I need to know.'

'Desk informed me there was a terrorist attack on your department in England.'

'Suspected.'

'Makes no sense at all to me, Toby. No fuckin' sense at all.' Zappa shook his head.

'Can you get me to these guys, Vinny?'

Zappa looked Ashe right in the eye. 'Look hard at these eyes, Mr Ashe, sir. In North Carolina, my family they hunt foxes. Ain't no pussy face gonna stop us neither! Unlike you guys, we don't think it sport to let the critters go. I'll find your source, *old chap*. And all *you* gotta do is sit right down there and rehydrate!'

37

Beck was panting when he entered Kellner's office at CIA Langley.

'Si'down, Beck.'

'Got here as soon as I could, sir.'

'CTC SIGINT has picked up another epistle from our "doctor" friend.'

'Trace, sir?'

'They're workin' on it now. Told they got a new female in there. Began work as an amateur in Wisconsin, tracing al-Qaeda internet links. Quite an operator.'

'Would she have gotten a job before 9/11?'

'One thing about a crisis, Beck. Brings out the talent!'

'And shows up the deadwood, sir.'

'Ain't no deadwood here, Sherman.'

'No, sir. God forbid, sir.'

'In God we trust, Agent Beck.'

'So does the enemy, sir.'

'We can't both be wrong, Beck.'

Kellner stood up and put his hands on his hips. 'I'm short of time so I'm not gonna tell ya everything right now. I'll leave that to Leanne Gresham. She's had to cope with a few surprises concerning her dear Sami al-Qasr. I'll give you a summary, 'cause I want your reaction here and now. The "doctor" claims to have been at Baghdad University with al-Qasr. Late sixties and early seventies. Friends even.'

'Could be personal, sir.'

'Yeah. But it's *motivation* we're lookin' for. They disagreed about politics. Student stuff. Al-Qasr joined the Ba'ath Party. Pan-Arab socialism. Party-knows-best kinda thing. He studied physics, biology, chemistry.'

'All that's in our al-Qasr file, sir.'

'Just bear with me, Beck. There's bound to be overlap. In 1974, his biology thesis got him the attention of Sir Moses Beerbohm in Cambridge, England. He's a world authority – I guess you know that.'

'Al-Qasr joined the MRC Laboratory of Molecular Biology on a Wellcome Trust research fellowship, sir. He assisted Sir Moses Beerbohm in Cambridge.'

'On what, Beck?'

'Research on the interactions of proteins with nucleic acids, the molecular structures of viruses. Al-Qasr assisted in the method of 3-D image reconstruction in electron microscopy from a series of 2-D tilted images. This work later formed the basis of the X-ray CT scanner. But Sir Moses's biggest hit was the discovery of the zinc finger family of transcription factors. These are used to regulate genes. Latest research – and al-Qasr is at the forefront of this – is in using the zinc finger design to engineer artificial factors to switch genes on and off.'

'Switching genes on or off. I'm impressed, Sherman Beck. And wondering if you're in the right line of business.'

'Thank you, sir. If that was a compliment.'

'Now, Beck, you can rampage through all the technical stuff when you see Leanne Gresham. I thought I was going to tell you something you didn't know.'

'Absolutely, sir. That's why I'm here.'

'OK. Now cast your mind back to Great Britain in the late seventies and early eighties. Al-Qasr is a wizzo in genes. But he's getting frustrated with his own research. Beerbohm's got him workin' on a long-term project. Highly statistical stuff. He's relating genes to specific diseases in specific areas. Lots of field-work in the flatlands of East Anglia, England. Ever spent a week

149

in North Dakota, Beck?'

'No, sir.'

'Not every young man's dream. Al-Qasr was more interested in what Beerbohm was doing. Beerbohm was flattered. Maybe he was thinking of an heir to his intellectual fortune.'

'Maybe he fancied him.'

'Think there's a sex angle here, Beck?'

'I thought we were looking for motivation, sir.'

'Don't be a smart-ass. Beerbohm started using al-Qasr as a kind of sounding board. Seems al-Qasr is turned on by the idea of rewriting genes. Then Sir Moses gets the Nobel Prize for Chemistry. That was 1982. Al-Qasr observes fame close up. Smells good. You could say the boy's straining at the limits of ambition. But he's in the old man's shadow.'

'So?'

'So the fuckin' Iran–Iraq war enters the scene. In 1983, al-Qasr gets offered a golden cheque as an inducement to go back to his homeland in its hour of need. The war is going badly for Iraq after early gains. Saddam's getting desperate. He's putting a lot of effort into unconventional weapons to give him the edge. It's December '83. Al-Qasr has just got back to Iraq from England. Don Rumsfeld meets Saddam. Normal diplomatic ties ensue between the US and Iraq. Trade benefits for Saddam include sales of chemical and biological agents.'

'Biological agents?'

'Yeah. Including anthrax. Don't they tell you these things in the Bureau? We don't live on Sesame Street, Beck.'

'No, sir.'

'March 1984. The UN reports Iraq used mustard gas and tabun nerve gas against the Iranians. As I said, Saddam was on his back foot. Now this is where it gets interesting, Beck. So pay attention, d'ya hear?'

'Sir.'

'Al-Qasr's workin' on... Well, from what we can gather from our guy in Iraq here, al-Qasr's workin' on fuckin' everything.

How to treat Iraqi troops if caught downwind of mustard gas. How to deal with anthrax. Perfection of gases for controlled use.'

'Controlled use?'

'You heard of Halabja, Beck?'

'Civilians?'

'Yes, Beck, five thousand of them, at least. Kurdish civilians, poisoned. Dictators don't distinguish. Al-Qasr is also engaging in DNA research. This is ultra, ultra secret and has never entered the public domain.'

'Why not, sir?'

'Think about it, Beck.'

Beck gripped his chin, unable to follow Kellner's drift.

'Let's just say for now, Beck, that it's been difficult to prove. Are you following me? Now, while all this is goin' on, Iran is busy on Operation Dawn V. It's early '84, like I say. Iran wants to split the Iraqi 3rd and 4th Army Corps near Basra. Iran pipes in about half a million men. The two armies clash. 25,000 killed in less than a week. This happened while the great American public was getting excited over Madonna's marriage to Sean Penn.'

'Phew!'

'Yeah. Now, all this time, our source in Iraq is still meeting al-Qasr socially. They're still intense young people, keen to convince the other they're doing the right thing. This would be consistent with what Fless was saying about our informant being a doctor.'

'Or in the same field as al-Qasr?'

'Can't be ruled out. Anyhow, this guy has a conscience. What's more, another friend of – let's call him "the doctor" – another friend of the doctor is captured as a deserter. According to the doctor, this man's the son of a religious figure.'

'An Imam? A Shia Muslim?'

Kellner shook his head.

'Sunni?'

'Nope. A *Yezidi*.'

'Sorry, sir. I haven't had time to go into that.'

151

'Start now. This guy deserts from the Iraqi army. He was a forced conscript anyhow. Traditionally, the Yezidis didn't fight alongside Muslims, for religious reasons. The Yezidi says he deserted in protest at the use of illegal weapons against the Iranians – as if anyone gives a damn. He's given a choice. He can either be shot on the spot, or offer himself to help the Iraqi medical corps.'

'Hospital orderly?'

'He thinks that's the game. Poor sap's sent to al-Tuwaitha.'

'Why haven't I heard of that?'

'How the fuck should I know? Al-Tuwaitha is Iraq's biggest multi-purpose scientific facility. Six kilometres across. Massive earthworks, bunkers and lookout towers protect it. And there's underground stuff. Nuclear, biological, chemical – you name it. The Iraq Survey Group have had more fun looking through that place than Saddam's private movie collection.'

'No way out, presumably, for the doctor's friend.'

'By a nasty twist, the Yezidi deserter is sent to the personal laboratory of Dr Sami al-Qasr, Iraq's scientific superstar, the genetic specialist whose word is law.'

'I presume the power he's been given is making up for the lack of a Nobel Prize.'

'He's got power over life and death. Something they never thought to give Sir Moses Beerbohm in Cambridge.'

'And the deserter?'

'Poor guy's subjected to dosages of chemicals, biological agents, even radiation. That is, according to our good doctor. Turns out the boy's got a curious resistance to an unnamed bacillus. Maybe anthrax. Al-Qasr subjects his guinea pig to every kind of test and DNA-mapping procedure. And that doesn't tell us much, because we don't know for sure what al-Qasr was capable of in Iraq.'

'How did the doctor know all this?'

'Seems in some unguarded moments, al-Qasr boasted to his old friend of breakthroughs that would make Iraq the global centre of microbiological research. Seems the doctor found out his friend was in al-Qasr's grip, because al-Qasr had started making enquiries about the boy's background. Drawing up comparative DNA profiles. Yezidi society being fairly tight-knit, this all got back to the doctor.'

'Our informant is a Yezidi?'

'That not obvious to you, Agent Beck? You surprise me.'

'Thank you, sir. I'll take that as a compliment too.'

Kellner looked at his watch. 'Oh shit, Beck! I've got to chair a Threat Matrix Report meeting with the President in ten. Look, I'll try to wrap this up, but you'll have to get on to Leanne Gresham. Now, how can I put it?'

'Sir, why not just call me tonight?'

'This ain't something I'll put over any phone, Beck. No matter how damn secure.'

'Any phone, sir?'

Kellner leant forward, face rigid, and looked Beck very hard in the eye. '*Any* fucking phone.'

38

'You'll need this, Toby. Just sign here.'

Major Richmond handed Ashe a SIG Sauer 9 mm pistol, small enough for the shoulder holster secreted beneath his jacket.

'And Toby...'

'Simon?'

'Body armour.'

'Check.'

Richmond sat on his plastic chair and surveyed his tiny, windowless office, covered from floor to ceiling in specialised maps of Iraq. 'Ready for this, Toby?'

'I feel a hell of a lot better knowing you're the driver.'

'You were lucky to get me. Thank Desk: his word reaches far.'

'What in hell's happened to Zappa?'

'What time did he tell you?'

'4.40.'

'And what time is it?'

'4.39.'

'Relax, Toby. Zap's a good man. Besides, he's had to pick up the interpreter. And that's not always as simple as it sounds.'

'Regular interpreter?'

'We've done pre-tests and Zap's fully checked the source background. We do it all the time – standard procedure and usually reliable.'

'Usually?'

'Nothing's perfect.'

There was a knock on the door.

'Who is it?'

'Vinny.'

Richmond turned to Ashe. 'Time?'

'4.40.'

The major grinned as he opened the door. 'Vincent!'

'Major Richmond, let me take your hand. Allow me to introduce Dr Zaqqarah.'

'Hello, Safi! Good to see you again.'

The slightly nervous, rotund academic gripped Richmond's hand. 'Peace be upon you, Major.'

'One of these days. May I introduce to you a friend from England?' Ashe was not to be introduced by name. Zaqqarah smiled sweetly and shook hands with Ashe.

As they emerged from the stairwell hatch into the light, Ashe struggled with the glare of the afternoon sun; the heat came hard.

An American sergeant saluted Richmond. 'We've gotten you a BMW, sir.'

'Class 5 or 7, Sergeant?'

'Class 5, sir.'

'I asked for Class 7.'

'The last one left the compound with Major Rudetsky, an hour ago, sir.'

'What's wrong with the Merc?'

'Fuel pump, sir. It'll be ready tonight.'

Richmond turned to Zappa. 'Class 5 today, Zap.'

'The Lord giveth, Major.'

Ashe looked quizzical.

'It's about adapted security features, Ashe. Additional batteries, secondary air-con systems, armoured chassis, bulletproofing, tracking features, weaponry. I'd hoped for the Merc Class 7. Apparently, we're not important enough. Or *you* aren't!'

The two men laughed.

'I suppose some are more indispensable than others.' Dr Zaqqarah's nervous laugh cracked audibly.

The sergeant opened the door for the three men and saluted. 'Good luck, sir.'

'Thank you, Sergeant.'

Ashe got into the back of the BMW with the interpreter. The doors slammed shut. This was it: Ashe's first operation in the field.

39

The grey BMW passed through the al-Kindi gate into the heart of Baghdad. A busy late afternoon and the streets were pullulating with hot, dusty activity. Most Baghdadis understood the 'live and let live' principle, Ashe was coming to realise, but that didn't mean someone was going to let them live.

Heading towards the Tigris along al-Mamoun Boulevard, the car turned sharp right, following signs for the Main Supply Route – or MSR as Richmond referred to the Basra–Baghdad highway.

Ashe enjoyed talking to Dr Zaqqarah. It turned out he had a cousin working as a surgeon in Burton-on-Trent, ten miles from Ashe's home. Ashe wondered if Zaqqarah's cousin might find better employment in Iraq.

'This is what I tell him, sir. And he says, "Come home? Is it safe?" What can I tell him? Here, criminals kidnap doctors and hold them to ransom every week. The rebellion must stop; we want normal lives.'

The car pulled up outside a café at a huge crossroads. The single-storey establishment stood out starkly against the barren site. The surrounding structures had been bombed and the debris bulldozed to make way for yet another car park. The positive point was that there was little cover for anyone contemplating an ambush, and ample means of escape should such a thing occur.

The air was still; Richmond checked his watch. Zappa muttered under his breath, 'Eyes peeled, TA.'

The American stretched his left arm down to an M4 carbine secured in a special pocket to the side of his seat. Richmond had his hand close to his jacket's inside pocket; he checked his watch again.

'Twenty seconds.'

'What's that?'

A red Toyota pickup skidded into the bay at the side of the café. A teenager emerged from the back of the building, spoke to the driver and went back inside.

'That's it, guys, we're off.'

Richmond put the car in gear.

'Hold it, Major. Look!' Zappa pointed to the café entrance. A big man in a dark-pink shirt and holding a newspaper came out of the café. He pulled a rag from his back pocket and blew his nose. At the same moment, the teenager returned to the Toyota at the side, carrying a huge plastic petrol container.

'It's OK. Black market.'

'Free market,' added Zaqqarah.

The man with the newspaper thrust a fat cigarette through the bush of his moustache. A match failed; he reached into his back pocket for a lighter.

'That's the signal.'

Richmond revved the car twice. The man walked slowly towards the BMW.

Ashe held his breath. It could be a set-up. He fingered the SIG, trying to recall a wet weekend's weapons-handling course at British Army Kineton. A dismally damp Warwickshire suddenly seemed a very attractive alternative to a car park in Iraq.

Zaqqarah depressed the rear-window control and spoke to the man in Arabic.

Before Ashe had a moment to grasp the exchange, the car had a new passenger and was speeding off south. Hurried, nervous conversation passed between the man and the interpreter.

'What's going on, Simon?'

'Confirmation of the price. Agreement of terms.'

'Price?'

'Replacement car parts mostly. Handy equipment, difficult to obtain. A car service. Nothing conspicuous. Maybe a little money. Petrol. That sort of stuff. Common things but bloody useful.'

The car sped on beyond the outskirts of Baghdad. In the distance, Ashe caught sight of a row of massive guard towers, spaced out some fifty meters from one to another. It looked like the outer limits of hell. As the car got closer and the towers loomed larger, gargantuan soil embankments 100 metres high blocked the eye line, leaving the perimeter road in heavy shadow.

'What the hell's that?'

'*That* is the al-Tuwaitha Research Facility.'

'And those mounds? Looks like archaeology.'

'Maybe in the future. This is just part of Saddam's protection investment.'

The car screeched to a standstill.

'Shit!'

Thirty metres down the road, a great plume of black smoke billowed from a cauldron of twisted metal and orange fire: a Humvee had hit a mine. A makeshift roadblock had been erected.

The source began to fidget awkwardly in his seat.

'Everybody, stay calm. Translate that, please Dr Zaqqarah.'

The source was sweating uncontrollably. Ashe's shoulder was feeling the damp.

An M16 was levelled at the car. An American private indicated for an interpreter to move forwards between himself and the vehicle. As the interpreter raised a battery-powered megaphone, he tripped over a corpse by his feet.

'Get down everyone!' bellowed Richmond.

The private looked startled, and released a three-round burst towards the car. Tiny shards of windscreen scattered as the car shook, echoing with the deafening shots.

'Christ!'

The private's interpreter screamed. 'No shoot! It's all right. I trip on body.'

The soldier, young, nervous, distracted, fired harsh words at the interpreter. The interpreter begged the driver and passengers of the BMW to get out, one by one, and lie on the ground with hands and legs stretched out in a cross pattern.

'What's he saying?'

'He says everyone out of the car, one at a time. Only one at a time, or they shoot. No questions.'

Richmond spoke under his breath. 'Thank God it's a Class 5 windscreen. OK, you first Vinny.'

'Why the fuck is it always me?'

'Yanks like to be first, don't they?'

The source lost control. Panicking, he flailed his arms about, kicking the backs of the seats.

'For God's sake, TA, calm him down!'

'Why not show him your pistol?'

'If they see me do that, you can kiss your life goodbye.'

'I not want to die! I not want to die!'

'Not you! Zaqqarah, tell the man we'll all be bloody dead if he carries on like this!'

The interpreter reached for his megaphone. 'One by one. Now!'

'Shit, Simon! If the source gets out on his own, he could blow the whole thing.'

Zappa turned to the source. 'Listen, man! You know some English, right?'

'Yes, sir. But I don't want—'

'Can it! If you're a good boy, brave lion, big man... your father's son, pride of your family, then we all live, OK?'

Zaqqarah translated for good measure. The man nodded and wiped his nose.

The interpreter with the megaphone repeated the orders in Arabic. Richmond put his hand on Zappa's shoulder. 'Come on, old friend.'

Zappa calmly got out of the car, his hands in the air. The private indicated with his rifle barrel that he should hit the deck.

'Next man out!'

Ashe was next. Gingerly, he opened the back door to see, in the distance, the private calling up a ground-mounted machine gun: a bright new M240B. The crew loaded it, itching to give the lethal weapon a road test.

Ashe held his breath, tried to smile, and lay down near to Zappa. Zappa whispered to Ashe. 'Why the fuck doesn't the soldier use his sight?'

Ashe whispered back. 'None as blind as them that won't see.'

Zappa closed his eyes and began running Beatles songs through his mind, trying to get the singles in order of release – an old trick he'd been using at the dentist ever since he was a boy. With any luck, by the time he'd got to 'The Long and Winding Road' the pain would be over.

The source had begun to shake again, and had developed a curious tick in his neck. Richmond implored the interpreter inside the car to do something. 'Tell him he'll be fine. I'll leave the car last.

'OK, now you, Dr Zaqqarah. Give 'em a big smile and raise your hands. Everything's going to be fine. Everything's going to be fine.'

'I'm afraid… I'm afraid I have…' Zaqqarah tried to edge his way out of the car; his trousers were stuck to the seat. He gave an awful look to Richmond and shook his head. A stomach-turning stench filled the car's interior.

Ashe, his body roasting on the tarmac, tried to move to spread the heat. He heard Zaqqarah's feet crunch on the loose gravel chippings. In the distance: two choppers, like spiders descending from a celestial web, buzzed through the smoke-filled sky to the burning Humvee.

Ashe could hear the machine-gun crew addressing the private. 'Christ!' he thought, 'a group of five men in an expensive car. US casualties on the ground. What was the crew thinking? Revenge? Something to release the tension?'

Ashe saw the machine-gun crew taking aim.

The source emerged from the car and stared into the barrel of the M240B, like a rabbit in headlights; he was paralysed.

'One at a time,' whispered Zappa from somewhere between 'She loves you' and 'I want to hold your hand'. 'Come on, boy!'

Ashe thought he heard something on the machine gun. The helicopters were now directly overhead, whipping up the gravel that danced along the road like demented locusts. The private and the gun crew started shouting at each other above the increased whirl and roar of 'copter blades. The crew pointed at the source, shaking by the back door. The man dropped to his knees. The private levelled his M16 downwards.

'Move away from the car!' pleaded Zaqqarah to the source.

'Shut up!' shouted the private's interpreter.

'Move away!'

The man would not move.

Richmond started audibly praying. The helicopter hovered overhead. Nothing he could say would be heard. The source would not move.

40

Richmond raised his arms in surrender to the car roof, his fists clenched; his nails dug into his hands.

The machine-gunners caught the movement inside the car and pulled the gun towards the windscreen.

'Oh, Jesus!'

The machine-gun crew screamed at the private. The crew sergeant got to his feet. 'Lower your weapon, Soldier! That goddamn guy out there is one of us! Why don't you use the fuckin' sight?'

'It's my shades, Sarge. Covered in blood. I was assisting wounded and this car's suddenly there, Sergeant. I couldn't see good.'

The sergeant told the interpreter he could use English. The interpreter was confused. The sergeant grabbed the megaphone and walked towards the car. 'OK you guys! There's been a mis-understanding over here. Stand up and approach the roadblock!'

Zappa, whistling 'A Ticket to Ride', hauled his weight off the tarmac and went round to the source, who was still kneeling, crippled with fear.

'Come on, pal, you're safe. You tell him, Doctor.'

Ashe, still apprehensive, rolled over onto his back and snapped to his feet. Feeling dizzy, he tried to stop holding his breath.

Medics were pouring from the 'copter and racing across to the wounded soldiers. Richmond approached the sergeant, showed his ID and shared a joke – both trying to ignore the cries of the men being strapped onto stretchers.

'You're damned lucky, sir. My crew here had you marked out as fuckin' terrorists. Excuse my language, sir; they're in no mood to be delicate about it. If you take my advice, sir, you'll be outta here as soon as possible. Lord knows what else is gonna come this way now. Those 'copters make mighty fine targets for rocket grenades. This whole damn country's a weapon of mass destruction!'

'That's what they'd like you to believe, Sergeant. Good luck.'

Richmond thanked the apologetic machine-gun crew for not opening fire. Zappa went back to the BMW and manoeuvred it slowly through the smoke.

Dr Zaqqarah removed his trousers and used Richmond's mineral water to wash his backside, drying it with the discarded garments.

And the source sat cross-legged by the car, praying out loud to Allah to deliver him and everybody else from the checkpoint inferno.

That night, Ashe drank himself sober. He lay still, gazing at the rough wool of the blanket in the bunk above his head.

Had he been frightened? Yes. Had he ever been as scared as that? No, he didn't think so. But had he ever been more alive? That he couldn't answer; he'd had some incredible experiences in the past, things so special that memory itself was inadequate to replay them. This was different – and what a bond had been forged in just a few hours between himself, Zappa and Richmond. He could see why many men found life outside the services difficult. Then he thought of poor Dr Zaqqarah going home to his wife that night: a pious Muslim, unable to drink, unable to speak, and with a new pair of ill-fitting trousers – and no explanation.

And what of the poor source? He seemed to have aged five years in an afternoon.

But, for all that, it had worked well. They'd taken the

softened-up source to the edge of a stone quarry near the al-Tuwaitha installation, close to a Hungarian field hospital. Desperate to get back to his own world, the source had spilled everything he had on Kurdish political activity in Baghdad. Zappa even picked up some useful information on unrelated investigations. The source had gabbed and gabbed, and Zappa had been happy. They threw in a microwave and a spare set of tyres for his trouble. He said 'Any time,' but 'could they meet in Baghdad next time?'

Zappa and Richmond doubted if they'd see him again – at least until his car broke down again for want of parts.

Both Yazar and Yildiz had been in Baghdad, ostensibly for discussions on the composition of the new Iraqi constitutional assembly, due to take control in the spring of '05. Their presence there could be seen as innocent enough. They could just have been getting the low-down on Kurdish chances for autonomy, federation or even independence from central Iraqi power in the new Iraq so many dreamed of.

There were hundreds of issues of importance to Kurdish politicians and the people they represented. For example, would the Kurdish militia be expected to amalgamate with a new Iraqi army? The Kurds, allied to US Forces, had been partially independent since the safe zone had been established in northern Iraq in 1991. Who would control an Iraqi army? How could a future military coup be prevented?

These issues also exercised the minds of Turkish security forces. Yazar and Yildiz were operating under assumed names; the source had only recognised them from photographs in Zappa's file. According to the source, Yazar and Yildiz had left Baghdad in a hurry. They'd gone north to Mosul.

Mosul was Zappa's territory; he liked the north of Iraq. For a start, the area had more supporters of the US effort than any other part of the Middle and Near East. Zappa got on well with the Kurds and enjoyed the complex politicking that happened in every corner of the region. But, frankly, as he put it to Ashe before nesting down with a bottle of JD, Harlem at its worst was better than Kirkuk at its best.

Ashe himself longed to get out of the DIA HQ. It felt like a bunker. This was doubtless due to the fact that it had once been a bunker. An Oddball's bunker, no less – one of Saddam's many lairs. It had been no surprise to learn that Richmond's 'office', in dull, lavatorial green, once was an interrogation chamber.

Ashe was beginning to think about getting back home; everyone was – except, perhaps, Zappa. Anyhow, no one voiced such thoughts too eagerly; the task lay before them, undone.

Ashe had, somewhat to his surprise, become a component in what Major Richmond called 'the intelligence cycle'. The idea worked like this: a certain number of objectives would be established. These would lead to a series of source interviews. The interviews would be assessed, checked, crosschecked, analysed and compared. New information would coalesce into a new set of priorities and a fresh intelligence cycle could begin.

There was no jumping the gun, no place for undisciplined mavericks or loose cannons. In theory, original minds were welcome, but one man's lateral thinker could be another man's nut. There were no freewheeling agents acting on intuition, going from one gun-toting adventure to another. This was not acting, and James Bond could only be found on the Coalition Camp DVD screens.

Intelligence-gathering was many things, but one thing it could not be described as was 'entertaining' – though it might contain the odd glimmer of light relief. The story of Zaqqarah's trousers would do the rounds for some time – as would a certain black humour associated with the private's shades, covered with blood.

There was even some lightness to be gained from full exposure to Zappa's extraordinary range of shirts. Like his shirts, Vinny's turn of phrase was rarely anything less than florid. Vinny was an acquired taste; Ashe had acquired it.

41

The morning hit Ashe like a wet flannel. Every limb in his body ached, his head an unholy hole of regret and pain.

Richmond burst into his room like a hammer to the temples. 'Hands off cocks, on with socks!'

The intelligence cycle had turned another crucial notch. A cog had slipped into place and while Ashe had slept the sleep of the just, an operation had been planned to get him up into Kurdistan.

'Shit, shower and shave, Toby!'

Ashe squinted at the naked strip light.

'Come on! You can try these.' Richmond withdrew a packet of hangover Eazers from the breast pocket of his US uniform shirt. 'They're pretty good if you have a big breakfast – give all that acid something to work on.'

'Do I have to get up?'

'We've got two armoured cars and four US guardsmen out there waiting to escort you to the wedding. Don't they deserve a little enthusiasm?'

Ashe struggled out of his bunk and tried to get his right foot into his shorts. He looked up at Richmond – dressed, for the first time in a fortnight, in combat uniform. It was a fine sight, set off by Simon Richmond's perennially encouraging smile.

'If you enjoyed our minor incident at the roadblock, you're going to love this little outing.'

'More friendly fire, Simon?'

'You'll be lucky!'

Richmond tossed Ashe a helmet, freshly camouflaged. As Ashe caught it, his shorts fell down. Richmond tutted. 'Limp cock. Bad sign.'

While Zappa, Richmond and Ashe were making their way quickly through the DIA forward-planning area, Richmond handed Ashe a Browning 9 mm with its canvas holster and belt.

'I forgot this, Toby. I hope you won't.'

'Trust me.'

The shadowy room flickered with dozens of LCD monitors. There was a positive babel of voices on phones and in radio communication with contacts throughout the Middle East.

'Say goodbye to civilisation, Toby!'

'You're kidding, Zap old boy! Civilisation is where we're heading. We're going to the land of Abraham!'

'I think you'll find Abraham's moved out, bud.'

'Must have seen you coming.'

'Fuck off, Toby!'

The trio mounted a series of cast-iron steps that led through the dark and up to the surface. An unfamiliar sound was tap-dancing its way over the closed steel hatch.

'Umbrellas, anyone?' quipped Richmond, as the three emerged into a torrential grey-and-brown downpour. An unpleasant green colour seemed to flash on and off as the banks of angry black clouds battled with each other for supremacy. The bullets of rain fell so heavily that soon every nose was dripping and every garment had turned into a soaking flannel. Ashe's head felt oddly cocooned in his helmet as the rain echoed about and within his head like a Walkman.

Richmond patted Ashe on the shoulder and shouted under his helmet rim. 'Like I said, Toby. Limp cock. Bad sign!'

'Hey! It's size that matters.'

'Then we're sunk!'

Through the barrage of rain and explosions of thunder, Ashe

could hear the vehicles revving up for the 150-mile journey ahead: a caravan of steel.

In front of him, reversing with great skill considering the conditions, were two US four-wheeled, four-door Humvees. The rear plating on one had been removed to accommodate two mounted machine guns, both wrapped in tarpaulin. The second vehicle had an enclosed rear with a winch attached at the back. Two privates, dressed in light-brown waterproof capes, directed the Humvees into position.

Ashe called over to Richmond. 'Are we going to get waterproofs, Simon?'

'Afraid not. I've not been issued with one and there's none left for you!'

'That's a— *Hey*! What's that?'

'You're a lucky man, Toby. That's our Merc. Class 7. Somebody's decided you're an important person.'

Ashe looked at Zappa.

'Don't look at me, bud. Class 5's always been good 'nough for me.'

'Anyhow, Toby, if you still want protection from this rain, may I suggest…?'

Richmond opened the front door.

'Front this time?'

'Hop in! Vinny – the back! What's that? Yeah, gear's loaded already.'

Richmond settled into the driving seat. Ashe stared at the unfamiliar dashboard and complexity of additional features. 'Very hi-tech, Simon.'

'Yes, a CD player. Anyone fancy Dolly Parton?'

'Must we?'

'How about *Wagner for Soldiers* – US Defense Special Issue?'

'You're fuckin' joking!'

'I jest not, Vinny. It's a psy-ops production. Look!'

'Fuck! Who's been in this wagon?'

'Francis Ford Coppola by the sound of things.'

169

Richmond tried out the high-speed wipers. 'We have vision, gentlemen. Now, here's something. Rolling Stones, anybody?'

'Just play "Start me Up", Major, and cut the crap!'

'I'm with Vinny. I want the Human Riff.'

'Coming up.'

'By the way, Simon, where's our interpreter?'

'Dr Zaqqarah was not available for duty. We've got Ibrahim on this trip. He's behind us in the Humvee.'

'Remind me again why they're called "Humvees"?'

'D'ya hear that? There's something this boy doesn't know. You explain it, Major.'

'Humvee, Toby, is a… what's that word? Diminutive?'

'Don't look at me, Major. Abbreviation?'

'Yeah, well, it's like that. Officially they're called an HMMWV, which, if you say it fast with a mouth full of cornflakes, sounds a bit like "Humvee".'

'And what is an HMMWV?'

'It's an acronym!'

'Now he tells us!'

'Thank you, Toby. It's an acronym for High Mobility Multipurpose Wheeled Vehicle.'

'Right.'

'OK, fasten your fears and lock up your doubts. Gentlemen, we're go, go, go!'

The Humvee in front led the way as a squad lifted a series of double razor-wire barriers. Ashe looked out of the window to see whether the Humvee behind was in step with the rest of the convoy. His spirits sank. Two familiar faces in British combat gear were approaching the stairwell hatch. The men stopped, looked over at the vehicles, and stared hard through the driving rain. Ashe pulled his head back in.

Bagot and Colquitt. Like some awful old firm of debt collectors. What the fuck were the beagles doing in Baghdad? What was more, had they sniffed him? Ashe dared not stick his head out again. No one could screw up his operation quicker than

Major Giles Bagot and Lieutenant Tony Colquitt. He prayed he would not hear the splash of running feet and a frantic knocking on the car door.

'Come on, Simon, let's get out of here.'

'Are you all right, Toby? Why the haste?'

'Let's just move.'

'Right.' Richmond put his foot down and rushed through the barriers as fast as he could, almost hitting the Humvee in front.

'Steady on, Major. We've a way to go yet.'

If anything, the weather was getting worse. Forks of lightning between the thunder claps made a dramatic if disturbing show over the ancient city.

Ashe jumped as a tortured-sounding voice echoed from a minaret overhead.

'You must be on edge if a muezzin startles you,' said Richmond.

'I'm fine,' Ashe said. 'It's just this filthy weather. There's something uncanny about the mix of Islamic pieties and the raging storm.'

'Good job the call to prayer comes from a pre-recorded tape these days, then, eh? You wouldn't want to be a live muezzin climbing up a minaret in lightning like this.'

Ashe nodded, and the pair fell into a companionable silence as Richmond drove the Merc out of the confines of the city, happy to leave the stress of Baghdad behind.

'So, Toby, you were asking me about the Humvees?'

'Was I? Oh yes. Those would be the High Mobility Multipurpose Wheeled Vehicles, would they not? Sometimes these acronyms go a bit far, don't you think? I mean, are there any High Mobility Multipurpose *Un*wheeled Vehicles?'

'Not on the road, bud.'

'I suppose they're trying to distinguish them from tanks.'

'Even so, but imagine if the Pentagon had to define a woman in similar terms. A High Mobility, Multipurpose Long-legged—'

'Thank the Lord they ain't on to that yet, Toby!'

171

The major quietly hummed the tune to 'There is Nothing Like a Dame'.

'That ain't how they see things at the Pentagon these days, Major. The way things are goin', the army would prefer to make no explicit distinction between males and females wherever humanly possible. They'd prefer some kind of hi-tech military-oriented hermaphrodite.'

'Really?'

'We got machines – robots – comin' in to man roadblocks.'

'If indeed "man" is the correct word.'

'The word is *appropriate*, not correct.'

'Are you saying it's not appropriate to be correct?'

'No, it's only appropriate when it is correct.'

'But I thought—'

'Listen, all I'm saying is, how long will it be before—'

'OK, Vinny, we've all seen *Terminator*! But it's a few years to go before robots do all the fighting.'

'But maybe it's only tomorrow when the robots do the planning.'

'Thank you, Toby. What you don't realise is that our friend Vincent Zappa here is, by and large, a very balanced, reasonable fellow.'

'I'm a regular guy!'

'See what I mean? But he does have his sensitive areas. He's scared of any technology that might make him redundant.'

'I'm just fightin' for my right to work, Major!'

'You have my full support. Now, Toby, to answer your question. The Humvee up front is the M1043 Humvee armament carrier.'

'Tell him what it weighs.'

'About four tons.'

'You won't be pullin' that with your teeth!'

'Behind us – or, as we jocularly say, "up our rear" – is the M1038 cargo and troop carrier with winch.'

'They throw the winch in extra!'

'Who do?'

'O'Gara-Hess & Eisenhardt of Fairfield, Ohio, if you must know.'

'And let us not forget, O smartass Limey, several models derive from AM General, of South Bend, Indiana.'

Ashe nodded with mock satisfaction. 'Well, gentlemen, I feel suitably enlightened. Is all the conversation on this journey to be of such sparkling and informative character?'

'Not if you leave it to us, Dr Toby Ashe. We'll leave the really smart remarks to you.'

'In that case, Simon, would you care to turn the music up?'

The convoy sped north out of Baghdad to the tune of the Rolling Stones' 'Tumbling Dice'. But as he tapped his boot to the old chestnut, the question uppermost in Ashe's mind was, on whose side *were* the dice loaded?

42

'This was a nice idea, Ms Gresham.'

'For heaven's sakes, Sherman, call me Leanne. My father did, and he never fell off his perch.'

Beck had taken a taxi ten miles south of Langley, McLean, through Fairfax County, to meet Leanne Gresham at a little Italian restaurant on the green outskirts of Annandale. The glare of the sun reflected off the plastic gingham tablecloth. Through the fine old windowpanes of the colonial-style establishment, they could see a quiet road and a tranquil pony ranch.

'That's where I used to take my daughter for riding lessons.'

'Where is she now?'

'Princeton.'

'I'm impressed.'

'Don't be. She's studying theology.'

'Could be useful today.'

'She thinks it will be even more useful tomorrow. Lord! How things change! I mean what use is theology in a laboratory? When I was growing up, theology was like studying antiquarian bookselling. Fascinating, but strictly for enthusiasts.'

'As you say, things change.'

'A law of the universe. And we in the Directorate of Science and Technology have as much trouble with it as anyone else. Take your boss. A fortnight ago, Lee Kellner could hardly bring himself to notice me in the corridor. Now he's all grace and charm. Makes quite a difference.'

'I guess he's suddenly realised your importance.'

'Well there *is* a change. And it isn't just smiles and courtesies. He's let me in on your story. Even asked me to finish briefing you before we – did you get that? *we* – go to California.'

'Is that an order, ma'am?'

'Objections?'

The question struck Beck as slightly compromising, especially as uttered by Gresham. There was just a hint of seductiveness, a tiny silver sparkle in the air between them.

'Not at all, ma'am. When duty calls, I follow.'

Gresham smiled. 'I do believe, Sherman, there's gallantry in your soul. Don't blush, honey. Paleness suits you.'

A large Italian lady, singing a Puccini aria to herself, carried two steaming earthenware dishes over to their table, balancing them like the scales of justice.

'Lasagne!'

'Thank you.'

'Grazie, madam. You both order salad.'

'Yeah. Caesar salad.'

'Now, if you'll take your eyes off that woman's derrière, Sherman, what did you want to know about al-Qasr? He's quite a looker, you know.'

'Kellner explained how al-Qasr used a Yezidi deserter for medical experiments at al-Tuwaitha.'

'Scientists often turn a blind eye to the human dimensions of what they do. I'm not saying this to excuse Dr al-Qasr. I mean, I was as shocked about that as you were. But sometimes the pursuit of knowledge seems to outweigh every other consideration. Did you know that Robert Boyle and Christopher Wren—'

'Who?'

'Boyle and Wren. Two English scientists who were around just before Lord Fairfax bought what is now Virginia. Late seventeenth century. Fairfax's house was where CIA Langley now stands.'

'So what did Boyle and Wren do?'

'They were interested in the way blood flows round the body. They understood that the condition of the blood is the clue to identifying illness. You could say these guys were at the root of what became genetic science.'

'It's all in the blood.'

'It's all in the blood. Anyhow, they drained a dog of all of its blood. Then they took a poor man, got him drunk, bled him, and transfused the dog's blood into him.'

Beck tried to take the idea in. It didn't go well with lasagne and salad. 'Yup. Sounds like science to me.'

'You get the picture. Well, like the poor sap used by the old scientists in my story, the Yezidi man at the mercy of al-Qasr eventually succumbed.'

'He murdered him.'

Gresham sighed. 'I guess so. The next thing is that the Yezidi man's family petition Saddam as to their relative's whereabouts. Eventually they're told he volunteered for the front but was now missing – the usual story given to Iraqi families to explain why sons didn't come home. Saddam didn't want anyone to know the full extent of the carnage. Men killed by Iranian bullets and shells were routinely listed as having been transferred to another front. Desperate people will believe anything. Saddam needed new fronts. This partly explains the attack on Kuwait. Also, Saddam owed Kuwait the fifteen billion dollars borrowed to wage war on Iran.'

'You're very well informed, Leanne.'

'Thank your nice Mr Kellner for that.'

'No one ever called Lee "nice".'

'Well, apart from Lee, no one at Langley ever called me "beautiful" either!'

'Was that appropriate?'

'Spare me the PC bullshit, Sherman. I'd call it courteous!'

'Forgive me.'

'Not at all. I mean, he didn't pinch my ass or anything!'

Beck laughed. 'OK. So what about al-Qasr?'

'Lee's informant knew – we don't know how – that al-Qasr's experimental victim had not returned to the guns and the fury. Apparently, the poor man was just as useful to al-Qasr dead as he had been alive. Al-Qasr had the body stored in a special freezing facility just north of Basra, protected by a missile bunker.'

'I get it. That's the place the British hit in 1992. The place mentioned in the informant's first communication. Makes you wonder what the British knew about it.'

'Right. All we know is the British Royal Air Force hit the facility in June 1992 as part of its holding operation in the no-fly zone after the end of the Gulf War. And that is when my department first heard of the great Dr Sami al-Qasr's desire to defect from Saddam. Naturally, we welcomed al-Qasr with open arms.'

'Why "naturally"?'

'That's a very good question, Sherman.'

'And?'

'And I'd need clearance from your Mr Kellner to answer that.'

'Touché.'

43

A black Mercedes limo drew up smoothly below the restaurant window.

'Looks like our taxi, Sherman.'

'That doesn't look anything like our taxi!'

'Wanna bet?'

Leanne Gresham and Sherman Beck slipped their jackets on, paid the waitress and made their way outside.

Gresham opened the rear door for Beck.

'Pleasant lunch, Agent Beck?' Kellner looked up from a report he was perusing, took off his reading glasses and smiled. 'Glad to have you aboard. And especially you, Mrs Gresham.'

Leanne Gresham slipped into the front seat and arranged her skirt. 'Thanks for the lift, Mr Kellner.'

'Call me Lee.'

'Lee and Sherman? I must say I would never have expected to be sharing a limo with two opposing Civil War generals!'

Beck grinned.

'Now, Lee. Agent Beck here was interested to know why my old department took such a keen interest in al-Qasr's offer to defect to the States in 1992.'

Kellner nodded slowly. 'Yeah. Right. OK… But before I go into that I'd like to tell y'all that—'

'Sir?' The driver interrupted them.

'What is it, Agent Keane?'

'Shall I drive to Langley, sir?'

'Yeah, but take it easy. Enjoy the ride.'

'Yessir.'

'Leanne, Sherman, I'm proud to tell you that we've traced our informant. The message about our friend in California came from Germany. Hamburg to be exact.

'Now, if you'll excuse me, Mrs Gresham, I'm going to put up the dividing screen.' Kellner pointed playfully at the driver and pressed a button. In a few seconds, Beck and Kellner were in a sealed environment.

'Now, Beck, consider this space a confessional.'

'Sir?'

'I'm not sayin' I'm guilty or anything, but you know a priest would rather die than reveal a confession.'

'In theory, sir.'

'Yeah. Well here is no theory. You get my meaning?'

Beck nodded.

'Good. Now take your eyes off the brown dirt and green leaves of north Virginia and look closely at my lips. You are going to hear some facts. Of a very secret nature.'

Beck took a deep breath and nodded.

'Good, Beck. I can tell you're taking this seriously. Now, many people have asked this question: why was it, when the Coalition had the Iraqi army on the run from Kuwait in the first Gulf War, that we did not finish Saddam off once and for all?'

'Are you asking me the question, sir?'

'Can you answer it?'

'A number of factors, sir. I mean, first and foremost, the Iraqi army was willing to surrender. Also, the terms of the UN Resolutions. They covered ejecting Iraq from Kuwait, but not toppling the regime. We had a famous victory with minimal loss of life. Invasion of Iraq had presumably not been planned for in any detail, and casualties might have been politically difficult to sustain. Then there's world opinion and the issue of the balance of power in the Mid-East, sir. Unpredictable consequences.

179

Relations with the Saudis. In short, sir, while the opportunity was ripe, there may have been too many unpredictable factors. There was of course the hope of an Iraqi uprising against their dictator. I guess there was talk of generals mutinying against Saddam and stuff like that. Restraint seemed appropriate. Colin Powell's style, sir.'

'I'm impressed, Beck. Again. Do tell me when you're applying for my job. I'd like to know in advance.'

Beck laughed modestly.

'All right, Sherman. That's a pretty good summary of what we might call the external position.'

'External position, sir?'

'There was another factor. Back in 1990, the CIA had intelligence – mainly from the Israelis – that Saddam was working on a new weapon.'

'The super gun, sir?'

'That's the one you could talk about, Beck. The Agency began to hear about an amazing dude workin' on the Iraqi chemical and biological programme.'

'Dr Sami al-Qasr?'

'You got it. Do you get the rest?'

Beck closed his eyes and thought hard for a few seconds. 'A DNA weapon.'

'A DNA selective weapon. Details varied. But Saddam was very clever. He could be, you know. He didn't threaten the United States directly. He didn't say, "March on Baghdad and I'll hit you with something you never even heard of." What he did was this. He knew the Israelis had a spy at al-Tuwaitha. So he seeded just sufficient information to get the Mossad on the hotline and give Uncle Sam the willies.'

'And did it?'

'You betcha. This was something we just hadn't bargained for. You could say this was the moment when the term "Weapons of Mass Destruction" came into its own. For the handful of us who knew about the situation, WMD was mainly a euphemism—'

'For Sami al-Qasr.'

'Right. You got it. Now, we couldn't go on air and tell the world about this thing. Why do you think that was, Beck?'

'Because we wanted it ourselves.'

'Right. *We wanted it ourselves*. And we didn't want anyone to know we wanted it. You may recall how much power having the atomic bomb gave us when nobody knew we had it. Well, we lost that advantage soon enough after we dropped the bomb, though for a while we were still ahead, because no one else had it. Then, thanks to the KGB, we lost that as well. Before al-Qasr, we hadn't experienced that kind of power for a long, long time. And what we wanted, it looked like Iraq had. But we couldn't just ask them, "Hey, do you have a terrifying DNA-altering weapon?" All we could do was try to find out if it was possible that they were so far ahead of us on that. Need I say that when information on al-Qasr started coming in, there were a lot of butts fidgeting around when it came to deciding: *Do we go for Baghdad this year?*'

'Jeez!' Beck shook his head in disbelief. 'You telling me that because of this guy…?'

Kellner nodded. 'I guess I am.'

Beck took time absorbing the information. 'But that means…'

'Go on, Beck. Do my thinking for me.'

'But when al-Qasr came over to the US in 1992, why didn't we invade?'

'You're on the right lines. Keep thinking.'

'OK. So al-Qasr comes over; he's debriefed. And he tells our people that he's left in a hurry and a lot of his work is still in Saddam's hands, and they're still workin' on it, and without him the US will never catch up.'

'Getting warmer.'

'And he says that in 1990 the threat was exaggerated, but the potential for development was there.'

'Boy, you're getting warm.'

'But the US would need to develop the counter weapon – and

there's no need to invade immediately because they're still a few years away from battlefield deployment. The heat's off. Anyhow, the UN has gone in. And guys like the Brit David Kelly are on the case.'

'You are hot, Beck. I'm thinking of promoting you right now.'

'But Saddam starts pissing with the UN inspection team. And we start wondering if he's got something up his sleeve. The Israelis are getting anxious. And – 9/11…'

'9/11. The issue of WMD shoots right up into the stratosphere. So the plan to invade is hatched. The ostensible purpose – well, you know all about that.'

'And the government has to allow the Iraq Survey Group to throw egg on its face.'

'Right, Beck. Because the US does not want it to be known that the weapon they were searching for *really does exist*.'

Beck's jaw dropped. 'So all that stuff about going to war on a false prospectus – and the Michael Moore film and all that stuff that suggested incompetence…'

'Just had to be taken on the chin, son. I guess it always will. Why d'ya think Colin Powell – in spite of everything – still supported the war?

'That's the thing you gotta understand about a secret weapon, Beck. It's only powerful when it's secret. Get it?'

'Just one question, sir?'

'Shoot.'

'Did the Iraqis have the weapon?'

Kellner smiled. 'What d'ya think?'

44

'Saddam certainly liked his highways, Vinny.'

'Yeah, Major. Like Hitler liked his autobahns.' Vinny gazed into the featureless desert as they raced along Highway 2 towards Mosul. He had a thought. 'Stalin was Saddam's hero, right?'

'Right.'

'So, Major, why didn't Stalin make a name for himself with highways across the Soviet Bloc?'

'Yeah... Interesting question, Vinny. Dr Ashe, why didn't Stalin make a name for himself in road transport?'

Ashe snapped out of the reverie induced by the dull hum of speeding along the well-metalled road. 'Two reasons immediately spring to mind.'

'Don'tcha just love this guy? Always something springing to mind! Jeez! You've got some fuckin' spring in there, bud!'

'I suppose the first requirement for a motorway is a car.'

Richmond stifled a laugh.

Vinny was agog. 'Boy's a genius!'

Ashe continued. 'I just don't think Hitler and Saddam were intimidated by private car ownership.'

Vinny cracked up.

'Quiet a second, Vinny!' Richmond's face froze. 'Something's happened.' The major tapped the side of his helmet. 'Come on! Fucking thing!' The transmission was faulty. 'It's... MND North. Blue Force in the vicinity. Call's gone out for Brigade Combat

Teams. I'm getting a coordinate.' Richmond magnified the scale of his electronic route plan, then hit the Merc's horn four times. The Humvee in front slowed down.

Zappa switched the CD player off.

Silence... as if the planet's loudspeakers had been suddenly cut. A violent peace. The desert was full of silence; nothingness.

A US soldier unwrapped the tarpaulin sheets from the mounted guns on the Humvee in front, then unclipped the leather case off the M249 squad automatic weapon. He unhooked an ammo box and started threading the magazine into the firing chamber.

Richmond opened the driver's door and called up to the driver in front. 'I'm getting out. Bring your Operation Map with you!'

A soldier from the Humvee behind ran up to the tail area of the Humvee in front and started preparing the larger-calibre M240B machine gun.

'See that, Toby?'

'I seem to recall seeing something like that at the roadblock yesterday.'

'Latest issue. It's got a range of about 1.6 kilometres.'

'Accuracy?'

'About 800 metres pinpoint lethal – with an experienced crew.'

'Rate of fire?'

'He'll get 600 rounds a minute. That's what Bob Dylan calls "a hard rain", Dr Toby.'

'Let's hope it's not going to fall. What about the other gun?'

'That's an M249, a one-man operated weapon. Good to 600 metres – but the firepower's more intense.'

'How much more intense?'

'750 rounds a minute. So you just relax there.'

'Thanks.'

'Before you do, try feeling under your seat... Yeah, that's it. You got it. Can you feel the clip?'

'I think so.'

'You've gotten yourself there an M4 carbine, Dr Toby. Know how to use it?'

'Did the course, Vinny.'

'Feel ready?'

'I don't think so.'

'Major Richmond will explain everything.'

'May I relax now?'

'Just keep your seat dry.'

Zappa unclipped his own M4.

'Vinny?'

'Toby?'

'What was all that about Blue Force?'

'They didn't tell you that?'

'I took the economy course.'

'OK, it's like this. Blue Force: good. Red Force...' Vinny shook his head. 'Red Force: *bad.*'

'I see.'

'See that box on the dash, just below the wheel?'

'Check.'

'That's a Blue Force tracker. Major Richmond has one attached to his epaulette.'

'Ah... That's what that was. I suppose it's replaced the customary parrot.'

'It's a global positioning system. It means someone knows where we are. It means we know when the bad guys are close. And it means we can call on the—'

'Blue Force.'

'Right. Blue Force – if we need assistance.'

'What's the method?'

'See those buttons there. Nice and finger-shaped. You press all four buttons, three times. Four and three. You got that?'

'Do I need to know?'

Zappa looked at him seriously. 'You may need to know, Toby.'

'Four buttons, three times. Right.'

'Now, what the good major is doing with the corporal in front there, is checking coordinates for the presence of Blue Force in the vicinity. On the basis that this probably means there's also something not good going on.'

'I get the idea, Vinny. We're in the shit.'

'If you mean we should prepare for all eventualities, you are correct.'

Ashe sat back in his seat. To the left of him: nothing. Sand, sand and more sand. And to the right? There might as well have been a mirror on the side of the road.

Sweating like a wet peach, Richmond climbed back inside the air-conditioned Merc.

'It would appear, gentlemen—'

'Here it comes.'

'That a British troop transporter, carrying mainly US troops, has gone down some miles west of here. There's a turn-off to the right in about fifteen kilometres – a turning for Irbil – which right now is a highly sensitive area. That's where the plane was heading. We've been requested to investigate the area where the aircraft lost contact with base.'

'By ourselves, Major?'

'No, there's a Blue Force presence already in the vicinity. Composition unknown.'

'That's strange.'

'Not necessarily. Anyhow, I could get no further details.'

Ashe closed his eyes. This was just the kind of open-ended scenario he'd been dreading. Then again, no one else was jumping for joy either.

'Just what is the mission here, Major?'

'Investigate the crash site – if there is a crash site; recover any survivors – if there are any survivors; submit a report on completion of task, and carry on to Mosul, pending further developments.'

'Like we get to play heroes, right?'

'We get to be soldiers, Vinny. Or, what is even more likely, nothing happens.'

'You wanna bet?'

'Corporal Pinsker's leading the way. Sergeant Bolton's following up behind. What could be nicer?'

The word 'nicer' rang in Ashe's ears. He thought of Melissa, then dismissed the thought.

'Major, you need two guys on the M240. Toby, are you listening?'

'What?'

'Are you listening?'

'Er… yeah, two guys on the M240.'

'Right. You need two guys on the M240. We've got four guys, plus ourselves and the interpreter. Basic math tells me that if we're gonna need the M249 as well, one of us should go up ahead.'

'Do I hear the voice of a volunteer, Vinny?'

'Me and my big mouth! I must be nuts!'

'No, Zap. We're all nuts. But your nuts are bigger than ours, that's all.'

45

Ashe stared at the flat horizon. That overused word 'infinity' dropped into his head; he recoiled from it. That which was welcome at death was no friend to the living. The word 'desert' was too close to the word 'lost' for comfort. Ashe became aware his teeth were grinding as he tried to get a sense of himself and where he was. What had appeared from the highway as sand was mostly hard-baked earth littered with loose stones and rocks. Sand was scattered over the surface like pepper on a pizza. It made for a bumpy ride and a nagging heckle of irritating gear changes.

The rocking and rolling made loading the M4 difficult; Ashe's fingers were shaking. Richmond told him there was a spare combat jacket stuffed into the corner under his seat: useful for additional magazines. Ashe looked for a quip to lighten the atmosphere, but nothing came.

The truth was dawning: Richmond was less than optimistic about returning to the main road without incident. The tension inside the vehicle rose; the CD was left switched off without comment.

Mile after mile, they advanced northwest to the coordinates of the supposed troop-plane crash site – or, hopefully, the site of a crash landing – halfway between the main road to Mosul and Tel Afar, sixty miles away.

Richmond, observing Ashe through the rear-view mirror, could see he was nervous. Richmond was an experienced morale-builder, but his techniques were normally used on trained soldiers. Soldiers could be reminded of shared training experiences, encouraged to remember that they were more than ready for action; they could depend on one another. Ashe had not imbibed the ethos of regimental solidarity, tradition and discipline.

'I'm going to stop the convoy in a second, Toby.'

'Why's that?' shot back Ashe, nervously.

Richmond surmised that Ashe was moving fast towards a knife's edge of anxiety, without the training to control it. The experience was entirely new to him.

'Tell me how you feel, Toby.'

'Sorry, Simon. It's a bit… I'm a bit hot in here, that's all.'

The air-con was on full blast.

'Vinny's a one, isn't he Toby? Always makes everything sound so easy. Look at him out there on that gun. He's loving every living minute of it. But, I tell you, he's as afraid as you are.'

'Really?'

'It's natural. He just knows a few tricks to keep it under control. Try something?'

'Yeah.'

'Take some deep breaths. As you do, make a picture of something here you're afraid of. Now let it come over you. It won't hurt you. Let it pass through you; don't resist it. It's a picture, a fear. How's the breathing going?'

'Difficult.'

'Gets easier. Don't bother resisting what you fear. Face it, but don't oppose it.'

'Fuck!'

'Yeah, *fuck*.'

Ashe tried to breathe deeply. He hadn't realised how short his breaths had become.

'You're doing fine. Give your brain some of that oxygen. Now hold it in. A few seconds. Now let it out very slowly. Slowly… Good. Trust me. Anyone can see you've got what it takes.'

'Are you sure, Simon?'

'As sure as you're gonna be.'

'I've never killed anyone.'

'Just breathe deeply. Let the air out slowly. That's it. The fear is washing over you. But you are a rock. You didn't know it before. But you're a rock.'

'And this… is a hard place.'

'Doesn't have to be. Make it your own.'

Richmond knew to let Ashe's own system take over the process of regaining control. He let the convoy roll on another half mile.

It was now two o'clock. Richmond suppressed a twinge of anxiety. Twilight descended so early in Iraq's spring, and he would rather not be returning from the target site in the dark. The men would be tired; vision poor. Experience told him that most accidents happened on the way down from the summit.

'Now, Toby, you need to consider the mission.'

'Become the mission: target-centred.'

'You've got it!'

'At the centre of the circle, the Master Mason cannot err.' Ashe remembered the great old line from the Masonic Third Degree lecture. Suddenly it seemed spot on.

'Yeah, we're at the centre of the circle, as you masons say. We're instruments of the mission. The mission will take us through. We have each other and, in case you thought we were alone out here, we're ringed by US airstrips, minutes of flight time away from here. It's not like the old days with legions disappearing in the desert!'

Ashe laughed. Richmond joined in. 'Poor buggers! I presume Vinny told you about the Blue Force trackers.'

'Yeah. Four buttons; three times.'

'You'll make a soldier yet. See the route map here on the right of the dash?'

'Yes.'

'That little dot on the screen there is us. See to the south?'

Richmond adjusted the monitor. 'That's Qayyarah West airstrip. Near the oil well, there at Tall 'Azbah. West of there: another one at Sahl Sinjar. North of there: Tel Afar. That's recently been reinforced. And thirty-odd miles away you've got the air base at Mosul.'

'Bloody busy the desert, these days! Can't you get any peace?'

Richmond laughed. 'Big Brother's everywhere. So long as that dot keeps flashing, they all know where we are. If I press this thing, choppers'll be here in minutes.'

'Shit! And I was thinking we were having a real adventure.'

'It's real, all right, Toby.'

'Just one thing, Simon old boy.'

'Yeah?'

'If those choppers can be here in the time you suggest, what the hell are we doing making the reconnaissance?'

'Standard procedure.'

'Standard procedure?'

'Yeah. Standard procedure to call in unengaged Blue Force in the vicinity.'

'But where are the choppers?'

'Glad you asked. Didn't I mention the action northwest of here?'

'Action?'

'There's been an attack on a village. I don't know anything else about it, but the position has drawn in the available local air power, short of base defence.'

'So what's all that stuff about pressing buttons and the air cavalry turns up?'

'If we encounter Red Force, Toby, they will send a detachment. You can take my word for that. Believe me, we'll get air support if we need it. Standard procedure. Now I'm going to switch the convoy round a bit.'

46

Richmond accelerated ahead of the lead Humvee and waved it down. There was no sense using horns out in a high-risk zone.

Concerned the convoy had no active firepower in the rear, Richmond ordered the tail Humvee into the middle. Now he and Ashe would bring up the rear. Ashe would be able to concentrate on lookout duty.

In front of them: Sergeant Bolton and Ibrahim the interpreter – a weak link in the chain. In the lead vehicle: Corporal Pinsker driving, Zappa and Private Laski on the big gun, and Private Dykins behind the M249 squad automatic.

If Richmond entertained doubts about the suitability of the firepower for the mission at hand, he kept them to himself, telling Ashe that convoys like this were known 'in the trade' as porcupines: too prickly to be messed with. He'd made that up on the spot.

Ashe eyed the shimmering thread that hovered between earth and sky: nothing. Then he noticed a speck – a black speck in the distance. Mangled by heat-haze, the speck grew in size. Behind it, distantly, he could see what looked like a grey band on the horizon – maybe a distant mountain, or an in-coming storm.

'What's that speck?'

'I can't see it, Toby. I'll drop back a bit.'

'It looks like… maybe a distant mountain.'

'How far?'

'I don't know. Maybe sixty or seventy miles.'

'You've got remarkable eyesight, Toby. But it can't be that far. It's probably the Jebel Sinjar.'

'Sinjar? As in Shinar?'

'What's Shinar?'

'It's the land where Noah and his lot came down to after the Great Flood. It's where Nimrod built the Tower of Babel.'

'Where all the races were divided?'

'Yeah.'

'Interesting. Come to think of it, from a distance, Sinjar does look a bit like the base of a massive ancient tower. It's an amazing place. A bit like Ayers Rock in Australia. Only far bigger. A little mountain range popping up out of nowhere. You got flatland, flatland... nothing; then: Bang! Jebel Sinjar.'

'Easy on the bangs, Simon!'

'Still a bit jumpy? That village I mentioned – the one under attack – that would be up in the Sinjar. That's where you'll find our choppers.'

'Comforting.'

'As for the speck, I'll bet it's an oil derrick. There's a drilling outpost at Tel Afar. Very close to the underground pipeline that runs south from Silopi, just over the Turkish border.'

'Turkey? We're that close?'

'The pipeline runs south through Qayyarah West, just south of here.'

'Wasn't there a car bomb attack on the US facility at Tel Afar in December?'

'Right. About thirty wounded. Could have been much worse. The guards did their job: approached the bombers and alerted the base. Even so, the suicide bomber detonated himself.'

'And the bomber? Local insurgent or Ansar al-Islam?'

'Tricky question, Toby. Last September, there was a new group announced.'

'Yeah, I remember. Ansar al-Sunna. Defenders of the Tradition.'

'Right. These guys are the main problem at the moment – at least in my sphere.'

'What happened to the old group, Ansar al-Islam?'

'Not entirely clear. Ansar al-Islam were mainly up in the Kurdish mountains northeast of here. Around Khurmal near the Iranian border. They threatened the Patriotic Union of Kurdistan forces, who are pro-democracy and modernisation, so they're aligned with the Coalition. In March '03, PUK *peshmerga* and US special forces mounted a joint op. You know how *peshmerga* vow to fight to the death? Well they pretty much took the Ansar al-Islam fighters apart. We thought we could rest a bit while the PUK exploited the gains.'

'And now?'

'To be honest, situation's much worse. Ansar al-Sunna forces have been creeping back across the Iranian border in the hundreds. Corrupt Kurdish guards have been taking bribes. And they've been moving into Mosul, merging with the population, and working as fixers for al-Qaeda-backed operatives coming in from the western border with Syria.'

'So you've got Ansar al-Sunna to the east of us, and al-Qaeda volunteers to the west of us. You could say we were—'

'In the middle of things, yes.'

'Shit.'

'Hmm... And then there's the problem with the reconciliation policy.'

'The what?'

'A nice idea. Major General Peter Atraeus, commander of the 101st Airborne, thought it might be wise to reintegrate some old Ba'athist Iraqi commanders – get them to work with the Kurds for the common good.'

'As you say, a nice idea. Bad in detail?'

'Maybe. The major general gave Syrian border security to General Muhammad al-Shiwah. He's a member of the al-Shammari tribe. The tribe spans the frontier with Syria. It's generally seen as being sympathetic to Saddam.'

Ashe observed how the speck seemed to be changing, like it was being smudged out, enveloped, yet somehow getting taller and taller.

'Whatever the reason, Toby, we've now got a fairly porous border, with al-Qaeda-stimulated volunteers coming in from both sides and Ansar al-Sunna as the welcoming committee.'

'That speck's getting bigger. There's a... what is it?'

Richmond reached into the glove compartment to his right and pulled out a telescopic sight. 'Don't bother mounting it on the M4, just tell me what you see.'

Ashe adjusted the focus. 'It's a... pillar of smoke.'

'Must be a mistake.'

'No, it's on fire.'

Thoughts raced through Richmond's head and they all crashed into one simple conclusion. 'They've hit the pipeline.'

47

Richmond stamped hard on the accelerator and sped out to wave down the Humvees in front. As the Merc skidded to block Corporal Pinsker, a sudden flash and grinding thud hurled Ashe to the left as the landmine explosion shot the front right wheel spinning into the sky.

A second blast. A Katyusha rocket tore up the earth next to the Merc. Rocket shrapnel smashed through the bulletproof windows, tearing off what to Ashe's shocked eyes looked like a piece of Richmond's shoulder. The casing embedded itself in Ashe's seat, inches from his head; Richmond's shoulder bled.

Pinsker's Humvee drew up at a 45-degree angle to the Merc's left, to provide cover so Ashe and Richmond could get out. Bullets strafed the Merc's side panels. With no one to protect it, grenades flew towards Sergeant Bolton's Humvee.

Ashe clambered into the front of the Merc as bullets ricocheted off the bonnet. He dragged Richmond down and opened the driver's door.

'The tracker!' screamed Richmond.

Ashe had a split second to think: three buttons, four times. No! Four buttons three times. Richmond's shoulder tracker had been smashed in the blast; the other tracker box had been propelled off the dash. Ashe pulled Richmond out, then reached for the underside of the dashboard. Bullets shattered the glass and thudded and whistled into the interior.

Ashe strained for the tracker box with everything he'd got.

'Don't!' screamed Richmond. 'Leave it! It's too dangerous!'

Ashe made contact with the box as bullets tore away the back seat. His fingers touched the four buttons; one was stuck.

'Stuck!'

'Hit it hard!'

Ashe pushed and pushed.

'Get out of there!'

A second rocket blast lifted the front of the stricken Merc up four feet, nearly ripping Ashe's arm out of its socket. Ashe was thrown over Richmond. Richmond screamed from the gash in his neck and shoulder.

At the rear of Pinsker's Humvee, Dykins, Laski and Zappa were giving the machine guns everything they'd got. There was a problem: the angle. The wrecked Merc was obscuring the main target area. If it pulled away, they would lose cover, and Ashe and Richmond would be exposed on the ground.

Ashe pulled Richmond's Browning out of the holster on his thigh and placed it in the major's left hand. He then rolled over and levelled his M4 under the Merc's chassis in the direction of the firing.

The firing ceased. There was no target: only rocks and stones and sand.

Richmond's wavering voice broke the sudden silence. 'Tell Bolton to come up to form a triangle.'

'Does he need to be told?'

Richmond's eyes pleaded for immediate action. Ashe nodded. 'Bolton!'

'I'm... dead, sir.'

'What?'

Nothing.

'Sergeant Bolton! Can you hear me!'

Silence again.

'Oh Christ!'

Richmond was starting to feel the pain. 'Get me some morphine, will you... Toby.'

Richmond passed out.

Ibrahim, alone in the cargo carrier, started singing out in Arabic. 'There is no God but Allah! Muhammad is his Prophet!'

'Dr Toby! You there?'

'Zappa!'

'Pipe down! Hey, Ibrahim! Cut it! They ain't listenin'!'

'What's going on, Vinny?'

'I guess they're waiting till nightfall. They know they've got the advantage. Did you get a chance to signal Red Force presence?'

'Sorry.'

'No tracker?'

'Chance in a million. Losing both.'

'There go the reinforcements. You're closer to the interpreter. Call for him to join you. He's no good on his own out there with no weapon.'

'Think he knows that, Vinny.' Ashe called to Ibrahim; he wouldn't budge.

'Ibrahim, try and make a dash for it. They could open up again any second!'

'I don't reckon that invitation would get me out of a hole, Toby! Hey, Ibrahim, move your goddamn ass out of that truck! Guy's frozen, I guess. What I can't see is, why don't they use another rocket?'

'Maybe they only had the two left, Vinny. Look to the left a second. That's what they must've done with the others.'

A hefty slab of RAF Hercules fuselage glistened as the sun kissed the horizon.

'How's the major?'

'Passed out. His neck's in a mess.'

Vinny said nothing.

'What's the tactic, Vinny? What are they going to do?'

'I guess they're gonna try and kill us, Toby.'

'The burning pipeline. That's going to attract Blue Force.'

'Three miles away – through the black smoke. You better start praying, Toby.'

'Praying?'

'You pray, son. Pray with all your heart.'

Ashe prayed. He prayed for Simon Richmond. He prayed for Sergeant Bolton. He prayed for everyone but himself.

Vinny broke the awful silence. 'You know, we got one secret weapon here.'

'What's that?'

'The accelerator. We got speed. I reckon that's our best hope. First you gotta get yourself and Major Richmond – and Ibrahim, if only the poor bastard will move his ass – into this truck. Without getting yourselves killed. And you better do it soon. Because it's gonna be awful dark in ten minutes.'

Ashe looked at Richmond, unable to staunch the blood that soaked his ripped shirt.

Not a medic in sight. Ashe called to the second Humvee. 'Ibrahim! Try and get over to me. We've got one chance. Ibrahim, save yourself... I don't think he's moving, Vinny.'

'Can you drag the major over here?'

'I think so, but if they're looking closely, they'll see us.'

'I'll cover you boys.'

A voice came from the gloom. 'Doctor Ashe! Doctor Ashe!'

'Ibrahim?'

'I try to come.'

As the Iraqi started to squeak open the Humvee's rear door, Ashe heard the sound of scurrying feet emerging from the shadows. He strained for a target. He couldn't see a thing. Smashed glass. Someone had climbed into the rear of the truck.

'Doctor Ashe! They're—'

Ibrahim screamed. Ashe, helpless, heard the sickening sounds of a desperate struggle – then the sound of running feet. Something was being dragged away.

Ashe was forced backwards by the power of the blast. The Humvee exploded – a parting grenade tore into the twilight, scattering debris and human limbs around the desert.

Zappa felt a sinking feeling.

'For Christ's sake, Ashe, get yer ass over here now!'

Ashe's eyes were suddenly blinded. Two huge searchlights shot across the site as two Toyota pickups drove up the sides of a depression. The lights scattered disorienting beams over the startled survivors. Now Ashe could see what had happened to the convoy.

The three vehicles had driven into a shallow dried-up river-bed. The late-afternoon light had obscured the true dimensions of the depression: perfect for an ambush.

An Arab voice boomed hysterically through a megaphone. 'Christians! Christian Crusaders in the land of Islam! You are prisoners of the holy jihad of the army of Ansar al-Sunna! There is no escape. The whole world will see! We have man with camera. Everything we do will be shown on your television screen. On the internet in the homes of your families. We film you even now! Surrender for the camera and for your lives! Allah is merciful to Crusaders who desert the armies of the Devil! No mercy for traitors who serve Jews and Christians!

'Christians say they love everyone. We have your servant here. Here is traitor Muslim who serves infidel! We cut his head off. No true Muslim will serve Jews and Christians! If you love this man like you say, save him. You show your mercy. Want to see this man with head hacked off? Leave your weapons now. Surrender to mercy of Allah now! Save him and yourself! One minute, Christian devils! One minute!'

48

Vinny's stomach was churning. A thought flashed into his mind. A US officer had recently been kidnapped. He'd been released after having promised to desert the army; he'd deserted and walked into Syria – which was more than he would have done had he defied his kidnappers.

'What the hell do we do, Toby? They mean what they say. Major come round?'

'Negative, Vinny.'

Ashe's will was pinched in a bottleneck. His mind began to fog over as if his life was suddenly crammed into a few seconds. Anger rose like a dragon in his soul. How dare these bastards use God's name for rank murder? What low, twisted, cynical, criminal barbarity – what kind of scum were these, to drag the name of the Almighty God into their vile, blood-drenched banalities? A poor young man, with his own life to live – the life God gave him to live – how dare they hold him with a butcher's knife to his throat, as if his existence were theirs to play with? Every fibre of Ashe's body shivered and shook with indignation and righteous anger. Where this energy came from, Ashe knew not, nor was he thinking.

Suddenly, Ashe was pulling himself forwards under the twisted chassis of the Merc. He wrenched himself out from beneath it and screamed at the black-masked faces hovering round the searchlights. 'How dare you? How dare you? How dare you call this God's work? What do you know of God? What do you know of God's love? Nothing! What you do is not the will of God! This is NOT—'

To the utter shock of the terrorists, he opened fire at the searchlights. He saw Ibrahim slump forwards. A bullet ricocheted off a lamp into the neck of the terrorist with the butcher's knife. He recoiled as Ibrahim's apparently lifeless body slid down the bonnet of the Toyota and fell down the stony slope. Ashe kept firing.

'Give 'em hell, Toby! Just give the fuckers hell!' Zappa turned to his driver. 'Pinsker! Pull out! Give us a look at these bastards!'

Ashe ran back around the wrecked Merc as bullets from the Toyotas flew into the darkness. Ibrahim – incredibly not dead after all – crawled for all he was worth towards the back of the Humvee.

Pinsker reversed the vehicle. As Ibrahim heaved himself up, Zappa and Private Laski opened fire with the M240. In five seconds, fifty rounds of 7.62 mm bullets tore up the windows, roofs and passengers of the Toyotas; Dykins on the 249 sprayed the surrounding area, blasting at the hooded killers with 750 lethal rounds a minute.

Zappa was screaming at the enemy: he was part of the gun, part of the fire. 'Ashe! Get Richmond into the vehicle! We'll cover you! Go!'

Ashe slung the M4 over his shoulder, took hold of Richmond's boots and dragged him across the open ground towards the throbbing Humvee. A grenade came over the brow of the dune right into the wrecked Merc. The explosion shot shrapnel and debris in all directions. Laski was hit in the face by razor-sharp torn bodywork.

'For Christ's sake, Ashe! Get up here! Feed me some ammo!'

'Need help, Vinny! With the major!'

'Private Dykins! Cover!'

'Sir!'

Dykins turned the 249 towards the brow and kept up the barrage. Zappa jumped down, pulled Richmond over his shoulder and dumped him in the armament bay of the Humvee. 'Feed me, Ashe! Get that fuckin' ammo in this thing! Pinsker!'

'Sir!'

'Head back east – full speed!'

Another grenade was launched at the Humvee, exploding by its rear. The back wheels leapt up like a stallion, sending Dykins flying out of the vehicle.

'Pinsker! Stop! It's Dykins!'

Dykins got up off the ground, dizzy, and ran, groping, towards the Humvee.

'Turn the fuckin' lights off!'

A bevy of terrorists, all in black uniforms, stormed over the hill, screaming and firing their AK-47s into the darkness.

'Shit! The bastards've got night vision!'

'Here, Ashe! Just pull the trigger! The trigger, Ashe! Squeeze it!' Zappa reached over the side. Bullets whizzed past and bounced off the armour plating. His hand caught Dykins'. 'Go, Pinsker! Dykins, hold on! Hold on!' Dykins ran alongside the escaping Humvee, grabbing desperately onto Zappa's arm. 'Jump, man! Jump! Now!'

Zappa had Dykins by the waist, his legs dangling over the side. A line of bullets riddled the side of the Humvee, thudding into Dykins' body armour, rocking his torso. As Zappa hauled him aboard, one of the bullets thudded through Dykins' armpit.

'Dykins!'

Dykins gurgled, blood in his mouth. Zappa pulled the limp Dykins onto the floor, next to Laski's by now unconscious body. Zappa then pushed Ashe back to the ammo feed.

'Open another box. Right hand! Yeah, you got it! Good! Now give it to me!'

Ashe struggled with the mechanism.

'For Christ's sake, Ashe!'

The 240 jammed. Zappa reached for the 249 and began firing wildly as the Humvee sped away east. Dykins was moaning, his lung punctured.

Ashe reloaded his M4 and sent bursts of bullets into the blackness beyond. 'Hit 'em! Hit 'em hard!' screamed Zappa like a madman.

Another Toyota pickup revved up and started in pursuit.

'Put your fuckin' foot down, Pinsker!'

Ashe, in a frenzy of fire, hit the Toyota's lights. The vehicle braked and skidded in a cloud of dirt and dust.

'That's fucked him, Vinny!'

Vinny was on his gun. Out of the darkness came an almighty smash. The Toyota had crashed into wrecked Hercules fuselage. The shouting and the bullets stopped.

In the far distance, US choppers were circling the Tel Afar oil outpost, searchlights sending weird, apocalyptic beams about the distant derricks, like the legs of some hideous creature from hell's U-bend.

Ashe was shaking, vibrating with elation; elated to be alive, to have faced the evil and channelled the evil in himself. No, it wasn't that. Something had come alive in him as if a stranger was in the driving seat of his mind and mindlessness.

In the starlight, Ashe looked into Vinny's flaming eyes, and saw himself. And the quietness of the night seemed to take over, as the groans from Dykins grew softer.

'We gotta get to Mosul!'

Richmond came to; the blood in his neck and shoulder had begun to clot.

'How ya feelin', Major?'

'What's happening? I thought I was dead. God, I feel sick.'

'You're OK.'

'Where are we?'

Ashe stared at him. 'We're here, Simon. We're *here*.'

Zappa turned to the interpreter. 'Ibrahim! Take off your shirt!'

'Yes, Mr Zappa.'

'Thank you, Ibrahim. Wrap it round the major's wound. Know first-aid?'

'No, sir.'

'Neither do I. Try and go easy.'

'It's OK, Vinny. I think the bleeding's stopped. I guess it looks pretty awful.'

'The red badge of courage, Major.'

'Courage?' Richmond laughed. 'I slept through the whole thing.'

Ashe looked to the ailing Private Dykins. Dykins screamed for his mother with every cruel vibration of the Humvee on the desert rocks.

Ashe held him in his arms. 'You'll be all right, Private. We'll be home soon.'

Ashe put his ear to Dykins' trembling lips. 'Where are we, sir?'

'See those stars, Private?'

'Sir?'

'Look up, they're showing us the way. We're all together, Private. You and us.'

Dykins seized Ashe's hand. 'Sir, did I do OK?'

'You did great, didn't he, Vinny?'

'Private Dykins, you've served man and God. Try to be peaceful till we're home.'

Ashe held the dying soldier. Ibrahim gave him mineral water and prayed to Allah.

Dykins pulled once more on Ashe's arm. 'Sir, I don't think I'm going to…'

'That's all right. You sleep now. We're safe.'

'Sir, is God…?'

The grip became a spasm, left behind as Private Abraham Lincoln Dykins died.

'You see that, Ibrahim?'

'Mr Ashe?'

Ashe showed the Iraqi a letter from Dykins' blood-soaked breast pocket. 'He's got the same name as you, Ibrahim. Abraham. *Father of nations.*'

Ibrahim handed the water to Zappa who gave it to the thirsty Richmond.

Ashe looked to the stars and thought of the ladder that links man to his destiny.

'Vinny, my friend. I was just thinking. Maybe the headlights?'

Zappa unclipped the rear window behind Pinsker's driving seat.

'Pinsker, how d'ya feel about front lamps, dipped? Doctor's getting jumpy.'

'Front lights only: dipped, sir.'

Pinsker hit the brakes.

'Oh Jesus! What in fuck's name is THAT?'

49

'Hey, Pinsker, where d'ya keep the night goggles?'

'Box in the rear, sir.'

'What fuckin' box?'

'Dykins knows, sir. He packed 'em.'

'Ibrahim, what you sitting on? Move your ass. That's government property, bud.'

'Pardon! Pardon!'

'Only kiddin', man. Yup, this is it.'

Zappa unclipped the box and withdrew a set of night goggles with adjustable sights. 'Holy Shit! Here, Ashe, take a look!'

About fifty metres ahead were two trucks packed with a crowd of Arabs standing up in the back, waving and chanting.

'Can you hear that, Ashe? What they sayin'?'

'It's a welcome party, Vinny.'

Ibrahim interjected. 'Welcome party, yes, sir. But welcome for Ansar al-Sunna – not US army.'

Richmond pulled himself up. 'Give me a look.'

'You sure you're up to this, Major?'

'Don't be an arse. Give me the goggles.' He focused his attention on the trucks. 'OK, chaps. What you have here is a very mixed bunch of illegal immigrants. I'll bet it's the usual collection of Moroccans, Yemenis, Saudis, Syrians. They'll have been brought over the Syrian border on al-Qaeda one-way tickets. I presume the guys we encountered back there were their welcoming committee, ready to tuck them into warm beds in Mosul, before a trip to suicide's paradise.'

'Suicide volunteers?'

'Yes, Toby. Though they might not all be aware of that yet. You can tell from that unreal, happy look.'

'Every insurance salesman's dream client.'

'Shit!'

'Shit it is. I reckon they think we're the welcoming committee.'

Zappa clicked shut the trigger chamber of the 240. 'They'll get some fuckin' welcome, man!'

'How many do you see, Simon?'

'Two trucks. About twenty in each.'

'Armed?'

Richmond strained to see the greenish images through the goggles. 'Not yet.'

'Four against forty?'

'Element of surprise?'

'Simon, what if we shut lights down, vanish into the night, no questions asked?'

Richmond sounded personally affronted. 'And leave forty suicide bombers, Toby? What d'you think we're here for? Just one of these guys can kill a hundred innocent civilians – women and children.'

'Cool it, Major. Dr Toby ain't chicken. You owe your fuckin' life to this guy, and so do I. So I say we leave it to him to decide what we do next.'

Ashe didn't need to think. 'I don't like suicide bombers, Vinny. Against my religion.'

Corporal Pinsker butted in. 'Trucks have started up, sir. Coming our way.'

'OK. I say we come real close, Major, duck down fast, and then let 'em have it!'

'I second that, Vinny.'

'Why, thank you, Major. You get the M249. Can you handle it?'

'Fuck off, Zap. I'm OK with my left.'

'Toby, you feed me the ammo. Keep it up and steady, right? When we're within fifty feet, I'll signal to Pinsker to—'

'Sir!'

'Corporal Pinsker?'

'I got this viewfinder thing here, sir. And I'd say they're wavin' AK-47s. And... they're heading straight for us, sir.'

'Right, Pinsker. Lights out. We'll race it. If they don't know who we are, they'll—'

'And if they do?'

'We do our duty, Corporal!'

'Yes, sir!'

'Skirting operation. Sweep round in a crescent. Give us a good view. Carry on.'

'Yes, sir!'

The Humvee revved up towards the advancing trucks. Suddenly, the trucks switched their headlights off and skidded to a halt. Amid a flurry of shouting, the men jumped off the trucks.

'Pull right! Pinsker! Right!'

The guns of the wannabe martyrs opened up on the Humvee. Zappa hit back, straight into the gunsmoke. Unable to load efficiently, the 249 jammed. Richmond grabbed the M4 and manoeuvred a fresh mag into position. As the Humvee skidded round the trucks, Richmond added wide bursts to the power of the 240.

'That's it, Pinsker! Round we go!'

A stray bullet hit a rear tyre. Collapsing instantly, the Humvee dived into an angled skid that tore a gash in the earth. 'Damn! Damn! Damn! We lost a goddamn wheel!'

'Engine off, Pinsker!'

Distant cries grew louder through the earth and billowing sand. Zappa spread some warning rounds in the direction of the voices.

'You there, Ashe?'

'I want to do some shooting, Vinny.'

'Fix the belt on the 249. Major, can you help me with the

ammo – left-handed? Just remember, Ashe, these fuckers are suicides.'

'Just remember, Vinny, they're deluded. Truth will prevail!'

'You better believe it!'

Ashe unclipped the firing chamber and reset the magazine of the M249. 'That's done it. I'm ready.'

'Then fire the bastard!'

'Ibrahim! You take the major's rifle. Only fire at the enemy!'

'I never use gun.'

'First time for everything, Ibrahim. It might save your life!'

Bullets thudded into the earth in front of the stricken Humvee.

'That was close.'

'We must have hit a dozen.'

'Sure?'

'Why not?'

'Sir!'

'Pinsker!'

'OK if I get my weapon, sir?'

'Permission granted.'

'Join the party, Corporal. We ain't goin' nowhere.'

'What's that?'

'What?'

'Those lights?'

'Not...'

'It's those fuckers from Tel Afar. There's more of 'em. How we doin' for ammo?'

'Enough, but...'

Ashe looked at Zappa; Zappa looked at Richmond. Richmond smiled. A shared moment of cold reality: they *knew*. This was it; their luck had just run out.

The headlights got closer and closer as AK-47 fire spat out of the blackness.

'What's that sound?'

'What fuckin' sound?'

'*That* sound. *Listen!*'

'*What the…?* Is that a storm?'

A whirlwind roar whipped its way around the Humvee – an ancient sound, elemental, pounding. A voice from history on the heels of memory.

'Weird fuckin' noise, man.'

'Sounds like—'

'Guns. Thunder.'

Richmond coughed. 'Haven't you ever heard horses before? I think our luck's in.'

In the distance, the jihadists started screaming out. They'd heard nothing about this in the madrasahs or on the videos. Ashe stared along the horizon. The black silhouettes of dozens of horsemen bobbed across the landline like demented shadow-puppets. The roaring force broke into two arcs: one hundred warriors on each flank.

'I don't fuckin' believe it! It's the Light Brigade.'

'No, Vinny. It's the Brigade of Light!'

Ashe's eyes stretched wider and wider. He had never seen anything like it. In seconds, the horsemen had overwhelmed the jihadists with snorting, fiery horsepower – a vision from history, terrifying the enemy with memories long forgotten, buried in the mythic subconscious of their parents and grandparents.

Horseman after horseman swung their British SA80 semi-automatics like scythes before alien corn, letting loose a tornado of firepower that shattered and scattered the screaming forces of the killer fanatics.

50

'Toby, there's someone I'd like you to meet.'

'You, Simon, are in no condition to introduce anyone.'

The silhouette of a man on horseback advanced towards them. Ashe jumped from the Humvee. Gracefully, the man dismounted. In the headlights' glow, Ashe could just make out a long-haired man with a long, thin face. Above high cheekbones shone large, dark eyes. He wore the baggy trousers common among Kurdish men and women, but sported what looked like English hunting boots. Over an American special forces combat jacket hung a silk cape, embroidered in gold and silver. Beneath the jacket he wore a white shirt, loose at the front, with a wide collar, and fastened at the back. He had a shaven chin and a young man's thin moustache lining his upper lip.

The man smiled warmly at Richmond, leaning over the Humvee's side panel.

'I am deeply honoured, Major Richmond. How may I serve you?'

'Done enough for one night, Captain. Permit me to introduce my friend, Toby Ashe.'

'Tobbiash! A friend of the Major Richmond is a friend of my heart and my people. I am at your service.'

Ashe clasped the man's hot, smooth hand.

'Toby, this is Jolo. Jolo Kheyri. I call him the Lord of the Mountain.'

'No, no, no! Please, Major Richmond! This honour belongs

to my kinsman, who is in Paradise. Hamo Shero. He is Chief of the Mountain!'

'The mountain being the Jebel Sinjar, Toby.'

'Hamo Shero fought with the British against the Turks in your first war with Germany. What your Lawrence of Arabia is to you, Hamo Shero is to us.'

'Jolo lives in Shero's image. We are blessed in... *Agh*!'

'What's the matter?'

Richmond clutched his shoulder: bleeding again.

'Major Richmond, you need the field hospital in Mosul. Hasil! Hasil!'

Jolo's deputy rode up to the Humvee. 'Hasil! Call special forces in Kursi! Medical helicopter for Major Richmond. Inform them of this action.'

'It is done, Captain.'

Jolo studied Ashe's eyes. 'I am from Kursi, Tobbiash, yes. Yesterday, as the sun rose, Kursi was a fine village. It sits on slopes of Sinjar mountains. We grew good tobacco on the terraces. Then, Ansar al-Sunna. Grenade launchers, guns, knives. They come to find me. I am not there. So the men defend women and children, you understand?'

'That's the attack on the village I told you about, Toby. Damn it! Pinsker's morphine's wearing off. OK, Jolo Kheyri is a relative of Sheykh el-Wezîr, the grandson of Hamo Shero, Chief of the Mountain.'

Jolo beamed. 'A great man, Tobbiash! Pious and brave!'

'A great man. We've been doing a bit of work round here setting up an irregular auxiliary force. In the past, we made the mistake of trying to fit Jolo's people into our ways of fighting.'

'Not good, Major.'

'Now we complement one another. Jolo plays on his strengths; we support him. They're very good at night, as you've seen. They've been doing great tidying up and reconnaissance work, and they know what's going on. They know who's new in the district.'

Jolo interjected. 'It is sinful, Tobbiash. Under Americans, safe haven very, very good for our people. British and Americans fight evil people. Saddam cannot kill more of us. Muslims cannot kill us. Then are coming all these foreigners – from Iran, from Syria. And Turks, these are spying on us.

'None of these outsiders care for Iraq or people of Iraq. They do not care for Kurds! And they do not care for us! They hate us and call us Devil worshippers! We do not worship Devil! They claim God is their master, but they do not understand things about God. They are given evil teaching. They kill women and children and will not fight face to face. They are like criminals. They use human beings as bombs and hide their face in black mask. They love guns and death and beg for money even when they are not poor. They have lost sight of God. They blame every-one but themselves. Their Devil lives inside their own hearts, for they are blind.

'We, not they, are the Defenders of the Tradition!'

Ashe was transfixed. Beneath the starry canopy of a northern Iraqi sky, not far from the ruined Assyrian cities and lost palaces of Nineveh and Khorsabad, Ashe was listening to an ancient voice. This was a voice whose strange, majestic, poetic beauty seemed to come if not from another world, then from the pages of *The Seven Pillars of Wisdom* or the *Rubaiyat of Omar Khayyam*.

It was not what Jolo was saying, so much as the hidden music and mind within and between his words. But why, Ashe won-dered, did this Iraqi man refer to the Muslims as though referring to something almost alien? Was he a Christian? There were many Christians in Iraq, and their churches were as old as any in the world, though their voices were seldom heard.

Could he be a Mandaean, one of those who claimed John the Baptist as the last prophet and who lived in the marshlands south of Baghdad? At least, that is, until Saddam wrecked the ecology of the marshes and persecuted the people there.

'Tell me, Jolo—'

Ashe suddenly stopped himself. Behind Jolo, the horsemen were rounding up the surviving Arabs, tying their hands behind their backs, treating their wounds. What with the horses, the men, the heightened atmosphere, the burning fire of the wrecked oil derricks in the distance – it was as if he was standing in the midst of some vast epic. Then he realised: he *was*.

Ashe had strayed into history, the kind of history that makes legends. To meet a man like Jolo – a man living *in extremis*, beyond natural limits – was to encounter a life in which something *other* is generated: something pertaining to the soul. Ashe could see how, when this quality collides with memory, legend is produced: naturally and poetically coalescing in the ancient forms of myth.

Hamo Shero was as real and present to Jolo as Major Richmond and himself.

'Tell me about the horses, Jolo.'

'Very good for night-time work. Very good for all work. Ezidis are great horsemen. We have fought on horse for hundreds of years, against Egyptians, Turks, Iranians, Arabs. We have fought in Russian cavalry! When Berlin falls and Adolf Hitler kills himself, two Ezidis there also – the first in Berlin since a hundred years. Before Jesus and Moses, we were there.'

Ashe enjoyed the heroic exaggerations but wished to get the conversations back down to earth. 'Where did the horses come from?'

'From Khuda.'

Richmond butted in. 'He's saying the horses are a gift of God. But in reality they were brought from the hills of the Transcaucasus – from Georgian Armenia – at very great risk to his people.'

'We are used to risk, Major Richmond.'

That word was ringing in Ashe's ears... *Ezidi*. Did he mean *Yezidi*? Ashe had read about these people before – an ancient tribe with mysterious customs and traditions.

'Is Jolo a... Yezidi, Simon?'

'Didn't I make that clear?'

51

Zappa returned from the group of captured jihadists carrying a large backpack full of passports and border permits.

'Yup, we got the usual shit here. We got Yemenis, Saudis, Jordanians, Syrians – just like you said, Major. We got some Iraqis from Tikrit. We even got us an Algerian. We may even have us a leader of Ansar al-Sunna. Won't that look nice in the report?'

He threw the bag up into the air; it landed with an empty thump on the ground. Jolo's horse began chewing at it.

'No, Bucephalus! Later!'

'Bucephalus?'

'Captain Jolo, this is Vincent Zappa, DIA, Mosul.'

'Honoured, sir!'

'Wasn't Bucephalus…?'

'Alexander the Great's horse, yes Mr Dappa. His spirit returns to us.'

'It's Zappa, Captain.'

'Yes, Dappa.'

'OK, it's Dappa! Pleased to meet you. And you must be the Scourge of the East!'

Jolo laughed.

'Like I said, Major. We got us a fine bag. Medals all round.'

'Medal?' Jolo's eyes lit up. 'I like a medal. I put it on my sash.'

Richmond started coughing, feverishly, then passed out.

'Hasil! Hasil! How long for helicopters to come for Major?'

Hasil shook his head and shrugged his shoulders.

'Then call again! Emergency!'

Ashe got on to the Humvee and found a blanket for Richmond. Hasil nodded to the contact on the other end of the mobile. 'They come soon! They come for Major!'

'Don't forget poor Laski here!'

'No one is forgotten. Come with me, Tobbiash, to friends in Bashiqa.'

'*Bashiqa*... That's in the Sheikhan, isn't it?'

'Not very far from Mosul. East. Good country. The Sheikhan is good country. Our country.'

'What about Vinny and the major?' Ashe was thinking of his task.

'Mr Dappa, will you join us?'

'Captain Jolo, I'd just love to join you and Toby and all the Yezidis at Bashiqa. Really I would. But I got work to do in Mosul. There ain't much time.'

'Oh yeah? Nice try, Vinny. I know you're fed up of me hanging round your neck. But I don't think my superiors are gonna be happy with my taking a paid sabbatical.'

'Hey, bud, don't get me wrong. You've done your share. And I love your company. But how about giving Vinny some arm- and leg-room here? I'm workin' best on my own.'

'But—'

'Listen, my clever friend, the second I got beans on our Turkish friends Yildiz and Yazar, you'll hear from me. Might even bring 'em to you direct! Express service, how about that? Now give Vinny a break. You head off with Jolo. Hell! You'll be a lot safer with him in Bashiqa than with me in Mosul. I don't want you slowin' me down.'

Jolo looked upset. 'Turks, Mr Dappa?'

'Not friends necessarily, Captain. But I'd know better if I could just locate 'em.'

'We help you. My people help you.'

'I'd appreciate that.'

For all his curiosity about the Yezidis, Ashe wasn't ready to part from Vinny and Richmond. 'Really, Vin, it's Mosul for me, come what may. I've got to see the major's all right and stay close to things.'

'Now, Toby—'

Jolo pointed to the skies. 'Look! Choppers!'

Three Chinooks from Tel Afar swooped down towards them. Seeking landing space, they hovered overhead, their lights darting beams across the desert floor.

Zappa waved at the chopper crews. 'Hey, taxi! Over here!'

The Chinooks landed and three US medics leapt out and raced over to Richmond. Zappa rushed to greet them. Pointing at Ashe, Zappa tried to say something to one of the medics, but couldn't be heard against the roar of the choppers. He steered the medic towards Ashe, then returned to help with Richmond.

'Dr Ashe?'

'Yeah. Hadn't you better help with the major?'

'He's gonna be just fine. My colleagues can handle him, sir. Hear you've had some trouble here. How ya feelin'?'

'Sorry?'

'Breathing, sir. Are you feeling breathless, Dr Ashe?'

Ashe was taken aback. 'Breathless? Well, since you ask, it's been a bit tight since the battle. I hadn't really noticed.'

'Yeah, I can see y'all been busy here. Wait there please.'

The medic ran over to consult his colleagues as they strapped the major's stretcher to one of the Chinooks. Returning with a stethoscope, the medic smiled. 'Shirt up, Dr Ashe! Now breathe in and out slowly.'

The Chinook carrying Richmond rose into the sky, whipping up the sand. The medic started coughing. Ashe was anxious to get away, but the medic held his shoulder, pressing the stethoscope diaphragm firmly to Ashe's chest and back. 'Now cough, sir. And again. Once more. Now breathe in slowly, sir. And out again.' He took the stethoscope from his ears. 'OK, Dr Ashe. If you're a medical doctor, I won't have to explain pneumothorax to you.'

'I'm a doctor of philosophy, Doctor.'

'OK. You've had quite a shock. Been knocked about? Heavy weight on your body?'

'You could say that.'

'OK, you've had more than the usual amount of air in your lungs. Abnormal breathing. I don't want you in the chopper, sir.'

'Not you as well!'

'I can't be sure right here, but I think you might have excess air in your pleural space – between your chest wall and lungs. The atmospherics up there could exacerbate a pneumothorax. I am not joking, Dr Ashe. You better stay on dry land, sir, and try to take it easy. Can you do that?'

Ashe nodded.

'If breathing is not completely normal tomorrow, or if you feel at all uncomfortable with it, or if you have a dry cough you can't explain, you get your friends to take you to an army hospital, d'ya hear? And, Dr Ashe, I recommend you keep far away from stressful situations. At least for a few days.'

'I'll try.'

Zappa returned to Ashe. 'What was that about stress?'

'Very clever, Vinny.'

'I was concerned for you, Toby. I knew you wouldn't take it from me. I've seen these things before.'

Ashe looked over to Hasil and his fellow horsemen as they lined up the Arab prisoners for the long walk back to the US base at Mosul. 'Couldn't I go with them?'

'Stress-free, Toby. Guarding terrorist prisoners is not what I'd call stress-free. Now I don't want to hear any more about it. And I gotta run. May the good Lord bless and keep you, Toby. You're in good hands.'

Ashe smiled. 'I'll miss you, Vin.'

'And d'you know somethin', you Limey bastard?'

'What's that?'

'I'll cope.'

As Zappa disappeared into the third Chinook, Ashe looked up to see Jolo waiting on horseback.

'Is destiny, Tobbiash. Come!'

With a final burst of energy, an exhausted Ashe climbed onto Bucephalus and he, Jolo and a detachment of thirty Yezidis rode eastwards beneath the stars to Bashiqa.

52

Long before the detachment of Yezidi irregulars crossed the waters near the point where the Great Zab River disgorged her bulging foam into the long-drifting Tigris, Ashe had fallen asleep. Some silent will kept his arm around Jolo's waist, his head resting on Jolo's tireless back.

Ashe woke as Jolo brought the horse to a standstill. The anvil-hot sun, glowing rich and red, rose from the horizon. Jolo dismounted and raced forwards to kiss the ground where the sun's rays touched the earth. He crossed his arms before his chest and bowed three times. He kissed his forefingers and brought them to his forehead. Then he pulled up the collar of his shirt and kissed that.

Ashe glimpsed this curious ritual between half-closed eyes. Was he dreaming?

Jolo rejoined his horse and apologised to Ashe. 'It was not I who woke you, Tobbiash, but Sheykh Shems. He brings you light.'

The words meant nothing to Ashe, but he had a vague sense of déjà vu. 'You know, Jolo, where I live in England, there was once a saint.'

Jolo listened eagerly. 'Yes? Who was this holy man? Was he Ezidi?'

'His name was Chad, or Caedda.'

'Caedda. This word is like Kurmanji name, Khidr. Like our word for God: Khuda.'

'I suppose it is. Chad, it is said, awoke at dawn and went outside to stand by a well. There he greeted the rising sun with hymns.'

Jolo's eyes lit up. 'Your saint in England. He is friend of Sheykh Shems. The sun is for everyone on earth. From here in the Sheikhan to you in England. When you visit shrine of Sheykh Shems, you may pray to your... Caedda. You may speak to him, and he will speak to you. Yes!'

'That would be something.'

'Your saint with Khuda in Paradise, Tobbiash. To him, years are nothing. Your Caedda is one of the living ones. He speak to you.'

Rain began to fall, heavily and sharply. Jolo led Bucephalus by the reins and his men followed in the blue dawn light. The detachment joined the old track west of Mosul, avoiding the new road that had brought so much harm. The track took them through wet cornfields and beanfields, their booted feet cushioned by the sweet-smelling clover called *nofil* that grew everywhere.

As the sun rose higher and ruddy continents of clouds streaked the sky, Ashe realised the desert was far behind – on the other side of the night; the blood and killing on another side of himself.

For the irregulars, the night had brought a small victory – amply justifying their recruitment and payment. The extremism of the jihadist – no stranger to the ways and history of the region – left Yezidi families with little choice but to resist where possible. Not being 'people of the Book', as Muslims are defined by the Koran, nor being Christians or Jews, Yezidis were continually exposed to ancient hatreds in Iraq, Turkey, Georgian Armenia, and Iran.

Ansar al-Sunna demanded an all-Islamic, fundamentalist state in Iraq. Christians might be subjected to *dhimmitude* – humiliating second- or third-class status – while Jews would barely be tolerated. For Yezidis there was no place at all: in the event of Ansar al-Sunna's fulfilling its dreams, the only options for Yezidis who wished to stay in their homeland, would be to convert to Islam or be butchered. Yezidis had never willingly converted, and their enthusiasm for life and their faith had kept them alive.

The men now resembled a posse of pilgrims come to some

sacred place, quite different from the furious force of the previous evening.

As they approached Bashiqa, Ashe was struck by the peculiar whitewashed cones, like little steeples, that adorned the shrines around the town. They rose out of the olive groves as if they too were paying homage to the sun.

Ashe felt a gentle hand touching his shoulder.

'Tobbiash! Come!'

A golden light cast dappled shadows across the tiny stone room in which his camp bed had been placed. Squatting on a Persian carpet was an old lady, wide-eyed and grinning. Her face was like an old stone, cut with gorges and fissures, her eyes like suns.

She removed the silk scarf from around her greying hair, dipped it in a bronze bowl of water and wiped Ashe's face as he perched on a low stool.

'Welcome to Bashiqa, English gentleman. English gentleman very welcome here in home of my son. My son, Jolo's cousin. He is with Khuda now. He waits for the Resurrection. He sit then in judgement on Saddam's soul. Saddam kill my son. Yes.'

Tears came to the woman's eyes. 'I am Gulé, Englishman. I wash your clothes.'

Ashe sat up. 'Gulé. You must forgive me. If I'd known, I would not have brought my dirty clothes into your good house.'

'It is God's will you come here. The Kochek tell us so.'

'Kochek?'

'He sees through this world. You have two eyes. He has other eyes, like peacock. Kochek know about you, Tobbiash! You come from bad happening in England. You are hurt, Tobbiash. You come to Sheikhan to find answer.'

The lady dipped her headscarf again in the bronze dish and wrung it out thoroughly before retying it about her hair. Gulé had once been a beauty. Now the beauty shone inside.

53

A growl of thunder shot across the dull green mountain to the north. Ashe looked at his reflection in the big muddy puddle in the centre of the street. It was dotted with dying buttercups, like poppies around a wreath, and Ashe thought he looked different. Large droplets of rain splashed in the puddle. The image was distorted.

Ashe hurried back to Gulé's house. Gulé was sitting beneath a stone archway decorated with olive branches that led to the courtyard, mending a white woollen shawl.

'Jolo waiting for you.'

'I like your cap, Gulé.'

She pointed to her little turban, ringed with bright silver coins. Ashe nodded. Gulé giggled. 'I have it when young girl. It is called *cumédravé*, Tobbiash.'

Jolo emerged from the courtyard carrying two glasses of tea. 'You don't see these things now. All girls used to wear them. Gulé has it for the Sarsaleh – our Spring Festival. You miss it. Every Nisan – that is, your April. You have April Fool; we have Sarsaleh!'

'And is foolishness permitted?'

Jolo laughed. 'Do you like dancing?'

'The English have forgotten how to dance.'

'Very sad, Tobbiash. We could teach them again! Bashiqa best dancing in the Sheikhan. Everybody used to come for Sarsaleh at Bashiqa! People come from Kirkuk and Mosul! Dancing here is best.'

Gulé nodded. 'Tell him more, Jolo.'

'There are buttercups round the doors and all the women wear red flowers in their hair. And the girls… they dance the *debka*.'

'*Debka*?'

'A mountain dance. In a circle. The arms are raised. Like this!' Jolo demonstrated. 'Everyone loves this dance! And the boys join in, and a lamb or a chicken is sacrificed. We put the sacrifice blood on our houses to remember. And the meat is cut and shared for the poor. See the graves! The women are at the graves, giving food to passers-by. And the *qewwals* play… Oh, Tobbiash! The *daff* and the *shebab* – music like you never hear anywhere else in the world.'

'*Daff* and *shebab*, what are they?'

'Our *qewwals* – they are sacred musicians. They play *daff*. *Daff* is huge, round, like drum, but in hand.'

'Tambourine?'

'Tambour, yes.'

'And the *shebab* – a flute?'

'Flute. Yes! Good! This is our happiness.'

'And I missed it.'

Jolo shook his head. 'This year, not very good year. There is sadness. Danger.'

Gulé coughed. 'Even in a war, there is time for joy.' She disappeared inside, leaving the men sheltering from the rain beneath the stone archway at the entrance to the house.

Ashe was about to compliment Jolo on the sweet-tasting brown tea when a man poked his turbaned head through the doorway. He looked at Ashe with solemn interest and scratched his beard. 'Tobbiash. My father used to serve Ismail Beg. You know him?'

Ashe shook his head.

'Ismail Beg great man. Ismail Beg believe in schools. He make friends with Christians in Armenia. He try to help his people. He is liking English soldiers – and he love English aeroplanes. The English are often friends with Yezidis.'

Jolo got up. 'Now you meet Jiddan. He is Kochek.'

'Ah! The dream genie.'

The Kochek was shocked. 'Me? *Jinn*? No! No! I Jiddan, yes. Jiddan.' He gripped a bundle of rope attached to the black sash about his waist. 'Jiddan – Kochek, not *jinn*.'

The three men sat themselves down on a low wooden bench.

'Why call Jiddan *jinn*, Tobbiash?'

'A dream genie is a—'

'A *jinn* who appears in a dream?' The idea seemed perfectly natural to the Kochek.

'Yes, yes, that would be it.'

'Then you see me in your dream? I see *you*, Tobbiash, sir…'

'Will you explain "Kochek" to me?'

'Excuse…' The Kochek went abruptly back inside.

'What is Kochek?' Jolo rubbed the soft black hairs on his chin. 'Is very difficult, Tobbiash. There are many things you must live with Yezidis many years to understand. Even after many years, you do not understand all. I tell you, Tobbiash, I do not understand. We ask *pirs*: they are our holy men. Sometimes they explain. We have… oh, many ways, different men can explain things. These things are learnt in the heart. No books.'

'I think you've put that beautifully, Jolo.'

'Thank you.'

'But what is a Kochek?'

Ashe's mind turned to Sarsaleh and to April Fools'. The fool is sacrificed – made a lord for the day, fooled into thinking himself important. The fool is the animal who is fed well, separated from the herd or flock, treated with care – until the day comes when his blood will decorate the doorway. The fool is like a blade of corn, before the scythe whips its arrogant crown off.

These were the origins of the April Fool. Spring and harvest were directly linked – underground. First the gilded crown of corn, then the cutting. For a few blissful minutes Ashe forgot that he was a government agent close to a war zone.

Jiddan returned, carrying a huge plate filled with food.

'Look! He is like Gabriel!' said Jolo.

226

'The angel?'

'When man die, Angel Gabriel carry *ruh*.'

'*Ruh*?'

'Spirit. When man die, angel carry spirit of good person to Paradise on tray.'

'Or to hell, presumably.'

The Yezidis looked shocked. 'No hell.'

'No hell?'

'Fires all gone!' asserted the Kochek. 'Little child empty jar of tears – fires all gone!'

'Now see, Englishman, we have *kleycha*! *Dolma! Nan! Kaub! Khubbaz*!'

Ashe tried the *dolma*, popping the vine-leaf rissole into his mouth in one go, the better to savour its delicately spiced rice-and-meat stuffing.

'Good!'

The Yezidis smiled. 'Try *kleycha*!'

Ashe picked up what looked like a mince pie. 'We eat these at Christmas!'

'Yes, birth of Angel Jesus from Holy Mary.'

'You…?'

'Like Jesus? Of course! There is Syrian Orthodox church in village. There are Roman Christians in the Sheikhan, and American Baptist missionaries in Armenia. All kinds of Christians telling different stories. We say: we hear it all before. Disciples of Jesus know our country when no one knows England or America! Jesus was good angel, very beloved of God. He come to earth to tell people what is good life and about day of resurrection.'

'You mean he's a prophet?'

'Many, many holy men are coming to Hakkari Mountains and to Sheikhan. Many holy men. But Jesus not buried like prophet, Tobbiash. If Jesus buried, every good person come to his *mazar*. No. Jesus angel. He fly, like bird, back to Khuda when Khuda tell him.

'Jesus must do as he's told.'

54

Sami al-Qasr stared at himself in Fiona Normanton's bathroom mirror. Did he look like an evil man?

He carefully applied the grey hairs to his face with theatrical glue; then the false irises, the thickened eyebrows, the silver earrings. He tried a selection of spectacles.

It was a perfect day: a gentle breeze was blowing eastwards from Bodega Bay, all the way to the clear, bright contours of the Sierra Nevada.

Leanne Gresham had turned the crimson Mercedes coupé off Highway 80 at Sacramento and was now speeding north in the direction of Yuba City, halfway to Paradise.

Sherman Beck's eyes lingered on Leanne's copper-tone nails resting lightly on the steering wheel. They followed the line of her browny-green worsted jacket to her shoulders, where her hair danced like a young Jackie Kennedy's. Beck admired her mature, sexy look. He admired the Egyptian-style gold necklace circling her graceful neck, the impeccable match of her copper-coloured blouse, open to the third intriguing button.

She turned and smiled at him. He looked at her brown eyes, the finely plucked eyebrows and the pale-lilac eye shadow.

'You ain't so bad lookin' yourself, Agent Beck.'

'I'm sorry I was just...'

'California dreamin'?'

'Is it OK?'

'Charming as ever. Said it had been a long time and he had a lot to talk about.'

'What did you tell him?'

'I said we were going to improve security around him, and could he bear having two agents around for a while. He was enthusiastic. Maybe too enthusiastic.'

'We could get the FBI onto the guy in the pickup.'

'Lee was emphatic, Sherman. Keep it internal.'

The Mercedes rested in a large puddle beneath a dripping pine tree. The air was steamy, hot. Beck looked at Leanne. They kissed warmly.

'Later, cowboy.'

'So at last I get to meet the bio-wizard himself.'

Beck helped Leanne avoid the puddle as she stepped out of the Merc. RIBOTech was almost deserted. Beck shook his head.

'It's Saturday, Sherman. Everyone's gone to the game.'

Gresham and Beck stepped towards the small reception area and pressed the buzzer. An old man in a light-blue uniform appeared behind the plate-glass windows. One hand gripped his reading glasses, the other gripped his side holster.

'I see they put their best man on the job.' Gresham nudged Beck, smiled at the man and showed her ID through the glass.

He looked carefully at it, scratched his bald head, then went back to his desk and picked up a microphone. The croaky voice echoed about the entrance.

'What's your business, ma'am?'

Beck looked to the grille below the buzzer. 'CTC, officer. Check your book.'

The old man fumbled with his daybook. 'Your name, sir?'

'Beck.'

'Christian name?'

'Sherman.'

The guard pressed the entry button and the front door clicked. 'Name's Starbuck. Everyone calls me Cliff.'

'How ya doin', Cliff?'

'OK. It's customary to search visitors, Mr Beck. But in your case, I guess I'd be surprised if you weren't carrying a piece. Frankly, I can't see why you've come. There's no one here except Mr Lowenfeld.'

'What about Professor al-Qasr?'

'I ain't seen him since yesterday, sir.'

Beck looked at Gresham. 'Don't tell me—'

'The pickup?'

Gresham checked the daybook. 'Look here, Officer. Al-Qasr came in this morning at six-thirty.'

'Ah right. Yeah, well I didn't get here till seven. You'd have to ask the night-man. I let Mr Lowenfeld into Professor al-Qasr's office at 7.30. He wasn't there then.'

'We'll check, Officer.'

'You know the way, ma'am?'

Leanne nodded. 'You keep an eye out, Mr Starbuck. Anyone arrive or leave while we're upstairs, just give us the word.'

'You betcha!' Starbuck saluted.

Beck hurried to join Leanne on the oak stairs to the first floor. 'Needn't panic yet, Leanne. We're still ten minutes early.'

Leanne Gresham did not look convinced. She knocked on the outer door of al-Qasr's office. She tried the handle; it was open. They walked in.

'Dr Lowenfeld! You there? Dr Lowenfeld!' She turned to Beck. 'You check the men's room. And don't be too long in there.'

Gresham knocked on the laboratory doors, then ran her omni-pass through the security lock. The doors clicked open. 'Dr Lowenfeld! Professor al-Qasr! Leanne Gresham here!'

A shiver shot up her spine: a smell around al-Qasr's desk.

Behind it was a row of long cupboards around two feet high. She bent down under the desk; the smell seemed stronger. A hint of almonds.

Gresham heard footsteps echoing loudly in the corridor.

'That you, Sherman?' She started pulling at the cupboard door. 'That you?'

The cupboard door scuffed open. God, that was bad! Must be the pipes.

The lab doors burst open. Gresham pulled at the cupboard.

'Hold it there, Leanne! Don't move!'

Gresham let go of the cupboard door.

'Get right away from there, Leanne!'

'All right. All right. I seen a corpse before, Sherman.'

'I'm talking about the wire.'

'Wire?'

'Booby-trapped.'

'I didn't see. I...'

'Trick of the light, Leanne. I'll call the disposal guys down at al-Qasr's house.'

'And I'll get on to Kellner.'

'Why?'

'Authority to detain Hasidic Jews leaving San Francisco airport today.'

'Still think it was him?'

'Would we be forgiven if we did nothing?'

56

Gulé stood solemnly by the archway and waved the men off. The Snatch sped northwards out of the village. Everything felt good. The road was good, the fields were full of wet, wild flowers and the weather was glorious: not too hot, with a sweet, cooling breeze rolling down from the Hakkari Mountains.

Major Richmond gave Ashe a sly smile. 'Mystery tour, Toby. Do you mind changing gear for me?'

'Amazing you can drive at all. It looked like your shoulder'd been torn off.'

'Thank God for the Blue tracker. Took the main force.'

'Who put you right?'

'Czech field hospital. Fantastic people. Tore a patch off my backside. How's your pneumothorax? Jolo told me the story.'

'Pneumobollocks! My breathing's fine. Never better. Vinny was talking out his arse, I reckon.' Ashe suddenly became aware of Zappa's absence. 'Where is Vinny?'

'That's the bad news. Maybe he was protecting you.'

'What do you mean?'

'Vinny failed to report. No codes received on any channel. Vanished. We're half expecting to see his face on some bloody video with an execution threat.'

'And?'

'Nothing, so far. The kidnappers like to time their broadcasts for maximum impact. Even so, something usually leaks out.'

'I can see him bending a few rules – if he was on to something.'

'Some rules you don't bend. He knows that as well as anyone.' Richmond cleared his throat. 'Unfortunately, Toby, this makes things difficult for you. Without your source handler, you're wasting your time here.' Richmond paused. 'And ours.'

Ashe sighed. 'Just as things were getting interesting.'

Richmond scratched the back of his neck. 'Desk has taken a remarkable interest in your welfare, Toby. Not that you heard that from me, you understand.'

'Crayke or no Crayke, I take it the mystery tour leads straight to the airport.'

'Not quite.' Richmond turned to the Kochek, who was sitting next to Jolo on the back seat. 'Tell him, Jiddan.'

Jiddan's face lit up. 'It leads to Lalish! The pilgrimage site all Yezidi must visit once in their lifetime.'

Ashe liked the sound of that. 'And the occasion?'

'A little ceremony. Jolo's horsemen are handling security. Watching the passes. I'm Crayke's representative. All part of my liaison work with the Yezidi community. Respect breeds security. You can often accomplish a lot more by showing up at a family event – provided you're invited of course – than with a squadron of tanks.'

Ashe pondered the situation. There was no way the British and American security effort in Baghdad could afford to part with one of its best officers for a community liaison exercise. There was obviously more to it.

'You sure that's the only reason for this journey, Simon?'

Richmond turned to Ashe and smiled a smile that felt like a wink. 'Need-to-know basis, Toby.'

The Snatch stopped at a T-junction. The metalled road continued to the left, signposted to Tel Kef. To the right, the road became a track: red earth, muddy, full of potholes. This route was signposted in Arabic, but an English translation had been painted beneath it: 'Esiyan'.

'Guess which way, Toby?'

'By the steep and rugged pathway must we tread rejoicingly!'

'Where would we be without *Hymns Ancient & Modern*?'

'Modern Britain, dear boy.'

Richmond laughed. 'That path leads to your pot of gold, says the little one.'

'Little one?'

'That's what "Kochek" means.'

'I'll believe it when I see it.'

'That's not believing at all.'

Richmond turned the Land Rover to the right.

'Did you know the Yezidis invented the Ark?'

Jiddan chipped in. 'Noah, he true son of the tradition.'

'The Yezidis have a story there was another Flood.'

'Like the one in the Bible?'

'They say there were two. They say the great ship started at a village called Ain Sifni. That's a few miles northwest of here.'

Ashe had the distinct feeling that they were driving across some vast, cuneiform-inscribed tablet; the tracks were like the ancient Babylonian letters. But what was its message?

'The water rose and the ship sailed off.'

'Any particular direction?'

'Who can say? Anyhow, it sort of ran aground on the peaks of Mount Sinjar, where a rock pierced the hull.'

Jiddan, who was trying hard to follow Richmond's telling of the story, interjected. 'Snake! Snake!'

'As Jiddan says, there was this great serpent in the ship. And the snake curled itself up into a cake. And that plugged the ship. Then the ship floated off again until it rested on Mount Judi, ninety miles northeast of here. Used to be pilgrimages to see the remains.'

The Defender ground its way northwards, passing groups of armed Kurdish fighters on the way. Some of the Kurds cheered at the sight of a Coalition vehicle; some just nodded. They all looked dog-tired.

After long miles of trundling northeast, the Snatch took a left at the crossroads. Direction: Atrush. Ahead, Ashe could see a cluster of gentle, green mountains.

'Why approach from the east? Lalish is north of Bashiqa.'

'If we'd come from the south, we'd have had to take the footpath from Ba'dre – through the mountains. Bit of a hike.'

In the distance, Ashe could see the shell of an ancient building.

'*Khana Êzî,*' said Jolo.

'*Khana Êzî?*'

'House of Ezîd. "Ezîd" is other name for God.'

'Sultan Ezîd,' added Jiddan.

'Yes. This was Yezidi caravanserai. Many pilgrims come to Lalish in old times.'

Ashe got the feeling Jolo could actually envision lines of camels and horses and pilgrims: richly dressed, poorly dressed, brightly dressed, happily approaching... But wait! thought Ashe, that is what *I'm* seeing – in my mind's eye. He looked round at the Kochek. The Kochek was staring at him, his face glowing.

'There!' Jolo pointed right, to the mountain rising in the north. 'There!'

'Mount Erefat,' added Richmond coolly.

'Yes, Erefat, Tobbiash. High on Mount Erefat is holy spring.'

'*Kanî Baykî.*' Jiddan nodded knowingly.

'This, Tobbiash, is where Sheykh Adi beat rock with his *gopal.*'

'*Gopal?*'

'Like stick for guiding sheep. He beat rock with stick. Water flow from rock. Living water. Holy water. Spring still there. *Kanî Baykî.*'

'And who was Sheykh Adi?'

The two Yezidis were astounded Ashe had never heard of Sheykh Adi. To them, Adi was clearly the most important being who had ever lived.

Jiddan put his large hand gently on Richmond's shoulder. 'Here, Major, we stop.'

The Snatch came to a quiet rest near a burbling mountain stream. Jolo pointed to a small, white, stone bridge. 'Pira Silat.'

Jolo and Jiddan took their shoes off and stepped to the edge of the sparkling water. They washed their hands, faces and necks. Ashe followed them.

Richmond gripped his Browning, holstered onto his thigh. His cotton trousers stuck uncomfortably to his leg. The holster had been rubbing it all day long. He looked about him, then reached for a pair of field glasses to study the dense woodland.

Rising from the water, Jolo shook his head dry, then pointed to the major. The Yezidis laughed. Jolo made an ear-piercing whistle. From out of the woods, on both sides of the road, emerged a dozen of Jolo's irregular cavalry. Forming a sixty-metre ring around the Land Rover, they dismounted, withdrew their M16s from their saddles, and vanished into the bushes and grasses.

Jolo and Jiddan then crossed the bridge three times, clapping. As they made their way back and forth, they solemnly intoned the words:

Pira Silat, aliyek doje, êk cennete

'We're leaving the car and travelling on foot, so I should stick your boots back on, Toby. Those guys will walk barefoot the rest of the way, but they're used to it. We don't want to have to carry you back.'

'Just getting in the spirit of things.'

'Think of yourself as an official observer, OK?'

'And this?' Ashe patted his sidearm.

'There may not be much verbal objection to your having it, under current circumstances, but keep it covered.'

Ashe looked over to the two pilgrims on the other side of the bridge. 'What did those words mean?'

Jiddan gestured permission for Jolo to answer. 'Being interpreted, Tobbiash, the words are saying: "On the one side is hell; on the other Paradise".'

Richmond nudged Ashe across the bridge. 'D'you hear that, Toby? *Paradise.*'

240

57

'This is Mrs Valdès, Agent Beck.'

Clay from Homeland Security pointed to al-Qasr's chubby housekeeper. 'Now she's out of a job, her memory's improved. Says she reckons al-Qasr had a little drive-in joint about a mile down the road, off track. That right, Mrs Valdès?'

'I'm not sure, sir. I think I see him drive into trees once maybe.'

'I've sent people down there. They're checkin' out Mrs Valdès' story.'

Gresham and Beck explored al-Qasr's house. It was neat, well furnished, a little austere perhaps. There was the odd enlargement of NASA's more colourful galactic adventures, and scattered sepia prints showing scenes from pre-Saddam Iraq.

'Seems our doctor was a bit on the dull side, wouldn't you say, Sherman?'

'The "banality of evil", you mean? Does that cover forcing cyanide down Fiona Normanton's throat?'

'Sorry, I mean there's nothing to suggest he was a fanatical type. No diaries with prayerful confessions. Not even a copy of the Koran.'

'Maybe taken it with him.'

They heard a shout from downstairs. It was Clay. 'Just got a call from your explosives people. Seems they got something. Can you take a look?'

Gresham looked to Beck. 'You coming?'

'I'll come down soon. I want to speak with this Mrs Valdès while the heat's on and the memory's warm.'

Leanne stifled the urge to kiss him. 'I'll check it out and call. Oh damn it, Beck! I left my cellphone in my bag up at RIBOTech.'

'Use mine. Maybe I'll call you first.' Beck winked.

Bob Lowenfeld had been found in al-Qasr's bunker. The investigators had lowered a brace into the bunker to lift out the body, in case of further booby traps. Lowenfeld was still lying on the ground, uncovered. Gresham noted Lowenfeld's swollen lips. Cyanide again.

The young explosives expert wiped the sweat off his hot brow and rubbed his eyes. 'Mrs Gresham, I'm sorry I didn't call you earlier. When we finally found the hatch to this thing, we thought of what happened to you up at RIBOTech. Lucky we did. Al-Qasr had booby-trapped the hatch. After we cleared that, we then found he'd fixed a vibration mechanism to Mr Lowenfeld's body.'

'How did you…?'

'We got all the al-Qaeda training stuff. Booby trap was standard.'

'Fingerprints?'

'We've swept the place. Take a look. If you really want to.'

Leanne hitched her skirt up around her hips. The young man looked away. She eased her way down into the tiny bunker and sat on al-Qasr's stool. She checked out the CCTV monitor linked up to the RIBOTech lab in the corner. She examined his table and noticed the staining around what might have been a laptop. She checked for a phone link.

'Looks like he had a secure link down here. That's why we never got anything from his office or home computers.'

The cellphone on the table rang. 'I guess that's Sherman.' Gresham picked it up.

Up at al-Qasr's house, Beck heard the muffled explosion.

Leanne Gresham was dead.

58

As Ashe followed the group down from the sacred bridge at Pira Silat towards the Lalish valley, he wondered what had happened to the Kochek.

'Jiddan cuts wood for the sanctuary.'

Ashe stopped dead. Gunshots. He reached for his Browning.

Jolo laughed. 'Pilgrims at Silavgeh.'

'What?'

'Place of Greeting. On Mount Meshet. South of the valley. Pilgrims at festivals fire rifles when they come to stone. This is when they see Lalish first time. They kiss special stone on the path.'

Ashe climbed a hillock and the fabulous valley of Lalish opened out before him. Two miles of winding paths, woodland, olive groves, vines, and the most extraordinary collection of buildings he had ever seen in his life. To the south, Mount Meshet rose like a host at a festive table.

'Our songs teach us this holy valley of Lalish came down from heaven. It is called the Site of Truth,' said Jolo. 'Tomorrow is Wednesday, our holy day, so the pilgrims make special fires tonight.'

The valley looked magical, aglow with little fires. Jolo pointed out the shrine they were headed for and explained that, like all Sheykhs, Sheykh Adi was a historical figure who trod a spiritual path, and was understood by the Yezidis as a kind of angel – a reflection of the divine. Before Ashe could ask him to elaborate, Jolo was eagerly pointing out the shrines of Sheykh Obekr, Sheykh Hesen, Pîr Êsîbiya, Sheykh Babik, Sheykh Tokel, Pîr

Jerwan, Sheykh Sheref el-Dîn, and Sultan Êzîd, each one lit by hundreds of tiny flames burning gently in bowls of olive oil set in the stonework. Ashe was enchanted. It was as though the valley was filled with falling snowflakes, ignited from within, flickering peacefully down.

The air was sweet and pure; Lalish was clean.

As the men walked down into the valley, Ashe's attention was caught by three conical spires resembling upturned ice-cream cones, topped by golden globes.

'What's that?'

'Ah! Those are the *qubbe*, the spires, of the *mazar* of Sheykh Shems, Tobbiash.'

'That's where you said I could speak to the English saint.'

'Yes. Wait! I go see if you allow in. Not much time before we must be at big ceremony at Sheykh Adi, Tobbiash.'

Jolo walked quickly on ahead, leaving Ashe and Richmond to make their way down towards the Shrine of Sheykh Adi.

'Know anything about this Sheykh Adi, Simon?'

'You'll have to look this up – not that there's much in English. As far as I know, he was a... What's that word in Islam? Oh, you know, whirling dervishes – the mystical thing.'

'Sufis.'

'Right. Adi was a Sufi. He came here in the 1200s. From the Bekaa Valley in Syria.'

'No border in those days, Simon.'

'What is a Sufi, Toby?'

'Comes from the Arabic word for wool. They wore white woollen robes – like Jiddan. Simple life, given to ecstatic communion with the spirit of God. The Sufis follow what they call a "path", a spiritual path, sometimes named after the teacher of that path. Adi started a path. People are still following it. Sufism has been called the *gnosis* of Islam.'

'Ger-nosis?'

'Yeah, well, the "g" is usually silent – like the "k" in knowledge. It means knowledge, actually.'

'Mystic knowledge.'

'The knowledge of how to extricate oneself from this world.'

'Say that again.'

'*The knowledge of how to extricate oneself from this world*: in Gnostic thinking, the one who is truly alive is the one who has died to the world.'

'You could argue that suicide bombing is a kind of perversion of that idea.'

'It's certainly a perversion.'

Simon laughed. 'You should be in the propaganda unit.'

'What's that sound?'

Ashe and Richmond listened hard. They heard water rushing beneath their feet. Beneath the path were tunnels that fed streams through the valley. The waters were collected in cisterns. They were used for baptising children, and for the initiation of *pirs* or holy men into the mysteries of the tradition.

Soon their feet were echoing on great, smooth flagstones that paved a large square. The walls were made of huge stones – older than the crusades, Ashe surmised.

Jolo came running into the forecourt. 'You are blessed, Tobbiash. Tonight, the guardian of Sheykh Shems Sanctuary is here. Remember we speak of Hamo Shero?'

'Chief of the Mountain?'

'The grandson of Hamo Shero is here. He is Khidr, son of Khudêda, son of Hamo Shero. He is representative of the Mir in Sinjar.'

'The who?'

'The Mir. Prince of the Yezidi people. Tehsin Beg. Major Richmond, he explain.'

'The man Jolo is talking about is Sheykh el-Wezîr, the Mir's deputy in the Sinjar. Fine man.'

'Tobbiash, Khidr say you come to him at Sheykh Shems after the ceremony at Sanctuary of Sheykh Adi – and you speak to English saint in circle. I have arranged this for you.'

'Why?'

'Gulé and Kochek say you are in need of God.'

'Who isn't, Jolo?'

'You need faith.'

Within the precincts of Lalish, the offer seemed perfectly natural.

'Who are those women?'

'*Fiqreyyat.*'

Ashe studied the aged women in all-white, toga-like woollen garments, with great turbans wrapped around their hair and under their chins.

'Nuns?'

'They serve at the sanctuary. Pure women. They spend their lives at Lalish.'

Ashe's eyes moved from the *fiqreyyat* to a striking image by the entrance to the Sanctuary of Sheykh Adi. A huge, coal-black serpent, tall as a man, slithered upwards in stone relief.

'Our serpent at Lalish! Every day, serpent is made black again. Dye is from *zirgûz* trees – and ash from fires of Lalish.'

There were other carvings by the door. Ashe stared at the combs and the images of the sun. The hexagrams – interlaced triangles – were like stars of David or seals of Solomon, he thought. There were also birds, a hatchet, what looked like shepherds' crooks, six-petalled flowers in circles, and the sun, moon and stars in circles.

Jolo shook his head. 'Many more carvings long ago. Before your year of 1892.'

'What happened?'

'Turks burn Lalish. They kill many Yezidis. Many in prison. They steal our holy things. Yezidis always attacked by neighbours. Muslims had no mercy. We are not in their Book. When Turkish army want to be paid, government send them here to steal what they want. Now Sunnis murder us.'

Richmond interjected. 'We're doing our best, Jolo.'

'Yes. Our best.'

A group of men stepped lithely through the sanctuary

entrance, looking like Arab sheykhs in the familiar headdress and long, woollen surcoats. Each carried something in a brown, cotton bag.

'*Qewwals!*' cried Jolo. 'You see? *Daff* and *shebab*!'

'Is this courtyard part of the sanctuary, Jolo?'

'Sometimes this is called *sûq me'rifetê* – the Market of Mystical Knowledge.'

Startled by the name, Ashe mumbled to himself. 'Wisdom is sold in the desolate market where none come to buy.'

'What you say, Tobbiash?'

'A poem by William Blake – an English Kochek.'

'Is very good. But here also are shops by the walls at festivals where you can buy olive oil and sweets for children. And this market is not in desert – but in Paradise!'

A contented-looking Jiddan appeared in the courtyard. Jolo patted Ashe's back. 'Now we enter *Qapiya Sheykh Adi*.'

As they opened the sanctuary door beneath a Roman arch, Jiddan and Jolo kissed the threshold. Having crossed it, they gave their payment to a nun.

The sanctuary hall was dark and cool. Five ancient pillars supported its centre. Above them hung chandeliers. A few candles were lit.

Jolo whispered to Ashe. 'See here! *Hewdê Nasir el-Dîn*.' He pointed to a cistern. 'Here Angel of Death come to clean his knife, when person dies in the world.'

'He must be here now then.'

Jolo shuddered. 'Do you see him?'

Ashe shook his head.

'He does not want you to see him. So you are safe, Tobbiash. See! Behind that curtain: *senjaq*.'

'*Senjaq?*'

'Holy image.'

'Can we see it?'

Jiddan interjected. 'Must be special person. *Qewwals* take care of *senjaq* on its journey. They show to faithful Yezidis. You not Yezidis.' The Kochek hurried to the end of the hall, then turned left into another chamber. 'There is tomb of Sheykh Adi.'

Jiddan and Jolo circled the long stone slab three times and each tied a knot in one of the many colourful pieces of silk and cloth draped over the tomb. Jiddan spoke to a nun standing by a door on the left. 'It is permitted.'

The door creaked open.

But for two rows of large earthenware jars, the chamber was empty. Ashe thought of the wedding at Cana.

'Olive oil from sacred groves. For holy fires.'

Jiddan and Jolo tiptoed to the bare rock that formed the sanctuary's north wall. They plunged their wrists down into two holes in the rock, saying '*behisht, dozhe*' three times.

'What are you saying?'

'*Behisht, dozhe*?' Jolo looked to Jiddan. The Kochek nodded. 'It means "heaven, hell".'

'Like when you crossed the bridge earlier?'

'A crossing, yes.'

'Why do you do this?'

'We always do this. It is right to do it. God knows the reason. What do we know of these things?'

Back in the tomb chamber of Sheykh Adi, they were shown another door. Jiddan looked through it, then called to his party. 'Tomb of Sheykh Hesen. Now you have seen.'

Ashe was intrigued. 'Not properly. May I look?'

'Nothing to see,' said the Kochek awkwardly. 'We must hurry.'

Ashe entered the small tomb chamber. Sheykh Hesen's tomb did not have the appeal of Sheykh Adi's, judging by the amount of cloth laid upon it.

There was a small, modest door to the right.

'What's through there?'

'Nothing.'

'May I open it?'

'Not allow,' said Jiddan, trying hard to sound friendly.

Ashe showed no sign of moving. He remembered Gulé's

words about how coming to the Sheikhan was his destiny. 'Can you tell me about it?'

'We have not seen tomb of Sheykh Obekr.'

'Can you tell me about this door?'

'Please, Tobbiash. Outsiders not allowed.'

Richmond called Ashe. 'Come on, Toby! Can't you see the man's upset?'

Ashe felt a powerful impulse to go through the plain door.

'Come on, Ashe! Or we'll leave you behind!'

'Please, Tobbiash. I must go.'

Ashe turned back. The Kochek looked relieved. 'We go back to *suq*.'

As they hurried over the cool steps, Ashe confided in Richmond. 'Any idea what's through that door, Simon?'

'Something to do with a cave, I think. But I never pursue the matter. It annoys them.'

'I wasn't trying to interfere.'

'Try and remember, Toby, these people have had to fight for access to this place. It's incredibly important to them.'

'It could be incredibly important to me too.'

'Curiosity, Toby, killed the cat.'

59

Beaming with pride, Jiddan pointed to two small braziers that lit the path across the stone forecourt. As Kochek, his job was to cut the wood. Around the braziers, the *qewwals'* faces, framed by grey hair and matted beards, flickered in the firelight. While the musicians tightened their instruments' skins over the flames, Ashe's attention was caught by a stone building behind them. He asked Jolo if it was another sanctuary dedicated to a sheykh.

'Here we have ceremony. Holy waters.'

'Where does the water come from?'

'*Kaniya Sipi*. White Spring.'

The Kochek nudged Jolo again, lest he say too much, then turned to Ashe. 'Zemzem Spring is miracle of Sheykh Adi. Listen to *qewwals*, Tobbiash.'

The musicians' leader raised his tambour, then began a low-pitched chant in a major key. The rhythm changed abruptly into a melody as wild as any jazz improvisation. The tambours were thrust upwards and outwards in unison and the bodies of the *qewwals* swayed in time with the words, rhymes, cries and melismas of the piercing pipes. The valley answered in echoed chorus. Ashe was captivated, his body strangely stirred as if from a long sleep. Richmond tapped his foot.

After the first chant, one of the seven *qewwals* began a prayer; others joined in.

A syncopated beat. The music climaxed. Jiddan disappeared into the shadows. Ashe noticed dozens of seated Yezidis; they seemed to have come from nowhere.

'What's the song about, Jolo?'

'Sheykh Adi established his path. When the path was made, on that day, the water of White Spring was made a… cure for all…'

'Sickness?'

Jolo nodded and passed glasses of dark coffee to Ashe and Richmond.

Again the music reached a pulsing, wild crescendo. Its sense of soulful abandon suggested a depth to this religion not easy to grasp. Yes, there was pious mysticism, thought Ashe, but there was also something more elemental and physical too: a marriage of 'heaven and hell'.

Richmond gave Ashe a nudge and pointed to a party entering the forecourt. Leading the procession and carrying a bronze candelabra was Jiddan, with his rope and his hatchet tucked into a white woollen cummerbund. Behind him walked an extremely tall old man wearing a loose white turban that fell over his eyes. His white robe, white gaiters and red sash, which was wrapped round his waist and diagonally across his chest, reminded Ashe of the magi.

Richmond whispered in Ashe's ear. 'Sheykh el-Wezîr – he's the Mir's deputy, what they call the *mendûb*, in Sinjar.'

Ashe stared at him. The sheykh looked straight back into Ashe's eyes: a clear, diamond stare. Ashe looked away.

Behind the sheykh walked a teenage girl, wearing clothes that might have come from any high-street store: flared black cotton trousers, black sandals, and a loose orange-and-black paisley-patterned blouse. The V-neck was open, revealing a pearl necklace. Her hair was long, thick and black, made even longer by dyed sheep's hair that had been tied in so that it flowed down her back almost to her ankles. Around her forehead the girl wore a bandana decorated with coins and red flowers.

Her eyes were large and bright, like many Yezidis Ashe had encountered. Burning within those eyes, however, Ashe sensed a terrible grief – pain too great for one so young.

As the little procession moved towards the stone building behind the *qewwals*, another figure came into view. Jolo grabbed Ashe's wrist. 'Laila! It is the princess!'

Attired in a sleeveless abaya embroidered with silver and gold wave patterns, moons and dolphins, Laila was regal in bearing and captivating in appearance. First to fall under the spell of her high cheekbones, pharaonic eyes and long black tresses was Richmond. He turned to Ashe. 'She's a cousin of the Mir.'

'Laila means "Morning Star",' added Jolo.

'Really?'

'Yes, Tobbiash. Laila is also name for Christian saint.'

'Which one?'

'You call her ... Mary Magdalene.'

The door of the stone building opened. Jiddan's face appeared; his eyes flew from left to right. Somebody pushed him outside. Spotting the major, Jiddan hurried towards Ashe's party.

'Tobbiash! You come. Princess Laila wills it.'

Ashe turned to Richmond. 'Why me?'

'Blame Jolo. He's told her something about you.'

'What?'

'Wouldn't tell me. Go on!'

Jiddan grabbed Ashe's wrist and pulled him away from the crowd. The assembly gasped. An outsider brought inside the mysterious building was unheard of.

Inside, the sheykh stood in a cramped space at the back, his hands crossed over his red sash, his eyes closed in communication with a higher power. Jiddan raised the candelabra above the heads of the assembly.

Standing in front of a raised basin area was Princess Laila, her dark eyes fixed on Ashe. 'Please do us the honour of witnessing our ceremony, Dr Ashe.'

Ashe was attracted to her superior smile and subterranean voice; the kind that could reach far into a man's soul. 'Delighted, Your Highness.'

'Dr Ashe, it is our wish that you understand that it is one of the five obligations on a Yezidi to choose what we call a Brother – or Sister – of the Hereafter. The sister must be from the family of a sheykh. I am of such a family, Dr Ashe. I am to be Rozeh's Sister of the Hereafter.'

'Rozeh?'

'The girl you have seen with us. The tie between us has existed before this life, and it will exist after this life. I will serve my Sister, Rozeh, and she will make offerings as she may and as custom dictates. I will care for Rozeh and she will seek guidance from me as she may and as God wills.

'I shall be present at her marriage and should she die before me, I shall be with her then. I shall know her after my death as I knew her before she was born.'

Laila then stepped back, revealing a stone basin surrounded by large slabs. At its centre, a small fountain of water bubbled up from below. Jiddan, steering Rozeh by the shoulders, brought her to Laila. Shy and respectful, Rozeh looked downwards, but Laila gently took her chin and raised her head. Their eyes met. Rozeh's sad face broke. Tears welled in her eyes as Laila said a few words, softly, in Kurmanji.

Laila reached her right hand into the basin, filling her palm with water from the White Spring. Rozeh stooped to drink the water from the palm of the princess. The door to the building opened and Rozeh left with Laila by her side.

Ashe went back to Richmond's side, in the forecourt. He turned to see Laila's gold-sandalled feet approaching him. Her face wore a look of concentrated interest that singled Toby Ashe out from every man in the world.

'Your Highness.'

'Please don't call me that, Tobbi. Call me Laila. I'm a modern girl.'

Laila tossed off her sandals, turned to the assembly, then called out a half dozen girls from the crowd, pointing wilfully. The crowd drew back to create space for dancing. Richmond's eyes could not leave the princess. Ashe whispered into his ear. 'I'm off to the Shrine of Sheykh Shems. It may be my last chance.'

Richmond nodded, his gaze fixed on the princess's nimble feet. Then he looked at Ashe. 'Toby, you don't *believe* that stuff about talking to long-dead saints do you?'

'I don't know.'

Richmond was mesmerised by the princess. Her arms were raised and she was slapping a small tambourine as her body entwined those of the other girls. So distracted was he that he failed to notice the small group of Yezidi auxiliaries who were pushing their way through the crowd towards himself and Jolo. Jolo greeted them warmly. Hearing their news, a huge grin lit up his face in the firelight. He turned to Richmond and began whispering. Richmond's face broadened into a smile of deep satisfaction.

'What is it, Simon?'

'Jackpot, Toby. But it can wait.' Richmond pointed at his watch. 'Exit in one hour.'

60

His mind racing, Ashe made his way through the flame-speckled valley towards Mount Meshet in the south. Aware of a presence, he looked behind him. Nothing.

The rising earth gave way to a series of stone steps. Stubbing his toe, he let out a suppressed screech. He felt a warm hand on his left shoulder.

'I think you need a guide. The steps up to Sheykh Shems are very steep. It is a holy walk. Pilgrims must suffer a little before the blessing.' She took his hand. 'You can't go through life as if you were afraid of its fire.'

'Think I haven't been burned already?'

'Little scars.'

'Probably.' She let go of his hand.

Ashe looked into Laila's eyes. She came down onto the step he was balancing on. The step was tiny, the slope severe.

Ashe could feel her breathing; he could feel her heart pounding. He could feel the heaving of her body. She touched his chest, and whispered, 'Will you hold me, if I fall?'

'Probably not.'

She raised her arms around his neck and pulled his face toward hers. 'I'm falling, Tobbi.' She kissed him on the cheek.

'There. I want to thank you, Tobbi.'

'For what? I don't know you.'

'I want to thank you. For something you're going to do for me.'

'Ah…'

'You have seen Rozeh?'

'She seems sad.'

'Her father, Saddiq, he was Jiddan's younger brother. Jiddan's brother was murdered last month, in Mosul. Rozeh's mother too. Her name was Qoteh. They were slaughtered, Tobbi, like beasts. Slaughtered by butchers.'

'Because they were Yezidis?'

'Because they were Yezidis.'

Ashe knew no words of comfort equal to such a loss.

'You don't have to say anything. I have seen into your eyes. I believe you can help. Help me do what is best for her. Rozeh is talented. She wants to serve people, to be a doctor. I want her to be a doctor, Tobbi. Please help me!'

Ashe sighed. 'I don't know, Laila. Honestly, I don't know how I can help. If it's money, I can—'

'Of course it's not money! Tobbi, take her to England with you! She can get her education. I will watch over her, through you.'

Ashe thought for a moment. 'I could speak to the ambassador, I suppose. If you wrote to him.'

'I will write to him. I will write to Prince Charles. I will write—'

'It's difficult. You know what happens with official channels. Anyhow, we're leaving for Mosul soon.'

'Mosul? I had hoped…' She clasped his hand to her breast. 'You do this service for me and for Rozeh and for your soul. The angel will smile on you. Now, go! Go to the *mazar* of Sheykh Shems. The guardian is waiting for you. Go! I will wait.'

The *mazar* door creaked open. Ashe closed it carefully behind him. The candlelit chamber was immediately filled with a great gong-like voice as the guardian's mighty grip enveloped Ashe's hands.

'I greet thee well, Dr Ashe. I am Khidr, son of Khudêda, Sheykh el-Wezîr. Greetings in the name of Sheykh Shems. A great pleasure for me to show you a treasure of my people.'

'Where my heart is, there my treasure is also.'

The sheykh smiled and bowed his head. 'Quite so. You think it is because of Jolo Kheyri that I agree to meet you here?'

'That is my information.'

'It is not entirely correct. You see, I know an Englishman who is in Baghdad. For many years he has been a friend. He is much interested in my people. I think you have met him recently.'

'Cray—'

'Please! Names can be dangerous, Dr Ashe. Security is important – even here in Lalish. You heard the gunfire in the valley?'

'Earlier this evening?'

The sheykh nodded.

'I thought—'

'Security. That is why the major has joined us this evening. That is one reason for your visit to us. Now, the Englishman in Baghdad knows you are here. It was he who first suggested we meet. He said that you would appreciate the life we lead.'

'True. I'm fascinated.'

'And in that fascination lies a deeper reason for your visit.'

'Maybe. But tell me, how did… "the Englishman" tell you I was here?'

'Really, Dr Ashe!' The sheykh patted his hip. 'We know what a mobile phone is for – even if we must communicate in code!'

'I'm sorry.'

'Forget it. It's easy to forget the modern world in Lalish.'

Ashe laughed. 'It's easy to forget everything in Lalish!'

'Quite. We come to Lalish to remember, to bring something special to mind we have forgotten. Now, when the Englishman tells me your name, it is not new to me. I remembered it.'

'How is that?'

'My people value knowledge. You write books, Dr Ashe. Our Mir, Tehsin Beg, is very educated, a university man. He has knowledge of the things you write: things of science and the spirit. I for myself follow the tradition of my forefathers. I do not rely on books.'

'We think that by writing we make things real and permanent.'

'Yes. But our words are in our eyes and our hearts. We learn

257

from mind to mind, from lip to ear. When we speak of holy things, this comes not from paper but from the heart of the tradition.'

'When I write, I try to get at the facts beyond the legend.'

The sheykh laughed. 'In these parts, Dr Ashe, fact becomes legend very quickly! Your people are concerned with what can be seen; we are interested in what cannot be seen. When a man dies, he disappears from here. We see only a very, very small part of a life. Legend makes up for deficiency of fact. Men have ceased to believe in the beauty of the impossible. They try to work miracles with explosives.'

The flame ate gradually into the taper, crackling about the bronze candelabra.

'I am the leader of the Shemsani sheykhs, Dr Ashe. Without Sheykh Shems, I am nothing. Sheykh Shems was also *wezîr* of Sheykh Hesen, whose tomb you have seen. He is also Sheykh Shemsê Tebrizî. Do you know the works of Mawlana Jalal al-Din Rumi?'

Ashe smiled with an ironic twinkle. 'The Sufi poet and mystic? Doesn't everybody?'

'Rumi's inspiration came through his knowledge of Shemsê Tebrizî. He was in the holy tradition of Sheykh Adi. How can the sun's divinity be also seen as a man?'

'I don't know.'

'One can only wonder at the beauty of the impossible. Jolo has told you that you may hear the voice of an English sheykh here at this shrine.'

'Saint Chad, yes. There is a shrine to him in England.'

'Yes, at the centre of England. It has three *qubbe*—'

'Spires.'

'Yes, spire. Like Sheykh Adi. And it has bronze *hilêl* at the top of spire. Like Shrine of Sheykh Shems. And your Sheykh Chad used to go to a sacred spring, at dawn. And he used to sing a hymn to Sheykh Shems.'

'That's the legend.'

'You English should look again at your legends.'

The sheykh rotated a ring he was wearing on one of his fingers and began scratching a circle in the dust of the shrine's floor. He then gathered the dust collected at the end of the tracing in his hand. He took a cup from a niche and sprinkled water into the dust.

'Water from Zemzem Spring, Dr Ashe.'

He rolled the dust in his hands into a kind of muddy ball, and smoothed it with his palms. Then he took a small piece of cloth from the niche and wrapped it around the globe of dust.

'We call this *berat.*'

'*Berat.*'

The sheykh then thrust the tiny parcel into Ashe's hand. 'A remedy for all ills, Dr Ashe. Keep it.'

Ashe held it for a moment, then pushed it deep into his trouser pocket.

'Thank you.' English always seemed a stingy language in which to express gratitude.

'Now, please sit in the circle.'

The reality of the situation struck Ashe with force. Was this a magic ritual, a prayer, a set-up – or what? What would happen? What could happen? Would it happen only if he believed? But he had forgotten how to believe; he was not a child any more.

Sheykh el-Wezîr began intoning the Hymn of Sheykh Shems of Tabriz. Ashe sat cross-legged in the circle. Above him, the figure of the sheykh loomed like an ancient statue come alive, his hands crossed over his chest, his eyes closed, his mind and soul inside the words of the hymn.

The words no longer seemed to come from his mouth but from the air around him, from the walls, from the circle, from Ashe himself; Ashe, Ashe, Toby, Toby Ashe was feeling extraordinarily hot; his body shuddered…

Oh Sheykh Shems, you have called us to this work of service,
Open for us a door of mercy,
Grant a light to us, and the people of the tradition
    everywhere

The sun at midnight... As Ashe's eyes closed, his inner eye opened. A blazing light. Ashe felt himself pulled towards it, like a meteor heading for the sun. There was no sense of fear, no will to resist: only to go.

The image of the *ankh*, the Egyptian sandal-strap meaning 'life', appeared to his inner vision: the sandal – to go! Only to go!

Something was pulling him back. He heard the sheykh's voice again: the echo in the chamber. *To go... To go...*

'We gotta go! Hey, buddy! Planet Earth calling! We gotta go!'

Ashe's eye opened slowly.

'What?'

'You ready for the human race? We're all packed up and ready to ride.'

'But... Vinny! VINNY!'

'It's me, baby! Back from the dead. Jeez! Some climb up here!'

'Did you see him?'

'Who?'

'The sheykh.'

'No, Dr Toby. No sheykh. And no rattle and roll neither. But I did see something... Wow! What a dame!'

'The princess.'

'Whoever she was, man, she was just sitting. *Still*, like somewhere else. She told me you were here. Then I find *you're* still as well. Like dead.'

'But... the Sheykh el-Wezîr. He was here a few seconds ago.'

'Look outside, Dr Toby.'

Ashe hauled himself off the floor of the shrine and poked his head through the doorway. Above him, the red disc of dawn had just arisen over Mount Meshet. He stepped outside and stared at the *hilêl*, the golden orb crowning the *qubbe*.

'Sheykh Shems!'

'No, Toby. He's gone.'

'No, Vinny.' Ashe pointed to his right temple. 'He's here!'

61

'Care to do the honours again, Toby?'

Ashe put the Land Rover into gear. The major eased off the clutch and the convoy set off from Pira Silat in the dawn light.

'What's with the two extra trucks, Simon?'

Richmond grinned. 'Remember last night I said we'd hit the jackpot?'

'Er… it's coming back to me. Yeah, just before I left the party. You said it could wait.'

'You got to hand it to Jolo's men. When they pull together, what a unit!'

'The shooting in the valley?'

'Yeah. Bit of a shooting match. Then some preliminary interrogation.'

'The prize?'

'Hafiz Razak.'

The name hit Ashe right between the eyes. He was in the Tower again – just before the explosion. The archdeacon was reading the summary of the November bombings in Istanbul. *Hafiz Razak*: the Syrian in the al-Qaeda cell. Hafiz Razak: one that got away. Dangerous man. Thought to be tied in with a new al-Qaeda cell in Fallujah.

'That's a hell of a coup, Simon. Many congratulations!'

'Thank you.'

'Razak's the forger and bomb-maker.'

'You're very well informed, Dr Ashe.'

'What do you think I do all day? Hafiz Razak's a prime

catch. And fresh from Istanbul too! This could be very exciting. What was he doing in the Sheikhan? His type tend to keep to the Sunni areas.'

Simon looked at Ashe, surprised by his naivety. 'You been reading newspapers again, Toby? Think these guys lack ambition?'

'Sorry, Simon. But aren't al-Qaeda concentrating on the south? Fallujah.'

'Come out of the dream, Toby. They're seeking support everywhere. Razak's been casing Kurdistan. Maybe even trying to establish a link with PKK units across the Turkish border. There are opportunities with Ansar al-Sunna crossing the Iranian border up here. Maybe, God forbid, Hafiz Razak had something atrocious in mind for Lalish. We'll have to see what further interrogation gets out of him. The Yanks want him of course. There's gonna be a lot of interest in Razak. One thing I *can* tell you already, if it's any help. Remember last week you were using me as a sounding board for some of your ideas on the Masonic Lodge bombing?'

'Yeah.'

'You mentioned a guy called al-Qasr, son of an anti-Masonic, anti-Semitic fanatic.'

'Yes. They showed up in some old files. Just a hunch really.'

'You may have got lucky. We had Razak over a barrel all night and of course he denies having anything to do with either Istanbul or al-Qaeda. The only thing he burbles on about is straightforward criminal activity. Seems he's been specialising in passports and identity documents of all kinds. Claims he's in on immigration rackets. After a little pressure, he claimed he had customers in America. Said he'd been assisting a guy he called a "famous American professor" with passport requirements. When pressed as to the professor's name, he mumbled something about "al-Qasr". Said he had immigration problems. Any use?'

'Maybe I'm not wasting my time after all. Can you get me in on the interrogation?'

'As I say, the Yanks have first call on this one.'

'But I'm an interested party.'

'Yeah, well.'

'I'll sort it out when we get to Mosul.'

Richmond looked slightly embarrassed. 'Maybe time to bring Vinny in.'

The major waved the convoy down on a precipitous ledge above a small gorge. Ashe heard a ramp come down from one of the trucks behind and Vinny's familiar voice.

'What is this? Men's-room break?'

Richmond called Vinny up to the Land Rover. 'Time for explanations, Mr Zappa. Hop in!'

'Delighted, Major. Those trucks are nut-crunching.'

The convoy set off once more.

'Do you want to tell him, Vinny? Explain what's happened and what it means for Toby's mission?'

'If there's shit, bud, I'm the fan.'

Ashe could feel it coming his way fast.

'What are you two on about? And what's happened to Jolo?'

'Tomorrow. After you've gone.'

'What do you mean "gone"? Vinny's back! Now we find Yildiz and Yazar!'

The major suddenly seemed to have developed a short temper. 'Look, Toby, after I hand Razak over to our American colleagues for interrogation, I've some rather pressing calls on my time. Like insurgency trouble right down the Syrian border – from al-Kara-bilah to Abu Kamal; from al-Qa'im to al-Ubaydi. Shitloads of trouble. There's 137 Egyptians crossing from Syria some time in the next thirty-six hours. Tunisians, Sudanese, Algerians, Saudis and even two blokes from Manchester training on the Syrian side. The Syrian government claims to be in the dark about all this.'

'Nothing unusual about that, Major.'

'Just tell him, Zappa, for fuck's sake!'

'OK. Well, ya see, Dr Toby, I guess there's been an… international incident.'

'Is he exaggerating again, Simon?'

'No.' Richmond turned the Snatch onto the main road west of Mosul.

'Your source handler here was in Mosul making best use of available sources – putting it discreetly about that I'm interested in the whereabouts of Resit Yazar and Ali Yildiz. All leads gratefully received plus modest remuneration package. So I start to get somewhere. And the trail is leading out of Mosul – which is a mercy 'cause it's getting awful cramped in there. There's over a million Kurds and Arabs in Mosul. And increasing numbers of uninvited immigrants are harbouring distinctly unfriendly intentions toward Uncle Sam.'

Richmond sighed.

'The downside is that the trail in question is leading south to Kirkuk. Kirkuk is not a friendly town. So, Dr Toby, I head there anyway, to the oil capital of Iraq – a truly sacred place, you understand – and one of the most bitterly contested little hotspots in the north. Naturally, I'm cautious. Then, would'ya believe it, I run into some cross-lines.'

'Crossed lines?'

'Yeah, Toby. Crossed and double-crossed. Seems I'm following a line well-trodden by Turkish military intelligence. And to be frank, there ain't quite as much dialogue going on between Turkey and Uncle Sam as one might hope to expect. I get the impression my presence in Kirkuk was not their idea of friendly collaboration. The trail hots up. I locate a source. We meet. Turns out he's working with the Turks. That's the motherfucker's day job. Takes me on a little ride.'

'Meaning?'

'The doors are locked. And I'm heading – against my will – 100 kilometres southeast to Suleymaniya. And you know what? They ain't got spare shades, so they give Vinny a big black blindfold to protect my eyes from the sun. Thoughtful motherfuckers. Turns out Vinny's destination is a basement interrogation room in one of the less fashionable suburbs of

Suleymaniya. Your friendly neighbourhood source handler has become a "guest" of Turkish intelligence. All for my own safety, of course.'

Ashe looked nonplussed.

'Seems they've got wind of some nasty killings that might be taking place in Kirkuk in the near future. "Mr Zappa," they say politely, "we wish to save you from the line of fire – and our national security requires you to be our guest for the short term." They also say they must check my ID. I might be a double agent for Ansar al-Sunna or the PKK or Vladimir Putin or Donald Duck. Any fuckin' excuse.'

'What Vincent is trying to say, Toby, is that he was kidnapped by a detachment of Turkish special forces.'

'I ain't *tryin'* to say nuthin'. I *was* fuckin' kidnapped!'

'But it was for your own safety.'

'Yeah, check. And don't it get messy out there in the field? And when denial time arrives, they can always say the detachment was truly detached – a rogue element now brought under control. So you can see why nothing came through to the US Defense Intelligence Agency in Mosul. As far as MND and the DIA were concerned, Vincent Zappa did not exist.'

'Ah! So, if your friendly captors realised you were missing, presumed dead…'

'You're getting the picture. Maybe a safe return to civilisation was also not in their national security interest. Vinny is beginning to get just a bit nervous. I might be in line for a "very regrettable" accidental accident that couldn't be avoided.'

'We should not have been surprised.'

'Can you imagine, guys, what it feels like, knowing your friends have not only given up hope but would be actually *relieved* if your body – headless or otherwise – were recovered?'

'We hadn't given up hope.'

'OK, Toby. But you'd've been relieved to find out what'd happened.'

'Frankly, yes. Disappearance is unbearable.'

'Especially for the one who's disappeared. But thanks for being frank. I'll do the same for you one day.'

'Well, Vinny, you obviously weren't erased from history. So what did happen?'

'It's always nice to know that you don't know everything. Seems DIA Mosul had independent investigations going on regarding some of our Turkish friends. Uncle Sam does not regard all Kurdish freedom fighters in the same light as the Turkish government. That is to say, friends, the war cannot be brought to a conclusion without Kurdish military support. The Turks thought that if they confined their obvious anti-Kurdish activities to their own side of the border, they might get away with some discreet tidying-up exercises on the other side, under Uncle Sam's nose. In this particular instance, this was, I'm happy – and alive – to say, a severe miscalculation.'

'Explain.'

'Seems Johnny Turk had it in mind to take out a high-up Kurdish representative in Kirkuk. The man in question had friends in high places, and the Kurdish authorities did not take kindly to Turks cherry-picking assassination targets from among their race on Iraqi soil. Especially when those very authorities had already declared their hostility to Kurdish terrorism in Turkey – plus they assisted in the defeat of PKK forces in northern Iraq in the nineties.

'So, one beautiful morning – yesterday to be exact – I was awoken by a disturbance upstairs in the free world. Special forces occupied what was described in the report as "an office of the Turkish army". They freed Vincent Zappa – humble operative of Uncle Sam – and arrested eleven Turkish officers and domestic personnel. The charge was plotting the assassination of a senior Kurdish politician. I think, Dr Toby, we can take it as read your friends Yazar and Yildiz were also in the firing line.'

Ashe raised his eyebrows.

'Which happy tale brings me to two significant revelations regarding Dr Toby Ashe's status in this part of the world. Sorry to be the bearer of bad news, Dr Toby, but there is now no question whatever that your Kurdish politicians have fled Iraq – pursued, I don't doubt, by Turkish intelligence. Anyhow, they're now way out of my remit. Sorry, bud! The buck just stopped.'

Ashe's heart sank. 'And the other significant revelation?'

'Now this is truly unfair, I grant you. But this is war, baby. Seems Ankara did not jump for joy when the US busted their butt in Suleymaniya. Apparently, Uncle Sam got it all wrong and well… pride is pride and national pride is something else. They've closed the border-crossing at Harbur.'

'Shit.'

'Just hit the fan. A little undiplomatic incident. Fuel and equipment supplies to the US up here are not getting through. This is inconvenient. And expensive. And it works. Turkey's little signal. They're pissed off. A line has been crossed and they're gonna want soothing. Seems a lot of Turkish voters don't trust Uncle Sam. According to Turkey, the US is soft on terrorism – except where its own interests are concerned. Can you believe that? And whose fucking interest is Turkey pursuing here – the international interest? Fuck! Do I hate politicians!'

'Our paymasters, Vinny.'

'Yeah. And aren't they supposed to be the servants of the people? Since when do the servants tell the lord what to do with his castle?'

'When they've taken it over?'

'You got it, Toby.'

'OK. Back to the point. You said the Turks have closed the border crossing at Harbur?'

'Right.'

'I can see this is an embarrassment all round.'

'Yeah! But look! There's some in the White House wonderin' why little Vinny Zappa was in the fuckin' hot house in the first place. "What's that?" they say, "A British intelligence operation? What's all that about?" Well, obviously Our Guy Vinny was just doin' his job – but who's this English guy chasing round northern

Iraq with Lawrence of Arabia here? Pardon your presence, Major. But they smell a rat.'

'Thanks a lot, Vinny. After all the tears we shed for you.'

'Sorry, Simon. You know I love ya – but these political guys never understand field priorities. It's one of those fuckin' tennis matches between Langley, the Pentagon, the White House, British SIS – and whichever national intelligence agency we've just rubbed up the wrong way.'

Vinny looked at Ashe. 'Anyhow, bud, seems you're the fall guy. Welcome to Shit City. Don't have to tell *me* it stinks.'

Ashe looked out of the window, watching Iraq float past him forever. Then he looked ahead, to the great city of Mosul, with its mosques, its murders and its magnificences – and saw it was for him the last station before an ignominious exit.

There would be no tearful Celia Johnson on the platform, no Rachmaninoff, just the bum's rush back to Blighty double quick.

Vinny patted him on the back. 'Sorry, Dr Toby. It's been great workin' with ya – keep in touch.'

'Never say goodbye, Vinny.'

All too soon the convoy was crossing the debris-strewn concrete bridge over the Tigris at Faisaliya, a few hundred metres from where Rozeh's parents had been murdered. Ashe pondered on what he could do now for Laila's 'Sister of the Hereafter'. This was war. Hearts got broken; things ended before their time; events ceased to make sense. People might claim innocence, but states sinned with impunity.

The convoy headed south through scenes of carnage. A suicide bomber had hit the police headquarters: there were roadblocks at the end of every street.

Passing slowly through lines of blast-proof concrete and hedgerows of razor wire, overlooked by snipers and lookout towers, the convoy rolled into the busy barracks.

As the Snatch drew to a halt in the parade ground, beneath the flagpole and its Stars and Stripes snapping against the clear blue sky, a pair of familiar faces strode out of the whitewashed admin office to greet the two Englishmen and their exhausted American source handler.

The men's welcome of Vincent Zappa was perfunctory. Zappa wrote them off as a couple of jerks and made his way to the canteen for a much needed beer.

'Bagot and Colquitt, I presume.'

'Dr Ashe. Back from his adventure.'

'What can I do for you?'

62

Bagot took the lead. 'Tony and I are most anxious you cease wasting department funds and join us in our vehicle for the short trip to Mosul aerodrome. Tony, get Dr Ashe's bags please.'

Richmond joined the men. 'Friends of yours, Toby?'

'They're from an escort agency called SIS.'

'Afternoon, chaps.'

'Major Richmond, isn't it?'

Richmond gripped Colquitt's hand like a vice; Colquitt winced. 'Now listen, you're to give Dr Ashe the very best treatment. He is a British hero. Get that? H. E. R. O.'

'I *can* spell.'

Richmond turned to Ashe. He blinked with a moist twinkle of fellow feeling. 'Cheer up, old friend. Things have a habit of—'

'Going pear-shaped?'

'Keep the faith.'

Colquitt butted in. 'Come on, Ashe. No time for niceties.'

'What about Vinny?'

'Never mind him. Zappa's in enough trouble as it is.'

Ashe was manoeuvred into the back of a Humvee troop carrier. It pulled out of the barracks and headed for the old aerodrome in the south of the city. Ashe stared at the metal floor, then looked up and faced Colquitt and Bagot. 'What's the charge?'

'Seems your interference with Turkish national security operations is not only an embarrassment to Her Majesty's Government, but was occasioned by no operational necessity we can possibly fathom.'

Colquitt chipped in. 'Heads will have to roll.'

The group got down from the Humvee and made their way to the control tower. There was a brief delay: an SAS detachment from Anbar Province was expected to arrive any minute for well-earned leave.

Colquitt and Bagot strode off to make calls and complete paperwork. Ashe squatted down and slumped back against a Coca Cola machine. He felt a hand on his shoulder.

'I hear you're leaving us, Tobbi. So I come here with Major Richmond and bring Rozeh to you.'

Behind Richmond stood Laila in smart jeans and a clean tee-shirt, her magnificent hair gathered up with a silver comb. Her eyes gazed at him through large, expensive glasses.

'One short flight to a British forces airport and Rozeh can claim asylum. Then you write to the ambassador and organise everything. This is her chance, Tobbi.'

Laila turned to the shy girl standing behind her. 'Here, Rozeh, this is Tobbi Ashe. He is a very good man from England. He makes sure you get your education.'

Rozeh nervously approached Ashe, who stood up. She extended her hand. He shook it. She slowly raised her sad eyes from the ground and met his own.

Ashe turned to his friend. 'What do you think?'

Richmond shrugged his shoulders. 'Not up to me. But since you want my opinion...'

Ashe read his face. It was a no-no. Anyhow, Ashe not only knew it was hopeless trying to appeal to the system, he also doubted the wisdom of the exercise in the first place. He hadn't promised Laila anything. She had presumed too much in all the excitement and heightened atmosphere of Lalish. 'It would've been better if the major here had stowed Rozeh aboard the plane.'

Colquitt came into the waiting area. 'What's all this then?

271

Farewell party? Hard to believe you've made so many friends, Ashe.'

Ashe decided to push Bagot and Colquitt as far as he could, regardless.

'I want to take this girl back with me.'

'Really?'

Colquitt dashed off to find Bagot.

Richmond looked apologetically at Laila. 'I feared this might happen, Your Highness. These two goons, Colquitt and Bagot, are actually here to escort Ashe out of the country.'

'Tobbi's a prisoner?'

'Not exactly a free agent.'

'Is this true, Tobbi?'

'Afraid so.'

'I speak to them.'

Bagot came huffing and puffing through the door.

'So, now you wish to compound your folly with a spot of illegal immigration.'

'It's important, Giles. This young girl, Rozeh. Her parents have been...' He looked at Rozeh. 'How's her English, Laila?'

'Very good.'

Ashe whispered into Bagot's ear. 'Murdered by terrorists in Mosul.'

'Dear oh dear. That's very sad. Do you have any more victims of the insurgency waiting to take the plane? We could fill it several times over with deserving cases. You really have left this a little on the late side.'

'Excuse me, sir.' Laila took Bagot's arm.

Bagot looked to Richmond. 'Who is this woman?'

Richmond cleared his throat. 'You're addressing Princess Laila of the Yezidi people.'

'This is outside of your professional remit, isn't it? Our orders are quite definite. Nothing here about illegal immigrants.' Bagot pointed to his departure authorisation papers.

'I'll take responsibility.'

Bagot laughed. 'You, Dr Ashe! *You*. I'm not sure responsibility and you travel in the same plane.'

'Now look here!' Richmond was getting annoyed. 'We're not asking you to do anything. Just turn a blind eye. This won't be the first time we've managed to save some very deserving cases! For goodness' sake, Bagot. Come off your high horse and do something worthwhile with your bloody life!'

'Listen, Major. You may think I'm deficient in humanity. But this sort of thing's got to stop. Last month we had some reporter from ITN bringing another deserving case with him back to Britain. And did he keep quiet about it? The thing got on the news. The prime minister's under a great deal of flak from the media about asylum seekers. He's promised a clampdown and a review. He's got to be very careful.'

'Look, Bagot, for Christ's sake, let Tony Blair look after his own interests – I'm sure he doesn't need your help.'

'You forget, Toby, that Tony and I serve the government of the day.'

Laila took his arms again, imploring him with tears. 'Please, sir. Let Tobbi take Rozeh on the plane. I've told her she's going to a great country where they care about real people. That is why you are in Iraq, is it not?'

Bagot looked to Colquitt. 'Is that why we're here, Tony?'

'Difficult to say, sir. Official policy was to rid the country of a dictator.'

'We *deliver* policy, Princess Laila, not invent it. I'm sorry. You'll have to try somewhere else. If Dr Ashe insists on letting this girl on the plane, we shall have to arrest him. Tony, get the bags. I think I see our jeep.'

Ashe exploded. 'You fucking bastard, Bagot! You little shit! Deliver policy, my arse! You just love the fucking power of it all!'

'And I love you too, Toby. You can calm down on the plane. Tony, the bags!'

Ashe looked helplessly at the princess and Rozeh and shook his head.

'Look, when I get back, I'll contact the ambassador. That *is* a promise. You can take it up with him while I try to bend his ear.'

'I'll second that, Your Highness. Don't give up hope.'

'I never give up hope, Major.' She looked at Ashe. 'There is something else you can do. I know you have the resources.'

'Go on.'

'Please, Tobbi, please find my brother Sinàn.'

'Your brother? Look, Laila, I'm not Father Christmas!'

'I know your heart, Tobbi.'

'My heart?'

'Please!'

'All right. Where do you think he might be?'

'He is in Europe. With the Baba Sheykh.'

'The who?'

'Baba Sheykh. We need them, Tobbi.'

'Ashe!' Colquitt bellowed from the door. 'Get a bloody move on!'

63

The flight from Las Vegas to New York had been hell.

It had been obvious to al-Qasr which of the other seven passengers was riding shotgun. Homeland Security insisted an armed man be present on all internal flights. This one had clearly been on one flight too many, like the Marlboro Man gone to seed. He kept fidgeting in his seat, tucking his nylon shirt beneath his fat stomach, getting up abruptly and walking around like a man caught short in a men's-room-free zone. What was more, he'd opted to sit across the aisle from al-Qasr. You'd have thought the guy had never seen an Hasidic Jew before.

Used to spying on others, al-Qasr felt acute distaste at being the object of another's interest. Whenever he'd looked across the aisle, the supposedly invisible guard had simply winked reassuringly, as if to say, 'That's all right son, Jews are safe on this flight.'

Al-Qasr's head was dizzy with nerves. He had no reserves of religious faith to draw on and nothing to calm him. Alcohol was restricted on Las Vegas–New York flights, it being reasoned that visitors departing Vegas had already had enough of everything. Why else would they go there?

At one point, the guard had leant over, slipped and grabbed al-Qasr's theatrical beard. The guard, sweating, had been profusely apologetic, then uttered the immortal question, 'Don't you guys like to get up and pray on these flights? You carry those... what are they called? Prophylactics?'

'Phylacteries?'

'Yeah. You like kiss them in the middle of the aisle. Seen it hundreds of times. You feel the need, sir, you just get right on up there and pray. Ain't no one's gonna stop you here, sir.'

'I prayed at the airport.'

'Sure is a good place to pray, sir. That's right. You'll be prayin' again at Kennedy?'

'God willing.'

The guard squinted. Something didn't sound quite right about that.

Now al-Qasr was standing in the departure lounge of New York Kennedy Airport, he would like to have prayed. But prayer had never made any sense to him. He could see it helped people, soothed them. But belief was the precipitate that made the chemistry work, and he had none.

If he believed in something, he'd be feeling guilty. Guilty for Fiona Normanton, guilty for that old bastard Lowenfeld – and for whoever else had turned up. He was proud of the booby-trapped body. It was mean, sure, but it showed creative flourish. It would give him credibility with his contacts. Soon he would be far from Judaeo-Christian sentimentality and back in a man's world. A few dead infidels would give him street cred.

But if he got caught – and, no question, he was aware of the risks – he knew it would be a lifetime in prison, hated by every inmate. He wouldn't last five minutes. There would be no flush of martyrdom for him.

He consoled himself with the thought that *his* sacrifice would be the greater one: greater than the average dumb martyr, tricked by false promises, manipulated by those who kept out of the firing line as long as possible.

Al-Qasr knew there would be no paradisal feast or maidens waiting for him. His only hope was that, some day, his people would understand what he'd done – maybe even why he'd done it. If they would not honour him, maybe they would remember his father. How could they have forgotten so quickly?

Standing in the packed lounge, surrounded by bright, stark lights and the strange, constant murmur he associated with being deep underwater, al-Qasr had never felt so alone.

And yet there was also excitement: a gathering rush of realisation that soon, very soon, his life's work would bear fruit. He took the thick-lensed glasses off, and squinted to focus on the departure board: Berlin Tegel, Lufthansa Flight 471 – twenty-two minutes to boarding.

He rubbed his moist fingers and looked up to the stainless-steel balcony above. *Who was that man with binoculars?* He was nudging his colleague. He was pointing down at al-Qasr. Something about the colleague looked familiar. Al-Qasr couldn't tell; he looked away. Al-Qasr prayed for a prayer: Hebrew, Arabic, Coptic, English – any damn thing. But nothing came – and they were still looking.

64

'Call through from Federal Agent Rice at New York Kennedy, sir.'

Beck took a deep swig of black coffee and picked up the phone in his darkened office at CIA Headquarters. 'Beck.'

'Sir, got a guy here dressed as a Jewish scholar.'

'Wha'd'ya mean, "got a guy"? You arrested him?'

'Sir, we read the notice you posted: "Suspicious looking Hasidic or Ashkenazi Jew". Raised quite a few eyebrows. It said "apprehend only on higher authority". That's why I'm calling, sir. The plane is sitting on the tarmac waiting for final clearance.'

'Destination?'

'Berlin. We've been trying to contact you for twenty-five minutes, sir.'

Beck bit his lip. Depressed at Leanne Gresham's murder, he'd had the phone off the hook, and had his cellphone off for an hour.

'What grounds have you got, Rice? Make it quick.'

'Guard on internal flight from Vegas reckoned suspect's conversation indicated Islam, not Jewish faith, sir.'

'Specifically?'

Rice paused, then coughed; it was a long shot. 'He said: "God willing".'

'In Arabic?'

'English, sir.'

As long shots went, this was stretching things. 'Checked the manifest?'

'Difficult, sir.'

278

'Why?'

'Happens there's a group of Talmudic scholars attending an academic conference in Berlin. Several members have similar names. Could be any one of them. Should we detain them all? Sir, we got less than a minute to put an agent on the plane.'

'Where'd the scholars come from?'

'Just a second, sir... Yuba City. California.'

'Yuba City? That's damn near Paradise!'

'That's not what I heard, sir.'

'One clever bastard... OK. Get a man on the plane. Do not apprehend. Repeat—'

'No need to repeat, sir.'

'We gotta know who he's meeting in Germany. Put a good man on the case.'

'All our men are good, sir.'

'Sure. Call me when the plane leaves – and don't let it go without our man!'

Al-Qasr shifted uncomfortably in his double-booked seat. He'd observed the commotion at the far end of the jumbo when the plane had reached the take-off runway. A late passenger? Unlikely to stop a plane at this point on an international flight, even for half a minute. Something was up.

Behind him, fifteen Talmudic scholars jabbered and joked with excitement and foreboding at the prospect of returning to the German part of Europe. Several had smiled warmly at al-Qasr, taking him for an associate. Al-Qasr had smiled in return.

This part of al-Qasr's plan was going perfectly. Having overheard the scholars' plans during a trip to Yuba City's public library, he had arranged to surreptitiously blend in with the group at Kennedy Airport. Hafiz had done a great job with the passport – like he always did. Practical problem? Contact Hafiz Razak. Man was a genius.

Al-Qasr peered over the edge of his *Washington Post* at the latecomer: a handsome young man in a dark business suit. Did he look just a little too fit for a man of the boardroom? Al-Qasr watched the man's eyes as he was directed to a seat at the front of the plane. The man carefully clocked the lines of passengers. Was he looking for his correct seat? The stewardess was offering him advice.

The red light went on, passengers fastened their seatbelts and said their prayers – some audibly. Al-Qasr had lost his interest in prayer. He glimpsed the newcomer at the front, casting his eyes around before he sat down. That man had a task – he was too calm by far for a man who, being late, would almost certainly have run through the terminal, held his breath through customs and should by now have been sweating with anxiety or at least sighing with relief.

The plane taxied into position. Then the engines' roar, the G-force and the shooting sensation of gravity-defying lift. The landing gear cranked into place, al-Qasr closed his eyes and thanked God he was leaving America, alive. If he wasn't arrested now, he figured he'd be safe until Germany.

Half an hour in and the plane was high above the eastern seaboard, heading towards Newfoundland. The passengers were settling down into movie watching, people watching, sleep, magazine reading, and music listening. The latecomer got up. He went to talk to the stewardess, then returned to his seat. What was that all about? Passenger manifest?

Al-Qasr looked around for the nearest bathroom. *Occupied*. He glanced down at the in-flight magazine. Small wisps of beard flecked the paper. Gingerly, he fingered his face. It was soaking with sweat.

The minutely applied beard, designed to look scruffy, was – like his plan – coming unstuck. The latecomer stood up again; he seemed to be counting.

Al-Qasr looked to the bathroom at the rear. Still occupied.

65

Unwilling to get up and walk about, al-Qasr pondered the agent's dilemma – if, that is, he was an agent. Best take it that he was. And the question for the agent was simple: which one of the Hasidic scholars was the odd man out?

Was the plan to arrest him on the plane, or wait till he got off? Had they not considered the possibility that he might have a bomb on the plane? If they approached him, he might set it off. *What were they thinking?*

The jumbo had become a prison. After an hour gazing out of the window at the clouds below, al-Qasr slipped to the bathroom to tidy up his beard. He had a terrifying thought: *what if one of the Jews behind him tried to strike up conversation in Yiddish or Hebrew?* Then he'd be sunk. He hurried back to his seat, gobbled down his in-flight meal, then pretended to go to sleep. Before long, al-Qasr was unconscious.

While al-Qasr slept, Agent Rice tried to figure out a way of finding which one of the Jews was the suspect. The flight manifest gave no obvious clues.

He couldn't simply go up to them and ask them who was a stranger. His orders had been straightforward: the suspect should be identified on board, if possible, but the suspect should not know he'd been targeted. Rice's best idea so far had been to brief the stewardess and ask her to tell him if anyone stood out. Long experience on transatlantic flights should have given her an intuitive edge – if she had any intuition to begin with. It was not as common a gift as many people assumed.

Before she did her inspection, Rice had asked her to first transmit the names of the group back to a number at Langley. By the time she was able to check on the men, half of them were asleep, hats over their eyes; she promised she'd return after a few hours. Meanwhile, Rice observed the group as best he could.

After two hours, the CIA had traced every name on the conference list and attempted to telephone friends, family and colleagues to check they were all expected to participate. The stewardess handed a note to Rice. 'Everyone kosher' read the message. Very funny, thought Rice. He was beginning to worry about his promotion prospects. She then whispered in his ear. 'That is, as far as they could tell. They couldn't get substantial traces on everyone.'

'Please underline the names with no absolute confirmation.'

The stewardess took the manifest and went back to the cockpit.

The jumbo was flying over the British Isles when al-Qasr awoke. He checked about him. The plane was relatively quiet. The seat next to him was still empty. Behind him, several members of the Talmudic party were still sleeping. The rest were reading copies of the Torah and various paperback versions of *midrashim* Bible commentaries. Al-Qasr wished he'd had the presence of mind to bring some Hebrew literature. It was an oversight: a bad one. He inadvertently caught the eye of the tired stewardess. He'd not meant to. The girl came towards him. At that moment, the agent turned round to see where she was going.

'Is everything all right, Mr…?'

'Huh?'

'Is everything all right? You're Mr…?'

'Weintraub. Mr Weintraub. Everything's fine, Miss. Really.'

'Sorry, sir, I thought you were trying to attract my attention.'

'No, no. I've just been asleep.'

'What are you doing in Berlin, Mr Weintraub?'

'Conference. On the Talmud. Scholarship.'

'That's fascinating. I always wanted to be a scholar.'

'Oh yes?'

'Yeah. But I wanted to get out of my folks' place and travel. Didn't like the homework, I guess.'

'I see.'

'Well, you have yourself a nice time.'

The stewardess looked over at the man sitting behind al-Qasr. 'Look after your friend here, sir. He's obviously very intelligent.'

'Oh, he's not my friend.'

'Really? Oh, excuse me, sir. I thought—'

Al-Qasr butted in. 'He means we don't know each other very well. But we have much in common, don't we?'

The man behind nodded in a serious fashion, and pointed to his Holy Book.

'Well, maybe you guys can become friends at the conference.'

Al-Qasr's eyes closed. That was all he needed: an invitation to talk.

The stewardess went back to the front of the plane. Several men behind al-Qasr started to look at him, curious to know who the extra man among them was.

Al-Qasr smiled weakly, excused himself and made his way quickly to the bathroom and locked the door. He reckoned there were maybe ninety minutes left before they landed.

The stewardess went straight back to Agent Rice. She squatted down out of sight in front of him. 'I don't know for definite, but there's something curious about the Hasidic gentleman who's currently in the bathroom on the right at the back of the compartment.'

'OK, good work. Did you catch his name?'

'Mr Weintraub.'

'Weintraub, you say? You've underlined his name – one of four unconfirmed. Can you get that name back to the number I gave you? Ask them to check again.'

'OK.'

Rice's promotion prospects went up again. His plan was working.

Al-Qasr felt the noose tightening. They were on to him. The guy at the front – he knew. And who else? If they didn't take him on the plane, it was because they did not want to. But would they take him in Berlin? Al-Qasr half-convinced himself they would. Once they could get him away from the other passengers. There'd be a welcoming committee at Berlin all right.

Damn! If only he could get onto his laptop and tune in to Agency e-traffic. But computer use had been expressly prohibited on this flight. He was still free, at least – whatever that meant. Or rather, he was alive. That's what mattered. That was as much freedom as most people ever got – himself included. If he could shake them at Tegel... It was a big if. So what! Genetics had taught him that 'if' meant everything. 'If' was change, and change... was hope.

Al-Qasr cursed his luck. Had everything gone to plan, he'd have been a different man by now – not a Jew skulking in a shit-house. Maybe there was still time. It all depended on one fact of nature – as true for Jews as it was for Christians, Muslims, pagans, Buddhists, Hindus, Zoroastrians, or atheists like him.

'Ten minutes to landing. Return to your seats.'

Al-Qasr pulled his trousers up and vacated the WC. The stewardess tried to look disinterested.

As he fell heavily into his seat, Al-Qasr felt a hand on his shoulder. 'You OK? You been away a long time. Luckily there's more than one men's room on this plane or we'd all be in the shit!'

Al-Qasr turned to the scholar and made the gesture of putting his fingers down his throat. The man behind thrust a sick-bag between the headrests.

Al-Qasr certainly looked pale enough to be airsick. What wouldn't he do for a comforting female arm around him? The sick-bag was a godsend. He buried his face in it.

The man behind patted him on the back. 'You hang with us when we get to the airport.'

Making a passable imitation of retching, al-Qasr nodded and put his thumb up. Maybe his luck had changed.

After what seemed an eternity with his mouth stuck in the bag, al-Qasr jerked forwards, crushing his hat into the folded table in front of him as the tyres gripped European tarmac. He sat up, leant backwards, and closed his eyes, dreaming of the days when he could have smoked his worries away.

Soon the passengers up front began filing off the plane, while the others congregated in the aisles as anxious travellers stalled over assembling their bags and cases.

Al-Qasr waited for the group behind him to move in front. Then he eased his way to his feet, reached for his blue canvas holdall in the overhead compartment and nudged his way up to the rear of the party. His new friend asked him if he felt any better; al-Qasr shook his head.

Step by leaden step, the passengers shuffled their way forwards. Al-Qasr felt the weight of the stewardess's eyes upon him. Where the hell was the agent? Maybe he hadn't been an agent after all! Maybe it was just paranoia and lack of sleep. Of course not. The agent was waiting for him, off the plane – waiting with his colleagues. It would be quick. Was it a trap? Maybe he could cut and run now.

No. Running would be pointless. He must hold his nerve. What would his father have done? Pointless to think about it. His father would never have been so stupid as to land himself in this mess. That's it: deal with it. Just fucking deal with it.

Have faith. Faith? Faith in what? Faith in the plan! Faith in science. Faith in Sami al-Qasr. Destiny. No point having faith in destiny. Destiny was destiny. You couldn't change it. Al-Qasr shrugged his shoulders. Accept. Submit.

Then he heard the stewardess. She called someone. 'Sir! Mr Rice!'

So that was the bastard's name. Rice.

Rice sprang out of the seat he'd been curled in; al-Qasr looked away.

'Message for you, sir. Urgent.'

Rice made his way to the cockpit.

Shit! This was it.

66

Al-Qasr stepped out of the jumbo onto the comforting rubber floor of the internal ramp. The air felt cool and fresh. No welcoming party. No guns. No shit. So what was Rice doing? Arranging something for immigration?

Rice emerged from the cockpit. He whispered to the stewardess, 'That's our man all right.'

Rice had just heard there were two Sol Weintraubs and one of them was dead: cold as stone in a San Francisco apartment. Rice ran off the plane, heading for baggage collection and the final immigration checkpoint. He wasn't alone. Beck had organised agents and soldiers at passport control and customs. All exits were being watched, and marksmen were in position around the airport. It was just a question of putting a tracer into his luggage and inside the binding of his passport.

Al-Qasr kept tight with the delegation, dazzled by the glare from the bright yellow-and-white signs that streamed around the terminal. The group passed the first men's room. Nobody stopped to go in. Al-Qasr's teeth began to grind. *What's wrong with these fuckers? Don't they use the john?*

Rice ran to the end of the long arrivals corridor. He could see the unmistakable posse of black-coated men. Where was the suspect? Was that him at the back? It was him all right. Rice hung back.

Al-Qasr saw the sign to the first security passport check. Security demanded an extra check before baggage collection. Staggering the influx gave the authorities more time; too much rush compromised judgement. The group passed a second men's room. *Shit!* He was going to have to show his passport.

'Hey! We're a group! I can collect all the passports.'

'Wait!' The green-uniformed official was not going to be rushed by the enthusiastic leader of the group. 'Wait in single file behind the yellow line, sir. You will be called forward one by one.'

Al-Qasr's blood turned to acid. His body was burning; his head was exploding in hideous slow motion.

'After you are called forward, present your passports. Don't speak unless I ask a question. When forward, stand behind the white line. Don't move until instructed.'

Al-Qasr waited. One scholar after another went forwards. Having to line up before German officials was fostering a dark – even angry – vibe. The hard-nosed official tried to look unconcerned, but he could sense the tension. Say something dumb like 'I'm only following orders', and there would be a bloody riot. He took his time. This allowed time for Rice's colleagues, watching from behind one-way glass, to pick out and photograph the suspect.

The official studied the contours of the faces, asked several to remove their glasses. Al-Qasr could now feel the presence of Rice behind him. Right behind him. Sami felt Rice's breath on his neck. Rice, suspecting he was too close, edged back.

'You! Next! Passport please. Name?'

'Weintraub.'

The controller looked hard at him.

'Enjoy your stay in Berlin, Herr Weintraub.'

Al-Qasr found himself walking forwards. The rest of the Jewish group had hurried down an escalator to the baggage reclaim area. He followed them. Behind him: Rice. All six-feet-four of him. The college hunk.

Lady Luck smiled again. The baggage transfer was subject to the usual delay. This gave an opportunity for the men from Yuba City to finally take a leak in the men's room.

288

Rice watched carefully as the bustling, talkative group hunched into the WC. He followed them. He in turn was followed by another crowd from another plane. The men's room was packed.

A chance. Al-Qasr made straight for a toilet cubicle, opened his bag, pulled off his overcoat, crushed his hat, ripped off his tie, unclipped the wig, stuffed the specs into the bag, and reached for the theatrical hair-removing lotion. While he slapped it on, he kicked off his shoes with his heels. These too were stuffed in his bag, next to his laptop. The lotion was stinging his face. He could hear the voices of the Jewish group congregating outside, waiting for their friends. Someone shouted round the men's room door. 'Baggage is coming through!'

Al-Qasr dipped his hands in the toilet bowl and applied the water to his face. He wiped it off quickly with toilet paper and ran a comb through his hair. He then pulled out a light cotton zip-up jacket, with a fresh passport in its inner pocket, slipped on a pair of sneakers, grabbed the bag, flushed the toilet and walked out of the men's room, leaving Rice still standing at the urinal.

Al-Qasr congratulated himself as he approached the customs passage. Double-booking as a Turkish businessman visiting family in Berlin was a master-stroke, thanks to Hafiz Razak's forgery and delivery skills. Al-Qasr's new name would almost certainly be on the passenger manifest sent through to Berlin, even though Rizgo Keser, a Kurd from Turkey's Batman Province, had 'missed' the flight.

He walked briskly through customs. All the staff had been told to keep a close eye on the Hasidic Jews from the New York flight. Lucky again.

Rice, meanwhile, was still waiting for his suspect to come out of the toilet cubicles. He had not seen which one al-Qasr had gone into, and the men's room had been packed ever since. His stomach started to churn. Maybe he'd missed him. *Fuck it! The bastard had somehow hidden himself among the group.* Rice dashed into the baggage hall. Most of the Jews had picked up their luggage and were approaching the customs area. He would have to delay them as a group.

Rice ran to the customs office and gestured they would have to detain the group as a whole, at least until he and his men had got a fix on al-Qasr.

Meanwhile, al-Qasr retrieved his passport from a pleasant immigration officer and headed for the airport exit. As Rizgo Keser, al-Qasr had achieved the impossible: he had flown invisibly across the Atlantic.

Al-Qasr hailed a taxi.

'Hamburg.'

The elderly taxi driver turned round. 'Sir, that's a four-hour drive.'

'And that's 200 euros.' Al-Qasr stuffed the cash into the driver's hand. 'I'm late for a meeting.'

The driver didn't argue: it was his lucky day too.

Al-Qasr smiled to himself. It would be at least eight hours before the taxi returned to Berlin. The security men would have a long wait.

He'd done it.

67

Ashe rolled noisily into the tidy village of Cudbury after a speedy drive through Berkshire's Lambourn Valley. Karla Lindars stood outside her home, The Old Forge, with a sponge in her hand.

'Do turn that engine off, Toby! Goodness, what a sound! You'll frighten the ducks!'

'Karla!'

'You may kiss me, darling, but I'm covered in muck.'

Karla's legs were encased in blue jeans, her slim torso barely covered by a short black woollen top, with black bra straps wrapping her shoulder blades. Her perfume was exquisite and her blue eyes glittered like a sun-kissed fjord. Even in household fatigues, Karla Lindars looked stunning.

She eyed Ashe's car. 'Haven't I seen this somewhere before?'

'Archdeacon's funeral. Saab 9-3.'

'Convertible too. Hmm... Rosso Bologna.'

'Painted specially.'

'Nice. Engine?'

'2.8. V6 Turbo.'

'I prefer it to the Maserati. Come inside.'

Karla placed a pot of coffee on the conservatory table. Ashe pulled out a letter from his jacket and passed it to her. Her sharp eyes took it in with gathering enthusiasm.

'Happy now, young man?'

'Hard to take in, isn't it? They've given me the whole department!'

'I suppose you won't talk to me now you're my boss.'

'You're my right arm, Karla. Now I can rid myself of impedimenta.'

'If you mean Messrs Colquitt and Bagot, Toby, I believe they've been transferred.'

'My God, things move fast! I wonder... You don't know a man called Crayke, do you?'

'My dear, nobody *knows* Crayke.'

Within the hour, Ashe had his foot down and was heading for Cranfield University's campus at Shrivenham, near Swindon, on the Wiltshire–Oxfordshire border.

Cranfield University introduced academic experts to officers of the armed forces. The Shrivenham campus served as the Royal Military College of Science, a leading world centre for research into disaster management, military vehicles, guns, ammunition systems, explosives, chemistry, communications, missile-control systems, solar energy and robotics.

Toby Ashe was given a small office in the elegant brick lecture-room wing of the establishment. He had already appointed Karla as his personal secretary, on the condition he could stay at her place when in the vicinity. Karla accepted, on condition he provide champagne and flowers on every occasion.

A lecture was in progress in Room 7. Lieutenant Commander Adrian Parsons was giving a talk on defending London from terror cells when Ashe gingerly eased the door open. Ashe caught Parsons' eagle eye as he tiptoed along the back of the lecture hall to the exit. Parsons nodded slightly at the rather Bohemian-looking figure at the back, without interrupting the flow of his troubling presentation.

Once through the exit, Ashe came to a plain white corridor, at the end of which was a double set of fireproof oak doors. A new card-swipe mechanism and a small pinewood plaque were fixed to the wall alongside. On the plaque was written 'B5(b)'.

Ashe swiped his security card and the doors clicked open.

The office was bare but for a plush black leather seat and a fit-for-purpose desk. Ashe picked up the phone. There was a dial tone. There were also three buttons for different lines: internal, domestic, and security (red of course). The walls were white; there was no window. An adjoining area, suitable for a secretary, enjoyed one high window: fine for ventilation, but poor for daydreaming.

68

A tape-recorded muezzin echoed about the centre of Istanbul, summoning the faithful to evening prayers. Aslan released his rear-window button and called out a greeting to the corner street seller. '*Merhaba!*'

The green-shirted surly young street seller noticed Aslan's suit and powerful car, and addressed him with the respectful honorific. '*Bey Effendi?*'

'*Simit!*'

'*Ayran?*'

'Ali!'

Ali nodded and Aslan put up two fingers. The seller poured the drinks from a large aluminium jug. Behind him, a lady leant out of her third-floor apartment window and let down a basket on the end of a rope to be filled by a girl from the corner bakery.

'*Iyigünler!*'

'*Salam Alukim!*'

Aslan passed a sesame-seeded bread roll and a yoghurt drink to Ali in the front.

'Hear what he said, Ali?'

'What's that?'

'The street seller. When I said "Goodbye", he said "*Salam Alukim*". You can't move for fundies these days!'

'May not be fundamentalist, sir. Just old-fashioned.'

'Sure, Ali. He's very careful to say "*Bey Effendi*" when he sees the car, but the look in his eye tells you everything.'

'What does it tell you, sir?'

'It shows, young corporal, this arsehole wants God to avenge his poverty.'

'And give him your car.'

'*My* car, Ali? Goes with the job. Maybe one day it'll be *me* selling *simit* on street corners! No, my friend, it's not the car he wants. It's the *country*.'

Aslan's personal mobile rang. 'Aslan here… Didn't I make it clear? *Never* call me on this line without notice.'

Ashe, taken aback, stared at the white walls of the Shrivenham office. 'Forgive me, Mahmut. But I expect your people know by now I've been on the trail of Yazar and Yildiz.'

'What can I do for you, Dr Ashe? NATO, wasn't it?'

'Are you not free to talk?'

'Oh yes, I'm free.'

'Yildiz and Yazar got away. We were too late.'

'Of course, Dr Ashe.'

'Why d'you say that?'

'Because I'm on my way to arrest them right now. Goodbye.'

69

Karla was lying on her back in the small pool. Ashe's trousers were rolled up to the knee and his tired feet dangled in the moon-kissed water.

'It's still bothering me, Karla.'

'Let's hear it.'

'My call to Aslan. He was so... so completely different to the man I met at the Hemlock.'

'I expect he wanted something from you then. Besides, you caught him while he was busy. You don't know who was with him. He was probably annoyed about something.'

'Me, probably. I forgot about his phone protocol.'

'Might not have been you.'

'He was *so* dismissive, Karla. You'd think... well you'd think that if he *was* about to arrest Yildiz and Yazar, he'd want to hear anything I had on them. I don't understand his attitude at all. Makes a complete nonsense of my time in Iraq.'

'Crayke obviously didn't think so.'

'If it *was* Crayke who arranged my promotion... You don't think that Tower bombing has really messed my head up, do you?'

'No, but it's been a shock for everyone. We can't even assemble ODDBALLS again until we know how the bomber discovered our meeting place.'

'Maybe my memory's been affected. Something's been bothering me.'

'So you said.'

'And I can't quite put it together.'

'Keep trying.'

'By the way, did you send that dispatch off to Mick Curzon today?'

'Your erudite plea for Rozeh will be on the ambassador's desk in Baghdad very soon, Toby.'

'I suppose that's *something*... But what I can do about the princess's other requests, I've no idea. She must think I've got spies everywhere!'

'Haven't you?'

Ashe laughed, then gazed up into the night sky. He thought of spy satellites looking down over Europe. Could they pick out Laila's brother? And the other fellow, the one her brother was supposed to be with... *What was his name? Baba something...* *Baba...* 'Oh! What *was* his name? *Baba...*'

'... the elephant?'

'BABA SHEYKH! Baba bloody Sheykh!'

Karla screamed as Ashe's legs splashed excitedly, kicking water into her eyes. 'Thank you very much!'

'Baba Sheykh! I knew I'd seen it before!'

Ashe padded his wet feet into Karla's house and dashed upstairs to the spare bedroom. Pulling open his briefcase, he dived into the Aslan file. There was Aslan's account of Turco-Kurdish politics, and there – his fingers gripped the sheets – was what he was looking for: the list of visitors to the Kartal Masonic Lodge the night of the bombing.

Yildiz and Yazar were on the list, their names heavily under-lined by Aslan. And, further down the list, obscured among obscure names: 'Baba Sheykh'. Before, the name had just looked like another New Age guru or whirling dervish on the Istanbul alternative philosophy scene. Guided by Aslan's emphases, Ashe had had no reason to pay the name particular attention. But there it was. It had something to do with Laila and her brother. And this Baba Sheykh was connected to the Kartal Lodge bombing. For was it not Aslan who had insisted the Lodge bombing was linked to the Tower bombing?

Aslan…

Ashe's mind was in turmoil.

A voice was calling him from downstairs. 'Toby! Call for you!'

Head buzzing, Ashe raced down and seized the mobile from the dripping Karla. She gave him a filthy look.

'Ashe speaking.'

'Pardon me for my rudeness today, Tobbi.'

'My… my fault entirely, Mahmut. Is this a secure line?'

'Of course. And you are taking me down a very thin line, Tobbi. What's your problem?'

'Did you arrest Yildiz and Yazar?'

'Internal Turkish matter, you understand. I'm under constraint of course. Should anything emerge of interest to your government, it's possible we can discuss the matter further.'

'Colonel, do you remember the list?'

'List, Dr Ashe?'

'The list you sent me. Yildiz and Yazar were invited to the Lodge. You underlined their names.'

'Did I?'

'There was another figure. One I never noticed.'

'Is that so?'

'Baba Sheykh.'

The phone crackled. 'Well… nothing in our game is obvious, Dr Ashe. I cannot recall that name.'

Aslan's manner seemed cold again. 'Is everything all right, Colonel?'

'Oh yes. Everything's fine. So what is your request? Interrogation of the Kurdish politicians has hardly begun.'

'Can you speak to the Lodge secretary in Kartal again? I'd like to know what this Baba Sheykh was doing at the Lodge the night of the bombing.'

'I see. I see… Don't make an official request, Tobbi. Leave it with me. I'm sure it's all perfectly innocent. I must go now. I'm a busy man. Goodbye, Dr Ashe.'

70

Dear Dr Ashe,

With respect to your enquiry concerning the incident at the Masonic Lodge, Kartal District. Further enquiries with the secretary of the Lodge show that the person you referred to did not attend the Lodge as a guest on the evening concerned, and is therefore irrelevant to enquiries.

For your further information, the invitation from the Lodge was issued in response to an enquiry from a man described as 'a Kurdish doctor of medicine' and known to a member of the Masonic Lodge. It was the belief of this doctor that the person who did not attend possessed knowledge concerning the origins of Freemasonry in the East. The Lodge was looking forward to an historical talk from the guest, a normal occurrence at Lodge meetings in Turkey. However, the talk did not take place, on account of the reason given above. Turkish authorities find no reason to investigate this matter further and are not authorised to provide additional assistance regarding internal Turkish affairs.

The letter was not signed, but the postmark was Ankara – the seat of the Turkish government. Since his journey with Jolo, Toby knew that a Sheykh was a Yezidi spiritual leader – and 'Baba' meant 'father', so he guessed this Baba Sheykh must be important. But that didn't explain why he was invited to the Lodge in the first place – or why he had then not turned up. And who was the Kurdish doctor?

‘Call for you on red, Toby.’

‘Who is it, Karla?’

‘It’s me, Dr Ashe.’ The deep, burnished timbre and tobacco-rasped tones could belong to only one man: Ranald Crayke. ‘Settling in all right, Ashe? I hear you don’t care too much for your new facility.’

‘A few pictures on the wall and it’ll be like home.’

‘Not meant to be like home, Ashe. I read a most illuminating report from Major Richmond. You did the service credit. And paid your office dues. Value it.’

‘Thank you very much, sir.’

‘No, Ashe. Thank *you*. Men of your calibre make my job not only possible, but infinitely worthwhile. How did you like the princess?’

‘Laila, sir?’

‘I dare say you will be on first-name terms with her. I should never have dared.’

‘You know her, sir?’

‘A most remarkable family, Ashe. The Yezidis are a remarkable people. I’ve been studying the Yezidi religion for many years. Did you know Lady Drower?’

‘Afraid not, sir.’

‘Very special lady, Lady Drower. You were following in her footsteps. Ethel Stefana Drower went to Lalish with a British officer in 1940. Dark times for civilisation. She came back to London and wrote a book about her experience. The British officer happened to be my father. I was a very young man when Lady Drower’s book first appeared on my desk. Soon it will be landing on yours. I’m also sending you some of my own personal papers – the product of many years’ research in the Near East. You will see soon enough how they chime with your investigations. Show them to nobody. Discuss them with nobody.’

‘Nobody, sir.’

'Nobody, Ashe. Not even me. At least for the time being. But cheer up! It's not going to be all reading. There are people you are going to meet. Old friends of mine.'

'Right, sir.'

'I have waited a long time for one such as you, Ashe. I don't intend to let you waste yourself on futile investigations. Or, for that matter, futile board meetings or so-called team-work, which all too often means less-work. Mrs Lindars may deputise for you. And by the way, Ashe, you will be interested to know that Hafiz Razak is once more on the run.'

'What happ—'

'Another suicide attack. With extras. They hit the US interrogation centre in Mosul. Messy business. Security's busted. Razak must be extremely valuable to our enemies for them to save him from interrogation like that. At least the Americans can't blame Major Richmond.'

'And all that work!'

'Not entirely wasted, Ashe. I believe Razak was able to impart something to Richmond and yourself that is unknown to our American friends. I trust you may find it useful in a friendly exchange with our cousins Stateside, for they surely know things that we do not. And we should not deny one another the things we need, should we? Good luck!'

Ashe stared at the blank notepaper in front of him. His pencil was sharp, but he had written nothing. When Ranald Crayke was speaking, you listened.

71

Thanks to Hafiz Razak's forgery skills, Sami al-Qasr was now Serif Okse, a Kurdish migrant worker from southeastern Turkey. He had shaved his head completely, wore thick plastic glasses and displayed a gold wedding ring. His base was an apartment in Antonistrasse, a steep hill that ran from the port and fish market right up to the Hein-Köllisch-Platz in the St Pauli district of Hamburg.

Al-Qasr sat down on a bench opposite the Babylon bar and lit a cigarette. He had a hunch that chance visits to the square, repeated randomly, might secure him a first glimpse of his prey. This time it had been a washout. He got up, shook his legs, and walked briskly round the sunlit square to a corner newsagent. He fumbled in his blue zip-up cotton jacket for the requisite money, bought a packet of Marlboro and a Turkish newspaper, then slipped into the Teufel Café for breakfast. He had just enough German and more than adequate English to make himself comfortable in the trendy bar; his escape from the Americans on the transatlantic flight had made him feel big again.

Al-Qasr had no doubt that the Baba Sheykh was somewhere in the city; he had a spy.

Cemal Goksel was a thirty-two-year-old Kurd who had worked as a border guard on Iraq's northeastern border with Iran. Unfortunately for Goksel, a large part of his family lived on the Iranian side of the border. It was short work for members of Ansar al-Sunna operating in the hills to find his family and threaten Goksel into cooperating with the insurgency. The

72

Lichfield

It was raining; autumn was in the air, crisp and moist by turns.
The elegiac sweetness of Richard Strauss's *Four Last Songs* filled
Toby Ashe's warm sitting room.

Scattered around the floor were sheets of paper covered in
large felt-penned words:

SETH

THOTH/HERMES

ABRAHAM

BRAHMIN

RA

BRAHMA

SHIVA

ARYAN

SERPENT

PILLARS

TOWER OF BABEL

MITHANNI

CHALDAEANS

KURDS

URARTU

UR

YEZIDIS

The results of a lifetime's research lay before Ashe's eyes: piles of Crayke's now yellow-edged papers occupied the floor. Some of the typed and handwritten notes dated back to the Second World War. The most recent additions had been written in the last few years. For Ashe, every page was a source of fascination.

Crayke's neat hand had embraced the most obscure textual resources, from the manuscripts of Arabic libraries in Istanbul and the Yemen to the private collections of maharajahs. The academic and private libraries of Europe and America had been thoroughly raked for anything that might sate Crayke's infinitely patient curiosity.

For the last few hours Ashe had been ploughing through acres of notes made by Crayke during a trip to Sri Lanka in the fifties. As far as Ashe could tell, Crayke had gone there to visit the island's many shrines dedicated to Shiva and the Shiva-lingam, the god's phallic symbol. As in India, it seemed that in Sri Lanka the Shiva-lingam was particularly important to Hindu women who were either praying for fertility or giving thanks for it.

Ashe already knew that Shiva, the Destroyer, was one of the Hindu Trinity, alongside Brahma, the Creator, and Vishnu, the Preserver. He was aware that Shiva had three eyes – the moon, the earth, and the sun, and that his third eye was always open. But Ashe was intrigued to learn that Shiva had close correlations with the Canaanite and Syrian god Ba'al, as well as to the Roman Saturn, the Phoenician El, the Greek Typhon, and the Egyptian Seth.

'Seth', it transpired, was Sanskrit for 'white', and Shiva rode a white bull. The white seemed related to the 'sour milk sea' from which, according to the Hindu *Vedas*, Creation emerged. The Yezidis called Creation's first beginning 'the pearl'.

Sometimes Shiva was depicted covered entirely in serpents. The word 'semen' came readily to Ashe's mind – the elixir of life scattered the world over. And he was often represented by a phallus: the Shiva-lingam. He was the father of the nations, and

his colours were white, black, red and yellow. He was the patron deity of esotericists, occultists, the creator and saviour of spiritual man.

Where did all this fit into his investigation? Or was the investigation supposed to fit into all of this? Ashe stared at the words surrounding him. If Crayke already knew how all this tied together, why was he wasting Ashe's time?

The phone rang.

'I want to speak to—'

'Laila!'

'Of course it's Laila, Tobbi. I'm in Cairo, with relatives. What of the Baba Sheykh – and my brother?'

'Your Baba Sheykh was probably in Istanbul in March. Perhaps with a doctor.'

'Sinàn is a doctor.'

'That helps. Any idea why they were in Istanbul?'

A pause. Laila seemed uncomfortable with the question.

'Laila, are you there?'

'I think I know. It was about Freemasonry and our faith. Baba wanted the world to know about us. But they cannot be in Istanbul now.'

'Why?'

'There is a Yezidi community in Germany. Near Giessen. Baba and my brother have visited recently. I think they are in Germany still, Tobbi. And in great danger.'

'Was anyone trying to hurt your brother and Baba Sheykh in Istanbul?'

'I cannot say. Please look after yourself. Please find them!'

'Laila, you know I'll do everything I can. But you need to tell me more about the Baba Sheykh so I can understand what danger he might face.'

The line crackled for a few seconds and Laila's voice emerged once more.

'The Baba Sheykh is like one of your saints. Like them, he is sworn to follow a path. He is *Ekhityare Mergehe*.'

'Which means?'

'It means "Old Man of the Sanctuary". "*Baba*" means "Father", Toby. He is father of the sheykhs. He must belong to the Fekhr el-Dîn branch of the Shemsani – the oldest clan of Yezidi sheykhs. The Baba Shekyh may not marry anyone except a member of this clan – and his son follows him. This is always the tradition. God be with you, Tobbi.'

Into the void of incomprehension crept a single word. Rising from within Ashe's brain, it spread itself over his consciousness like the tail of a glorious mythical bird.

The word was ENDOGAMY.

Endogamy. The Shemsani sheykhs were endogamous. That was the key Ashe had been waiting for: the key to understanding Crayke's long quest.

73

Oxford

Having temporarily swapped his desert fatigues for dark, worn tweeds and a moss-green tie, Crayke puffed on his glowing pipe. Beneath a halo of brown-grey cloud, his taut face and gnarled throat blended with the grained panels behind them. Even the hairless dome of his head had an oaken feel, like a barrel of mysterious rum or the rounded knob of a curious, graven wand.

With Crayke occupying one of its nooks, The Eagle and Child pub on St Giles had the air of its pre-war glory days, when C. S. Lewis, J. R. R. Tolkien and Charles Williams would convene there for beer and talk of the fictional and the mystical.

'Endogamy, sir.'

'Marriage restricted to within a family or clan. A formal means of genetic reincarnation. Find the subject especially interesting, Ashe?'

'I do, sir.'

Crayke closed his eyes. His mind seemed to be ascending to the smoke-cloud above.

'I'm not asleep, Ashe. I am visualising what you are going to say to me. You are going to refer to the pharaohs, how they preferred to marry inside their family, notwithstanding some attendant misfortunes in the form of simpletons. You are going to say something about the protection of a certain race. A certain race of human beings.'

Ashe shook his head. 'How the hell do you do that?'

'It's a gift, in the first instance. Then one can work on it – train it, if you will. Please continue the discourse – and do stop to drink occasionally. There's nothing worse than coming to the end of a point, only to find one's glass is still full. A pint per point is a sound rule of thumb.'

'Have you ever read *The Three Steles of Seth*?'

Crayke's eyes cracked open. 'Promising title.'

'It's a book that was discovered in Upper Egypt.'

'Ah yes. The so-called Nag Hammadi Library. Christian and non-Christian Gnostic writings. Most of them previously unknown before their discovery in 1945.'

'The book was written by a group who called themselves "Sethians".'

'They might not have called themselves that, Ashe! Were they not known by their enemies as "Ophites", or serpent worshippers? Fascinating things, snakes.'

'They called themselves the "immoveable race".'

'Why was that, Ashe?'

'Well, sir, they reckoned that an original divine knowledge was entrusted to Seth, Adam's new son, born after Cain murdered Abel. Seth's genetic line went on. It was preserved in Noah's family – particularly in the case of Abraham. He had the secret knowledge of God.'

'A fine tale. The Ark *could* be a kind of womb, couldn't it? The preserver of a secret. Didn't the Yezidis have a story about a leak in the Ark being blocked by the appearance of a serpent, coiling itself into the hole, and allowing the Ark to roll on to new heights? Mount Judi wasn't it? In the kingdom of Ararat – or, more properly, Urartu.'

'Are you sure you need me to—'

'Don't be so egotistical, man! We need one another's minds! Go on!'

Ashe drank deeply from his pint. 'So the Sethians decided that Jesus was an incarnation of the original Seth. Seth was the progenitor of divine knowledge.'

'Was not Seth also credited with knowledge of science?'

'He was, sir, as were several other persons, gods or groups. They all seem to have had something to do with a special aristocratic tradition, which was later called "Aryan".'

'"Aryan" is Sanskrit for "high-born", an aristocratic people. That's all it means.'

'Not to everyone, sir. Wasn't Abraham an Aryan?'

'You've been reading my notes, Ashe. Good. What did you learn?'

'Abraham came from "Ur of the Chaldees". That is, "Urartu", the biblical Ararat, where Noah's Ark rested in the Bible story.'

'And what people did Abraham come from?'

'Well, according to your work, sir, all that stuff about Abraham being a wandering shepherd is romantic rubbish.'

'Certainly. Abraham was a Mithanni prince, around 1450 BC. I presume you read Flavio Barbiero's paper on the subject? I included it with my notes.'

'It's a brilliant paper, sir. Barbiero shows that the Mithannis were "Aryans". Abraham's father, Tareh, had been at war with Pharaoh Thutmosis IV, and lost. So, as the royal son, Abraham was obliged to settle close to the Egyptian border in the south, the so-called "promised land", as insurance against further rebellion. That explains Abraham having a private army, and why he – and especially his wife Sarai – had close relations with the pharaoh's court. It explains how his descendants came to see themselves as being in captivity in Egypt – and why their faith was different.'

'Right. They had a tradition that they came from special stock.'

'And the family carried the old Mesopotamian stories with them. They took the stories into Egypt and out again. And Abraham probably worshipped a god whose equivalent in Egypt was Seth, the old god of sun and moon, of night and day, whose image was the extraordinary desert hare. This mighty Seth was later demoted by the Egyptians into a kind of wicked uncle, a usurping Richard III-type, because he'd been worshipped by hated foreigners. Later, Seth becomes a model for the Devil, and the desert hare's ears were turned into horns.'

'Good, Ashe. Go on.'

'Well, you then get all these traditions where the Egyptian god of science, Thoth, the Graeco-Egyptian mastermind, Hermes, and the Hebrew Seth are all identified. Stories like the pillars of Seth preserving all the wisdom of the arts and sciences. You get that in old Freemasonry.'

'And?'

'And I suppose it's got something to do with the ancestors of the Yezidis.'

'Only suppose, Ashe?'

'Well, the Yezidis come from the same part of the world as Abraham and the later Chaldaeans who conquered Babylon from the north. From the Transcaucasus, around Lake Van and the borders of what is now Turkey, Iran and Georgian Armenia. And then there's the fantastic snake at Lalish. The Sethian Gnostics called Jesus "the Great Seth", and depicted him as a serpent.'

'Why not? Jesus depicted himself that way. Gospel of John, Chapter 3: "And as Moses lifted up the serpent in the wilderness so must the Son of Man be lifted up, That whosoever believes in him may have eternal life."'

'Eternal life, yes. Remind me of the background, sir.'

'The Great Seth was doubtless quoting the Book of Numbers, Chapter 21, verses six to nine, at the time. God sent serpents to bite the children of Israel as punishment for blasphemy. The cure, following repentance, was for Moses to make a bronze serpent. The brazen serpent was raised high on a staff. It cured the sick that gazed upon it. Clearly a story with a story behind it.'

'Which appears to have been lost.'

'I wonder, Ashe. Does not the serpent represent wisdom? Think of the Garden of Eden. There is the story of the serpent who is wrapped round the tree of the knowledge of good and evil, whose fruit Eve mischievously did eat.'

'With catastrophic consequences. In the Gnostic myths, the fruit offered by the serpent is gnosis, knowledge of the person's divine identity: high or highest consciousness.'

'Indeed, Ashe. And for this the serpent is condemned.' Crayke inhaled pipe smoke, then blew his nose onto a red silk handkerchief. 'Funny thing, the Bible. One minute the snake is condemned, the next he's raised up as the source of a divine cure. The snake is ambivalent.'

'Like the Egyptian Seth, sir. He's ambivalent too. There's a duality. Sun and moon – good and bad. He's got a seriously dark side.'

'Have you read the story of Adam in the Yezidi text, the Meshef Resh?'

'Thought they had no written tradition, sir.'

'Only two short texts have emerged, so far, Ashe. Read them as soon as possible. You'll find transcripts in among my notes. According to the writer of the Meshef Resh, the "Black Book", the Yezidis come from Adam through the line of Seth.'

'Bloody hell!'

'No, it's a quite straightforward fact of their beliefs.'

'But the implications—'

'Are interesting, yes. In the Meshef Resh, the Yezidis' god, or rather their angel, called Melek Tawus – sometimes called the Peacock Angel – visits Adam in Paradise. Lord Tawus teaches Adam he will have to learn to fend for himself. He will have to make his way in the world from his own ingenuity.'

'Sounds up-to-date. Reminds me of the story of Nimrod and the Tower of Babel – an ancient Mesopotamian story, if I'm not mistaken.'

'How so, Ashe?'

'You remember the story: Nimrod tells Abraham's ancestors they needn't give thanks to God now they're capable of doing mighty things for themselves. So they start building the Tower, the Tower of Babel. But the way the Bible tells it, Nimrod's attitude is condemned.'

'Interesting. Perhaps the Yezidi story has more to say to our times. Are they telling us why we need genius? Lord Tawus gives Adam a helpful kick up the backside. Not to punish him, but to encourage him to get out and learn what he can do. And should the sons of Adam just keep at it, they'll come to work miracles.'

'The beautiful big black serpent at Lalish! I've seen it. It must be—'

Crayke put his finger to his lips. 'Please! Don't say too much – at least, that is, until I've brought you another pint of this happy intoxicant.'

Outside, heavy rain flushed away summer's accumulated grime. Ashe recalled distant student days; they had never been as good as this.

'There! Drink deep, man. Deep.'

Ashe drank; no better advice could he recall from a man of learning!

'I sense you have an urge to speculate.'

'Sir, could it be possible that once upon a time, as it were, there was a man... let's call him Seth or Shiva, for the sake of argument.'

'Which?'

'OK. We'll call him ProtoSeth. And ProtoSeth lived before there was recorded history. Because he, ProtoSeth, was the first to have the idea of recording it.'

'A master spirit.'

'Yes, a master spirit. And then he had an insight into nature. A marvellous image from his subconscious appeared to his mind's eye.'

'You are describing what is loosely called a vision.'

'Let's say this vision was the image long associated with Hermes or Mercury, and which, I suspect, is a true Sethian image. I refer of course to the caduceus.'

'Two serpents entwined about a "tau" staff. Yes.'

'I'm sure I'm not the first to detect a similarity between the caduceus of Hermes and the DNA double helix. The reconciliation of opposites into a higher unity.'

'Are you saying ProtoSeth saw the double helix we associate with DNA?'

'Well...'

'This is not the kind of thing, Ashe, you should be heard muttering at High Table. You might be considered eccentric.'

'Then it's lucky we're not at High Table.'

'But we shall be presently. There's someone I want you to meet. And I shall be your guest as well. Is not Toby Ashe a member of Brasenose College? And is not today the day when Sir Moses Beerbohm becomes an honorary fellow of that establishment? A grand ceremony at the Sheldonian Theatre on Broad Street – winding up even as we speak – swiftly followed by lunch in hall at Brasenose. Drink up!'

74

Crayke and Ashe reached for their coats and hurried out into St Giles. The rain had stopped and as they crossed into Broad Street, the stone glowed like amber in the sun.

Crayke paused to relight his pipe. 'It's good to be a peripatetic philosopher again. You've no idea how being stuck behind a desk can stunt your growth! So, what's next, Ashe, eh?'

'OK. Now let's imagine our original Aryan, our ProtoSeth. He's woken up to something no one else has ever seen. What he's got is an image for the origin of life and the universe. He's got some kind of intuitive knowledge of what we now call DNA. He doesn't understand it from the outside – the chemistry of it – as we now do. He understands the "sour milk sea" of Creation from the inside – as an expression of a mind.'

'He sees a pearl: the mind expressing itself in matter through chemistry.'

'Right. ProtoSeth has entered into one of the mysteries of life, maybe *the* mystery of life. He sees that creation and destruction are one complementary process; they belong together like day and night. The contradictory world of Creation points to a higher, invisible level. And it's the beginning of architecture!'

Crayke marvelled at Ashe's intuitive leaps. 'Architecture?'

'Yes. This power comes from beyond the stars. So the first proper architectural works are the columns and towers, the geometry of elevation, the high erections that link the whole life of mankind to the higher universe. These weren't just buildings, they were rockets! And what does the Bible suggest? Tall buildings are an affront to God! After Babel is destroyed, different languages come into being, different races emerge and divide – as a punishment for building with excessive pride, or too much high consciousness!'

'Hmm… Hubris is rarely the intelligent option.'

'Well, that's the moral applied to the story, sir, that the builders tempted God's wrath because they were building under their own initiative. Anyhow, if we use the Babel story as an image, rather than a morality play, we can see it's saying that the seed has been dispersed. Isn't it interesting, sir, that Babel – Babylon – was linked in the minds of the writers of Genesis to the Chaldaeans, the people who ruled Babylon when the Judaean aristocracy were imprisoned there? Maybe the Jewish exiles didn't realise the Chaldaeans, with their magical astrology, were their own long-lost cousins, the remains of the Mithanni aristocracy.'

'Fascinating, Ashe.'

'When unenlightened minds see great buildings, they have two impulses. One: worship the totem. Two—'

'Fly aeroplanes into them. I get it, Ashe. You're talking about the fear of Seth.'

'Great phrase, sir. "Fear of Seth". The "Fear of Seth" has dominated our culture. It dominates all of us.'

'Very true. Very true.' For a few seconds, Crayke's mind tripped into the ether. Then he smiled and turned to Ashe: 'So what about our man? Where's old ProtoSeth?'

'ProtoSeth believes the genetic line that has preserved the divine knowledge, or high consciousness, must be kept inviolate, so that the Aryan, or high-born consciousness, might serve as a leaven to raise the world.'

'Or subdue it, Ashe. ProtoSeth may have been less idealistic than you imagine! Maybe he, or his descendants, didn't *want* to "turn us on".'

'Benevolent or not, he or his followers form a tight aristocracy, a militia.'

'To what end?'

317

'As I say, they believe they must raise the original race, which has been scattered in the world.'

'You're doing it again. Most people hearing you now, Toby, would think this was some kind of Nazi race theory.'

'Well, the Nazis twisted the whole Aryan thing. Completely perverted the idea. Sick minds make sick ideas. Even if we imagine Aryans as some kind of super tribe, "the Germans" certainly weren't their representatives! Anyhow, Hitler's so-called Aryan gods were treated like sheep, not men.'

'And of course, Ashe, let us not forget that if Abraham was Mithanni, and the Mithannis were Aryans – as they have been called – then, my dear boy, the children of Abraham are the descendants of an Aryan aristocracy! So Hitler's mob murdered the true Aryans. Ironic, is it not?'

Ashe paused, the profundity dawning on him. 'My God! What would people think of that? The Jews – as Aryan as the ancient Iranians and Brahmins! From this standpoint, the Nazis had to fabricate the whole Atlantis-Nordic legend to make up for the fact they weren't real Aryans! They must subconsciously have felt inferior to the Jews.'

'The inferiority complex can be a very dangerous and very powerful thing. It has turned many a man into a raving lunatic. God help us when the lunatics seize the reins of power! That's what ODDBALLS is all about, Ashe: catch 'em while you can!'

The two men were halfway down the dark, narrow passage of Brasenose Lane. Glorious Radcliffe Square, with its great domed library chamber, the Radcliffe Camera, opened before them. But as he entered the porter's lodge of Brasenose College, Ashe was oblivious to his environment. His thoughts were at last becoming clear. He had to go on.

'The thing is, sir, what your work adds up to is this. What the world has been taught to accept as true is a pack of lies. And these Yezidis, they're really onto something.'

'Is that why they have been persecuted, Ashe?'

318

75

The college scouts were already delivering the prawn cocktail starters to the guests seated at High Table. Crayke stood at ease, surveying Brasenose's 500-year-old hall until he caught Sir Moses Beerbohm's restless eye. Smiling broadly, the rotund Nobel Prize-winner summoned Crayke to sit beside him.

'Ran! Ranald Crayke! My dear chap, how marvellous to see you! Glad to know that Baghdad does let you get away on occasion.'

'There's life beyond, dear friend. Do you know Dr Toby Ashe?'

'Delighted. Didn't you write a book, Dr Ashe? *The Generous...*?'

'*Gene*. Yes, Sir Moses. All my fault.'

'Come, come! It wasn't strictly science, but it wasn't rubbish either. What is your current field?'

Crayke interjected. 'For the moment, let's call it "aspects of Mesopotamian civilisation". Ancient, mostly. Toby has a question for you.'

Ashe winced at being put on the spot.

'Don't let old Crayke take liberties, Ashe. What's the question?'

Ashe looked at Crayke. Crayke's eyes widened. 'What was that extraordinary story you told me? The one about Adam and Eve.'

'Sounds like Genesis, not genetics, Ran, old boy!'

'Same concept, surely, Moshe!'

'Come, come! Must keep science and religion apart.'

Crayke nudged Ashe in the ribs, discreetly.

'Well, Sir Moses, it's... it's about people... a people I've been studying. They have this legend about Adam arguing with Eve.'

'How very true to life!'

'Eve insists she can have children by herself; she doesn't need Adam.'

'Eve – the original feminist!'

'And Adam says she's wrong. She needs him.'

'The original fantasist!' Beerbohm's massive frame bobbed with laughter.

'So, Sir Moses, Adam and Eve decide to test the merits of their convictions by conducting experiments.'

'I don't know who these people are, Dr Ashe, but they sound like proper scientists.'

'So Adam and Eve both place their respective reproductive—'

'Not over lunch, surely!'

'Pardon me. They put the product of their fertilities into separate jars and leave them for the prescribed period. After the gestation season, the jars are opened.'

'Is that the question, Dr Ashe – what was in each jar?'

'No. That's been answered. Eve's jar was opened. Inside they found a putrid mess.'

'How disappointing for her. And in Adam's jar?'

'Two healthy, bouncy children. A boy and a girl.'

'The question?'

'What do you think was the story's original meaning?'

'Goodness! Well, my dear boy, if I didn't know any better, I'd say this old tale constituted an ancient insight into the relative significance of X and Y chromosomes. An intuitive realisation that a sperm bearing a Y chromosome makes an embryo into a male. A gene on that chromosome leads the growing embryo on the road to masculinity, regardless of the number of X chromosomes. It's something in the male's sperm that does the job.'

Ashe stared at Crayke; Crayke smiled, raising his eyebrows.

'May I enquire, Dr Ashe, as to the provenance of this mythological titbit?' Beerbohm picked up a loose prawn, and swallowed it.

'It's a Yezidi story, Sir Moses.'

'Yezidi? Where have I heard that?'

'From me, you old duffer!'

'Of course, Ran. Kurds! Northern Iraq. Armenia. Now I remember. Was a time you talked of little else.'

Beerbohm went quiet for a while. Goblets of wine were filled and Dover sole was served.

Ashe could hardly believe his direct hit. He was about to get another.

'Ran, old boy! Perhaps your friend Ashe here would be interested in some of the latest research concerning the Kurds.'

'Research?'

'Their genes, man! Not really my field, but there's an interesting link between some Jews, and some Kurds and Armenians.'

Ashe slapped his silver cutlery on the polished table.

'Please, Ashe!'

'Sorry, sir. Please, Sir Moses. I'd like to know more.'

'We all would, my dear fellow. That's why we're still here. Well, as I recall – and that's not much – the work in question is being carried out by Michael Hammer, who's a fine geneticist, and a nephrologist, Karl Skorecki. The team's been building on a study by Ariella Oppenheim, carried out at the National Academy of Sciences in the USA. Can't be sure, but I think there was a contribution from my old protégé and plagiarist, Sami al-Qasr.'

The name 'al-Qasr' stuck out like a sore thumb. Al-Qasr, the son of the fanatical anti-Semite and anti-Mason; al-Qasr, the beneficiary of Istanbul bomber Razak's forgery skills. Now, al-Qasr the geneticist, whom Sir Moses accused of stealing ideas! Ashe began to wonder if he had been chasing the wrong fox altogether.

'Are you there, Dr Ashe?'

321

'I'm sorry, Sir Moses. I was just taking in what you were saying about the genetic link.'

'Between some Jews and Kurds, yes. Well, the team discovered a haplotype.'

'Haplo...?'

'Haplotype. Surely you remember? Genetic mutation in the chromosome, or what we call a "marker". The team called their new one the Cohen Modal Haplotype.'

'Sounds like a sixties psychedelic band, Sir Moses.'

'Well, you'll know more about that sort of thing than I do.'

'Why the "Cohen" bit?'

'The Cohen bit, Dr Ashe, comes from a Jewish word for "priest". It was a fairly common Jewish surname, indicating descendants of Judaean priests of two thousand years ago, when the Jews had their priesthood and temple in Jerusalem. Something like 56 per cent of Sephardic Cohens have the haplotype. Sephardic Jews have ancestors that can be traced to southwest Europe, North Africa and the Middle East. Anyhow, a lot of geneticists got quite excited about it. There's a chap here in Oxford, David Goldstein. He reckoned the chromosomal type was a constituent of the ancestral Hebrew population.'

'Amazing.'

'Interesting, certainly. Anyhow, it turns out the Cohen Modal Haplotype was not specific to the descendants of Jews.

'Dr Levon Yepiskoposyan at Armenia's Institute of Man in Yerevan found the haplotype in some Armenians. Looking further into the Transcaucasus region, Dr Brinkmann found the haplotype was actually common among Iraqi Kurds. And Ariella Oppenheim found the dominant haplotype of the Iraqi Kurds was only one microsatellite-mutation step away from the Cohen Modal Haplotype. Pretty significant. So, to sum up, the haplotype evidence supports the view that Kurds and Armenians are close relatives of today's Jews. That probably means the majority of Jews today have paternal ancestry from the northeastern Mediterranean region.'

Ashe could hardly contain his excitement: solid scientific support for his hypothesis. 'Let me get this right, Sir Moses. You're saying, in effect, that the Jews and the Kurds are related.'

'Going on the haplotype evidence, absolutely. A lot of Jews and Kurds are related – distantly anyway.'

'Could Abraham have come from what is now Kurdistan?'

Sir Moses thought for a moment. A twinkle appeared in his eye. 'Yes, I suppose he could. And from what I remember of the Bible, that would make sense of a lot of his movements. I don't know what difference it would make to anyone, but yes, it's more than possible that ancestors of Jewish people began their existence in an area within or near to Kurdistan. Is that useful at all, gentlemen?'

Two hours later, Ashe and Crayke stood on the step outside the Brasenose gatehouse. Eyes red from drink, their hearts were euphoric.

'Must be the wine, Ashe. Let's pull ourselves together. Do you know Lee Kellner?'

'Director of the Counter Terrorism Centre, CIA.'

'Right.'

'Never met him, sir.'

'Time you did. Zappa's been trying to wheedle intel from me about Sami al-Qasr. Seems al-Qasr's disgraced himself again and quit the US. The CTC must be desperate if they're nudging Zappa in my direction.' He seized Ashe's shoulder and whispered, 'Time's come to nudge you in theirs.'

76

Only a few minutes' drive from the centre of Washington DC, the Morrison House Hotel in South Alfred Street, Alexandria Old Town, was the perfect place for Ashe to collect his thoughts. A fine Federal-style red-brick house with arched sash windows, the hotel resembled nothing so much as a grand survivor of the 1864 Atlanta burning immortalised in *Gone with the Wind*. It was General Sherman who ordered the Atlanta conflagration and Ashe enjoyed the irony that it was another Sherman who introduced him to the warm Southern hospitality of the 4-star Virginian hotel 140 years later.

Having fixed a meeting with Kellner for later that afternoon, Beck left Ashe sitting quietly in the warm sunlight of an early eighteenth-century-style parlour 'Grille'. A genial black pianist played not 'As Time Goes By', but Debussy's 'Danse Bohémienne'. Even so, Ashe could not but dream that from among the immaculately dressed, refreshingly discreet ladies who sipped champagne on polished antique Windsor chairs, a latter-day Ingrid Bergman might yet appear with a story and an ache for meaningful adventure. Finding little inspiration in the large splashes of colour framed like Picassos to encourage enthusiasm for cocktails, Ashe looked to the pianist's fingers that acrobatically surmounted the tones and semitones, sharps and flats of the shiny keyboard.

While Ashe had felt hot on the trail where Crayke's researches were concerned, it was by no means obvious how to apply his new knowledge to the key questions.

Who was responsible for the Kartal Lodge bombing?

How was Kartal linked to the attack on the Tower?

The picture was a tangle and the clarity of his surroundings mocked his attempts at untangling it.

There had been disappointments. Trust in Colonel Aslan might be misplaced; Aslan had his own concerns, lodged, it seemed, within Turkish security priorities. Though he had grounds to suspect Aslan had used him to locate Yildiz and Yazar for internal Turkish purposes, he could not prove it. Had Aslan misled him? That might be going too far, but there was something suspicious about Aslan's reticence where the Baba Sheykh's presence on the Lodge guest list was concerned; Aslan's changed attitude struck Ashe as significant – but what did it signify?

If Aslan was not to be trusted, what of Aslan's belief that the Kartal Lodge atrocity was connected to the Tower bombing? Was this a blind? Maybe, but a new concern had emerged: Sami al-Qasr.

There was certainly a British angle to al-Qasr. He was a contact of Hafiz Razak's, the pro-al-Qaeda terrorist linked directly to attacks on British interests in Istanbul. Al-Qasr had significant British experience, including acquaintance with high-level scientific figures with intelligence contacts, such as Moses Beerbohm. Al-Qasr had quit Britain in the eighties to undertake secret work for Saddam and subsequently for the US. The British had tried to frustrate al-Qasr's military-scientific work in 1992, when the RAF had bombed a facility he used north of Basra. That much was clear from al-Qasr's old file. If al-Qasr followed his father's beliefs, hatred for a so-called 'Jewish-Masonic conspiracy' could have been a motivator, as well as a grudge against Britain whose air force might have wrecked his plans.

Ashe looked at his watch. The meeting at Gadsby's Tavern with Kellner and Beck was scheduled for 3 p.m. With only a quarter of an hour in hand, Ashe declined the hotel's generous offer of a car and chauffeur, stepped down from the hotel's pillared portico, and headed east along King Street, past the village-like colonial houses and overgrown grass verges towards the centre of Old Town Alexandria. Only the parked cars spoilt the near-illusion of a vanished America.

Ashe's thoughts were racing. As Sami al-Qasr loomed larger in his investigations, he also had to contend with the emergence of another mystery figure. How had the Baba Sheykh entered the scene, and what did that mean?

It had been Laila who had mentioned him first. In her anxiety to find her brother, she had brought the sheykh to Ashe's attention. Now the sheykh and Laila's brother were in Germany, or so Laila believed. Meanwhile, Crayke's work pointed to endogamy in the sheykh's family, a fact of genetic importance still obscure to the overall picture.

Then there was Aslan.

Aslan either regarded the sheykh as insignificant, or else wished to deflect Ashe's attention from the sheykh's place on the Lodge guest list. But there was another possibility. Any link between the sheykh and the Lodge bombing might have been coincidental. After all, had it not been for Laila, Ashe would never have heard of him. Perhaps the Baba Sheykh was a red herring. But then there was the genetic side of the picture: an ancient link between Jews and Kurds. And genetics was al-Qasr's territory.

An odd connection with Freemasonry ran through the picture. While al-Qasr may have been motivated to attack Freemasonry, Laila believed the Baba Sheykh wanted to harness Freemasonry in support of the Yezidi cause.

More confused than ever, Ashe turned into North Royal Street, opposite Alexandria's Market Square. Feeling nervous, he approached the multi-storey Gadsby's Tavern, opposite Alexandria's City Hall with its splendid clock-tower. Ashe could only hope Kellner would shed light on the conundrum. If Kellner could not, Ashe had better keep his expenses to the minimum.

77

Dubbed the 'finest old tavern in America', Gadsby's was a fabulous survivor from pre-industrial times. It had been a tavern since at least 1785, and by the end of the eighteenth century had been developed into a successful hotel by English entrepreneur John Gadsby. During a colourful history, it had played host to George Washington, Thomas Jefferson and John Adams. It had also played host to Toby Ashe. Ashe had been invited by Washington's Alexandria Masonic Lodge No. 22 to address their annual St John the Baptist Festival some years previously. Happy memories of that occasion encouraged Ashe to suggest it as a suitable venue for his first meeting with Lee Kellner. A Mason himself, Kellner agreed to the location with alacrity.

The sight of two conspicuous limousines and a pair of obvious secret service operatives outside the tavern brought a smile to Ashe's face. In America, it seemed, even the secret service relied on advertising. Recognising Ashe, the agents checked his ID and led him inside, across the polished white-oak floor of the old-time downstairs bar and restaurant to a private conference room upstairs. The candlelit dining room had hardly altered since 1814, when, across town, a British army had burned down Washington's White House and Capitol in retaliation for US support of Bonaparte and a planned invasion of Canada. How times had changed!

Kellner and Beck rose, smiling, from their seats round the antique table as a well-frisked Ashe was shown in by the two alert agents guarding the room and corridor.

'Welcome to Washington, Dr Ashe! I must say I admire your taste. Good of you to get me and Agent Beck here out of Langley. Care for a snack? Beck and I just ordered a Chesapeake Bay crab-cake sandwich.'

Ashe observed the bottle of Rapidan River Merlot on the table.

'A glass of the local vino will do very nicely, thank you.'

'Not eating?'

'Prefer to eat after the meeting. I was hoping you'd join me at the hotel.'

Kellner looked at Beck. 'Cancel the sandwiches.'

In spite of the rumble in Beck's stomach, the meeting got off to a good start. There was an instant spark between Kellner and Ashe. Beck, on the other hand, was wary and a mite suspicious of Ashe's charm; it eclipsed his own. Beck couldn't help feeling that Ashe would have preferred to speak to Kellner alone. In this he was correct; Ashe had requested a head-to-head, but Kellner wanted the factual backup and didn't want to have to repeat whatever might pass between himself and the Englishman. Unlike Beck, who was fond of admonishing others to 'Beware of Greeks bearing gifts', Kellner was not unduly suspicious of Englishmen. If the Brits were the new Greeks and the Americans the new Romans, that was fine; roots mattered.

Kellner had intended to get the ball rolling by explaining the concerns the US had about sharing intelligence with the British. Doubts about British security went at least as far back as the catastrophic disclosures of Burgess, Philby and co. Furthermore, there were voluble US critics who saw Great Britain as hampered by human-rights legislation, a soft-option hang-out for jihadists and anti-Americanism. However, one look at Ashe's smile and knowing eyes, together with the thought of his old friend Ran Crayke, told Kellner that Ashe knew all this anyway and they might as well put at least some of their cards on the table and cut to the chase.

Ashe very quickly realised the CIA was up a gum tree regarding al-Qasr. Not only had they physically lost him, but on weighing up the expense of all those years in California, they had to accept they had not got a great deal out of him, perhaps because never having grasped fully what he was capable of, they never had a straight deal in the first place.

It was soon clear that the British and Americans had been coming at the al-Qasr problem from opposite directions. In view of this, it made sense to complement each other's work, if possible. Ashe produced his expurgated copies of files on both al-Qasrs, father and son, while Beck produced the late Leanne Gresham's expurgated file on al-Qasr's work at RIBOTech. As Ashe began to grasp the dimensions of al-Qasr's role in advanced weapons research, the conversation hotted up considerably.

Kellner was fascinated by the idea of a link between the Kartal Lodge bombing and the Tower attack, but couldn't help feeling it was a red herring as far as capturing al-Qasr was concerned. However, when Ashe finally let Kellner in on intel regarding al-Qasr's connection with Syrian terrorist Hafiz Razak, his eyes lit up. He and Beck could now see perfectly how al-Qasr had eluded their grip. Taken together with their own file on Razak, they could confirm Mati Fless's warnings about al-Qasr's links with Ansar al-Sunna. Even more significantly, they could now confirm the so-called 'doctor' messages they had been receiving through SIGINT on al-Qasr.

The bombshell for Beck and Kellner was when Ashe explained about Princess Laila's desire to find her brother, the Yezidi doctor, and his companion, the Baba Sheykh, who for some reason were in danger, probably hiding in Germany. That set the bells a-ringing. Now al-Qasr's appearance in Berlin just might add up. The CTC could get onto Germany's secret service with some real meat.

Two bottles of Virginian Merlot later, Kellner was beginning to wonder how he was going to deal with Ashe. He would dearly have loved to sign him up on a full-time basis. That was not going to happen. He decided to put it directly.

'Dr Ashe. What do you want from us?'

'Apart from another glass of your excellent wine, I should like to come along as something like an observer on field operations in Europe connected with al-Qasr, Laila's brother and the sheykh. I would assist you all I could, subject to my superior's approval.'

'An "observer" you say?'

'Means I'll pay my own fare.'

Kellner laughed and turned to Beck. 'D'you think we can handle a deal like that, Beck?'

'I'd say, sir, that it's probably an offer we should not refuse. Dr Ashe clearly comes with the confidence of involved persons who could be of great use to us. This doctor guy, for one. Ashe can use familiarity with his sister as bait. I'd like to speak to him as soon as possible.'

'Just a minute, Sherman. I don't like the sound of that word "bait". I couldn't cooperate with Laila's brother being led into an "extraordinary rendition" scenario. I want his safety guaranteed.'

'I said I'd like to speak to the doctor, Toby, not torture him.'

'So long as that's understood.'

Kellner saw the need for a little mollification. 'OK, guys. I think we all understand one another. Subject to conversation with our mutual friend in Baghdad, Dr Ashe, I think we can join hands in amity on this one.'

'So mote it be, Lee!'

'So mote it be, Toby! Welcome to the United States!'

Kellner, Ashe and Beck shook hands.

Kellner turned to Beck. 'And now, Sherman, I hope you don't mind if I accept Dr Ashe's very kind offer of dinner at his place – to toast the Queen you understand.'

78

Sinàn tapped his fingers on the sunlit windowsill. From his third-floor vantage point he watched mothers lifting toddlers out of pushchairs to enjoy the late-summer morning's play in the August Lütgens Park.

One of Hamburg's smarter districts, Altona lay a few kilometres west of St Pauli. The Chemnitzstrasse apartment was a vast improvement on the discomforts of the past six months. The Baba Sheykh, whose health had improved, was enjoying a cup of strong coffee while watching *Mr Bean* on daytime television. He laughed repeatedly.

'Just like you see in Bashiqa! Only here you don't need a satellite dish.'

'Maybe we need a Yezidi channel, Baba.'

'But would the children want to watch it? They'd rather watch Bean than listen to me. I don't blame them. How can the old stories compete with this?'

Sinàn tapped his fingers on the windowsill again. 'I have to go out this afternoon.'

The sheykh looked up, anxiously.

'A message from the Kurdish centre in St Pauli. A sick woman. New arrival from Iraq. She has problems.' Sinàn pointed to his stomach.

'Why don't they use their regular doctor?'

'Immigration irregularities. They said, so long as I'm here, maybe I could help. Better than doing nothing. I'm getting tired of doing nothing.'

'You could get into trouble.'

Sinàn laughed. 'Trouble?' He shook his head, smiled, and laughed to himself. He couldn't remember a time when he was not in some kind of trouble.

'Let me come with you, Sinàn.'

Sinàn looked into the Baba Sheykh's imploring eyes, then back to the park.

Everything seemed so normal.

A white Mercedes van trundled up the cobbled Antonistrasse from the docks, coming to a halt outside al-Qasr's apartment block. From an upstairs window, al-Qasr counted the new arrivals. Two men got out of the front, and two more emerged from the rear of the van, all wearing clean blue overalls.

Al-Qasr's apartment bell rang. Donning thick-rimmed spectacles, he hurried down two flights of cool, stone steps to the dark vestibule. An elderly resident, owner of a gruff terrier, poked his head out of his ground-floor flat.

'*Guten Tag!*'

Al-Qasr shuddered, then turned to pacify the nosy neighbour. 'They've come to do my kitchen and bathroom. Best grab them while you can, eh?'

The old man nodded. The dog barked. Al-Qasr unlatched the door and two clean-shaven Iranian heads peered inside, watched closely by the old man.

'Okse?'

The old man let the terrier run towards the group at the door. It sniffed at the men's heels. The old man babbled anxiously. 'You can't leave the van here. Tell them, Herr Okse! Tell them they can't leave the van on the street! It's against the law!'

Al-Qasr nodded. 'I'll tell them.' He turned back to the tall driver. 'There's an underground car park on Lincolnstrasse. It's off the Reeperbahn.' Al-Qasr pointed. 'Round the corner. Up there. Can you see? But it's pedestrianised. You'll have to drive back down to the docks and round the long way. Got a map?'

'I find it.'

The old man persisted in being a nuisance. 'Lincolnstrasse! Herr Okse. Tell them! Car park!'

'They're just parking the van.'

The old man nodded again. Bugged, al-Qasr wondered when he'd have to fix him.

'What about tools, Herr Okse? They must have tools.'

'Yes, yes. Tools. Good point. Hey! Better leave your tools here!'

'What?'

'Your tools. No point carrying them all the way from the car park.'

The old man noticed the pause and saw heads shaking behind the dimpled glass. Generally suspicious of people who looked like Muslims, he moved out from his doorway and approached the entrance. He pulled open the door to take a better look at the four men. 'Don't look like plumbers, Herr Okse.'

'Students. Pocket money. For the extras, you know.'

'Extras? On the Reeperbahn?'

'Yeah. Holidays and luxuries. I got them cheap through the university.'

'University!' The old man shook his head. 'So now you need a degree to be a plumber! What's happening to Germany? Here! Let me help you with your tools!'

'No, no. It's all right.'

'No trouble. I know what it is to work.'

'Please! Please let me deal with this, sir.'

The old man looked hurt. The Iranians shuffled around on the step.

'Please yourself!' The old man sloped back to his door, muttering, and returned to his daytime TV.

The vestibule echoed as the old man slammed his wooden door shut, leaving fresh dog-shit on the cold floor. Barking could still be heard from inside. One of the Iranians looked at al-Qasr and motioned his finger across his neck.

79

The four men shuffled awkwardly around al-Qasr's sitting-room coffee table. Al-Qasr checked their names off a list on his laptop: Abu Ja'far Suyuti, Muhammad ibn Abu Talib, Ahmad al-Din bin Ali, and Hashim Bukhari. Suyuti was the tallest and clearly the leader of the group.

'OK to smoke?'

'Please. Sit down. I'll bring the tea.' Al-Qasr served tea in crimson glasses.

'Good tea!' offered Suyuti.

'British.'

'Great.'

Al-Qasr laughed. 'Tell me, how did you get here?'

Suyuti turned to Muhammad ibn Abu Talib, the youngest of the group. 'You tell him. You're the talker.'

Muhammad's eyes had a tired, glazed air. Just twenty-one, he had seen his share of fighting. 'We're all Arabs from the Iranian side of the northern border. We were about to leave Chechnya for northern Iraq. So we were looking forward to seeing our families again. Then we got the order to join an Iranian-Russian educational exchange. They said we looked like students. One day we're killing Russians, the next we're taking lessons from them! We were in St Petersburg a bit, then we got the order to head for Estonia. We had internal passes and stuff. I speak Russian.'

'Weren't you missed in St Petersburg?'

'Summer holidays!'

The other three men laughed. 'Travel broadens the mind!'

Suyuti chipped in. 'We got a ship from the Baltic to Hamburg. No problems.'

'Customs?'

Suyuti shrugged his shoulders. 'When do we start?'

Al-Qasr sat back in his armchair. 'Today. Soon you will meet my friend. Cemal Goksel. Trust him.'

'A Kurd!'

'He's a Kurd. So am I – for the moment. You'd better like Kurds round here, Hashim! They're everywhere.'

The other three laughed. Suyuti chided Hashim. 'You're small-minded, Hashim. Most Kurds are believers.'

'Shia!' snorted Hashim.

'Not all of them.'

'Kurds kill our brothers in Ansar al-Sunna.'

'And Kurds let us into Iraq to get revenge.'

Al-Qasr was dismayed to hear the old hatreds and rivalries. It had been a long time since he'd shared tea with fellow Arabs. 'Come on, brothers! I thought we were united in our cause! Allah is one. The Arabs are one.'

The men looked unconvinced. 'So, what do we do?'

'Goksel has made contact with a Kurdish doctor. He is coming to the Kurdish Centre close to here at six.'

'Then we take him!'

'Hold on, Muhammad! Not so fast. He's not the one we want. One of you will follow him home, with Goksel.'

'What do the rest of us do?'

'You, Ahmad? You can fix up my kitchen.'

80

'Mmm… That's nice. I think I like that one better.'

Ashe gently ran the black leather glove down the curve of Melissa's pale back.

'Yeah, that's definitely better.'

He smiled as his fingers clipped under the elastic of Melissa's black knickers.

'Don't stop.' Melissa lifted her face out of the sofa cushion and looked directly at Ashe. Her eyes widened. Ashe averted his gaze and took in the tidy flat Melissa was sharing with a friend in Paultons Square, London SW3.

'So you're a Chelsea girl now.'

'What does that mean? Think I'm a party tart? Smack addict?'

'It means I like your new hair, and I like the way you look at me.'

Melissa smiled. 'Amazing the effect a dab of black hair dye has on a man.'

Ashe laughed. It was true. Melissa had never looked so desirable. She turned onto her side, her hip luxuriating in the soft cushion.

'You know there's something really intense about your breasts.'

'Intense?' Melissa's bright eyes narrowed.

'Yeah. Try this.'

'Oh Christ!'

'Thought so.'

'Kiss me.'

'Where?'

Ashe kissed her passionately on the lips, running his hand down her warm body. What a fantastic wife Melissa would make, Ashe thought to himself. There was something voluptuous, even Italian, about this Cheshire rose. Large family... passionate nights... big fights... fierce loyalty... full-blooded – quite a future. They could move to the sun together, bask by the sea – were it not for the world.

'I was thinking about the Iraq situation, Melissa. Have you realised how close it's getting to the Bible?'

Melissa shook her head. 'Oh God, Toby! Is now the time?' She pulled his head towards her large eyes and full lips. Ashe resisted.

'No, no. Just wait a second. I put this down to you. You've turned me on.'

'And this is the result? A lecture?'

'In the head. Thoughts. Inspirations.'

'Screw that, Toby. Let's see how well you think now.'

Melissa rolled off the sofa onto the thick carpet and began playing with the fly on Ashe's black jeans.

'Yeah, I mean if you change the characters around a bit. You've virtually got the Christmas story.'

'You've got a gorgeous cock.'

'The Roman eagle marching up and down Palestine – that's the US army, taking the census. Getting control of the bureaucracy. Herod is, if you like, the Iraqi government – currently in waiting. The government favoured by Rome (the US) but hated by a lot of the population – the Zealots, so to speak. Herod was an Idumaean Arab. An outsider from mainstream society, just like the Kurds. Rumour has it the first Iraqi prime minister next year might be a... a Kurd.'

Ashe was having some trouble keeping to his train of thought. Melissa looked up at him. 'Like that?'

Another side to Melissa; he liked it.

'Mmm... Yeah, like I was saying. You've got the eagle bringing what it considers civilisation – the Pax Romana – to a troubled part of the empire. God, Melissa! Now, it's called freedom and democracy. Pax Americana. Point being that the Romans were utterly convinced they were doing the Right Thing. Couldn't understand the suicidal determination of the Zealots. Anyhow. Then you've got the massacre of the innocents in the Christmas story. A lot of children are dying in this thing. You've got people expecting the end of the world.'

Melissa reached her hand up under Ashe's shirt and tickled his chest.

'Melissa!'

'Still thinking?'

'Then there's... there's... a... Well, the only thing you need now is the totally unseen element. Totally unseen. Unexpected. A sort of Joseph and Mary dodging the violence. Two little people carrying destiny in their... Maybe taking refuge in Egypt. Interesting place.'

'Yes, Toby. So when are you taking me?'

'Why've you stopped?'

Melissa slipped off her knickers and wrapped her legs around Ashe. She took him in her arms and kissed him. 'So, Toby, you reckon the Second Coming is imminent do you?'

Ashe cracked up. 'All right, you win.'

'At last!'

Ashe's mobile rang. He reached behind the sofa to his jacket.

'No! Don't answer it!'

'I'm expecting something.'

'So am I, Toby Ashe!'

Melissa jumped off Ashe and tried to get to the phone first. Both their hands seized the mobile as it continued to bleep. Ashe pushed Melissa away.

'Right, you bastard! You take your bloody call. I'm going out. Make sure you're gone when I come back!'

Melissa gathered her clothes and stormed into her bedroom, slamming the door. Ashe could hear her sobbing. He clicked on the phone. 'Here we go again...'

'I'm sorry?'

'No, no, not you. Who is it?'

'Beck.'

'Ah, yes. Kellner said I'd be hearing from you.'

'Can you get over to Hamburg, Dr Ashe?'

'Now?'

'If you wanna find your man. Pull some strings – and be here by 1800 hours, OK?'

Ashe looked at his watch. 'That's…'

'Call me. The minute you got an ETA, I'll give you a location. Adios, friend.'

81

Ashe slammed the taxi door, pulled his jacket lapels up round his earlobes and cast a cautious eye around the chilly Hein-Köllisch-Platz. It was one of those sudden autumn afternoons that felt more like February: empty and disorientating. His watch said 17.37.

Gazing around the little square, Ashe spotted a grey Ford Mondeo parked opposite the Babylon bar. He approached it and looked casually into the driving seat. Empty. A tap on the shoulder.

'Don't look now, Dr Ashe.'

It was Beck.

'Just walk to your left in the direction of the café – not the Babylon, the Teufel Café.'

Ashe soon found himself in the warm, orange-coloured confines of the 'Devil's Café'. A few students and a couple of solemn salesmen occupied comfortable sofas by the toilets. The harder window seats were all empty. Ashe moved to the window. Beck ordered coffee from the tired-looking ex-punk behind the counter.

'Sherman Beck at your service, Doctor—'

'Toby.'

'Toby. How d'ya get here so fast?'

'Strings.'

'RAF?'

Ashe nodded.

'Great. I gotta say that stuff on al-Qasr just blew our minds.'

Ashe gestured to Beck to keep the volume down. 'Expecting a party, Sherman?'

'I got men at every exit. Snipers on the roofs.'

'Snipers? Grenzschutzgruppe 9 in on this?'

'German security's holding back. Our people have strict instructions, Toby.'

'I bloody hope so.'

Ashe was struck by the apparent recklessness of Beck's operation. The area was full of civilians; children were playing all over the streets. One stray bullet...

'They ain't shootin', Toby. We need their eyes. This Baba Sheykh guy – always accompanied by the doctor, right?'

'Sinàn.'

'Right. Sinàn. Knows a lot about this al-Qasr fuck.'

Ashe could sense the bitterness in Beck's eyes. 'This isn't personal is it, Beck?'

Beck bit the inside of his cheek. 'Yes and no. This guy's cold, man. Psycho.'

'Pity you didn't know that before you set him up in California.'

'I had nuthin' to do with that. Al-Qasr's bad. Bad seed. Bad every-fucking-thing.'

'Maybe a little black and white there, Sherman.'

'Guy's a cold-blooded killer.'

'Certainly that. As for whether the doctor's always with the sheykh, I can't vouch for every move. Why are you so sure we're going to see them?'

'We suspect a set-up. The doctor's been called to treat a woman at the Kurdish Centre near here. As the doctor protects the sheykh, we expect the pair of them.'

'Why the set-up?'

'Al-Qasr's sidekick. Nervous guy. Cemal Goksel. Been seen with a stranger. Might be al-Qasr.'

'Might be?'

'In disguise. Sitting in these here seats.'

'Did you get a picture of al-Qasr?'

'Not enough for a positive ID. He's so fucking devious, man.'
'Shame. Don't you think we're taking a risk, sitting here?'
'Al-Qasr doesn't know either of us.'
'He's probably better connected than you think.'

82

Two minutes later, Ashe and Beck were sitting in Beck's Ford close to the Kurdish Community Centre in Silbersackstrasse.

'How the hell did you track the sheykh down?'

'Guess we owe you there, Toby. Your information on Sinàn matched up with our checks on his background. Then the messages he's been sending the Agency about al-Qasr and the Yezidis. Clearly this sheykh guy ties in somewhere with al-Qasr's interest in Yezidi genetics. That guy's in danger. We also pulled favours from Yezidis in the Kurdistan National Assembly. They did what they could to track down the sheykh.'

'Who handled the negotiation, Sherman?'

Beck was reluctant to reveal sources.

'Wouldn't have been a certain Vincent Zappa, would it?'

'Well...'

'Please give him my best wishes. How did you pin all this down to Hamburg?'

'Hamburg police picked up an illegal taxi driver. He'd been racing round like a crazy guy. Turned out he'd carried two Yezidis from Giessen to Hamburg. Then we located a Berlin taxi driver who'd carried what he thought was a Turkish businessman to Hamburg. The timing matched al-Qasr's arrival in Berlin. This gave us a match with an invisible guy who never boarded al-Qasr's plane.'

'Impressive work, Sherman.'

'We got a lotta help. Since 9/11, Hamburg's been a German intelligence hot spot. We got good relations. They got an agent in the Kurdish community here. That led us to St Pauli. That's how we heard about the—' Beck stopped in his tracks.

'What is it?'

'See that guy?'

'Goksel?'

Beck nodded. 'You got a piece?'

'Will I need one?'

'Keep your head down, Toby. Could get unfriendly.'

Ashe felt hemmed in. 'We staying in the car?'

'Got a better idea? Watch Goksel,' Beck whispered. 'Guy on the corner. Briefcase.'

'Doctor?'

Beck's eyes followed the man approaching Silbersackstrasse from Hein-Köllisch-Platz. Ashe registered the man's fine, olive features: educated Yezidi; must be Sinàn. *Where was the Baba Sheykh?*

The man approached Goksel. The Kurd pointed to the Centre's side entrance. More discussion. The man looked cautiously behind, then followed Goksel into the alleyway at the side of the Kurdish Centre.

Beck licked his lips. 'I smell al-Qasr.'

'I smell a rat, Sherman.'

'Yeah. A rat.'

'It's a trap.' Ashe was out of the car in a split second, pulling away from Beck's restraining arm. 'Cover me.'

'Shit, Ashe!'

He ran into the alley. In the darkness stood the Yezidi.

'Doctor?'

The man turned to see Ashe's silhouette against the dull light.

'Laila wants you.'

The man said a few hurried words to Goksel and walked towards the figure in the light. Ashe whispered, 'Sinàn?'

The man nodded slowly. 'And you?'

'British intelligence. You know a man called al-Qasr?'

Sinàn shuddered.

'Your man in there works for al-Qasr.'

Sinàn went pale. He turned to Goksel, still waiting by the side door. 'Go in. Tell the woman I'm coming. Be kind to her.'

Goksel protested.

'Go in, or forget it!'

Goksel shuffled his feet, then, reluctantly, pushed the Centre's side door. The thick odour of over-spiced cooking swept into the alleyway.

'Where's the Baba Sheykh?'

Sinàn said nothing.

'I know you're protecting him. Al-Qasr's in Hamburg. This is a set-up.'

'Set-up? That's why he's... not here.'

'You left him alone?'

The truth dawned.

'Please get in the car. You direct us. Take us to him, Sinàn, please!'

'Us?'

'Before it's too late.'

'Why should I believe...?'

'Don't believe. Work it out for yourself.'

'Where is Laila?'

'Cairo. At least... she was last week.'

Sinàn's eyes brightened. Ashe grabbed his arm and pulled him towards Beck's car.

'Ashe, you asshole!' bellowed Beck. 'You've fucked up the whole scene!'

Ashe prodded the doctor gently into the back seat, then got in himself.

Goksel appeared at the Centre's front door, a picture of malice and confusion as he helplessly watched the Ford reverse and screech out of the side street into Hein-Köllisch-Platz.

Desperate, Goksel looked to a man in blue overalls loitering across the street. The Iranian trailed the car, his pace increasing into a jog. *Where were his friends?*

Inside the Ford, Sinàn pointed to the Iranian in the rear-view mirror. Seizing his radio, Beck alerted the men on the roofs to the man hurrying after their car.

'Do we apprehend suspect, sir?'

Beck bit his lip.

Ashe interjected. 'Apprehend! You need a lead.'

'Who's running this operation, Dr Ashe?'

'Right now, I'd say Sami al-Qasr.' Ashe ignored Beck's anger. 'Look, Sherman, just follow doctor's orders. Where the Baba Sheykh is, al-Qasr will be close.'

Beck grunted and reversed the car over the cobbles of Hein-Köllisch-Platz. He then headed back into the one-way system on Silbersackstrasse, just as the Iranian was cornered by two plain-clothes agents. They bundled him into a Nissan 4x4.

'You better be right, Ashe!'

83

Followed closely by Ashe, Sinàn raced up to the Altona apartment. Beck inspected the smashed lock. In agony of frustration, Sinàn poked under every visible item of furniture. Ashe pulled a suitcase out from behind the TV. He rattled it. 'Sounds interesting.'

Sinàn froze. 'Too late. The Baba Sheykh is gone.' He took the suitcase from Ashe and clutched it to his heart. 'Nothing could have separated the Baba Sheykh from this.'

'Al-Qasr did. What is it? *Senjaq*?'

Sinàn was surprised.

'I was at Lalish, Sinàn.'

'Then you are thrice blessed.' Sinàn studied Ashe's face. 'Who do you really work for, Mr Ashe?'

Beck frowned. 'Goddammit, Ashe! You're supposed to be an observer!'

'As every student of popular quantum theory knows, observers can exert a major influence on what is observed. Anyhow, we've lost al-Qasr, and we've lost the Baba Sheykh. I've observed that much.'

Sinàn put his head in his hands. 'My fault! It was all my fault. He begged me to take him. I left him.'

As Beck's forensic contingent arrived to scour the apartment, Beck made interminable phone calls. Delighted to have bagged at least half the intended brace, Ashe listened to Sinàn's story.

Beck was in despair. Ashe patted him on the back. 'Come on,

Sherman, I know you're fearing a rocket from Lee, but, truth is, al-Qasr has foxed us because he's fucking clever. And being the guilty party – and being clever – always gives the bastards a temporal advantage. *Nil desperandum.*'

Ashe finally won Beck's attention. 'Two questions bug me, Sherman.'

'Shoot.'

'One. How did al-Qasr know the Baba Sheykh was here? Two: who arranged this apartment for Sinàn and the holy man?'

'You better ask Sinàn here.'

'I have.'

'What did he say?'

'Guess.'

Beck rubbed his eyes. He wondered who had turned the lights out in his mind; nothing always felt like nothing.

Leanne looked hard into his eyes, found something she trusted and smiled again. 'Yeah. It's OK.'

Beck placed his hand just above her knee and gently squeezed.

'You know, Sherman, I'm not sure this interview thing with al-Qasr has been properly thought through.'

'I guess Kellner places a lot of faith in your intuition, Leanne. Anyhow, while you're having your appointment with the evil doctor, our internal security people are gonna give his place a last sweep. Kellner's agent reckoned he was still hiding stuff.'

'D'you think al-Qasr suspects?'

'I'd be surprised if he didn't suspect something. But we've made it very clear to him that if he wants Israeli assassins kept from his door he's got to accept the downside.'

'Hmm… Maybe he doubts how long his protection's gonna last.'

'Yeah. We better move fast.'

'You're right.' Leanne moved her right hand off the steering wheel and placed it gently on Beck's. Beck felt something he hadn't felt in a long, long time.

She drew her slender fingers though her hair. 'But I don't see why he's left the decision to me as to when or whether to bring al-Qasr in. It seems he can't make up his own mind. That's not good, Sherman.'

Beck took a deep breath. 'I guess he kinda wants affirmation. I guess he wants your support. He's afraid if we bring him in too soon, we'll lose good leads. But if we leave it too late… We gotta know who he's been talkin' to, and what he's been saying. Personally, I gotta say I admire Kellner's choice.'

She squeezed his hand. 'It's a tough one. But I don't feel like seeing al-Qasr today.'

'What do you feel like?'

She looked at her watch.

The car skidded into a lay-by, next to an empty picnic site. She pulled the handbrake and turned, wide-eyed, to Beck. 'Make a move.'

His hand glided up her leg onto the silk of her blouse, over her breasts to cup her neck and bring it towards him. They kissed, excitedly, as nervous as first-timers. His heart beat faster, his hand touched her chest, unbuttoned her blouse clumsily, determinedly. He slid the blouse over her shoulder, revealing a classy black bra. He kissed her breastbone. Her skin reddened. She pulled her jacket off and grabbed Beck's face, covering him with kisses.

Beck's hand followed the line of her hip and soon found itself beneath her skirt. Leanne's breathing became passionate, heavy, free. Beck felt her leg, the fine silk stocking. His finger caught beneath the lacy suspender.

A voice came over the short-wave radio. 'ISF time check. Over.'

Beck's body fell back into his seat. 'Take it, Leanne.'

'That's OK, honey, it's over.'

Beck laughed, resignedly. 'Before it even began.'

She grabbed the mike. 'Beck and Leanne. Over.'

The Toyota pickup rumbled south down the Sacramento Valley. Al-Qasr looked at himself in the rear-view mirror. Who the hell was that? The shock and suppressed excitement made him laugh out loud. This was a damn sight better than staring at chromosomes and base sequences from one end of the day to the other, wondering all the time when he would be released. It had been hell. He hadn't even realised how bad it had been. He felt like a slave whose shackles had been smashed.

Al-Qasr put his foot down and giggled, exhilarated at his newfound liberty, careless of his life and everything else. He felt great. He didn't notice the red light and ringing bells where the road crossed the Sacramento to Redding railroad at Marysville, north of Yuba City. He didn't notice the railroad crossing barrier coming down in front of him.

The pickup screamed as tyre rubber burned into the tarmac. The barrier hit the windscreen. Al-Qasr cried out as a great crack appeared in front of him. Shaken, he reversed the pickup into a long-distance truck that had edged up behind him. The incensed driver jumped from the cab to inspect the damage.

Al-Qasr bit his lip and closed his eyes. Opening them he glimpsed a couple waiting on the other side of the tracks. Was the woman pointing at him? Who was that man staring? He knew that face. She was staring too. Leanne Gresham.

The truck driver banged on al-Qasr's nearside window, mouthing something al-Qasr couldn't hear. A silver Amtrak passenger train rattled up the line. He wound his window down.

'You're sure as hell lucky this time, bud. What are you, some kinda religious nut?'

'You're confusing me with someone else.' Al-Qasr looked to his glove compartment. One shot and... the police would be all over him.

'Hey, fuckhead! I ain't confusin' you with nobody! I thought you'd wanna know this ain't gonna cost you nuthin'.'

'Delighted to hear it, sir. Is it money you want?' Al-Qasr didn't know what he was saying. The bells had stopped ringing. The barrier was opening, and she was still staring at him.

'I don't want yer fuckin' money, man!'

'OK, OK. I got the message. Now I'm in a hurry.'

'So take your time at a fuckin' crossing! Think of the next guy!'

Al-Qasr slammed his foot on the clutch and rammed the pickup into first, trying not to look at the car coming towards him. He looked to the right to obscure his face.

'I dunno what you mean, Leanne. I always thought those Hasidic Jews looked the same. I thought that was the idea. No vanity. You know, like a uniform. The homburg hat, the ringlets, the steel-rimmed glasses, overcoats. Still, I gotta say I never saw one in a Toyota pickup tryin' to smash his way into a railroad crossing before.'

'Well, there was something about him. I got the feeling he recognised me. I'm sure I've seen him before somewhere.'

'Intuition?'

'Yeah. Isn't that why you said Lee Kellner wanted me to interview al-Qasr?'

'Sure. And it's an Arab suspect we're lookin' into, not a... Unless...'

'Unless what?'

'How did al-Qasr react when you spoke to him about today's meeting?'

terrorist network had arranged for Goksel to be brought to Germany via Chechnya, and Goksel had got himself a job at the Babylon after the regular cook had disappeared. He consoled himself knowing his family was better off with the extra money he received, but he missed his life at home. Here in Europe, the Yezidis were suspicious of the Muslim Kurds. That wasn't so surprising considering that, in the homelands of the old days, Yezidis would be threatened with death if they didn't convert to Islam, and their children would be indoctrinated in Muslim schools to reject what their teachers called 'Devil worship'. But the reality nowadays was very different. In Goksel's experience, generations of living in close proximity had created acceptance and tolerance – just last month he had attended a Yezidi rite of circumcision where a Muslim had held the baby boy.

The Babylon was popular with Kurdish Turks, and Goksel had already established contacts within the Yezidi community, which was based in a converted aircraft hangar and disused government supply centre near Giessen in the state of Hessen. There was currently great excitement in the community as two men had recently arrived from Istanbul, bearing the ancient bronze image of the Peacock Angel: the symbolic representation of Tawusi Melek, the Supreme Angel, whom Yezidis believed governed this world. These two men were named Sinàn and the Baba Sheykh.

Al-Qasr watched as Goksel crossed the cobbles towards the Teufel Café. Goksel entered, swept back his greasy black hair and surveyed the bar. The manager poured him an espresso. Goksel took the cup and ambled over to the narrow wooden table where al-Qasr was sitting.

Goksel took out some cigarette papers and rolling tobacco. He laid a cigarette paper out on the table. Al-Qasr looked over his newspaper at the rolling paper. On it was written a message in pencil:

Doktor. Freitag. 18.00

Goksel tipped out a finger-full of *halfzware* shag into the paper and rolled it up. As he lit it, al-Qasr turned two pages of his newspaper: an agreed code; they would meet at the same time in two days.

84

'Must you use Blu-tack, Toby?'

Ashe had just fixed a blow-up of an old sepia photograph to the plain white wall in front of his desk in his Shrivenham office: a sixty-five-year-old image of a group of Yezidi girls dancing the *debka* in their velvet caps.

'Very striking. Still dreaming of the princess you left behind, Toby?'

'No, Karla. It's the dance. Round in circles to ecstasy. Rather sums up the investigation so far.'

'Ever-decreasing circles?'

'Promising circles.'

'And ecstasy?'

Ashe looked cheekily at Karla's crimson velvet miniskirt and matching tights. 'Hmm...'

'Flirt.'

'Have you tracked down Sir Moses?'

'Nearly, maestro. Expected at his club shortly – the Savile.'

'Sounds about right. Old-style liberal with a hint of the raffish.'

'Just like me.'

While Ashe studied the bulky Beerbohm file, he was also thinking about Hamburg and Sherman Beck. Clearly, the CTC's primary objective was getting al-Qasr back; the Baba Sheykh was incidental to that.

Who was al-Qasr working for? He'd worked for the Americans. He'd worked for Sir Moses Beerbohm. Now it seemed he was wrapped up with Ansar al-Sunna. Over dinner in Alexandria, Lee Kellner had let it slip that there was an Israeli angle to the story: still a jigsaw – or a jig. Ashe looked up at the image of the young Yezidi girls dancing, then back down at Beerbohm's career summary.

Sir Moses Beerbohm. Born 15 April 1927, Lithuania. Raised and educated in Australia. Left University of Melbourne on overseas scholarship, 1951. PhD in Physics, University of Cambridge, UK. Joined the MRC Laboratory of Molecular Biology, University of Cambridge, 1963. Director of MRC Laboratory, 1985–7. President of the Royal Society, 1997–2001. Member, Order of Merit. Foreign Associate, US National Academy of Sciences; Foreign Associate, French Academy of Sciences. Honorary Fellow, Trinity College, Cambridge.

In the fifties, Beerbohm began to study viruses. In the seventies he used electron microscopy and structural modelling to study the three-dimensional nature of polio and other viruses. The more Ashe read about Beerbohm's groundbreaking research into the interactions of proteins and nucleic acids, leading to his discovery of the transcription factors used to regulate the expression of genes, the more Ashe realised what a unique research guinea pig the Baba Sheykh represented to someone like Al-Qasr.

'Your call to Sir Moses Beerbohm, Toby, on red.'

'Sir Moses?'

'Is that the young Dr Ashe who made such an impression over a college lunch? Ran Crayke intimated you might be in touch. Cloak-and-dagger stuff, eh? What can I do for you, my dear fellow?'

'I wonder, Sir Moses, if you recall referring to Sami al-Qasr in the course of our conversation?'

'Oh, *him*: the Thief from Baghdad. I'm sorry if I sound

disappointed, but Sami al-Qasr can have that effect on people. Works at RIBOTech, California. Very hush-hush. He was after the family jewels, Ashe. In more ways than one.'

'Sounds quite something.'

'Oh yes. He could impress. That talent was obvious from the start.'

'What was he doing when you met him?'

'Linking genes to diseases. I presume you already know that one of the common differences between the DNA of one person and another comes in the form of a single nucleotide polymorphism, known as a "snip".'

'Sounds familiar, Sir Moses. What exactly do you mean by a "snip"?'

'Wasn't it in that book of yours… *Generous Gene?*'

'You flatter me, Sir Moses. But that was a while back. More philosophy than fact.'

'All right, let's put it this way: why is Person A going to get Huntingdon's Disease but not Person B? Can it be predicted? Seems pretty old hat now in some respects, but in the sixties and seventies it was foundation work. Al-Qasr was good, no mistake. But the little bum seemed to get bored easily. And I always had the impression he was looking over my shoulder. Curious. Always wanted to cut corners. He was, I suppose, as unstable as many young gifted people. That's why I wouldn't let him marry my daughter.'

'Your daughter?'

'Esther. Al-Qasr said it was because she was Jewish and he was an Arab. Race prejudice. And God, don't I know about that! I told him I was only half Jewish – on my mother's side. My father was East Prussian. He said, "Oh, it all comes through the mother" – which is racial tradition, not first-class genetics. I mean this Jewish thing was one of the reasons my parents left for Australia in the twenties. I wouldn't have thrown it at al-Qasr. But he never believed me. I tried to tell him he just wasn't ready for marriage. But he felt I was trying to keep him down. For heaven's sake, he was my student! He could hardly be my equal.'

'Chip on the shoulder?'

'Or "snip" on the shoulder. Who knows? More of a mountain. As big as his ego – which was big enough, Dr Ashe, believe me. Al-Qasr wanted to be the star. The number one star. Then, when he couldn't have Esther to himself, he wanted to prove he was bigger than me. And, like a fool, I suppose, I encouraged him. Maybe to compensate for the heartache he seemed to be suffering. Don't get me wrong. Al-Qasr was not as horrible as he may sound. We all liked him. But you never felt entirely comfortable with his...'

'Ambition?'

'Yes, ambition. I mean, he joined us at MRC in 1974, just after the Yom Kippur War, and we all knew he had a thing against Israel.'

'Did he include you in that, Sir Moses?'

'Didn't seem to. He recognised a difference between politics and personal matters. After all, he was happy enough to ask a Jewess to be his bride.'

'But not happy to be refused. What did he take from you, if not your daughter?'

'Amusing way of putting it, Dr Ashe. I suppose you could say he ran with the whole ZFP research – you know, the zinc finger protein stuff I was working on. He was close to all the research prior to the big discovery in 1982. He had a hell of an apprenticeship. I should have been so lucky! Then, the following year, he runs back to Iraq. He'd always told me science was bigger to him than any nation, but, when I think about it, Sami al-Qasr probably meant more to him than science.'

'He was an egomaniac?'

'In Iraq, he could be the star.'

85

Beerbohm cleared his throat. 'I never thought Sami al-Qasr was a nut. He's not that different to many other ambitious people in the profession. He's not unreasonable.'

Ashe kept thoughts of the great man's evident naivety to himself. 'Tell me about this zinc finger stuff, Sir Moses.'

'All right, Dr Ashe. But not too long, eh? I'm expecting a friend.'

'A pencil sketch would be helpful.'

'A zinc finger protein, Dr Ashe, is pretty much what it sounds like. They look like fingers. They're projections of protein. They're held in shape by a zinc atom. You find them in all cells. The... well, we call them "fingertips" are configured to match a particular gene sequence. I suppose we could have called them something else. "Gene monitors", or something. Amazing things. When you think there are some 30,000 genes in our DNA! But they don't all work at the same time. If you imagine a kind of "shift" pattern you'd be close to the mark.'

'Like clocking in and clocking out?'

'There is a rotation of sorts. ZFPs pick out the genes that need activating, or the ones that need turning off. For example, we don't all eat at regular times. So in stomach cells, the genes in charge of enzyme production – for digestion – get switched on only when food is on the way.'

'Ingenious.'

'Yes, it is. And yet it's just like everything we experience in the visible world. That's the great thing about science. The rules that control stars also control our fingernails.'

'As above, so below. That's what the alchemists and magicians used to say.'

'And they're right, of course. There's a whole system of natural attractions and correspondences. We can learn about things on Mars by looking at things on Earth. There's a principle that operates in all systems. Science deals with the systems. The principle may just be philosophy.'

'Just philosophy?'

'Well, in science we try to deal with what is actually happening. Effects are easier to see than causes, as you know. For example, when zinc finger proteins find a gene sequence that matches their fingertips, they lock on. That's what they do. They lock on! I can't say I really know *why*. They just do. But I suppose there's a principle at work in there somewhere! Anyhow, as the fingers go into this lock-on mode, what we call a switch molecule gets activated. The switch molecule has been trailing behind the ZFP. This molecule switches the gene on or off.'

'Brilliant stuff, Sir Moses. But how does all this relate to viruses and diseases?'

'You ask all the right questions, Dr Ashe. You'd have made a good pupil.'

'Did al-Qasr ask the right questions?'

'Al-Qasr grew frustrated with the idea of relating genes to disease. But he did cotton on to the implications of zinc finger proteins. It was his eureka moment. As it was mine, in a sense. So, yes, he asked some good questions. These questions led him into a specialised sphere.'

'I'm intrigued. What is this sphere, Sir Moses?'

'Rewriting genes. *Actually rewriting genes*. Altering the building blocks – to some extent anyway. I mean, this is what we're about, here! We want to get right in there and see if we can use this knowledge to help the human race.'

'Did Sami al-Qasr share that ideal?'

'Difficult to say. There's always some self-interest. In Sami's case, I suppose there was more. But he was still making a contribution. We were laying the stones for what would become known as gene therapy. This reached a stable state, more or less, by the mid-eighties, but by then al-Qasr was in Iraq. And I don't honestly know where he took the fairly limited technologies we then had at our disposal.'

'It might help if you could tell me where you had got to?'

'Look, Ashe, could we do all this on another occasion?'

'Forgive me, Sir Moses. I understand, but this enquiry is a matter of some urgency. Lives could be at stake.'

'*Lives*, you say? All right, Dr Ashe. Where were we?'

'Gene therapy.'

'Right. Conventional gene therapy compensates for a genetic fault rather than corrects it. It adds working copies of genes to cells. Viruses have ways of kidding cells to let them in. Once they're in – well, they're in! And there's nothing much you can do about it. Gene therapy took the road of exploiting this cunning.'

'Imitating it?'

'If you like. If you can't beat 'em, join 'em! You can't really beat nature. The aim was to get genetic material incorporated into that of the host. You've got to establish a virus delivery system. New genes have to be smuggled into cells. The human body is a world of covert operations – just up your street, my dear fellow!'

'Thank you.'

'When trying to cure diseases, you want to smuggle in a retrovirus engineered so its genetic material contains the correct version of a faulty gene.'

'Does it work?'

'Limited successes. It was a bit of a scattergun approach. The idea is not unlike the original principle of Jenner's bacteriology. Set a thief to catch a thief. You immunise by getting the system geared up to accept the enemy – in small doses. The body can be deceived. Nature is the great deceiver – and the great deceived.'

'Sounds like philosophy, Sir Moses. I'm not sure I understand yet.'

'Let's put it like this. Patients have their cells "infected", as it were, with these manipulated viruses.'

'Isn't that dangerous?'

'Yes. It's not been a complete success. Far from it, really. Scientifically, it's been very useful, but the process is not very efficient. Only a small number of cells actually take up the new genes. The process can be unstable and you can't be sure the right cells have been targeted. Worryingly, the new gene can insert itself anywhere in the person's DNA. The worst case, I suppose, occurred among a group of French children undergoing gene therapy. Some scientists think the genes inserted too close to those regulating the cancer might have caused leukaemia. There was a delay in trials. But now the technique has been taken further.'

'Did al-Qasr have anything to do with new developments?'

'He probably has some involvement with the new technique.'

'Do you think he may have developed his own techniques?'

'One hears rumours. Science never sleeps. I know he's been involved in gene editing. And this is where ZFPs come into their own: the result, I'm proud to say, of my discovery.'

While Ashe scribbled notes, Karla leant over his desk with a memo:

Melissa telephoned. A misunderstanding.

Are you available today?

Ashe smiled and scrawled 'NO' over it. Karla whispered in his ear, 'On your head be it, maestro!'

Sir Moses picked up on the interruption. 'You got yourself a girlie in there, Dr Ashe?'

'Er, no, Sir Moses. My secretary. You were explaining about gene editing.'

'Can't we discuss your secretary instead?'

'I'm just trying to grasp what direction al-Qasr might be heading in.'

'Speak to RIBOTech, California, though they probably don't want to talk. To be honest, the only person who knows where al-Qasr is right now, is al-Qasr.'

'In more ways than one, Sir Moses.'

'I shan't ask what you mean by that. Off the record, I'd say Sami's involved with advanced gene editing. Hot stuff. Gene editing gets to grips with the DNA's own repair system to correct a faulty gene. It's like hijacking a natural function.

'DNA, as I'm sure you're aware, is the chemical instruction manual for our bodies. One unit in that system is a gene. One small fault in a gene alters the sense of an instruction. These faults or errors are called "single gene defects". They may result in anything from sickle-cell anaemia to Huntingdon's Disease. Some genes control how cells divide. Single gene defects here – especially in later life – cause a range of cancers.

'As I said, in gene editing, zinc finger proteins really come into their own. Now I don't know what al-Qasr's been up to but I can tell you something about the scientists at Sangamo BioSciences, another gene research lab in California. They've had the decency to put their discoveries in the public domain. I can only suspect your man's on strictly government work.'

'I suspect so. Possibly military applications.'

'Hmm… We have people on this sort of thing too. You might find someone to ask about it at one of the government institutions. Talk to Ran. He's your best bet there.'

'What's happened at Sangamo, Sir Moses? I just want to grasp the principle.'

'Ah, yes. As far as I can tell, the scientists there have attached a specially made ZFP to a molecule. This molecule can cut – or edit – DNA. Getting into the cell in the manner of a virus, the zinc fingers locate "their" gene. Then they splice themselves into the genetic movie, as it were. The DNA editor cuts the defective gene. The act of cutting the DNA triggers the cell to repair the damage. Because the cell needs the right bit of DNA to make a repair, fresh copies of the right gene are sent in with the zinc fingers.

'And then, dear friend, by the magic of nature, the cell takes the good genes and uses them as templates for the repair operation. The faulty parts are exchanged for fresh parts. And once repaired, the cell divides normally with all the new cells carrying the correct gene. Quite something, isn't it?'

'Sounds like a cross between a film editor's suite and a commercial garage.'

Sir Moses laughed. 'I suppose it is. It always sounds easy after some poor slave to science has spent years sweating to make it happen! Having said that, Dr Ashe, as far as I know they haven't reached the level of statistically verifiable certainty.'

'Not fully tested yet?'

'No. But they're very close.'

'How close?'

'Six months. But even if they can test it, I'd reckon it will be only a portion of cells – maybe 15 to 20 per cent – that can have faulty genes corrected. Still, what a start!'

'Would you be surprised if I suggested al-Qasr might have made a breakthrough?'

'Of course it's possible, but where's your evidence? You'll need to be sure of your facts. People claim extraordinary things in this field all the time. I'm sure al-Qasr will have seen some of the problems with the earlier gene therapy. He was on to my discoveries pretty damn quickly. But, like I said, he went to Iraq – out of sight, out of mind. And then, the question of motivation comes in.'

'In what sense?'

'Well, if you follow my line about him wanting to be the star. You'd expect him to publish his discoveries and make a great name for himself. You'd be hard pressed to keep him quiet about it – even if he was under a no-disclosure contract with the government. I mean, this kind of discovery could save millions of lives. Imagine the publicity: "Brilliant Arab Saves the World!"'

'Unless…'

'Unless what, Dr Ashe?'

'Well, unless he had even bigger fish to fry.'

'I'm not sure I can help you there. It starts to get science fiction. I mean, what happens when you fall off the cutting edge?'

'Quite.'

Ashe thought hard, trying with all his will to get into the mind of al-Qasr, trying to understand what might be driving him, pushing him, leading him. The information he'd received from Beck was painfully inadequate. What was worse, it seemed well at odds with the picture he was receiving from Sir Moses Beerbohm.

'Are you there, Dr Ashe?'

'Yes, there's just…'

'I think I see my friend. Yes, that's him. I really have to go now. I'm—'

'Sir Moses. A quick question.'

'Is there really such a thing?'

'It's most urgent. I can't put it more strongly than that.'

'Hold on a second.'

86

Sir Moses left the phone to ask his friend to wait for the call to end, but returned swiftly.

'Dr Ashe?'

'Sir Moses, it seems you've something here with this retroviral penetration concept that could be turned into a weapon.'

There was a pause. 'Anything can be turned into a weapon, Toby. That's true. And very frustrating it is for we scientists who prefer to remain moral virgins.'

Ashe laughed.

'I wish it were so funny, Dr Ashe. So many of our revelations turn into nightmares. But as regards your question, well, I suppose the problem here would be *delivery*. How do you get the virus to the target? Still... if that wasn't a factor... I mean, yes, if you can change genetic factors for health, then you can change them for... But it's so hit and miss.'

'Like many weapons, Sir Moses. But what... what if you, for the sake of argument, wished to annihilate a race?'

'Use a bomb! Much quicker!'

'That's not what I mean.'

'Of course. Have you heard that old chestnut that some Israeli politician was harping on about some time ago? A race-targeted weapon.'

'Is that... is that really *possible*?'

'Well Ashe, if you do more homework on the subject, you'll soon find that race is a very complex thing and not really a question of say, a single genetic pattern. Certain races have things in common, like certain families or individuals. But there's no common racial genetic pattern that defines a person genetically as being a member of an ethnic or racial group. We've pretty well all got a bit of each other in us, if you go back far enough. What's that line of John Lennon's? Remember him? Mad but brilliant too. Can't recall exactly but it went something like: "I am he and you are we and you are me and we are all together." Wasn't he saying that from a cosmic perspective or something, he could have been a walrus? Who knows? But it kind of sums it up in a surrealist way. I mean, the idea's preposterous really. Not just the walrus, I mean, but this whole idea of targeting a race from the inside, so to speak. And quite devilish too.

'But whichever way you look at it, Ashe, it's totally impracticable. Many Jews have some genetic components shared, as it were, with Arabs; many Arabs have Jewish or other characteristics. I mean, you might be waving different flags on the outside, but wrapping yourself up with the same one on the inside – and that flag is probably nothing like the one you're waving! I mean, genetics does have something to say about all divisions in the world.'

'A mixed message, I think.'

Sir Moses laughed. 'Yes, of course. But, seriously, a race-based weapon would be no weapon at all, really. I mean, why use genetics? Hitler used gas.'

'But in principle—'

'Well, now you're talking principles again. Philosophy. All right, just for you. A second of speculation. Don't quote me! You'd need... oh I don't know, some kind of control – control specimen – or template. An original genetic map: a primary pattern from which the diversity proceeded. Then I suppose you could track the fundamental mutations. That would, in theory, be like having the key to a safe. But after the Tower of Babel, as the Bible story pictures it, all the races got mixed up.'

'Don't you mean *separated*, Sir Moses? Whereas before they'd been more or less a single entity, the story says after Babel – or Babylon – the peoples could no longer speak the same language.'

'My dear fellow, are we discussing theology here, or science? My point is that since some unknown primordial time, gene pools have been shared around. Everyone's been swimming in everyone else's pool. Gets a bit murky. Our current ideas of race came very late in the day. I mean the Jews weren't even a race before... what is it? Moses? Abraham? It was a belief that separated them, not a skin type. Now I'm only prepared to say another word if the question is strictly scientific and not speculative. My friend is in his eighties – seconds are precious.'

'As they are to me, Sir Moses, believe me. If you had the template – a kind of original genetic template – of a major gene system that is fundamental to a number of races that have stemmed from it, would you be able to learn from it what constitutes the deviation from the original?'

'If you had the template... it's feasible.' Beerbohm paused again. 'Big question... I mean, you might then be able to target families, clans, micro-groups. But, my dear fellow, I suspect it's quite impossible. Where could you get such a template from? It was all too long ago.'

'Thank you, Sir Moses. You've been tremendously helpful.'

'Well, I can't see how, but good luck!'

Ashe replaced the receiver gently, a swell of pride welling up inside him.

'Karla!'

'Yes, maestro.'

'Tell Melissa I'm available. I suddenly feel better about life.'

'Too late. Told her you couldn't speak to her. Said she was going to Dublin with friends and had no idea when she'd be back – *as far as you're concerned*, that is.'

'Me and my big mouth.'

'Depends where you put it. I told you not to play around with that particular young lady. You may have lost her forever.'

'Lost her? I never really found her.'

'Too bad.'

87

Massoud's little house in Shariya was surrounded by villagers, all clamouring to see the relative of the Mir.

Sinàn, a junior member of the Chols – the Yezidi royal family – was nervous. From out of the much-travelled suitcase he carefully took the three components of the *senjaq* and assembled the bronze pieces. A sheykh of the Qatani clan watched closely as Sinàn screwed together the large circular base, the smaller middle disc and then the bulbous, bold-breasted bronze peacock with its stunning fan-like plumage. At the end of each feather was an eye, symbolising the all-seeing lordship of Tawusi Melek, the Peacock Angel.

The Qatani sheykh smiled and kissed the base of the *senjaq*. Women outside the house in long velvet skirts and round linen turbans trilled with excitement. The *senjaq*, or standard, was the sacred image of the Lord of the Earth's destiny, the invisible patron of the Yezidis, the world's secret governor, the greatest angel of them all, given control of the universe by the highest god, whose spirit dwelled in everything. Several villagers shook with emotion to see the sacred peacock, the focus of devotion, a signifier of the divine presence, his all-seeing will. It was a symbol of continuity and of the future blessings guaranteed to faithful Yezidis, God's special people – born to suffer, in a unique way, the miseries and trials of the centuries.

It had been a long time since these people had witnessed the parade of the peacock through their village. Their village – as most people would understand the term – was gone.

The inhabitants of seven villages from the surrounding mountains had been forcibly relocated to Shariya by Saddam Hussein during the seventies, obliged to start again in a unified cluster of spare, concrete nests constructed by the government on a cruelly arid plain. Yet the identities of each of the seven villages had remained intact. So much so that during this, the annual visit of the Baba Sheykh to the Yezidi villages, the spiritual guest had to stay for seven nights, with a host from each of the original seven villages.

A Yezidi village, like the sheykh, was a spiritual as well as a physical entity. The official map said 'Shariya', but in their hearts the Yezidis were still linked to their own mountain pastures, with their crops and goats.

But where was the Baba Sheykh? The villagers expected him. This was tradition and Tawusi Melek willed such things to be.

A meeting with the Mir in Baghdad had decided the issue. News of the Baba Sheykh's kidnap was to be withheld from the *murids*, or followers of the sheykhs, as long as possible. Such news could only dampen morale, already at a low ebb. Worse, the news would surely lead to rumours and then to vivid but fictional accounts; there would be cries for revenge. Someone would be blamed.

The sheykhs, in the absence of their leader, were particularly concerned. Rather than have one of them deputise for the absent Baba – which might give rise to speculation that the Baba had been replaced high-handedly by a rival – it had been decided to dispatch Sinàn, a much respected close friend of the Baba Sheykh.

As a doctor, he could provide immediate and much-appreciated assistance. And, as extra compensation for the absence of the Baba Sheykh himself, it had been agreed that the Sheikhani *senjaq* would be 'walked' through each 'village' of Shariya – a special privilege, much envied by surrounding Yezidi communities.

The story put out was that the Baba Sheykh had remained behind to offer special spiritual service to the absent Yezidi

364

brethren who were undergoing difficulties in Germany. The Baba Sheykh's presence in that country could be confirmed, at least for the time being, by relatives of German-based Yezidis still living in Kurdistan.

This was the reason Sinàn had driven fifty kilometres north-west from his much-neglected apartment in Mosul to this dry and dusty satellite of the big, bustling city of Dohuk. There were added responsibilities, and these too made Sinàn nervous.

It was the custom for the Baba Sheykh, while staying in the houses of the village hosts, to try to solve disputes and feuds. Since 2002 there had been a particularly painful feud going on which had already claimed several lives and threatened more. Lacking the spiritual authority of the Baba Sheykh, with his conduit to the will of Tawusi Melek and the judgement of the ancestors, Sinàn was thrown back on variations of the 'you must look at the bigger picture' argument. This authoritative strategy was artfully combined with moral injunctions carried, it was believed, from the mouth of the absent religious leader.

The previous night, Sinàn had told visitors to Massoud's house that just as they were now watching the bigger world, through their antennae and prized satellite dishes, the bigger world would be watching them also. They had entered a new era, an era that demanded exemplary behaviour. The reputation of the Yezidis was at stake. They were a special people, called to a higher destiny. The spiritual integrity of all Yezidis would suffer from the follies of the few.

Sinàn was not at all sure that his words – coming from one in a smart Western suit with a silvery silk tie – carried much weight with people who were suffering great anxieties and hardship, as well as the peculiar pressure that comes with great hope. If only he knew what had happened to the Baba Sheykh.

Amid the chatter of the excited women, Sinàn could hear the gathering beat of the massive tambours held by the *qewwals*. Then the flutes began their transcendent melismas. The *qewwals* began to sing. Sinàn raised the standard aloft. As he emerged

through the front door into the dusty street, the *qewwals* began
singing 'The Morning Prayer':

> *Amen, amen,*
> *The blessing of the faith.*
> *God is the best of Creators.*
> *Through the miraculous power of Shem el-Din,*
> *Fekhr el-Din, Sejadin,*
> *Nasir el-Din and Babadin,*
> *Sheykh Shems is the strength of the faith,*
> *Sultan Sheykh Adi is the crown, from first to last.*
> *Truth, Praise be to God. Oh Lord of the Worlds,*
> *Give good things, avert evil.*
> *We long for a moment of the Presence.*
>
> *Light comes from the light of dawn,*
> *Praise to you, my Creator.*
> *The Angel is facing us.*
>
> *From house to house,*
> *Sheykh Shems is the lord of lustre...*

Past the cream-coloured houses, the procession continued.
Ahead of Sinàn marched a flautist dressed in a long black embroidered waistcoat and baggy black trousers. Children gathered,
running cheerfully alongside the growing procession. White-
bearded old men joined in too, wearing Arab-style red-chequered
headdresses bound with black rope. Fathers in white linen robes
had wrapped checked turbans about their skull caps; some
sported pointed black beards. A few visitors from the Jebel Sinjar
still wore the long black ringlets of days long gone, framing their
handsome faces. Old men with huge moustaches – a sign of religious devotion – waved on the procession with their walking
sticks. Teenage girls in Western-style blouses and sandy-coloured
cotton trousers cheered along the *senjaq*'s 'walk' as Sinjari

matriarchs in massive white headdresses bound at the chin by great swathes of cotton clapped their hands and trilled along with the pulsing prayer.

On every side and surface of the uniform concrete houses the flash of the morning light added to the colour.

Sinàn began to relax; things seemed to be going well. He joined in with the prayer he had heard so many times in this life.

From pillar to pillar,
Sheykh Shems is the lord of mystical knowledge, of the
*   pillars of the faith,*
And of discernment.

From eye to mouth,
The baptism of Sheykh Shems falls on one,
The Great Ones are busy; they do not allow you to sleep.

From head to feet,
Oh Sheykh Shems, you designed us and set us on our paths...

88

The procession turned a corner into an identical street and there in its sun-drenched centre, shimmering gloriously, stood Sinàn's only sister: the Morning Star – Laila. The princess was accompanied by a group of smiling, bearded sheykhs, impossible to miss in their distinctive turbans that looked like miniature white mill-stones. Red sashes hung diagonally, right to left, across their chests and they wore white woollen capes that reached down to their knees.

Laila's heart leapt as she saw the princely figure of her brother approaching. Sinàn wanted to thrust the *senjaq* into someone else's hands and run to embrace his sister, but he could not. He had to go on to the next village host.

Laila stepped aside as the sheykhs joined the procession one by one. As Sinàn passed Laila, his eye was caught by a girl standing in her shadow. After the last sheykh had joined the procession's serpentine path, Laila grabbed the girl's hand and led her to the back.

The festivities continued throughout the day and into the evening. The new host slaughtered a goat to feed the many men and women from his village who came to converse with the unexpected guest and to kiss the base of the Peacock Angel. They all left money, as was customary, for the Baba Sheykh, and for the absent Mir.

Late in the evening, when the men of the village had left the host's rug-filled living room, the princess entered and introduced Rozeh to her brother.

'My Sister of the Hereafter. She wants to be a doctor.'

'I know.'

'Will it happen?'

'She's the niece of the Kochek of Bashiqa.'

This was considered a sufficient answer to the question. He looked at her intently; the girl covered her face with her long black hair and blushed. 'Please don't be shy. I'm so sorry to hear what happened to your mother and father. Another tragedy.'

'Did you know them, Sinàn?'

'The Baba Sheykh told me about them. We had so much time to talk. We discussed many things. Important things. Little things. They were good people. True Yezidis. Faithful to the tradition. I do not think Baba knows yet what evil befell them on that day. He will be very sorry.'

He looked again into Rozeh's wide, moist eyes. 'Please don't cry. You want to be a doctor, don't you? You will see many terrible things. Many terrible things. Things you would never believe. You will hear the cries of the lost and the cries of those who fear losing. You will look into the eyes of death and find life. You will look into lively eyes and see things, things you wish you'd never seen. You cannot cry every day, or you will see nothing.'

'I want to serve the people, like you have done, sir.'

'Very well, young lady. I'll see what can be done.'

Rozeh smiled. 'I thank you, sir. May I go now?'

'Of course, Rozeh! You run along and enjoy yourself.' Laila patted her spiritual sister on the back. 'Yes, it is time to go and gossip with your new friends in Shariya.'

'Have you got the tape, Highness?'

Laila looked into her handbag and brought out the cassette of Madonna's *Ray of Light* album she had bought in Cairo.

'Do you like her, Sinàn?'

'I've only just met her.'

'You seem to know a lot about her.'

'The Baba Sheykh knew her parents well. He spoke of her.

Not very much. I knew she wanted to study medicine. Her family had very high hopes.'

Mamo, the host, brought coffee to his guests in tall glass goblets.

'Is there anything I can do for you, Highness?'

'May my sister and I be left alone for a while, Mamo?'

'Of course.'

Mamo, a serious-looking man of about thirty with a short wispy moustache, tightened the thick cotton sash around his robed waist, backed away to the door of his house, then slipped into the darkness. The day had been long, and had cost him much – even more than his satellite dish. Now he might have to sell it. But to have given shelter to the *senjaq*! This was ample recompense.

'I thought I might never see you again, Sinàn.'

'I don't understand how you found me here so quickly. I've only been in Kurdistan a few days. Toby Ashe told me he thought you were in Cairo.'

'What did you think of him?'

'I cannot say, Laila. It was very strange in Germany. He has a good mind. I think I like him. He knows a lot about us. Perhaps he has saved my life. But it is all so complicated. There are Americans involved and strange things happened in Istanbul. But, yes, I think somehow Toby Ashe may have saved my life.'

'We owe him much.'

'The Baba…? '

'I'm sure he will help find him. He found you.'

'But I'm lost, Laila. I'm being asked questions all the time. What can I say?'

Laila put her arm round her brother. 'You're tired.'

'I've been tired for a long, long time. And I failed. I was supposed to protect the Baba Sheykh. With my life. My hands. And I allowed myself to be tricked.'

'Stop it! Stop it, Sinàn! This will get us nowhere. Here, drink this!'

370

'Forgive me!'

'Nonsense. I thank you. We all thank you.'

Sinàn shook his head and looked around the simple house. 'It's another world here. They will not understand. The Autumn Festival's coming – the Great Assembly at Lalish! What can we say? Only a few weeks. And no Baba Sheykh! We have never held the Assembly without the Baba Sheykh! It is unheard of! People will think the world is falling apart! Everyone knows he would never stay in Germany while the lights of Lalish are lit for the Assembly!'

'Don't worry! What were we singing this morning? *Amen, amen, The blessing of the faith*. The angel wills it; good will prevail for our people. This is a test! Every generation is tested somehow. I tell you, brother, I believe in this Tobbi Ashe.'

'Ridiculous woman! He is not one of us.'

'No, but…'

'But nothing.'

'Whatever you think of him, you must speak to him. He says he must speak to you.'

'Why didn't he ask me his questions in Hamburg?'

'He says you were whisked away by the American—'

'The amiable Mr Beck!'

'And before Tobbi knew it, you'd been flown back here in a US plane.'

'And interrogated for days.'

'Did they hurt you?'

'No, but I would have preferred to be somewhere else.'

'What did you tell them?'

'That it was not me they should be interrogating, but another.'

89

Did Ashe believe in coincidences? Coincidences happened, but had no essential meaning. If you could see the meaning, then it would no longer be a coincidence. Why was he back in Iraq? Coincidence? Of course not.

Major Richmond turned to Ashe. 'You've been quiet for the last two hours. Silent. We've enough graves in Iraq, right now. This road's pretty boring, y'know.'

Ashe looked about him. The route north from Baghdad through the Sunni heartlands and on to the Kurdish Autonomous Region looked the same as it had on his last visit, but the whole thing felt entirely different. It was as though he had been dreaming on his last visit. Was he a different man?

'You're losing your romanticism, Ashe. Happens to all of us.'

'Temporary, I'm sure, Simon. Just a bit more focused, I think. Keen to get to the point. I've just been philosophising. To be honest, you don't seem the same either.'

'Tired, Toby. Just fucking tired. It's been getting worse while you've been away. Remember we were trying to plug holes in the western border with Syria? It's like an open wound now. Not enough men really.'

'Morale, OK?'

'Pretty good, Toby. Good things have been happening. But it's the carnage. I don't think we expected this kind of civilian death toll. The retribution killings. The strength of the opposition. The bloodlust. Continual murders. It's unnatural. It's like a plague's hit the land. Don't get me wrong. We'll win out here. There are elections coming up in the new year. That's our focus. As long as you've got focus, the random events have meaning. When you've got meaning, you've got purpose.'

'Funny you should say that, Simon. I was thinking the very same thing.'

Richmond smiled, his taut features softening for a few seconds. He did look that bit thinner, that bit more worn, that bit older. His steely nerve seemed a little frayed.

The Mercedes sped north at 70 to 80 mph. Having passed through the Kurdish checkpoints with little difficulty, Ashe noticed that Richmond reduced his speed. Iraqi Kurdistan had a far better security record than further south. There were even tentative plans to get Kurds to come back to their homeland from Europe. The Kurdish Democratic Party was setting up a website. That sounded hopeful. All the same, Ashe instinctively felt for the loaded SIG pistol beneath his bulletproof vest.

As they headed north, past the spreading city of Mosul, Ashe's heart warmed.

He looked east, to the Sheikhan, home of the Yezidis.

At the busy T-junction fifty kilometres north of Mosul, Ashe studied the new Kurdish sign: 'Duhok, 10 km'. He was due to meet Sinàn at a new bar in the centre of the flourishing city. Time was running out.

'I'll pick you up in five hours, so you'd better get a move on. I've an arrangement to meet an old friend of ours at Shariya, not far from here.'

'Old friend?'

'Jolo Kheyri.'

'Give him my warmest regards.'

'And er... I believe a certain Princess Laila will be there. Now isn't that a coincidence?'

'No, Simon. That is fate.'

90

The name was clever. 'Welcome to The Future', 'We have seen The Future – and we love it' read the advertisements, in Kurmanji and in English. Against all the odds, there was a hopeful spirit in the air.

The moment Ashe sat down at the bar, Sinàn appeared, looking worried. He ordered two Carlsbergs and suggested they move to a table at the rear next to the kitchen door and the lavatories. 'It's cooler.'

'You mean safer.'

'Nobody comes here until late, I think, Mr Ashe.'

'Please call me Toby.'

'If it pleases you. My sister is already on familiar terms with you, I believe.'

A pretty waitress in a light silk scarf, jeans and white sweat-shirt brought the drinks to their table. Sinàn smiled at her. It was clear she didn't recognise him from Adam. They were all Kurds now and the status, or lack of it, of the Yezidi royal family had little meaning in Kurdish politics. Ashe couldn't quite stop himself from seeing this handsome scion of the Chol family as something of a spiritual exile in the fast-reshaping Kurdistan.

'My sister wants me to trust you, Toby. I don't know why I should. But I trust her.'

Ashe noticed the pain in Sinàn's face. 'Whatever you tell me, Sinàn, has one objective: to recover a certain person from the hands of a very wicked man. What do you know about the man who has taken that certain person from us?'

'I don't know much. There were men I met in Turkey. Guinea pigs from Saddam's laboratories. They saw the wickedness. It's hard to believe. I remember hearing about that bright young man at Baghdad University when I studied medicine. Many admired him. They were admiring a monster, but they did not know it. An enemy of God and our people.'

Ashe signalled to Sinàn to lower the volume of the conversation. Sinàn got up, went to the bar, and whispered something to the girl. She nodded and turned to the CD player below a shelf of glasses. The latest Coldplay anthem was soon pounding through the room. To Ashe's ears, this future sounded like the past.

Sinàn resumed his seat. 'I asked for British music. She seemed pleased to provide it.'

'It's OK. Your visit to Istanbul, Sinàn. What was that all about?'

Sinàn laughed at the thought. 'Istanbul!' For a moment, the melancholy in his face vanished. 'Before all this business started, you'd be surprised how lively the Baba Sheykh was. Always bubbling with ideas. A very special mind, Mr Ashe. But like so many men with a well-defined social role, he could not always show it. I've known him since I was a boy. Even then he told me his ideas. He could be very funny. Always saw things from a higher perspective, like he was on a mountain. I think if the Yezidi people were better known, he could have been a world figure. Like the Pope maybe. But more surprising. His spirit was very free. But always, always his feet are on the ground. I miss him so much.'

'But why go to Istanbul?'

'He had an idea. Subtle. Maybe too subtle! Show the world the terrible plight of my people. But he would not beg. He did not want to say, "Look, we can't help ourselves. We need the UN or something." We can help ourselves, but we need some help too. What God has sent us, we accept. We must use our brains. We must be clever. If we have a problem, maybe it is sent by God to test us. This is the sort of thing the Baba Sheykh would say to us. So the question was, how to show the truth to the world without it being just another cry from an oppressed people with a begging bowl. He believed the strong attract the strong.'

'Strong in spirit?'

'If the spirit is gone, the rest follows. Now, Baba knows that most people are like children. Even leaders of the world talk like children. They even have tantrums and throw things about. But like children, they love stories and mysteries. The Baba Sheykh wanted, as it were, to put a mystery into the pot – then let the way of the world stir it up a bit. The Baba Sheykh knows that there has always been a great fascination with Freemasonry. There is a mystery there. There is secrecy and the hint of something...'

'Supernatural?'

'Perhaps. The penalty for being a Freemason under Saddam, of course, was death. Why? Many of our Arab neighbours have condemned Freemasonry in the last fifty years. I think the Palestine–Israel conflict has a lot to do with this change in attitude. Crazy talk of Zionist-Masonic conspiracies.'

'I think you're right.'

'We know that extremists who are dictating to people in our country and now dictating to people around the world insist Freemasonry is a Western creation, an evil creation. That it is somehow against the true God and people of faith.'

'So what did the Baba Sheykh have to say?'

'A different point of view.'

Ashe looked out through the open doors of the bar to the Duhok rush hour, chugging past the new bar like the passage of history.

'A different point of view, Sinàn?'

'His view. Baba's view. He said it was consistent with the tradition he embodies.'

'Tradition?'

'That is how we refer to our beliefs.'

'What was the Baba Sheykh's point of view?'

'You must read the text, because it is the way he expresses it that is so special. His mind was in his words. If I try to say it, you will only see the outside.'

'Can you give me a clue?'

'The Baba Sheykh intended to prove that Freemasonry is not a Western creation, but is older than Islam, older than Jesus. He wanted to show that when people understand it properly, it holds a promise, not a threat, for the world.'

Ashe was disappointed. The idea that Freemasonry came from the ancient world was hardly new. 'But why did the Baba Sheykh want to make his statement in Turkey?'

'Baba understood that interest in the mystique surrounding Freemasonry could make Westerners curious about the Yezidis. In Turkey, Islam is the religion, but Freemasonry is not forbidden. Turkish governments have not always been as just to Yezidis as they have to Freemasonry, so there would be a little controversy. Baba thought choosing a Turkish Lodge would help the message get into the public sphere. He was excited about the internet because it carries truth as well as lies. If a story is good, news travels fast.'

Ashe felt tempted to say that bad news travels faster, but knew he would have to keep Sinàn on a positive note. He feared Sinàn might withdraw into himself at any moment. Ashe thought about his next question carefully.

'Was there a ... political aspect to what the Baba Sheykh had to say?'

'The Baba Sheykh would not have made the speech unless he believed it to be true. That was its secret power.'

'But he never made the speech.'

'He wrote it, Toby Ashe. And friends of mine in Istanbul ensured that he would be invited to give this speech.'

'Can you tell me the names of these friends?'

'I would not do them such a disservice.'

'Are the names Yildiz and Yazar familiar to you?'

'No.'

Ashe could see from Sinàn's eyes that the names were indeed familiar to him. Ashe knew that if the Americans knew Sinàn was friendly with Kurdish separatist politicians suspected by Turkish authorities of sympathy, or more, with the PKK, Sinàn would be interrogated once more, and not quite so humanely. Satisfied Sinàn was no stranger to Kurdish politics in Turkey, Ashe knew better than to poke further into an issue that would probably terminate the conversation.

'So tell me, Sinàn, why didn't the speech actually take place in Istanbul?'

'The Lodge Master in Istanbul requested a copy of the speech in advance. You can't just say anything in a Lodge meeting. I was told it was sent to the Grand Secretary of the English Grand Lodge because Britain is the home of Freemasonry. That is where the leading scholars and historians of Masonry live. The Turkish Lodge wanted the approval of English Freemasons.'

'Presumably because the United Grand Lodge of England dispenses Masonic authority in many parts of the world.'

'That is true. The largest Masonic jurisdiction in Turkey is in fellowship with the English Grand Lodge. That is to say, Toby Ashe, that the United Grand Lodge of England *recognises* Turkey's largest Grand Lodge.'

'You seem to know a lot about it, Sinàn.'

Sinàn cleared his throat. 'My friends in Istanbul explained this to me. They said that a Lodge that is not "recognised" by the English Grand Lodge is not accepted as pure Freemasonry. They told me that in France there is a "Grand Orient" Lodge that does not require people to believe in God. Because of this, the Grand Orient is not "recognised", as they call it, by the English Grand Lodge. Are you a Mason, Toby Ashe?'

'I haven't visited for many years. Was the Baba Sheykh a Brother?'

'You asked me about the speech. It was sent to London. We heard nothing. Nothing. Not approval. Not disapproval. All was still set for the meeting in March but then—'

'Yes?'

'We received a warning. Definite warning, Toby Ashe. Very convincing. Baba was informed someone wanted to kill him. He must leave Turkey. He was also warned he would not be safe in Iraq. Germany was better for him. We have friends there.'

'Who gave you the warning?'

'People I trusted. Well-informed people.'

'Did you inform the Lodge you would not attend?'

'We were told not to do so. We went west, Toby Ashe. And there you found me.'

91

'Tobbi!' It was Laila in the doorway, a star in the afternoon sun.

Ashe was taken aback by the sight of the princess in a khaki military blouse tucked into desert slacks, her black hair tied right back and covered by a red polka-dot scarf.

Laila kissed Ashe on the cheek; Sinàn looked on jealously.

'Excuse me, gentlemen. I am your chauffeur for Shariya!'

'I was expecting Major Richmond.'

'He sent me, Tobbi.'

'Not alone, I hope.'

'No, Tobbi, I have two bodyguards. The major is with Jolo. New developments. He wants you to know about it, Tobbi. I will wait outside for you.'

The two men sat down again as Laila left the bar; it seemed darker without her.

'She likes you a lot, Toby Ashe.'

Ashe feigned indifference and said nothing.

'You know we do not permit marriage outside our tradition.'

'It's one of the many remarkable things about your people.'

'You do not wish to marry my sister?'

'Your sister, Sinàn, is a person of dignity whom I respect as a friend.'

'If you respect me, you will respect my sister as a Yezidi.'

'Of course. Now there is something I'd like to hear from your lips, Sinàn. When did the wicked man first become a threat to your people, and to the Baba Sheykh?'

'Like I told the Americans at the interrogation, it was more than ten years ago. There was a rumour around the Yezidi villages.'

'Rumour?'

'That this wicked man killed the Baba Sheykh's son.'

'His *son*?'

'Yes, his only son. His only son… was used, the rumour said, to test the effects of diseases, or poison gas. Wickedness. So, it was decided by some people to kill the wicked man.'

'On a rumour?'

'I mean stop the wicked man. When we had him, then we would know. But we could never get close to him. It was after the first Gulf War. There was an uprising. An uprising in the south and an uprising in the north. We believed the Americans would help us. In the confusion, some people tried to find the wicked man in Baghdad. Then we heard he was gone. He ran away. Now he has come back. And now I ask a question of you, Toby Ashe. I am thinking that this wicked man wants revenge because of the plan to take him that made him escape from Baghdad. But now I am thinking… Why should the Americans and the British want him so much? What has he done to them? And how do you know that this man wants to… I think he wanted to kill me in Hamburg, and you saved me. But then why did he not kill the Baba Sheykh when he found him? Why, Toby Ashe, why do you think this wicked man has taken our holy man? What does he want with him?'

'You really have no idea at all?'

'Please! Please, Toby Ashe! What does he want? If it is money, we will find money!'

Ashe squirmed uncomfortably in his seat. In a sense, the Yezidi leaders had a right to know. But Sinàn was not obliged to keep secrets. Promises would be worthless.

'OK, Sinàn. Let's get this straight. I understood from Mr Beck that you were making contact with his department in the USA during your trek with the sheykh. You seemed to know a lot about the wicked man's work when he was employed by Saddam.'

'*Contact*, Toby Ashe? What contact? I never make contact! How would I know how to make contact with American secret services? That's what I kept telling them at the interrogation! Why would they not believe me?'

'Did they...? They didn't...?'

'Torture me? No, not torture. Just hours and hours of the same questions. And always I gave the same answers. The same things I am repeating to you today. They're probably watching me now. They want to know who I will contact, I suppose. Surely, Toby Ashe, you are working with them? So tell them, Toby Ashe, tell them I would never think of sending messages to the CIA! That is why I agreed to see you. My sister says you are a good man, and you tell your American friends that what I have said to them is the truth.'

'I can tell them. But if they don't believe you, why should they believe me?'

'They kept saying their messages came from a man who called himself "the doctor". And that that was me, because I was in Hamburg and they had traced a message to Germany. I had nothing to tell them. I have nothing to tell you, except please, please find my friend! Tell us where he is!'

Ashe sighed. 'I'm sorry, Sinàn. I only wish I knew.'

92

Beneath vast skies, Princess Laila continued to cast Ashe appreciative glances. Ashe was conscious that Sinàn, sitting moodily in the back seat with two of Jolo's militia, was catching every look with ill-disguised contempt. Was it sibling jealousy? Seemed unlikely. Perhaps he was just the moody type. Sinàn showed no interest in talking to the militiamen either. The taciturn Yezidis respected Sinàn's silence and instead concentrated on closely observing every house roof, alleyway, passing car and cart.

It seemed most likely to Ashe that Laila's brother was suffering from depressive anxiety since losing contact with the Baba Sheykh. Nevertheless, he could not entirely shake the conviction that Sinàn somehow held him, Ashe, personally responsible for the Baba Sheykh's predicament – both before the kidnap, and since. He knew Ashe and the Americans were hiding something.

The open Land Rover 110 approached Shariya. The collective village was low-lying, situated beneath rolling terracotta slopes. Laila's long fingers squeezed Ashe's knee. Uncomfortable, Ashe felt himself itching to get back to Europe. He had an old friend who worked at Freemasons' Hall. What the hell had the Baba Sheykh been going to say to the Turkish Lodge that necessitated English Masonic approval? Furthermore, the time had come to use Aslan's arrest of Yildiz and Yazar to help the investigation. If it *was* Yildiz and Yazar who had warned the Baba Sheykh in Istanbul, how did they know about al-Qasr's intentions against him? Was it certain al-Qasr was behind the threat to the Baba

Sheykh's life in Istanbul? And if it was, who told him the Baba Sheykh was on the Lodge guest list that night?

The sight of Shariya did nothing to encourage Ashe to linger in Iraq. The whitewashed warren of single-storey concrete boxes was clearly Saddam's idea of a village for people he did not trust. But the Yezidis had made a home of it. Vital electricity buzzed through a network of crooked wooden pylons that criss-crossed the village like a cat's cradle. Ashe couldn't help noticing the satellite dishes bent back to receive the media vision, like mini Easter Island gods squatting on the roofs.

Children cheered the returning militia as the Land Rover dodged the occasional pickup truck. Richmond's armour-plated Mercedes was unmistakable. Inside, Richmond, Jolo and an excitable interpreter huddled over a series of maps, enjoying the air-conditioning and the tension of fresh intelligence.

Inside the house opposite, a small line of villagers queued up quietly to kiss the sacred base of the *senjaq*, watched by a stone-faced sheykh who collected the devotees' money.

'I'm afraid I must leave you, Dr Ashe. I have disputes to settle before I leave. Are you coming with me, Laila?'

'You promised to take Rozeh into Duhok this evening, Sinàn.'

'I've not forgotten. I shall... leave you here then. Goodbye, Toby Ashe.'

Ashe gave him a firm shake of the hand and looked deep into the Yezidi's eyes. 'We *will* find the sheykh, Sinàn. Believe me.'

The doctor nodded with a faint smile. 'That is more than we have a right to expect.'

Inside the Merc, Richmond continually congratulated Jolo on his achievements. Having an interpreter meant that Jolo heard each congratulatory utterance twice, and this made his youthful face twice as proud. Jolo was also delighted at the latest provision of new armour, ammunition and transmission equipment. Major Richmond had been as good as his word.

There was a good deal of shaking of hands and very soon

Jolo, who hugged Ashe warmly, was out of the vehicle and on his way. Richmond turned to the young interpreter. 'Take a walk. If people want to talk to you, make yourself available. Could be useful.'

Ashe looked down at the map spread over the dashboard, covered with large felt-pen detail of divisional movements and coded military dispositions.

'OK, Toby. There's something come up might interest you. As you know, most security work done in this sector is US-controlled. And done pretty well too, by and large.'

'Glad to hear it.'

'Still, we have our uses. Jolo's detachment has been invaluable out in the western desert between the Jebel Sinjar and the north Syrian border. Recently though, I thought he needed a change of air and space, so I organised some reconnaissance missions for his detachment here.'

Richmond pointed to the far northeast, close to the Iraqi border with Turkey's Hakkari Province. 'You see here, Toby, the Hakkari Mountains respect no border. This seems to have inspired our Turkish friends.

'We expect Turkish special forces activity in this area. Their argument is strong enough to satisfy themselves: if the US won't come down on the PKK – though they are known terrorists – then it's Turkey's responsibility to pursue the "war on terrorism" beyond its borders, as the US and Britain have done.'

'Yeah. I can't see it making headlines anywhere.'

'Now, have a look round here.' Richmond waved his finger over a seriously mountainous area some seventy kilometres to the northeast of Duhok. 'Jolo started a series of observation sorties from this point.'

'Al-Amadiyah?'

'The Kurds call it Amadiyye. Now, see this fan from Amadiyye north to the Turkish border post at Üzümlü, then follow the line of the border about twenty-five kilometres east to the next Turkish border point at Khwari, then back down to Amadiyye.'

'Looks like tough terrain.'

'It is. We need Jolo. His eyes see things differently to the rest of us. Extraordinary. I reckon he could give the Gurkhas a run for their money – in their own country! Now, you see these little Kurdish villages and townships?'

'I can just make out Betfa, Kara, Rashi, Baytka, Nerva Zheri—'

'That last one, Nerva Zheri. You need the satellite map to see this properly, but within a five-kilometre radius of the place, Jolo's seen some unusual activity.'

'Unusual?'

'Turkish special forces. Carrying supplies mostly. Not much surprising in that, though it seems more intense than what we've seen before.'

'Something else going on there?'

'It's odd. In the same territory, they've observed small detachments of Ansar al-Sunna forces training there. Now it's been all I can do to persuade Jolo and his men not to blow these guys into the next world.'

'So what's your point?'

'The point, Toby, is that given the proximity of their respective operations, the Turkish special forces and the foreign insurgents are literally moving in each others' footsteps!'

'They could be tracking one another. But why are you telling *me* this? I mean, if you're asking my opinion, I'd say at the worst what you've got here is Turkish special forces co-opting Ansar al-Sunna terrorists into their war on renegade PKK forces over the Iraqi border.'

Richmond was surprised how comfortable Ashe was with this thought. 'Well, that would be a startling new development wouldn't it, Toby? I mean, mighty embarrassing for the Turkish government, to say the least, if that's what we're looking at here! Can you see the headline? "Turkey uses al-Qaeda allies to kill Kurds." That would do nothing for their hopes of joining the EU. The US might reasonably regard them as a legitimate target.'

'I don't suppose the world at large would hear about it. Stakes are too high.'

'You have a point. Anyhow, let's not jump to conclusions. We need to keep a very close eye on this.'

'It's nice to be kept informed, Simon, but why tell *me*?'

'Crayke said I should.'

'What?'

'Keep you informed of developments. On the Turkish border.'

93

Royal Military College of Science, Shrivenham, Wiltshire

Ashe slapped a large black-and-white photograph of Colonel Mahmut Aslan onto his secretary's desk, then grabbed his blue overcoat and opened the door of his office. 'Get this faxed off to Hamburg, will you please, Karla? I've spoken to the Hamburg letting agent.'

'Who he?'

'One Gerhard Fitzthum, of Fitzthum & Nietzsche. They deal in property and antiques. Question is: can he positively identify the image of this person? Was the person depicted involved in the letting transaction for the Altona apartment? Need an answer today, Karla. Details in the covering note. Call you from London. Adios!'

Ashe stepped over the large brass pentagram embedded into the polished-stone threshold and entered the marble reception of Freemasons' Hall, 60 Great Queen Street, London WC2.

The reception was vast and dim. Ahead: a grand staircase, carpeted in the distant past. Ashe approached the reception desk. A uniformed man with a passionless demeanour looked him up and down for signs of Masonic engagement. Ashe was not wearing a black tie. His trousers were black, his shirt was black, his jacket was an encouragingly blue cashmere, but his hair was rather long and unruly.

'Yes, sir.'

'I've an appointment with Julian Travers. Your information officer.'

'I know what he does, sir.' The man looked around for his phone and groped about for a printed list of internal numbers. 'Travers, is it, sir?'

'Yes.'

'Here it is: Travers, J., Information Officer.' He prodded the internal number. 'Gentleman here to see you, Julian. Excuse me, what's your name, sir?'

'Ashe.'

'Says 'is name's Ashe. Right. Mr Travers says to go up to 'is office. First floor.'

Ashe turned and headed for the staircase.

'Excuse me, sir. I'm s'posed to ask for ID now, sir. Security thing.'

Ashe turned to the man and looked him in the eye with a twinkle. 'I was taught to be cautious.'

The security guard winked. 'Right, sir. First floor, sir.'

Ashe tore up the staircase to the floor housing the Library and Museum of Freemasonry and turned right, down a narrow corridor opening off into dozens of separate Lodge rooms. He was amused, as always, to remember that this public building housed the largest collection of lavatories in central London, and he popped into one to check that the unmistakeable smell of damp and cleaning powder had remained unchanged. Like many things in the lodge, the lavatories had an air of faded grandeur; their vast powder-blue basins, magnificent urinals and purpose-built brass ashtrays speaking of an old-fashioned, masculine sensibility.

Rounding a corner, Ashe narrowly avoided crashing into a battalion of old ladies emerging from an ancient-looking cleaning cupboard. He stopped briefly to congratulate them on the high shine on the lapis-lazuli-coloured linoleum flooring, which stretched, seemingly endlessly, down to the shabby grey lift, and took another right towards the library gallery.

As he passed a cleaner's cupboard decorated with newspaper pictures of the royal family, not updated since the 1980s, Ashe reflected that, like the edifice of English Freemasonry in general,

Grand Lodge seemed to be in a state of denial. Instead of mysticism, magic or spirituality, here was a granite ideology of empire and enterprise: a brotherhood of trust, a sober cult of moral rectitude. It was a building that should have been constructed with eternity in mind. Instead, it belonged to the twenties and thirties and seemed to have stayed there.

Change, inertia's gift, would surely come to Grand Lodge, but what kind of change would it be? Given the character of the times, and the spiritual vacuity of the influential, any change was likely to involve further reduction of spiritual substance, probably to cold-zero. The end of modernisation was likely to be a hierarchical social club with historical frills whose genuine roots had been lost, and, where not lost, ignored by those with the most to lose from their revival.

As Ashe approached the library gallery, Julian Travers came bounding towards him, his polished Oxford shoes squeaking as he moved. Travers was a well-knit package of indefatigable enthusiasm, his gaunt, kindly face set off by thick black 'Harry Palmer' specs.

The men shook hands.

'We've been out of touch too long, Julian.'

'That's life. Hey, how's Lichfield? Still writing? Lectures? All that stuff?'

'Less and less. I'm into travel. Research. Look, are we meeting here, or outside?'

'Prince of Wales OK?'

'You can't get away from Masonry, can you?'

'They say it's the best fun you can have with your trousers on!'

'Or rolled up.'

The two men chatted briskly about old times at Oxford as they made their way out of Grand Lodge and onto the pavement of Great Queen Street in Covent Garden.

'You know, we Magdalen chaps used to come down to your bar at Brasenose because the beer was always better.'

'I thought it was the girls.'

'Yeah! The girls were friendly at Brasenose.'

'You have a creative memory, Julian. We called our bar "the sewer".'

In the crowded pub, Ashe and Travers found window seats with a view of Drury Lane. There was an aroma of steak-and-kidney pies mixed with Italianate dishes of indeterminate provenance. Italian customers seemed to prefer the pies.

'OK. Did you get it?'

'You know this could cost me my job.'

'Never. I'll take a digital photo in the loos and give it straight back.'

'I took it from the Grand Secretary's desk.' Travers reached for the folded wad of typescript, bound by a paper clip, in his inside pocket. 'This isn't on file.'

'Why not?'

'Don't know. Matters pending? It's not unknown for documents of historic significance to be destroyed in Grand Lodge.'

'The sign perhaps of a confident institution.'

Travers caught Ashe's irony and smiled. 'Well, I hope it's what you wanted to see.'

'Have you read it?'

'Are you kidding? I'm the information officer.'

'I thought you ran the publicity.'

Travers laughed. 'My dear Toby. I'm run *by* the publicity.'

'Travers!'

Julian shuddered; it was the booming voice of the Grand Secretary himself, Bob Foulhurst.

'See who's here!' Foulhurst turned to two other men, also wearing black ties, dark suits and waistcoats, and carrying briefcases. 'Look! It's Tigger – out for a crafty lunch!'

Ashe folded his hands over the document, covering as much of it as possible.

'Afternoon, Tigger!' boomed the balding provincial grand secretaries accompanying the Grand Secretary for a lunchtime drink.

'Shouldn't you be on a working lunch today, Tigger?'

Ashe looked up at Foulhurst. 'Your brilliant information officer is just being brilliant.'

'Who might you be?'

Ashe showed the Grand Secretary a Cranfield Royal Military College of Science card. Foulhurst perused it, sceptically. His eye caught the document under Ashe's hand.

'Not passing information on to outsiders are you, Tigger? Pro-Grand Master won't like that.' He pointed to the papers under Ashe's flattened hand. 'Not one of ours, is it?'

Ashe interjected. 'As a matter of fact, Grand Secretary, I'm passing information on to your library and museum. Wonderful stuff about Service Lodges. Means a lot to veterans. I believe it involves the Duke of Kent. Was it his request, Julian?'

'Er…'

'Anyhow, the Duke has in the past taken a keen interest.'

The reference to the Duke of Kent settled the Grand Secretary somewhat. The Duke of Kent, being Grand Master of the United Grand Lodge of England, was entitled, Foulhurst surmised, to do things even he, the Grand Secretary, did not know about.

On the other hand, Foulhurst felt a right to know about everything that passed within the Craft. 'The Duke, you say? I'll have to have a chat next time we meet.'

'Come on, Bob!' The Provincial Grand Secretary for Lancashire patted Foulhurst on his shoulder. 'We'd all like a drink before we go into Lodge.'

'Sorry. Sorry, Peter. Right. Be sure you're back in the office by two, Tigger. Goodbye, er… whatever your name is. Not one of us, is he, Julian?'

'No, sir.'

'I see. Well, keep it brief.'

As the three men moved to the other side of the bar, Ashe noticed sweat beginning to gather on Travers' forehead.

'How the fuck can you put up with shit like that, Julian? And you an Oxford man!'

'That's the whole trouble, Toby. None of these guys went to a decent university. But Masonry gives them rank. And in their little world, they're like kings.'

'That's sad. You deserve better. No one should have to put up with crap like that in this day and age. And what's all that "Tigger" stuff?'

'You know. I run around, always doing something.'

'And they laugh at you?'

'Their little joke.'

94

Ashe's hunch had been right. Herr Gerhard Fitzthum of Fitzthum & Nietzsche recalled the face. He was sure: this was the man who called himself Mustapha Atbash. This was the man who had arranged the lease in Altona, Hamburg.

Colonel Aslan had set up the whole apartment.

All morning Karla Lindars had tried to reach Aslan in his Istanbul office. No one was answering the phone. The switchboard operator in Ümraniye could give no information. Ashe tried Aslan's mobile: no answer.

And all the time, the contents of the Baba Sheykh's curious speech raced round Ashe's mind. Had the Baba Sheykh quit Istanbul because of al-Qasr? Or could it be that the warning was somehow connected to the Baba Sheykh's speech?

Tired of making Ashe coffee, Karla stood in front of his desk, put her hands on her hips and screamed his name.

'Good. I've got your attention. Toby, I have come to listen. I have come to be mummy.'

'That's all I bloody need!'

'Maybe it is, at this moment. Just tell me what is going on in your head? And see if I can help, just a bit. First, what, if I may ask, is in that document there?'

'Which one?'

'The one you've been fiddling with since last night. The one you had in the bathroom. The one you had at breakfast. That one. There. What's it all about?'

'That, darling Karla, is a very original account of the origins and development of Freemasonry. Freshly swiped from the United Grand Lodge of England.'

'So, kindly explain its contents. It will make you feel better.'

Ashe took a deep breath. 'All right. The Grand Lodge of England was the first "Grand Lodge" of Freemasonry anywhere in the world. According to its *Constitutions*, which were published in 1723, four Lodges got together in a Covent Garden pub in 1716, and decided to join together as a "Grand Lodge" the following year. What does that tell you?'

'I don't know. What are you driving at?'

'There were four Lodges. Then there was a Grand Lodge. When did Freemasonry start?'

'Oh, I get it! For four Lodges to come together, there must have already been Freemasonry in 1716 – before there was a "Grand Lodge".'

'Right. Freemasonry already existed. It was an adjunct to the skilled trade of masonry and architecture. A "freemason" was the English term for one who worked in "freestone". And freestone was another name for sandstone and limestone that was good for carving. Try carving granite and you'll see what I mean. These freestone masons, or "freemasons", belonged to companies. By the time of James I, the London Company of Freemasons had been active for some two centuries. They fixed their own wages, and had their own rituals and traditions.'

'OK. Did you get this from the Baba Sheykh's speech?'

'No. This is just basic history.'

'Basic!'

'And the Baba Sheykh, it turns out, knows it much better than I do. Now, some time between that alleged meeting of four London Lodges in 1716, and the year 1723, when the supposedly new organisation published its *Constitutions*, something odd happened. The so-called "Grand Lodge" removed the old stipulation that an actual working stonemason should be present at the meetings of Lodges of Accepted Masons.'

'Hold on. Why's that odd? And what's an "Accepted Mason"? And why weren't all the members working masons?'

'I'm coming to that. Before the new "Grand Lodge", special meetings were held in the City of London by the leaders of the London Masons' Company, formerly known as the London Company of Freemasons. Senior master masons, what we would now call "architects", could attend, as well as gentlemen with an interest in the practical and mystical aspects of building and geometry. They were usually friends of senior members of the Masons' Company. We know from records that one very special meeting was called an "Acception".'

'Is that where "Accepted" Mason comes from?'

'Right. Scholars think that it was at this meeting – the Acception – that brother masons celebrated something symbolic about their craft: a higher, more esoteric insight, based on very old traditions of masonry. Evidence suggests that the spiritual and intellectual aspects of architecture were more of a focus at these meetings. When you'd been initiated at the meeting, you became "accepted". That is, you'd accepted something.'

'What's this spiritual and intellectual side you speak of, Toby? Weird stuff?'

'I'll let the Baba Sheykh enlighten us on this matter in a minute, Karla. But first I want you to understand why it is so significant that the so-called "Grand Lodge" separated itself from the science, art and trade of masonry.'

'Are you saying that they hijacked the Acception meetings from the old order of craft Masonry?'

'You're very quick on the uptake today, Karla. There's a body of evidence to suggest that yes, something of the sort happened. Because by 1730, English Freemasonry had become a self-contained Order available for export – and it was completely separate from the trade. So something fundamental had obviously occurred.'

'Fascinating. But if I was organising a new Order, I think I'd want people to know it was very old.'

'That's one of the contradictory things about modern British Freemasonry. By the time of Queen Victoria, leading Freemasons were distinguishing between "speculative" and "operative" Freemasonry. Grand Lodge Freemasonry was "speculative", which seems to have meant "symbolic and philosophical", whereas the old builders, carvers and architects knew only "operative" masonry. That way, the new Order could have its cake and eat it! True Freemasonry started with the Grand Lodge, but it was *also* very ancient! Operative equals old; speculative equals new.'

'Sounds like a class distinction. Tradesmen's entrance and all that.'

'Well, the Victorian era saw Masonry in England becoming more and more a bourgeois phenomenon: a badge of acceptability in some quarters.'

'Yuck!'

'Quite. Or one could say Freemasonry had become positive social cement with a healthy interest in charity. Anyway, back to the contradictions... It was not discouraged during all that time for Freemasons to think of themselves as belonging to an Order with roots in academically respectable ancient civilisations – Greek, Roman, Egyptian, even Druid, with their links to Stonehenge. That sort of thing came to be tolerated as part of the romantic ethos of "the Craft" – as the brotherhood of Freemasons is known. But by the twentieth century, leading members of Grand Lodge began to disassociate themselves from this picture. They began to stress that there was a very clear line to be drawn between what preceded Grand Lodge Freemasonry, and what came after it. Effectively, real "speculative" Masonry was the intellectual property of the United Grand Lodge of England.'

'OK. So what does the Baba Sheykh have to say on the subject?'

'Frankly, Karla, in a strange and subtle way, he throws a massive spanner in the works.'

'How so?'

'This sparkling genius – for such I think he is – has gone right back to first principles. What is this spiritual side of Freemasonry? Where did it come from? Where does it come from?'

'I can't wait. Just let me get another coffee.'

Ashe looked up at the picture of the Yezidi girls for inspiration. On the sheykh's lips the speech would have sounded like the words of an old prophet, speaking from far distant times to a lost and confused present.

Karla came up behind him and squeezed his shoulders. 'I can't tell you, Toby, how attractive you are when I can actually see you thinking.'

Ashe took her hand and kissed it. 'You're a good listener. And you ask sensible questions.'

'Thank you, Professor. And here's another one. What's all this got to do with the Baba Sheykh?'

95

'The Baba Sheykh says that what became known as Freemasonry came from the Yezidis.'

'From the Yezidis! That's some claim, isn't it? I mean, how could he say that? I'm guessing it's not written anywhere, is it?'

'Most Yezidi philosophy is learned as an oral tradition. There are very few writings.'

'I remember from my granddad that Masons had to learn all their rituals from memory. That's a sort of oral tradition, isn't it?'

'Good point. Anyway, the bulk of Yezidi thought is found in their hymn tradition. The *qewwals* – their holy musicians – learn it and pass it on. You know, Karla, in the hymns of the Yezidis, Creation begins with a pearl. And from out of the pearl come the cornerstones.'

'Cornerstones?'

'Cornerstones.'

'Sounds a bit Masonic, I suppose, Toby. What other philosophy have you found in these hymns? And how come you've been party to it, anyway?'

'Professor Philip Kreyenbroek of Göttingen University in Germany has teamed up with some Yezidis and written down many of their traditional hymns.'

'Pity.'

'Pity or not, Karla, there's philosophy in them there hymns. Spiritual philosophy. We can learn about the Yezidi tradition from them.'

'Go on.'

'Well, I think the first aspect of the Yezidi tradition is contemplation. Contemplation and meditation on the act of Creation. In this tradition, there are three architects. There is God, who made the pearl from which all things came. Then there is the eternal word, which is God's mind in his Creation. This "word" you can call the "inner architect".'

'Because it's in all things?'

'Right. And the *third* architect is man.'

'I'm a bit sick of man. But I like the sound of this "inner architect".'

'The inner word is the spirit of things, present but invisible. The word is the secret or hidden principle in Creation, in the smallest atom, in the largest planet, in the sun, and in the eye. It is like the genes on the DNA helix. This "word" or *logos* is the inner architect, the inner driver, the inner—'

'Programme?'

'Yes! Like a computer program. The hidden word. The code that makes the thing work. Not on its own, but in tune with everything else. The smallest part encapsulates the whole. The whole is the union of the parts. But there is "one word " in all things—'

'"All things are one" – that's the basis of all mystic perception, isn't it, Toby?'

'Yes. This inner architect that men do not see.'

'Unless they look for it.'

'Right, Karla. So that's the second architect. The third architect is man. Sorry. It means the idea of man, not a male.'

'Maybe, but "man" sounds to me more like a man's idea of "man"!'

'Can't help that. Anyway, he stands between the Great Architect and the word, or the inner architect – at least, in potential. And man contains the inner architect within his being, because God is in him. This is how man becomes an architect as we know the term. His mind extends through the application of geometry and he becomes a geometrical microcosm.'

'A what?'

'Microcosm. Little cosmos. A little universe, reflecting the greater universe.'

'The kingdom of the heavens is within him? Interesting, Toby.'

'But man needs to be woken up to it. Opened up to his hidden identity. He needs to look hard inside himself. When he is in tune with this dynamic word—'

'He is the word made flesh!'

'Yes! Gospel of John, Chapter 1! That's partly why Saint John is the patron saint of Masonry. But in us, this "word made flesh" concept is only a possibility. We can't make the whole journey because we've still got one foot stuck in the sleeping, or confused state – the way we ordinarily are: half asleep. Or drunk. Freemasonry teaches that life is a journey towards perfection. There is the rough stone—'

'And the perfect stone! I think I'm a Mason without knowing it.'

'Saves on fees! So, darling Karla, the perfect stone is the inner architect. It is the reflection of the Great Architect. This stone can be realised within every person. The Yezidis talk about it as a luminous cornerstone. This may be the *true* Philosopher's Stone.'

'I love it!'

'Then – as the old Masons did – you can start turning the tools that shape the stone into symbols. The square, the dividers, the plumb line, chisel, maul, rule. The tools are ethical principles: truth, righteousness, goodness, strength, personal integrity, purity, charity, love, and the willingness to be tested.'

'It's beautiful, really, but very idealistic.'

'It doesn't appeal to everyone. Anyhow, the Baba Sheykh makes all this pristinely clear in his speech. And he demonstrates that these essential principles lie within the traditions of the Yezidis.

'He makes a number of powerful quotes from Yezidi hymns. For example, one hymn refers to Sheykh Adi, who is an historical figure from the 1200s, a teacher or master of a spiritual path, but also a kind of angel or reflection of the divine for the Yezidis. In the "Angelic Sheykh" he is called "the master builder". "You are the master builder; I am the building." I mean, just in this little quote you have the tradition of the temple being within us. The church of the spirit is constructed within the soul, while at the same time, every Mason is also to be a stone in the greater temple. There is a hymn that talks of the four cornerstones that are one. One cornerstone for the holy men. These cornerstones are also angels. Streams of light. And the "Hymn of the Faith" asks: "What is the colour of the faith? It is the pre-eternal word, it is the name of Sheykh Adi."'

'But why is Sheykh Adi this pre-eternal word?'

'Because Sheykh Adi realised in himself his identity with the inner architect. With God. This was the aim of the Sufis – or Gnostics – of Islam: to become a mirror of God. When they do, they start identifying with the holy men and women of all religions. They break the bounds. That's perhaps why Freemasonry has this tolerance of different spiritual and religious traditions. Freemasonry is rooted in Gnostic traditions but often won't admit it. That's why it's so threatening to people whose concept of God is particular to their own brand, so to speak.

'Sheykh Adi was called a heretic. It's the old story. But Sheykh Adi says in the hymn. "For your column, I am a good cornerstone." This is the language of spiritual Freemasonry. This is the tradition the Yezidis kept alive. They even say Lalish, their holy valley, is a pure cornerstone, "the cornerstone for mankind". Somehow, human destiny depends upon it.'

'And you've been there?'

'Bodily and spiritually.'

'Coffee?'

Ashe nodded, suddenly recalling the magic of his night at Lalish, the night he met Laila and the guardian of the sanctuary: the night he experienced true timelessness.

Ashe's thoughts drifted back to the archdeacon's funeral at Peover in Cheshire, the day he'd met Melissa. He remembered how Colquitt and Bagot had showed up, and nearly spoiled everything. Then he remembered the call from Colonel Aslan. The call from Aslan... The call from Aslan... *Where had he called from?* 'KARLA!'

'No need to scream!' Karla hurried back into Ashe's office. 'Not another history lesson, darling. I'm still trying to get through to your friend in Istanbul.'

'Peover, Cheshire. The archdeacon's funeral. He called me.'

'Who did?'

'Aslan. He called me. He said he was visiting relatives in St Pauli.'

'So?'

'St Pauli, Hamburg. It's where the Kurdish Centre is. *That's* when he must have arranged the lease of the apartment for our Yezidi friends!'

Ashe stared at the copy of the Baba Sheykh's speech. 'But *why?*'

'Obvious, Toby. Aslan must have known al-Qasr wanted to kill or kidnap the Baba Sheykh.'

'WHAT?' The idea that Aslan could have known al-Qasr had never occurred to Ashe. He was startled.

'Karla, do you know what you've just said?'

'Sorry, did I say something wrong? I take it all back.'

'I mean, did you think about it? Was this Karla lateral thinking?'

'No, maestro. Just a guess. I'm trying to keep up with you.'

'And vice versa, darling. Shit! You know, if you're right, it could've been Aslan who gave the tip-off to Sinàn to get out of Istanbul quick. Or... maybe he gave the word to Yildiz and Yazar. That might explain why...'

'Why?'

'What if...?' Ashe seized Karla's arm. 'What if it *wasn't* al-Qasr who kidnapped the Baba Sheykh? What if...?'

96

'And how is Baghdad this morning, sir?'

'Hotting up as usual, Ashe. Now let's leave small-talk for small people. I've recently had the pleasure of a meeting with Lee Kellner at Fort Bragg, North Carolina.'

'Big talk, sir?'

'Amusing but irrelevant, Ashe. Time is of the essence. Among other things discussed was my concern that your friend Sherman Beck is not sharing candy. Lee assured me he doesn't let Beck in on everything, so what I have to say to you...'

'Understood, sir.'

'Right. First question. Did the CTC have a lead on al-Qasr's current whereabouts? Kellner tried fobbing me off with some drivel about four different sightings of a stranger with a bearded kidnap victim.'

'Bearded? Hardly a distinction in the East!'

'Quite. I warmed him up after that: possible sighting in south Waziristan; another in Aiwaz, Pakistan; another near Kandahar; and one on the Iraqi–Syrian border. None confirmed, but all being followed up. I thanked Lee politely. We then proceeded to the business of the day: tracking down bin Laden. He's still top of the list, Ashe. In this matter, British and US cooperation has proved fruitful. You may recall Brigadier Radclyffe from your nasty experience at the Tower. He was on hand to observe US special forces training. Something was being cooked up with Pakistan's Directorate of Inter-Services Intelligence. Kellner couldn't be entirely open with the ISI. In some respects, the ISI is a security liability. So Kellner looked to me for support there.'

'Anything come out of that, sir?'

'You're ahead of me, Ashe. Kellner informed me about mobile phone intercepts linking bin Laden with a certain "al-Qasr". This revelation should add a fresh dimension to your investigation.'

'I should say so, sir.'

'One last thing. It didn't pass by me what Kellner let slip to you in Washington.'

'About Israeli intelligence, sir?'

'Mati Fless. Name mean anything to you?'

'Matthias Fless of the Mossad? Old acquaintance.'

'And recently released from CTC custody.'

'Custody? Where held, sir?'

'Chicago. Arrested in California while on a mission. The Mossad deny all knowledge of course. And some mission, Ashe! Seems Fless was trying either to kill or kidnap Professor Sami al-Qasr.'

'Why the hell didn't Beck tell me?'

'You didn't ask. That was the reason Lee gave. And I had to accept it, and so will you. Keep up the good work, Ashe!'

Karla slapped a note down onto Ashe's desk.

'Right, I'll take it.' Ashe picked up the phone. 'That you, Julian?'

'Sorry 'bout the delay, Toby. I found a few things. Could be useful. By the way, if the line goes funny, it's because I'm walking up Drury Lane. I couldn't make this call from inside Grand Lodge.'

'Understood. Julian, I've read the copy of the speech.'

'Nice, isn't it?'

'Why do you think the Grand Sec sat on it?'

'You should see the draft memo I found.'

'Found?'

'You could say that. From the Grand Secretary of the United

Grand Lodge of England to the current Grand Master of the Grand Temple of Free and Accepted Masons of Turkey. Hold on a second.'

Julian Travers stopped outside the box office for *Cats* and manoeuvred a packet of Silk Cut towards his mouth.

'And?'

'Just a second.'

Travers lit the cigarette. 'Phew! Now, to cut a long story short, our Grand Secretary concluded, after discussion with the Librarian of UGLE and others, that, first, the history outlined in the Baba Sheykh's speech was highly spurious—'

'Spurious? It's bloody good!'

'And, second, that it might be bad news for the Masonic status quo in Turkey.'

'Why?'

'Masonic politics. Except, Toby, in Turkey, Masonic politics has, in the past, overlapped with state politics.'

'In what sense?'

'Freemasonry is controversial in Turkey. There's a population of 70 million, and only about 14,000 Masons. Nevertheless, Turks know what small numbers of well-organised people can do. In the minds of some people who resent the secular Turkish state, modern Turkey is the product of a kind of Masonic-influenced coup.'

'You're just saying that Masons are associated with secularism. But Masons, *as Masons*, have no political position at all.'

'*We* know that, Toby. But try explaining that to the Islamists. Look, before 1909, Turkey was ruled by a sultan, who ran a Muslim caliphate. Then the so-called "Young Turks" kicked him out. Twenty years later, Turkey had become a secular state, supported mainly by educated metropolitan people, and by the army. Ideas about liberty, equality, fraternity and all that appealed to the educated as being progressive and European: something to work towards in a national context.'

'Right.'

'But these same ideas were also enshrined in Grand Orient Freemasonry as *Masonic* ideals.'

'So there *is* a link between secular ideals, Masonry and Turkish politics!'

'Tricky one. The Young Turks set up a "Committee of Union and Progress" to achieve a new, progressive Turkey. It was from that committee that Mustapha Kemal – Atatürk, father of the Turks – emerged. As far as I know, Atatürk was a Mason.'

'Jurisdiction?'

'Atatürk was associated with Italian Grand Orient Lodges in Thessalonica. And it was from members of these Lodges that political opposition to the old sultan, Abdul Hamid, came. Most of the committee were Freemasons, initiated into Grand Orient Freemasonry, based in France and Italy.'

'And the United Grand Lodge of England does not recognise Grand Orient Freemasonry, does it?'

'Right, Toby. Because the Grand Orient has been associated with political movements. Also, the Grand Orient system doesn't require members to believe in God. So, anti-Masons in the East argue that Freemasonry is atheistic and materialistic. In Turkey's case, Freemasonry's opponents insist Masonry is political, driving the split between state and faith. Whereas, as I needn't tell you, Toby, in British Lodges and recognised Lodges abroad, political and religious argument is forbidden, even though belief in the Supreme Being is required.'

'So, Grand Orient Freemasonry's secular tendency makes it a natural target for some Turkish Muslim opponents. And they tend to lump all Masonry in with it.'

'Right, Toby. They see secularism as a calamity for traditional Islamic Turkey. They'd like to turn the clock back. Now, all this conflict over Turkey's future was vexing for Atatürk, modern Turkey's founder-hero. So Atatürk side-stepped the issue of Turkey's religious past by promoting *pre-Islamic* Turkish identity. He declared that the ancient Turkic peoples were the original Aryans.'

'The WHAT?'

'Yeah. He reckoned the Turks were the original Aryans. He

reckoned the ancient Greeks got their culture from ancient Turks. Atatürk had a group of selected scholars write this book—'

'What book?'

'A book called *History*. Taught in all Turkish schools. You can still meet people in Turkey familiar with its basic idea.'

'Which is?'

'That the Turks are the heroes of world history. The book insists the Turks grew from the first race of scientists and philosophers in the world. In short, Aryan Turks are the source of civilisation. Atatürk transformed the appellation "Turk" into something glorious, something to be proud of. Turkish identity had been a glorious secret that only needed to be uncovered and revived. Well, Masonic ideas of ancient hidden knowledge, and universal brotherhood, can easily get mixed up in all of this. And the United Grand Lodge of England knows this only too well. It does its best to foster the kind of nice, friendly, charity-giving Freemasonry we're familiar with.'

'So what's all this got to do with the Baba Sheykh's speech?'

'Look Toby, I can only give you my opinion. You know how important recognition policy is. It's the only means the United Grand Lodge of England has to exercise a measure of restraint over quasi-Masonic waywardness or error. Freemasonry's been through a lot of changes in Turkey since the days of the Young Turks. In 1935 Atatürk himself closed the Masonic Lodges because of widespread fears of foreign interference. But after the Second World War, Masons met in their old buildings, though unofficially. Lodges were officially re-opened in the sixties and operated in a national association.

'But in 1965 this national association split. Some of its members founded the now larger Grand Temple of Free and Accepted Masons of Turkey. This jurisdiction is recognised here in London. It conforms to the English Masonic pattern, and it supports an openness policy. The Lodge attacked in March, in Kartal District, Istanbul, was under this recognised jurisdiction.'

'I wonder if that was a factor in the bombing? Any other jurisdictions in Turkey, Julian?'

'I was coming to that. There's the Liberal Grand Lodge of the Freemasons of Turkey. The Liberal Grand Lodge is in amity with the Grand Orient of France. It doesn't require any religious statement from its members. They say such a requirement hinders the universality of the aims of Freemasonry. It's an interesting argument—'

'It is. But why did London sit on the Baba Sheykh's speech?'

'OK. My opinion is that London believed the Baba Sheykh's speech could be used to undermine the authority of the recognised Grand Temple of Turkish Freemasons.'

'And presumably of England, too.'

'I... I suppose so. Hadn't thought of that.'

'The reason being, dear Julian, that the Baba Sheykh regards developments in Freemasonry after the establishment of the Grand Lodge of England as deviations from a more profound tradition that stems from the East.'

'It's a view. And I've got to say, Toby, I have sympathy with the Grand Secretary's decision to dissociate regular Masons from the speech. This whole question opens up a vast can of worms. Every unrecognised Grand Lodge in the world would love it to be proved that it had as much right to reform itself according to some ancient principle as any other. While some Grand Lodges appear indifferent to London's claim of premiership, they would not be indifferent to new evidence suggesting the Grand Lodge of England was illegitimate. It could get very messy – and who, really, would benefit?'

'Not the Grand Lodge, that's for sure.'

'Exactly. At the moment, it all works fairly cosily. The Grand Lodge of England doesn't claim jurisdiction over any other Grand Lodge. If Grand Lodges abroad balls things up, that's their problem, and London can always – and often does – remove recognition.

'Look at Turkey, Toby. There, Freemasonry is problematical.

Members of the army are associated with it. What if an internal Masonic conflict in Turkey got out of hand? This would be ammunition for every critic and enemy of Freemasonry in Turkey. Anything which puts Freemasonry into the newspapers makes Masons in the army uncomfortable. On the other hand, there are other members of the army, I believe, who are anti-Masonic, associating Masonry with foreign interference. Do you follow me, Toby?'

'I am experiencing enlightenment, Julian.'

'Good. I can do no more. At least, I hope you can see that my employers are not entirely to be condemned.'

'Check.' Ashe thought for a second. 'Just one thing, Julian.'

'Shoot.'

'From what you're saying, if the Grand Lodge of England had been able to have everything its own way from its establishment until now, there would never have *been* a Grand Orient Freemasonry, French or Italian, and therefore, there would never have been a modern, secular Turkish state.'

'It's a thought, Toby.'

97

Ashe sat back in his chair, his head spinning. He looked up at his Yezidi dancing girl poster. Round and round, with no centre in sight. No secular state. No Atatürk. No... Mahmut Aslan.

Aslan.

What about Aslan? In intelligence circles there was often talk of good links between Turkish secret services and Israel's Mossad. As the thought curled itself into Ashe's head like a cat before a fire, Karla slipped a memo behind his ear. 'Busy day, maestro – getting somewhere?'

'If only I knew where "somewhere" was.'

'This might help. Overheard your chat with Mr Crayke. I checked past records.'

Ashe examined the memo. 'Mati Fless's number!' Ashe blew Karla a kiss and phoned the number. It rang and rang: no message-taking facility. A click.

'Matthias Fless?'

'Who is speaking?'

Ashe immediately recalled the Israeli's deep, gloomy voice.

'Toby Ashe. We—'

'Toby!'

'You remember?'

'The Shmuel ben Yackai case. You helped us with that creep who wanted to blow up the al-Aqsa mosque and rebuild Solomon's Temple. Mad.'

'Madness is my business.'

'No shortage of work.'

'I hear you've recently suffered an interruption to your activities.'

'Really?'

'In Chicago.'

'All part of the job, Toby. How much do you know?'

'I gather that if you had pursued your job without interruption, both the CIA and myself would not be quite so harassed by circumstance as we presently are.'

'I do like your English understatement. If they had let me do my job, Toby, they wouldn't be in the shit, and I wouldn't be in Tel Aviv being roasted alive by my superiors, and you wouldn't be speaking to me during my toilet break. I presume you're not calling to reminisce?'

'Simple question.'

Fless laughed.

'I understand, Mati, that you intercepted messages from a guy who called himself...'

'Go on!'

'Called himself "the doctor".'

'You got this from Beck, or from Kellner?'

'Both.'

'What else do you know, Toby?'

'Like to know more.'

'Look, this is something I need to check up on with higher authority. I'm in enough—'

'I understand, Mati. But before you check up on me, just remember that although you failed in *your* mission, and *we* have not yet succeeded, we all have a common interest here. You really must help me if you can. You do want al-Qasr stopped, don't you?'

'Stopped from what, Dr Ashe?'

'From... murdering people.'

'That was the intention, Dr Ashe. And I believe, still is.'

It was late afternoon when Karla called Ashe in from a walk around the dull campus.

'Tel Aviv, Toby.'

Ashe smiled. 'Thanks, Karla. You never fail.'

Ashe sat on his desk and picked up the phone.

'Ashe speaking.'

'Congratulations on your promotion.'

'Thank you. I deserve it.'

'Agreed, Dr Ashe. Now ask your question.'

'Does the name Mahmut Aslan mean anything to you?'

The line crackled. 'Mati, you there?'

'I'm thinking. Remarkable man. Do you know him?'

'Yes, at least I thought I did.'

'Then you probably know Colonel Aslan is a specialist in Kurdish relations, or, if you like, the lack of them, from the Turkish point of view.'

Ashe laughed.

'So, he has had a finger in northern Iraq for a considerable time, on account, you understand, of the succour shown the PKK by a minority of Kurds there. And we, of course, have a vital interest in Ansar al-Sunna and all the other anti-Israeli forces operating in the same area.'

'You've shared intelligence.'

'We have shared intelligence, of course.'

'I have another question.'

'Is this one simple too?'

'I hope so. Has Aslan ever shown any interest in Sami al-Qasr?'

'Is that what British intelligence wants to know? Interesting.'

'I hope so. And I hope I've come to the right place.'

'Some years ago, Dr Ashe, Aslan attempted to pressure one of our informants at Baghdad's al-Tuwaitha facility.'

'Informants?'

'You know what I mean. This was in Saddam's time. And al-Tuwaitha held all Saddam's secrets. Aslan, a very resourceful man, contacted our informant, which, you can imagine, was for him a great surprise.'

'I can imagine!'

413

'Aslan wanted information on al-Qasr. We told our informant what he could safely disclose to Turkish security. That information gave Aslan negotiating leverage later on.'

'Negotiation?'

'I'll come to that. But I believe the colonel first heard about al-Qasr through Yezidis who had crossed the Iraq–Turkey border one way or the other. That wouldn't give Aslan many hard facts about al-Qasr but it certainly stimulated his interest. I think Aslan got most of his knowledge about al-Qasr from us. Part of a shared-intelligence arrangement. He was very helpful in other matters. Jihadists in northern Iraq. Insurgents from Iran. Anti-Zionists in Turkey. It all helped to grease the wheels. The interest in al-Qasr was a very small part of what we shared.'

'What did you tell him?'

'Enough. Everything short of a personal introduction, you might say.'

'Aslan's angle?'

'Aslan's angle was straightforward: counter-insurgency.'

'Where did he think al-Qasr fitted into that?'

'Good question. At the time, I was a little surprised by his interest, but then he was curious about our interest in al-Qasr too. There's always a bit of cat and mouse. You know how it is. He talked about hunches, but nothing concrete. It seemed like professional curiosity. Then we discovered independently that al-Qasr *did* have terrorist contacts. At which point Aslan's interest in al-Qasr made sense to us. He was right to be concerned. He was simply keeping his sources secret. And you must remember this, Toby. Aslan is popular with my colleagues. He is useful to us. Colonel Aslan is respected. If it were not for our concern about al-Qasr, you and I would not be having this conversation.'

'Did Aslan know you knew about al-Qasr's links to terrorism?'

'Aslan has his ways. When he realised we knew about it, he congratulated himself on having got there before us! We asked

414

him if he would share what he knew with the Americans. He said talking to America was our business, but insisted that further cooperation from him required that his name be omitted from any communications with the US. He said he was cautious of giving intelligence to Americans unless Turkish national interest was involved. He insisted the Americans were too tolerant of the PKK in northern Iraq. So we stepped lightly. But once we were certain al-Qasr had terrorist contacts, we started concocting the "doctor" scenario.'

'It was you! Not a question of intercepts then? There is no real "doctor"?'

'I should not be surprised if Kellner and Beck have realised that by now.'

'Why?'

'Oh, I think you can work that out, Dr Ashe!'

'OK. Let me get this straight. With al-Qasr protected by US security, you had to find a way of undermining his position. But why didn't you just pass on your information?'

'If I might say so, that's exactly what we *have* done, in our own way. I told Kellner and Beck what I know to be true. Al-Qasr is working with al-Qaeda. Of course we in Israel want to take al-Qasr out of the picture! We are sensitive to his kind of craziness – or science, if you insist. Do you remember that phrase Churchill used when describing what the doctors were doing in the Nazi camps?'

'"The lights of perverted science"?'

'Yeah. That's al-Qasr. The lights of perverted science. There were discussions over the best way to deal with the problem. We knew the Americans would resist giving up such an important scientist, even if he *was* in contact with terrorists. They'd just tighten things up. Of course we remembered how America was ready to employ scientists who had worked for Hitler's war-machine. Would there have been an Apollo programme without Wernher von Braun – the very man who designed the V2 rockets that brought about the deaths of thousands of civilians in London

415

at the end of the Second World War? So we cooked up the "doctor" story, based on someone we had on file who was known to have had a relationship with al-Qasr in their student days and who, as far as we could tell, was on the run in Europe. We had messages sent first from Iraq, then Turkey, Austria and Germany. It was as close to the truth as lies can get.'

'I get it… I get it. You wanted the CIA and FBI to investigate the matter for themselves. Create enough steam so it couldn't all be swept under the carpet. Did you hope to force al-Qasr's hand? Make him panic, or quit?'

'We didn't want him to quit like that of course. And the doctor scenario was only one idea. The other idea was mine. It became clear to us that al-Qasr might at any moment flee, especially if the CTC bungled their investigation in any way. We didn't want al-Qasr to disappear.'

'And when you failed, the doctor messages became your only hope.'

'Not our only hope, Toby! Contrary to rumour, we cannot tell the Americans what to do.'

'Did Aslan know anything about the doctor messages?'

'We're not sure. If he didn't know to begin with, he probably does now. He has his ways, as I said.'

'Do you know where al-Qasr might be?'

Fless laughed. 'Afraid not, Dr Ashe! Of course, if we did, we might keep it to ourselves. But we are very interested in your call. I cannot help wondering, now I have heard what you have to say, that the best way to find al-Qasr might be—'

'To find Aslan.'

'I didn't know the colonel was lost.'

'He isn't. *We* are.'

98

'Call waiting for you, Toby.'

'I don't believe it! It's like hitting the jackpot today. Who is it now? The Sultan of Brunei?'

'Brigadier Charles Radclyffe. Calling from London.'

'Shit! The Director of Special Forces!'

Ashe took the call. 'Good afternoon, Brigadier.'

'Heard good things about you, Ashe, from Richmond and from Crayke. Pity our last meeting was cut so short.'

'Indeed, Brigadier.'

'Oh, call me Charles or DSF for God's sake. You're not in uniform are you, Ashe?'

'No, sir.'

'Well, you can tell me to fuck off, if you like.'

'Rather not. Got a feeling you've something important to say.'

'Bugger your feelings, Ashe. I don't know if you're familiar with the way we work in the SAS. Doesn't matter. Listen. I'm in receipt of information sent by Richmond to our Operational Intelligence cell at Stirling Lines.'

'Hereford.'

'Correct.'

'You call it "the Kremlin".'

'Correct again. Then you'll also know that they disseminate intelligence to their operational planners. If the information calls for an operation, they contact me for my point of view and authority to proceed. If I agree with their assessment, I then task the Kremlin for a feasibility study. Now, Ashe, I have read their report concerning suspicious military activity in Iraq's Hakkari Mountains. I have consulted with senior authority and have requested the Kremlin go ahead with plans to be submitted to the sortie commander. The sortie commander is Major Richmond.'

'May I ask who is the relevant authority in this case?'

'The relevant authority in this case is not unknown to you. He's requested you be informed and liaise in strictest secrecy with the sortie commander. Am I making myself clear, Ashe?'

'Very clear. Except for one thing.'

'And that is?'

'What's the information, sir?'

'Don't ask me, Ashe! Contact OP/INT and do as they tell you. One more thing.'

'Yes?'

'How's the investigation going?'

'Investigation?'

'Admiral Whitmore's bloody Tower! Any closer to finding out who blew it up?'

'Nothing certain yet.'

'Well, I don't know if this is any use, but I've been sent a curious message. Got it here in front of me.'

'Care to share?' Ashe was intrigued.

'It's a bugger of a thing. Cheap drawing paper. Written in charcoal. Rough capitals. Reads as follows: "THE TOWER OF BABEL IS NOT DESTROYED. AS CAIN SLEW ABEL SO WILL YOU DIE BAD. ABEL DIED SO SETH CAN LIVE. I SETH, THE IMMOVEABLE RACE, JUDGE." Make anything of that, Ashe? Bloody foxes me.'

Ashe had a strange sense that he'd seen something like it before, but when? 'I'll give it some thought, sir.'

'I've had a go. What's all that stuff about Seth?'

'It's in Genesis. The Bible says that after Adam's son Cain murdered his brother Abel, Adam and Eve had another child. This new child, Seth, was seen as a new hope for the human race after Cain's crime. Seth had "the knowledge of God" and was a patriarch of science and wisdom.'

'News to me, Ashe. What's that "immoveable race" stuff all about? Sounds a bit Nazi.'

'Some time after Christ, various groups appeared who claimed they were the Children of Seth, that they were the guardians of something pure, which had survived through time to reappear at the end of time. They saw themselves as the unmoveable or "unchangeable" race. A group that had held the true torch burning from the beginning of mankind. The original, undivided, inspired race.'

'True torch burning? Sounds like some bloody weird cult. I'll send this crap to you at Shrivenham in the diplomatic bag. Sounds right up your street, Ashe. Good luck. Over and out.'

99

Kurdish Autonomous Region, northern Iraq

Ashe was soaking. It had rained all the way from the airport at Mosul – a steady drizzle, persistent enough to dampen any good feelings.

The Land Rover 110 splashed its way along the winding mountain roads. On the approach to the village of Kurahmark the gradient increased and the earth got browner and browner as the sky got filthier and filthier. Traces of green slowly faded away as they made the last twenty kilometres to the RV, the rendezvous point near the village of Kurku. Just outside the village, the road stopped abruptly. The Land Rover carried on along the rough mountainside for another kilometre, until it became too steep.

'This'll be it, chum.'

The driver – a Mancunian – Kev 'The Blade' Norton (signals), gave a one-sided grin and jumped out of the Land Rover. He was swiftly followed by Pat Scrabster (linguist and sniper), Derek Hayes (demolition), and Andy Tongue (medicine).

The men had worked as a team for two years in Afghanistan and Iraq. All of them were used to prolonged periods of silence and seemed to know what the others were thinking. Quietly, they started loading equipment onto their backs.

Three Pink Panther – 'pinkie' – desert vehicles were waiting for them under camouflage, which also gave some shelter from the rain. Out from under the camouflage, dressed in Kurdish costume, stepped Major Richmond. He shook hands with Ashe.

'Welcome to the RV. This is where we'll regroup after the show. I hope you're ready for a walk, Toby.'

'How far?'

'About eight kilometres, as the crow flies.'

'And we're not crows.'

'It'll seem longer. We need to move out in four minutes, so I'd like you to get some extra kit on. We're all adopting some aspect of Kurdish style. This will help Jolo and his men identify us. But first I want you to get into this vest and a few other things.'

'What's that?'

'That's the Kevlar body suit. It can take a bullet, and it's got ceramic inserts, which really do save lives.'

Ashe pulled off his desert fatigues and hauled himself into the body suit.

'You'd never think this stuff would stop bullets.'

'Science doing the soldier a favour for a change. Once it's on, you don't have to think about it.'

Richmond threw Ashe a green sleeveless garment. 'This is the Dowty Armourshield General Purpose Vest 25, Toby.'

'What's this one got, apart from an extraordinary name?'

'It's got a blunt trauma shield.'

'Purpose?'

'The rest might stop a bullet from piercing your body, but you need the shield to lessen the trauma of being hit. Weighs four kilogrammes, which you'll notice after a while.'

'Better than being dead.'

Richmond smiled. 'That's the idea.'

Ashe slipped on some grey baggy trousers and a buff-coloured light cotton jacket while Richmond helped him with a blue-and-white-striped turban.

'Important thing is to get its tail to flow backwards, not in your face.'

'Got it.'

'Now, in this pack you'll find a survival kit, some stun grenades, an SF10 respirator, a specialised helmet adapted to it, some plastic bags to put your shit in, a few other things I'll talk about later – and a map. Important thing. Never mark the map or fold it in such a way as to give anyone finding it a clue about anything that matters.'

'Over my dead body.'

'That's where they'd find it. Right. Weapon. As this sort of trek is new to you, I thought you might like to get to grips with this.'

Ashe admired the factory-fresh submachine gun. 'Heckler & Koch MP5 SD. Silenced version.'

'Very good. Don't want to frighten you with loud noises. If you'd prefer an assault rifle to the submachine gun, just say so.'

'This is fine.'

'Here's the ammo belt. The holster carries a 9 mm Browning High Power pistol. You can keep your boots.'

'I should think so. Cost a bloody fortune.'

Ashe and Richmond emerged from beneath the camouflage netting to find themselves surrounded by a ring of human steel. This mission clearly had high-priority status.

100

Simon Richmond was in command of sixteen men from 22 SAS Sabre Squadron G, Mountain Troop, and a further sixteen men from D Squadron's Air Troop: a formidable force.

Each man carried at least 100 kilogrammes of equipment, but the combined muscle did not hang lead-heavy as Ashe might have expected; rather it seemed to shimmer in the rain, bristling like a porcupine and ready to take its cargo of death right into the unsuspecting face of the enemy.

'Where the fuck did they all come from?'

'These are the invisible men, Toby.'

'Quite a sight for invisible men.'

Richmond addressed them. 'I hope you're all comfortable. Any outstanding issues or questions about equipment, this is your last chance. Good. Before we go, I want to introduce you to Toby Ashe, whose name you have just forgotten. He's with intelligence, and the higher-ups want him here to help with identification and interrogation procedures.'

Ashe looked somewhat apologetic, only too aware that he owed his place on the operation more to Crayke's insistence than strict operational necessity.

'Toby's not undergone specialist training, but take my word for it, he has distinguished himself in field operations. Bastard even saved my life.'

Richmond awaited the expected mild amusement; it didn't come.

'Right. He doesn't expect anyone to wait for him, or carry

him. He's aware that if he's incapacitated, he will have to make his own way to the RV. Needless to say, we'll take a diamond formation on the open stretches, and single file when we reach the foliage.'

There was a murmur of 'Needless to say, Major', and 'Tell us something we didn't know'.

'As we discussed this morning, there is a high risk of anti-personnel mines and booby traps closer to the target, so bear that in mind. OK, we shall depart RV at five-minute intervals. Note there is to be no Morse or any electronic signalling whatsoever within five kilometres of the target area under any circumstances. Before that, high-speed transmissions may be used. It's likely the enemy has direction-finding equipment installed in their facility. Signalling may resume in the event of engagement. I think that's it. Good luck.'

There was some good-natured nodding from some of the troops, but most had their minds fixed firmly on the operation objectives. The men, divided into groups of four, would each follow a different route to the target area. Each route had been planned meticulously to offer a consistent strategic arrival pattern. Each group of four had a specific set of objectives to accomplish before the attack on the facility proper began.

Richmond and Ashe set off first, with the four men from Squadron G Mountain Troop who had brought Ashe in from Mosul. Already, Ashe's shoulders were beginning to ache. Richmond turned round and noticed his discomfort.

'It'll improve, Toby. Now, before we spread out, I think I'd better explain what's been going on.'

'I'd appreciate that, Simon.'

'Yes. The planning stage is usually like that. We don't like to dwell on an operation. Just get on with it.'

'Feet first, is it?'

'Deep end.'

'Right.'

'I wasn't going to mention it, Toby. But that submachine gun you have there is not a fashion accessory. I've lost four from my allotted force.'

'Casualties?'

'You've heard of the Ken Bigley kidnap?'

'Al-Tawhid wal-Jihad group.'

'Yeah. Abu Musab al-Zarqawi. He's threatened to execute the poor chap. All on video. It's one of those Iraq stories that newspapers really go to town on.'

'Presumably why the kidnaps keep happening.'

'Yeah, well. The PM has pulled out as many stops as possible. So I've lost a unit trying to find him. Of course, if they get to Bigley in time, they'll also get the most-wanted terrorist in the region, so it's worth the effort.'

'D'you think our effort will make headlines?'

'Rather doubt it, don't you? Still, this operation makes sense. Remember last time you and I looked over a map of the region?'

'In Shariya. You said there was the possibility of joint Turkish special forces and Ansar al-Sunna activity – weird though that sounded.'

'Jolo's men picked up one of the Ansar al-Sunna men in the area.'

'Picked up?'

'Abducted. Borrowed. Lifted. Took bloody prisoner. Anyhow, they got him talking. And he started gabbing about a bearded Yezidi brought in from Europe. Special hostage. He also identified a photograph of this Sami al-Qasr guy we and everybody else seems to have as a high-priority target. I've got to say though, Toby, it's weird him turning up in these parts, given my briefing about him.'

'Did the prisoner mention anyone else?'

'Only a senior Turkish officer.'

Ashe felt a rush of excitement. He tried to sound unmoved. 'Name?'

'Didn't know the name.'

'Pity.'

'Seems, Toby, this guy's been running a special operation of his own.'

'I'll bet!'

'Know this guy?'

'Maybe.'

'Well, he's something special. He's apparently turned about fifty captured Ansar al-Sunna volunteers into his own private force. They're targeting PKK rebels operating inside northern Iraq. Some of the rebels are cooperating with American special forces, some are just hiding out in places the Turkish special forces can't find. The Turkish justification is simple. It's the war on terrorism.'

'Of course it is. But Turkish style. Using Ansar al-Sunna volunteers distracts terrorists from killing Americans, while assisting the global war on terror by locating and/or liquidating Turkey's internal enemies. Clever.'

'And it keeps to a diplomatic minimum the number of Turkish special forces operating over the border. Now, Toby, you can answer a question of mine. We've been told this isn't a simple blat-and-splat mission. There's the hostage-release aspect.'

'That's just part of it, Simon. I presume you know that if this comes off, your command will have found the only significant WMD in the Iraq conflict.'

'That aspect's been rather muted. We can't be sure what we're going to find, if anything.'

'So what's your question?'

'Why no US forces? Does Blair want the honours – save his career and trounce his enemies?'

Ashe laughed. 'I doubt it. Maybe the prospect of US forces going out to hit Turks is embarrassing for all parties. On the other hand, a regular mission against Ansar al-Sunna forces by Kurdish irregulars, albeit with some SAS backup – which also *happens* to locate some Turkish forces – I suppose that could be dressed up rather differently. But there'll be diplomatic problems if the Yanks find we've gone after al-Qasr without telling them. Success will be our proof.'

Richmond squinted, not entirely convinced. 'Is that the only reason our allies are in the dark on this one, Toby?'

Ashe thought it best to avoid the question. 'Of course, there's the capability factor.'

'Capability, Toby?'

'I'm told cave-bashing operations like this normally get US AC-130 Spectre Gunship support with deep-penetration bombs targeting the cave entrances. But in this case, we can't risk killing either the hostage or those in charge of holding him.'

'That's been made clear. Who's the hostage?'

'They didn't tell you?'

'It was made clear there was no guarantee the hoped-for hostage would be there at all. Crayke suggested you would know.'

'And this mission was okayed on that basis?'

'That's how it is sometimes. Uncertainty complicates things, Toby, but sometimes you just have to go.'

'I presume hostage release is nothing new to you.'

'Never done it from inside a bloody cave in the mountains before! It's the worst of two worlds.'

'That's life.'

Ashe found the going easier now the blood was flowing and his mind was active. As the men curved round the brow of the mountain and headed towards a stunning serpentine valley of gentle serrations, streaked by a gushing tributary of the Great Zab River, the autumn sun poked out from behind the clouds. Its cleansing beams flooded the valley.

Richmond turned to Ashe. 'Know something?'

'What?'

'You've changed.'

101

The day wore on like a heavy sack. The mountains that had seemed so brown now looked blue in the distance. As he placed one weary foot in front of another, Ashe noticed that the rocks were not brown either, but covered in a rusty-red lichen. The Martian character of the mountain suited the operation, but just as Ashe had got used to the redness, psyching himself up for the unknown that lay ahead, the troops rounded the base of a low mountain and entered a lush gorge.

On either side of its bank grew may bushes, terebinth trees with jade-coloured berries rotting on the boughs, oleanders, poplar trees, rock roses and sturdy little oaks. The stony ground was pocked with thistles and weeds. This route had been traced by tired soldiers since the days of Alexander the Great.

Richmond had told Ashe that four SAS men were already in the target area, establishing OPs. These observation posts were known as bashas – damp, desperately uncomfortable holes that were more suited to ascetic hermits of extreme persuasions, or psychopaths.

The men had been told that in addition to their minimal rations, they might, at night, also pick an edible weed called *khubbaz*. This could be supplemented by the milky-white *kivar* thistle, which could be warmed up on their elementary stoves but was best chewed cold since cooking smells were to be avoided so close to the target.

Richmond signalled for Kev Norton to approach with an update from the entrenched advance party. The long Afghani dagger flashing under Norton's vest explained why his oppos called him The Blade. Norton noticed Ashe's interest and quickly covered his personal weapon.

Hayes, Tongue and Scrabster darted over rocks into foliage on opposite sides of the stream, gripping their Colt Commandos and covering the distracted major, who was bent over Norton's PRC 319 radio system. Ashe knelt on one knee, his submachine gun at the ready, ten metres in front of the major.

Two minutes later, Richmond signalled Ashe to join him, then signalled the other three men to climb as far up the banks as possible, making use of the trees and bushes. It was perilous to be so close to the target area in daylight, but the strike had been agreed for dusk, after dinner, when the enemy was likely to be least alert.

A dead-of-night operation had been discussed but was rejected because the enemy also had night-vision equipment provided by Turkish special forces. Furthermore, the entrance to the cave facility was already extremely dark due to rock overhangs and dense forest.

Complete surprise would be their trump card, and the mist that rose off the streams at dusk would also help. It had also been observed that night guards were posted to the facility's perimeter just after nightfall.

Two of the advance group were sniper specialists, trained to kill at up to 1,000 metres. Geoff Barrow and Tim Blakeley carried Accuracy International L96A1 rifles with Schmidt & Bender telescopic sights. They had already spent thirty-six hours dug into the dampness and cold, monitoring the positioning of facility guards. When the time came, ice-cold nerve and steady hands would ensure success.

Some three kilometres north of Richmond's position, four groups of four from D Squadron's Air Troop had advanced to assess the enemy's likely escape routes and set up a maximum of two ambush sites. The plotting of potential routes had been assisted by Jolo's men. They had discovered four possible paths. Available troop numbers ensured only the two most likely routes would be covered. Should things go badly at the target site, they could respond to calls for reinforcements.

Jolo's enthusiastic irregulars covered remaining routes using M16s with attached 40 mm M203 grenade launchers. The D Squadron troop had also carried two 81 mm mortars to the anticipated contact area – an amazing feat of strength, given the weight of operational loads.

The ascent of the gorge had been gruelling, but the last half-kilometre was even worse: the men now had to crawl through the scrub on their stomachs, negotiating the rocks and endless thistles in complete silence.

The plateau ended abruptly at a mossy slope that ran down into a narrow gorge. God knew how Jolo's men and the advance group had been able to position themselves there without being caught. As the sun hovered over the western horizon, Ashe heard noises.

Below Ashe and Richmond, at the foot of the gorge, some thirty Ansar al-Sunna terrorists had gathered round a large fire and were eating goat, raisins and rice. Some wore black combat suits with full-face balaclavas rolled up over their foreheads. Others wore blue cotton *thobes*, the male robe common in Arab countries, under green combat jackets. Many sported the Palestinian headscarf, folded on a diagonal, with tassels at the corners. Others wore red Arabic headscarves with the familiar zigzag pattern. All sported bandanas, side pistols and belts laden with AK-47 magazines.

The timing was perfect. Hardly any of them had their hands on their guns. Above the sharp voices of the terrorists, Ashe barely heard the two sniper shots that took out the two tired guards positioned on the sides of the gorge. From further up the lip of the gorge, short bursts of GPMG fire, lethal shots from M16s and Colt Commandos and a sudden barrage of grenades turned the dining party into a mangled, bloody mess. Some more snipers' shots, a brief strafing of machine-gun fire, and the gorge was quiet, but for the flow of the tiny stream as it flowed red over its stony bed. Smoke rose like a veil over the scene.

Richmond whispered, 'Fucking good. Stage one done. Wait here.'

As Richmond eased his way gently down into the gorge, there was a brief wait. At the end of the gorge was a dark rocky over-hang, with dripping moss and ivy cascading down. That was the entrance to the cave. Whoever was inside would be very confused.

There were groans from the gorge. One of Jolo's men hurried around the massacred corpses and delivered swift death to the wounded.

The first four seconds of a hostage-release scenario always belong to the SAS.

An explosion at the far end of the gorge. The demolition guys were on the job with PE4 plastic explosives. The outer door to the cave was now twisted metal. Two Remington 870 pump-action shotguns blew the hinges off the inner doors. The SAS entered with stun grenades, CS gas and deadly shots from hand-guns. Dazed guards came tumbling out of the cave entrance, scraping their eyes and crying, wildly firing rounds from Kalashnikov submachine guns. Hayes was hit in the leg. His body fell onto his bleeding stump, which trailed the shattered limb. Scotsman Andy Tongue ran to Hayes' aid with his medicine bag and reached for morphine. Hayes had passed out.

Richmond screamed to Norton, 'Check arrival time for the Chinook! We've got wounded.' Richmond was knocked back-wards as two shots bounced off the ceramic plates in his Kevlar suit.

'You all right, sir?'

'Just send the message!'

Norton checked the coordination digits with his handheld GPS receiver. Richmond got back on his feet as the last of the main-gate guards fell to sniper fire.

Scrabster, his face encased in a helmet and respirator, emerged from the cave entrance. 'Ready inside, sir. We got a brace.'

'Hostage?'

'Not yet, sir. Looks like the Turkish SF reserve have taken to the tunnels.'

Richmond reached for his Acme Thunderer and blew a piercing whistle that resounded across the gorge. The remaining SAS force and a dozen of Jolo's irregulars emerged from the undergrowth.

At that moment, heavy machine-gun fire sprayed across the gorge from a ridge in the side of a deep gully.

'Christ! It's the suicide squad!'

Richmond blew his whistle again. The firing stopped. There were casualties.

'Get that bloody position!'

Richmond reached for Norton's M16. 'Hayes! Grenade!'

Hayes tossed Richmond a grenade. Richmond loaded it into the launcher on the underside of the M16, pressed the trigger and fired at the flashpoint.

'Fuck it! Give me another!'

Looking down, Ashe caught the flash of a mighty explosion as a huge cloud of smoke enveloped the cave entrance. 'Shit! They've got a Fagot!'

The 9K111-2 Fagot M-type was a Russian-made rocket launcher of deadly accuracy. As the smoke cleared, it was obvious things at the cave entrance were desperate. Hayes and Norton were dead. Richmond, shielded from the blast by the shattered door of the facility, was pinned down.

Ashe checked the aiming projector sight on his MP5. Now the image intensifier and infra-red feature came into its own. He scoured the area from which the rocket had been fired. He could see it. He could see the emplacement.

A burst of heavy machine-gun fire resounded across the gorge. The enemy quickly retaliated with another rocket. This too was accurate. The machine-gun fire ceased.

Richmond knew that to move was certain death. He could only hope his men inside the cave complex had assessed the situation correctly and would not attempt to emerge from it. The enemy would be waiting for them.

More heavy machine-gun fire spattered across the gorge, keeping Jolo's men crouching in the undergrowth. Another grenade shot across the gorge, narrowly missing the enemy. Seconds ticked by.

Ashe could see the best means of getting to the enemy was from above. He unstrapped his heavy pack, took out two stun grenades and hooked them to his vest, then got up out of the grass and ran as fast as he could round the edge of the lip until he was above the emplacement.

An SAS sniper, biding his moment on the opposite side, saw what Ashe was trying to do and gave him pin-accurate covering fire.

Ashe lay down, checking the viewfinder as his submachine gun dipped over the edge. *Damn!* He'd have to go down. Suddenly his legs became jelly, and dizziness swept over him. Bile rose into his throat, but he was already half over the edge, his boot dangling in search of a foothold. God! Please, a ridge! Just a fucking ridge. Anything! His foot found purchase; another foot, a hand. He slid down. He carried on sliding. He couldn't stop. He'd had it. He couldn't stop himself. Ashe kept sliding. He tumbled down hard onto the ridge, then rolled over into the gully. Two militants gripped a captured Minimi. In shocked surprise, they turned. The Minimi's tripod was tangled up in camouflage netting. They panicked. Lying on his back, Ashe delivered fatal rounds into the faces and shoulders of the men.

A great cheer swept across the gorge. Ashe had won his spurs all right. But would he ever have the greater courage to admit his victory had been a complete accident?

102

'Just getting a signal in from D Squadron, sir.'

'Yes, Hadley?'

'Retreating troops all Turkish SF, sir.'

'How many?'

'They count twenty-five, sir. Can they ambush?'

'No, Hadley, arrest and search. I want a video.'

'Are we returning to RV, sir?'

'We're waiting here for the Chinook from Mosul to airlift casualties. Details to follow in forty-five minutes.'

Richmond turned to Ashe, still elated after his narrow brush with death.

'We've got some tidying up to do. Bury the enemy combatants. Clear the site of mines and booby traps. Record the scene. Gather evidence. Perhaps you'd like to interrogate your friends while we wait for the Chinook.'

'Delighted.'

Two figures emerged from what was left of the cave entrance, blindfolded, coughing and with their hands tied. They were forced to kneel at gunpoint. Ashe pulled off his turban, wiped his sore eyes with it and signalled for a soldier to remove the blindfolds.

Sami al-Qasr, squinting in the dusk light, glimpsed Ashe and the enveloping chaos, then closed his streaming eyes, still coughing. Aslan inhaled and stared at Ashe.

'Not exactly the Hemlock Club, is it Tobbi?'

The figure kneeling before him in green battle jacket and cargo trousers was a hundred years away from the sensitive character with whom Ashe had shared wine in St James's. Now he really looked like his name – *Aslan*: defiant as a lion. Ashe did not know whether to smile or scowl. Behind those bright, hard-soft eyes was a complex character beyond Ashe's understanding.

'A few questions, Colonel.'

'First, Dr Ashe, before you congratulate yourselves on your professional heroics, you should know the full price of your victory.' Aslan observed Ashe's narrowing eyes. 'Yes, Tobbi. Your decision to strike here today has blown to pieces the greatest opportunity the West has ever enjoyed of capturing, and delivering to justice, the fugitive Osama Bin Laden.'

He paused for effect. 'Is this not true, Sami?'

Al-Qasr nodded.

Ashe's stomach wound itself into a knot. There was such a conviction in Aslan's face and eyes that Ashe instinctively knew that this was no face-saving boast, no blind to shake off the shame of defeat.

'Yes, Dr Ashe, it's a real British victory for "Cool Britannia". But it is not Trafalgar, Tobbi, and I am not your Napoleon. The fools have rushed in, yet again. You see, the thing about intelligence is, it has to be employed intelligently.'

'Where is the Baba Sheykh?'

'Safe in the cave. No need for alarm.'

Ashe looked at Richmond's blanched face. Richmond gave a slight nod.

'Just where might we find Bin Laden, Colonel?'

'You won't. He'll have sent an advance party to assess security. Who knows where he's coming from. Soon, it's going to be dark. You've missed the chance of a lifetime.'

'I can alert satellite reconnaissance. Checkpoints. Reinforce border posts. How do we keep this from the Americans now?'

'You'll find a way, Major.'

Richmond hurried into the gorge to find a signals operator.

Ashe squatted down. 'All right, Colonel. Explain.'

'Would you mind untying my hands? It would help me unburden myself.'

'Prove your innocence, Colonel.'

'I will establish my innocence. It has not escaped me that the man who brings Bin Laden to justice will be richly rewarded. He will find a path to the very centre of power. Who would ever have thought that Turkey could – as you might say – *bring home the bacon*?'

Ashe grimaced.

'Not only that, Dr Ashe, but our good genius here, Sami al-Qasr, has formulated a weapon of such extraordinary and subtle potency that simply possessing it would mean a vast increase in respect accorded us. Even from those nations who have affected friendliness towards us. America, for example. The president speaks of a war on terrorism but treads softly with Kurdish rebels who've brought death and misery to my country.'

Aslan glanced around the scene in the gorge.

'I see you've killed my little private band of terrorist hunters.'

'Everyone knows, Colonel, that the position of the PKK in Iraq is an anomaly.'

'An anomaly to you, but an insult to those who believe in Turkey.'

'What will Turkey's having a DNA weapon prove?'

'If nothing else, we should deny it to the Americans. Do something positive for the balance of power in the world. Turkey is the balancing point for peace around the globe. It always was. You see, Dr Ashe, my country has a destiny. It is not a pawn in the international game. We are finding ourselves again.'

'Get to the point, Colonel. What about Bin Laden?'

'I dreamt up a plan. In my grubby little office, in a not very inspiring quarter of Istanbul. With only a picture of Atatürk for company. From my work in Hakkari Province, during the war with the PKK.

'From my good contacts in Israeli intelligence, and from my

own operations elsewhere, I knew about Sami al-Qasr: Iraq's lost genius. And I have also learned a great deal about the Yezidis. Enough to regret many things I did when I was in eastern Turkey. My job was to lure Sami here out of his comfortable role as a CIA lackey in California, and get him to do something I knew burned in his heart. So I created a charming little al-Qaeda recruiting and information website. It was called... What was it called, Sami?'

'The Daggers of Righteousness.'

'That's right. This was my creation – along with my good colleague, Ali, who is very skilled at the computing side of life. Daggers of Righteousness has hooked many into the cause of Bin Laden. Or rather, the cause of Aslan. This gory little website, packed with coded material, is the best counter-terrorism operation in the world today! Why? Because it is the bridge between many groups of al-Qaeda supporters and the leadership of al-Qaeda itself! My troops have been *turned* without even realising that they are working against their supposed masters!'

'Brilliant, Mahmut. Worthy of you.'

'Thank you, Tobbi. You are a good man, but still a beginner in the game. Now, I have played a waiting game, a careful game. To bag your prey you have to take infinite pains. You do not tell people, "I have lost patience with Saddam", or al-Qaeda, or anyone like that. You never lose patience with your enemy. You must learn to love him in order to defeat him!

'And so... whilst I covered my own tracks, this one here–' he gestured to a surprised-looking Sami '–was encouraged to believe that Bin Laden was paying for a secret research facility in the Hakkari Mountains, created especially for him! And Osama, meanwhile, was given to believe that he and his colleagues could purchase a weapon here of such force that the mere threat of its use would get him almost whatever he wanted. It might be used, for example, to persuade General Musharraff in Pakistan to change his policies towards the United States. The weapon need never be actually employed. And if it ever was... Well, it's very psychological. No blood. No scenes of railway station massacres. No grieving families. No burning skyscrapers. No headlines. Just a silent, painless defeat of… how can I put it? *Expectation.* Targeted precisely at the genetic pool of choice. Clans. Tribes. Musharraff's family, for example. Or Bush's. Or Blair's. The new, subtle way of bringing your enemy to its knees.'

Al-Qasr's eyes lit up for the first time. Ashe immediately spotted the strange, telltale gleam of the blind idealist who has gone beyond himself, into the bottomless hinterland of egoistic fantasy.

'This far from charming weapon was enough inducement to persuade Osama to pay us a call.'

'The caves?'

'His facility, Tobbi. This very evening! You see, you bloody fool, your timing could not have been more insane. Had you only waited till dawn, history would have been different. Now it is too late. Your actions here will have sent him rushing off at full speed to a fresh hiding place, right out of the country. I *had* him, Tobbi! Almost in my grip!'

'Which direction was he coming from?'

Aslan slowly shook his head. 'You can forget it. You've missed your moment. Blown it, you might say. Take my word for it. He's gone.'

103

Night was closing in. In the firelight, Ashe could see pain in Aslan's eyes. Ashe knelt behind him and loosened his cords.

'For God's sake, Dr Ashe, untie it properly! You have your lost scientist. At least you can brag about that to the Americans. I'm not going anywhere. You've seen to that.'

'I'm sorry, Colonel.'

'Don't be sorry. Destiny.'

'Still a few things I don't understand.'

Aslan laughed. 'A *few* things, Dr Ashe! You want to know about the Baba Sheykh. Let's not beat about the bush. You know the genetic advantage held in the body of the sheykh.'

'Took some finding.'

'This was the key inducement to get al-Qasr to quit California. There was also the pressing fact that US and Israeli agents were closing in on his comfort zone. Al-Qasr had become a security risk. He was getting scared. He was even driven to do some very bad things to individuals who stood in his way. Weren't you, Sami?'

Al-Qasr shrugged his shoulders.

'But what does death matter to an ambitious scientist? To turn the screw on Sami here, I lured the Baba Sheykh and his trusting protector to Hamburg. A safe house. I checked up on him, pretending my mission was an attempt to arrest Yildiz and Yazar. Ah! How destiny favours the prepared mind! What a stroke of luck, or fate, it was that Yildiz and Yazar were present at the Lodge the night of the bombing. That pair have been so useful. As my cloak!

'And then, in the fullness of time, our ever-resourceful scientist "kidnaps" the sheykh. You must have thought you were brilliant, eh, Sami?'

Al-Qasr nodded.

'Yes, he kidnapped him all right. With agents provided by me! Right from under the noses of you and your American colleagues. And then Sami brings him right into my lap. All in one piece. Safe and sound, as you English say. Of course, it's taken a short while for Sami to adjust his huge mind to dividing the spoils, but he is sensible enough to see the advantages in sharing his discoveries – not with al-Qaeda, but with a country that has a more golden future.'

'Clever, Colonel. I've got to hand it to you.'

'Thank you.'

'You obviously get your kicks from humiliating your friends.'

'On the contrary, Tobbi. Is it humiliating to serve a higher purpose?'

'And how did this higher purpose include bombing the Kartal Lodge?'

'The attack on the Lodge at Kartal, Istanbul, was not my accomplishment. In fact, it nearly wrecked my plans!'

'Who did do it then, Colonel? Who hit the Lodge?'

'General Koglu, my highly decorated superior.'

'Why?'

'It had come to the general's attention that a problem existed within a Lodge in Istanbul: a little Masonic lecture from the Baba Sheykh promised a lot of trouble. The English Grand Lodge warned of "consequences" if the speech was permitted. While the sheykh appeared all innocence, Koglu suspected devious motives. He naturally feared the speech could be inflammatory in our country. I wonder, Toby Ashe, if you understand just how inflammatory such a speech can be, and how divisive the question of Freemasonry has been in our country!'

'I do have some idea.'

'Then I give you another idea. *Koglu*. Koglu is an idea. He embodies an idea of my country. Koglu and men like him do not want publicity for Freemasonry. Nor do they want the world to know about the Yezidis or any other Kurds. In our country, most people, if they ever think about it at all, think Turkish Kurds who don't accept they *are* Turks are, if not necessarily dangerous, a fussy lot. They attract too much attention to themselves, and should accept the facts of life – that being born in Turkey, they are Turks first and foremost. As for the Kurdish Yezidis in Iraq, they have always been seen as a nuisance. They will not conform. It is true that my country has not been kind to the Yezidis. I am not Koglu, Dr Ashe. Koglu hates Freemasonry. He hates Kurds. And he does not have a very high opinion of Jews.'

'So what did Koglu do?'

'He arranges a little exercise of his own. To accomplish it, he decides to use my resources. This is how I got to know of his plans.

'Over the last few years, I have "turned" some of our own, homegrown Islamic militants to serve the state's purposes. But though I say "turned", they themselves do not know that their orders come from their enemies. They are still convinced they are fighting for the cause! You see, Ashe, it's hard to find a traitor when the traitor is unaware that he *is* a traitor.

'Koglu ordered me to release some of these agents of mine for his purposes. I was of course suspicious. Koglu planned to get them to kill the Baba Sheykh, and make a nasty, threatening scene at the Masonic Lodge – all of which he could then manipulate as propaganda. This explains the curious nature of the chaos that occurred that night. The terrorists turned up, could not find the Baba Sheykh – I had ensured he and the doctor quit Turkey of course – got confused, fired a few shots, and then, apparently, blew themselves up! Which was fortunate, as I presume that in their anger and frustration at not finding their target, they were about to exceed their original instructions. Koglu had not fully realised he was playing with fire. Not all of my operatives can be described as "stable". So, after that, it was even easier to say that this was an amateurish attack and of no concern to other countries. That was the story given to the public, more or less.

'But even without murdering the sheykh, Koglu got pretty much what he wanted. He's still pushing his secret and not so secret agenda of intensifying the observation of minority groups. He tried to persuade me to fabricate evidence against those he sees as enemies – putting me, I must say, in a very awkward position. Koglu hates a lot of things. And anything he hates is, by virtue of this, a mortal threat to Turkey's future. And is that not your Chinook I can hear in the distance?'

Ashe looked up into the blackening skies and listened for the Chinook. Feeling an extraordinary relief, he turned to Aslan.

Aslan shuffled about painfully. 'Would you mind if I got off my knees now, Dr Ashe?'

'*You* can. But al-Qasr stays where he is. I'm afraid you're staying in custody, Colonel. For all I know, everything you've just told me is bullshit.'

Richmond returned to the cave entrance. 'We'll have the wounded out in no time, Toby. You can take yourself and your friends back to Mosul in the Chinook, if you like. The rest of us are pulling out and heading back to the RV. We still haven't located your sheykh.'

Aslan shrugged his shoulders.

The Chinook hovered noisily over the gorge, its twin rotors creating storm-like waves among the bushes and trees along the ridges.

'There's something else you need to know, Tobbi. Thanks to my work here, I have some papers. When you know what they contain, you'll see I have the interests of humanity at heart. And you will trust me.'

'Don't count on it.'

Aslan reached for his breast pocket. Ashe pulled out his Browning and pointed it at Aslan's head. 'Slow down, Colonel.'

Ashe reached forwards with his left arm and patted Aslan's breast pocket.

'Don't be stupid, Tobbi. Your men have frisked me already. These papers come from our enemies!'

'One can never be too sure.' Ashe reached into the pocket and brought out a folded bunch of papers. He replaced the Browning.

A flash... Another flash! An explosion! The whole gorge lit up as the Chinook's fuel tanks ignited.

'Hit the floor!' screamed Richmond as the long shoe of the helicopter separated itself mid-air from the twisted, whirling blades, then tumbled out of the night, crashing with an unbearable roar into the narrow sides of the gorge.

Silhouetted against the rippling night sky, a group of Taliban fighters from Bin Laden's advance party, holding a Katyusha-bearing SAM rocket launcher, shot several rounds into the night air before disappearing into the blackness.

The quivering Chinook creaked with busting rivets as it hung suspended halfway down the gorge sides. Another explosion ripped apart its body. The remains slipped, groaned, then crashed violently into the riverbed, swiftly followed by wild spinning chopper blades and torn tyres.

Ashe and Richmond kept their hands over their heads, their faces sunk into the earth and their eyes closed, as flaming debris shot everywhere. Burning petrol flowed into the stream, lapping against the sides. When the heat became too much to bear, Ashe looked over to Richmond, then to Aslan and al-Qasr.

They'd gone.

Ashe pulled at Richmond's jacket and screamed at his friend above the noise. 'Inside the cave! The cave!' Richmond nodded. The two men crawled on their bellies, the backs of their legs singed by the heat, towards the cave entrance. They made their way under the twisted metal and, finally, into the foul gloom of the now-stinking interior.

A third explosion: this time from inside the cave complex; then another, followed by a rapid series of smaller detonations that rocked the covert labyrinth. The facility had been booby-trapped: a final, bitter adieu from Aslan and al-Qasr.

104

Rain was beating against the high window in Karla Lindars' office at Shrivenham. The dreary autumn light cast phantom shadows across the pale room. Ashe's secretary was on the phone.

'No, Melissa. No news at all. It's been nearly a week now. Anyway, darling, what do you care? Fucking off to Dublin like that with your girlfriends.'

'Seemed the right thing to do, Karla. The strain gets to you, you know.'

'Yes, but it's how we cope with the strain, isn't it?'

'Maybe I'm just not made for this sort of thing, Karla. Anyhow, I've met someone.'

'I don't want to know. I'll call you if I have any news. Goodbye Melissa.'

US Field Hospital, Mosul, Iraq

A beautiful face. Jolo Kheyri was looking down at Ashe.

'I try to grow a moustache like my uncle's, Tobbiash. But is no good.'

Ashe's eyes adjusted to the sight. 'You're looking… fine, Jolo. Where's the party?'

Jolo stood up and twirled his sumptuous gold-edged black robe. His spotless linen headscarf, bound by an elaborate pitch-black *ogal*, caught the hard light of the strip-bulb. Ashe squinted. His head was pounding. 'Very nice.'

'The men of the Sinjar always wear best things for the Jema'iyye.'

'The…?'

'The pilgrimage.'

Ashe realised Jolo was talking about the all-important Autumn Festival at Lalish, the Great Assembly feast. He knew that thousands normally attended, and that it always took place in the first week of October. 'Starts today?'

Jolo counted on his fingers. 'This is five day.'

'Fifth day?' Ashe sighed heavily. 'I've been in hospital for over a week?'

'Yes.'

'I don't feel so well, Jolo. Where's Simon?'

Jolo sat down again. 'Very sick.'

Ashe closed his eyes. He thought of his friend's open, lightly freckled face, the warm smile, the kindly, no-nonsense voice: the man he could trust with his life.

'Like you, Tobbiash, Major Richmond is caught in… cave. Rock falling on body. We dig you out. Major Richmond very, very sick. You have… operation. You have metal, here.' Jolo pointed to the back of his skull.

'Great, Jolo. Now I'm bulletproof.' Ashe tried to laugh, but it hurt.

'For Major Richmond,' Jolo shook his head mournfully, 'is very serious. American doctors here in Mosul try very much, but he is sent back to Britain.'

'The other guys?'

Jolo looked very uncomfortable. 'Yes. It was hard day. Evil things are happening.'

'How many?'

Jolo smiled. 'D Squadron. All are safe! Very good!'

'The others?'

'Very good for eight men.'

'Eight killed?'

'Yes, but many Ansar al-Sunna dead! And Tobbiash! Very, very good! Baba Sheykh is found! Yes! Thanks to you!'

'Me?'

'When Major Richmond is attacking. Many explosions. Sheykh is lying down. He has guards but bombs are too much for them. They are scared and don't know what to do. Sheykh tells them, "Go outside! Help your friends! If you cannot help your friends, now is the time to run away because the soldiers have more guns, and they kill you." Then they are thinking to kill the sheykh. And the sheykh looks in their eyes and says, "I am dying. I pray to God for you." And the men leave the sheykh. And the sheykh is not dying. He still has strength. And he follows way through caves. All the time guns, explosions, and men are running. Now Baba Sheykh know these caves near Nerva Zheri in Hakkari Mountains. Our people have hidden in them many centuries. He is not well. But he finds way! And he climbs and he climbs, out into the mountainside. All the time he is thinking of his people and of the pilgrimage. And he sees the stars. And he goes to sleep in love of God. And British soldiers find him. And they bring him here.'

'Where is he?'

'He is at Lalish of course! Without Baba Sheykh, no Jema'iyye! Now, is thanks to you, he is with Yezidi people! You are servant of Tawusi Melek, yes! Thank God! Thank God! Tobbiash!'

Jolo's excitement caught the attention of a passing US airforce flight surgeon.

'I think you'll have to leave now, sir.'

Ashe looked over to the doctor in the steel-rimmed pilot's glasses and glimpsed the name sewn onto his sleeveless, darkgreen surgeon's shirt. 'Captain Hong.'

'Yes, Dr Ashe?'

Ashe extended his hand.

'How do you do, Dr Ashe?'

'Can I get up now?'

Hong looked surprised. 'Since CASEVAC brought you in to the field hospital here, you've had serious surgery on your skull, sir. The stitches have dissolved now, but you should be taking it

446

easy for a few weeks. You had a hole in your skull the size of my thumbnail. We've been very concerned about possible brain injury.'

'You got the piece out.'

'Pieces, sir. We got them all out. You should be taking it easy.'

'On my back?'

'Well, you've come round… May I take your pulse, sir? And your temperature? Here, don't swallow.'

Hong put a thermometer on Ashe's tongue. 'I don't know if you're up to it, sir, but there's been a guy from home seconded to the DIA up here. He's been in and out. Damn keen, sir, to speak to you.'

'Name wouldn't be Beck, would it?'

'Yes, sir. Sherman Beck. Nice fella. Now, if you can sit up, I'd like to take a look at the scars.'

Hong deftly felt along the lines of the surgical wound. 'Pretty good. Very good! You shape up well, Dr Ashe.'

'Did Beck say when he was coming back?'

'Well, he's been coming back every four hours or so. So… I guess he'll be here… pretty soon. He'll be delighted to see you back in the land of the living.'

'And the dying.'

'Well, sir… we do our best. I guess he's got a lot to say to you, Dr Ashe.'

'I bet he has.' Ashe took Jolo's arm. 'Jolo, give me a hand! Got my kit, Dr Hong?'

'I'm not sure I'm authorised to let you outta the hospital, sir.'

'Listen, Dr Hong. I'm a British citizen, on a very important mission for a very important man in Baghdad.'

'Covert work, sir?'

'Would I tell you?'

'I'll get your kit, sir. But you better be taking it easy. And I want to see you back here for a check-up and X-ray in twenty-four hours, d'ya hear?'

'You're a brilliant man, Dr Hong.'

'I doubt it, sir. But if I was you, I wouldn't be getting out of bed like this.'

'No choice, Doctor. Here, Jolo! Help me on with what's left of my trousers!'

Ashe reached for his combat vest, still caked in dust and myriad fragments of carbon. He felt a bulge in the breast pocket and withdrew a sheaf of dusty papers: scan-copies of printed Arabic.

'What on earth are these? I don't remember seeing them before. How's your Arabic, Jolo?'

'No problem.'

Jolo seized the papers. His eyes darted down the sheets. 'Ansar al-Sunna! Tobbiash, these are plans. Who give this to you?'

Ashe shook his head. 'No idea.'

As Jolo studied the papers more closely, his body began to shudder. He looked up at Ashe in horror, hands shaking. 'Tobbiash! We must go! We must go now! I must warn my men!'

'What the hell is it?'

'Plans to attack the Yezidi people! At Lalish. You see here! On the fifth day: at the Assembly! Six agents.'

'Why Lalish?'

'We always fear it. In our hearts. Many hate us. They say our tradition is not true, that we worship a devil. You know Arab word for "tradition" is "al-Sunna". By killing us, they claim to be guardians of tradition. Is propaganda for al-Qaeda. We have heard warning before. Who find this?'

'I can't remember. My head's too…'

105

Jolo's knuckles were white as the pinkie SAS desert Land Rover stormed north to Lalish. The three SAS-trained irregulars carrying M16s with grenade launchers in the back seat were tingling with fear for their people.

'I am sorry for your head, Tobbiash, but we must do everything to save the people.'

'You've radioed ahead. You've got guards at all the entry points. Patrols on the mountaintops. Men in the streets. At the shrines.'

'You not understand, Tobbiash. There are thousands of Yezidis in the holy valley. Also on the hillsides. At the tomb of Sheykh Adi. At the shrines. At the sacred springs. There is dancing. There is singing. There are people selling. There are Muslims there who come to watch. The Baba Sheykh. Where do we begin? Will they bomb the shrines? Snipers against the prince? People have tried to kill him before.'

Suddenly, Ashe realised that the return of the Baba Sheykh and the presence of the prince – both vital for the Autumn Assembly – would almost certainly bring Princess Laila and Sinàn to the valley. He felt something of the panic that had enveloped Jolo Kheyri.

'Look, they only have six agents.'

'Six agents. Six bombs.'

'I understand that. So, if you had a limited number of agents and you wanted to make the biggest impact, what would you do?'

Jolo looked bereft, shaking his head.

'Think, man! *Think!*'

Jolo thought hard. 'Tobbiash, today is the five day. Today sacrifice of bull.'

'Perfect. Ansar al-Sunna must know this. Describe it!'

The men in the back pointed to the mountains in the north. 'Mount Meshet!'

Mount Meshet bounded the holy valley to the south. The men urged Jolo to put his foot down. The pinkie could go no faster.

Jolo shouted to Ashe, 'On day of sacrifice. Always in afternoon.'

'What time?'

'Every year is different. No special time. Head *feqir* and prince decide on day.'

Ashe looked at his watch. 13.10. His heart raced. He took three of the painkillers given him by Dr Hong. He felt dizzy. Jolo continued the description.

'You know Market of Mystical Knowledge?'

'The walled place in front of the Sanctuary of Sheykh Adi?'

Jolo nodded. 'Men come with guns. They line up round walls. Even the holy men and the nobles in the sanctuary guesthouse. They stand to see.'

'Who's in the guesthouse?'

'The nobles and holy men. They stay there. Sleep on mats on floors. It is fine pillars and good stone floor.'

'Are they all there?'

'Most, yes.'

'That's where they'll strike! Alert your guards, Jolo! They must search the guesthouse!'

'The nobles will not like this!'

'Can you persuade them?'

106

The road towards the valley from Meshet was packed. Battered old cars from the days before the first Gulf War, held together with string and hope, jostled for every available place. There was no way the pinkie could get through.

Jolo's men had brought horses. Even so, the hundreds of men, women and children from the Sheikhan, from the Jebel Sinjar, ancient Nineveh, Mosul, and even Syria, made it impossible to get any speed up.

Everywhere Ashe looked he could see *qewwals* with *daff* and *shebab*, playing and singing as the pilgrims hogged the narrow paths towards the Shrine of Sheykh Shems.

Ashe was repeatedly jostled by late-comers carrying the striped tents they would erect at the traditional *ojakhs*, the camp-sites where the clans spent their week at the holy valley, cooking, playing and sleeping.

To Ashe's astonishment, Jolo's men had already rooted out five terrorists attempting to conceal AK-47s in tents. They'd been dragged outside Lalish, given a beating and tied up, pending interrogation. The method of capture had been simple. Gathering round a group, Jolo's men would suddenly request the people to crouch, in Kurmanji. Arabic speakers would immediately stand out, literally, from the crowds. Given the conditions, the irregulars' efficient operation was little short of miraculous. But then, miracles had always happened at Lalish, and none but Ashe was surprised.

Miracle or not, that still left one agent – and one determined agent of Ansar al-Sunna would be more than enough to wreck the entire community forever.

Jolo told Ashe to dismount and remove his boots and socks. They must all walk barefoot in the valley, security or no security.

Down the valley, the call had gone out that the ceremonies culminating in the bull sacrifice were to begin soon. Jolo, Ashe and over a dozen of Jolo's irregulars ran up the stone paths, dodging dozens of startled pilgrims. From among the trees, young men in Western gear and girls in lace and gold and silver brocade pointed at them, wondering what was going on. One word in the wrong ear, and there would be massive panic, a stampede, and death.

Finally, they arrived at the courtyard outside the sanctuary. The place had been thoroughly searched. Jolo bowed to the prince. There was a tap on Ashe's shoulder.

'Laila!'

She kissed him on both cheeks. 'Oh, Tobbi! What you and Major Richmond have made possible! Look!' Laila pointed to the Baba Sheykh, who was sitting beneath a wooden gazebo in a corner of the courtyard, deliberating with visiting Yezidi headmen. 'My brother is overjoyed. He is so sorry. He wants to speak to you.'

'Please, Laila! Not now! Please, leave the area!'

'No one leaves now, Tobbi. We have our guards.'

A group of men dressed in baggy trousers and white shirts appeared with sticks, striking people lightly in a well-understood gesture to clear the square before the arrival of the guns.

Ashe strained to see. He looked over to Jolo; Jolo shrugged his shoulders.

There came the echo of fast-moving feet on stone. The crowds began to quieten. Some twenty-five Yezidi men in cream-coloured surcoats over black sweaters and trousers ran into the courtyard and lined the sides, raising their AK-47s above their blue-chequered turbans and into the air. Jolo ran over to Ashe. The crowd gasped.

'What's going to happen?'

'Any time now, guns fire to signal beginning.'

'That must be the time. That's why they chose this day. Everyone's in one place.'

Jolo pulled Ashe into a crouching position. 'Look at the people's feet! Follow me!'

Ashe followed Jolo, who pushed through the crowd with his unwelcome M16. Foot after foot. It was maddening. 'What am I looking for, Jolo?'

'Anyone who is not naked foot.'

They approached the sanctuary guesthouse. Ashe saw pools of goats' blood, glistening. This was where the goats gathered to be slaughtered and then fed to the guests.

'Look! Look!'

'Where?'

'Look there! A man with a goat! His feet.'

Ashe saw a pair of feet in thick woollen socks.

107

An urgent wave of expectancy swept through the crowd. Everyone stared at the great coal-black serpent at the sanctuary gate. Suddenly the murmur ceased. Shuffling feet on stone. Jolo whispered quickly to Ashe, 'Muslims, when asked to remove their shoes, often take only the shoes away. We do not ask them to remove sock.'

The two men stood up to inspect the suspect who'd entered the courtyard in socks. Several Muslim dignitaries had been invited. They wore socks also. But this man was dressed like a Yezidi. He was leading a goat towards the interior of the guesthouse.

'Look at his eyes, Tobbi. Something is wrong.'

Ashe looked at the cord attached to the goat. Not the usual rope. It was a cable. Ashe grabbed Jolo's shoulder and pointed to the goat. 'Look at it!'

Staring intently through the shifting gaps in the wavering crowd, Jolo could see the goat had been shaved. A new coat of goat's hair had been carefully bound around it.

'The cable's the detonator. In his hand.'

Jolo nodded. He stepped gently into the guesthouse.

A great cry went up. Jolo screamed in Kurmanji. 'To the ground!'

The guns in the courtyard fired a death rattle into the tense air. The goat bleated wildly as it trailed the severed hand of the terrorist behind it, dragging it into a blood-soaked heap of goat's flesh. With a single stroke from his knife, Jolo had hacked the terrorist's hand clean off. The terrorist, his right wrist spurting blood like a fountain, ran madly after the goat. The goat turned and raced in panic towards the Baba Sheykh, then into the courtyard.

The terrorist fell to the hot flagstones and grabbed the cable with his left hand, his amputated right hand still swinging from the flex. He stood up, fumbling desperately for the detonator. Behind him, the door of the sanctuary flew open. The sacrificial bull was about to be released for his last run, down to the Shrine of Sheykh Shems. For a second, the terrorist stared into the Baba Sheykh's eyes, but before he could plunge the detonator pin, the rampant bull charged and impaled him on its horns.

Jolo ran after the fleeing goat as the men in the courtyard fired more shots. The sacrificial bull thundered down the valley towards the shrine of Sheykh Shems, the limp body of the terrorist bobbing from left to right over its head, the crowds parting to let the animal through.

Ashe, breathless with relief, caught Sinàn's eye. Around them, the holy men and Yezidi nobility cheered.

'Now you must meet the prince. Please, come.'

'Sorry, Sinàn. I must see the Baba Sheykh. Urgent.'

'But the prince!'

'Tell His Highness we can meet later. I ask one thing. That bull deserves a medal, not to be sacrificed.'

'There is always a sacrifice today at the shrine of Sheykh Shems!'

'From where I'm standing, Sinàn, you've just had it.'

Ashe broke away. He brushed aside Princess Laila, stunning in her blue-and-gold embroidered abaya, and pushed his way to where the sheykh had been standing. The Baba Sheykh was gone.

Ashe had seen the look in the sheykh's eyes when he had confronted the terrorist. The sheykh had blamed himself for attracting danger to his people. Ashe saw intuitively that something terrible was happening in the Baba Sheykh's mind. He must find him, before someone else did.

108

The next few minutes passed in a blur for Ashe, as if the colours of the world had been left in place, but all its substance removed. The world was in the wind, scattered in the sky.

He remembered Laila clutching his arm, pulling him close, calling to him, as the liquid tapestry of people flooded down the valley towards the Shrine of the Sun. He saw her mouth move, her eyes imploring.

He caught sight of a grey head as Baba Sheykh marched forwards, children all about him. He heard a call from behind. He turned. Amongst the bouquet of faces was Sherman Beck's, out of place, out of time. Laila tugged at Ashe's arm, pulling him on. Beck was shouting. 'Ashe! Dr Ashe! I gotta speak to you. You gotta speak to me!'

Ashe stopped. Was he running away? He wouldn't run away.

'This Aslan guy, Toby. You shoulda told us! God! All these people!'

'Take your shoes off, Beck!'

'What?'

'Take your fucking shoes off!'

'Who's the guy on the bull?'

Laila called to Ashe. 'You must come!'

Beck grabbed Ashe's arm. 'Listen, man, I gotta see this Baba Sheykh guy! I ain't taking my shoes off until I do. D'ya hear me, Ashe?'

Ashe looked down at Beck's fist, gripping his arm. He stared Beck in the eye. 'This valley is holy, Beck.' He pushed Beck back hard into the crowd.

Ashe ran on, past the crowds, past the bull now surrounded by pilgrims, past the Shrine of Sheykh Shems, into the woods, among the olive trees and tiny oaks. A flash of colour in the distance. The voice of Laila, screaming. 'Tobbi! Please!'

Ashe came to a ridge. Laila was sobbing on the ground. 'He ordered me to stay here, Tobbi. He told me, for my own soul, I must wait.'

'Where is he?'

'There! Down there!'

'Well what is it?'

'There is the last sight of the Zemzem stream. Then it flows underground, into the mountains.'

Behind them, they could hear the singing of the pilgrims, gathered around the bull, building to a crescendo: the drums beating hard, the flutes insistent, the voices ecstatic.

Ashe caught sight of the Baba Sheykh. He stood tall against the sky, his back turned, his arms outstretched, greeting the sun.

In the valley behind them, all was suddenly quiet, as specially selected men from the Mamusi, Qa'idi and Tirk tribes raised their swords before the eyes of the beast. The sun hid behind a cloud.

A cry pierced the calm. 'From the earthly Lalish to the heavenly Lalish. From the world of men to the abode of the angels!'

The sun's rays suddenly enveloped the body of the sheykh as he crossed his arms over his heart. Then, greeting the Peacock Angel at the second of sacrifice, he hurled himself into the whiteness of the Zemzem stream to be borne swiftly into the mountains.

'Hey Toby, I gotta talk to the Baba Sheykh!'

Ashe turned to the sweating Beck, footwear dangling by laces from his raised arms.

'Look man, I took my fuckin' shoes off!'

'Yes, Beck. But you left your socks on.'

109

On 8 November 2004, US troops entered Fallujah in force to flush out and destroy a stronghold of the Iraqi insurgency. Major Richmond, limping slightly but otherwise recovered, was on hand to help identify any rebels who tried to blend in with the civilian exodus from the city. One of the prizes was Hafiz Razak. Thanks to Richmond's positive identification, the Syrian terrorist had made his last bomb and forged his last passport.

That same day, Ashe was instructed to attend a cursory MIT briefing in a secure room at Ankara Esenboga Airport. Also invited were Matthias Fless and Sherman Beck. The dull meeting turned out to be merely a prelude to a ride in a four-seater jet to the furthest reaches of eastern Turkey.

From the Turkish air-force base at Hakkari, the party was driven by military truck to a barren crossroads near Güzeldere, only ten kilometres from the Turkey–Iraq border. As a private from a platoon of regular Turkish soldiers waved them down, a black Mercedes limousine emerged from behind a covered troop-carrier. The limo's rear door opened and the party was ushered in.

To the right of the chauffeur sat the rotund figure of General Ahmet Koglu, representing the Foundation for the Strengthening of the Turkish Security Forces (TSKGV), the army's economic development wing. Koglu signalled the driver to follow the military truck. The convoy soon left the road and headed up a farm track that skirted a dull grey escarpment.

Koglu turned to his guests. 'Today is an auspicious day, gentlemen. A special day for you and for my country. It gives me very great pleasure to demonstrate three things that bring credit to my country.'

Beck interrupted. 'And will the press be seeing what we are about to see, General?'

'Naturally, the press will in due course see what is of most significance to the public. You, however, will be privileged to report to your superiors the essence of three facts. First. The Turkey of today will not tolerate surprising developments that threaten the principle of national progress and democracy. Second. Our great army is fully in accord with this principle. Third. We shall show today that where the United States and Great Britain have failed, my country will succeed.'

'I only wish Major Richmond were here,' Ashe muttered to Beck.

'Didn't you know? He's confounded the surgeons and is back in his boots!'

Ashe's heart rose.

The car stopped at a temporary checkpoint. Ashe had the awful feeling that they had been dragged in to witness some appalling show-trial, the kind of thing Bolshevik Russia used to arrange for compliant foreign journalists.

Koglu spoke animatedly to the checkpoint officer. The officer pointed out the perimeter of a distant facility. Koglu nodded with satisfaction.

The truck continued up a hill. The limousine followed, its suspension tested to its limits. Fless began rubbing his fingers, anxious for his absent firearm. Beck tapped the sides of the windows. The general turned to them with a milk-curdling smile.

'You are perfectly safe, gentlemen. The limousine is bulletproof.'

Ashe, seated uncomfortably between the two agents, was not reassured.

As the limo approached a breezeblock gatehouse, the party had its first view of the intended destination: a flat-roofed concrete army base, the size of a village school. Covered in cracked grey plaster, the facility extended from a main block to a small barrack block at the rear. A barn-like structure, next to the barrack, was still under construction.

Bursts of submachine-gun fire echoed from behind the main structure.

'Please be calm, gentlemen.' Koglu drew his pistol and stepped out of the car. He approached the gatehouse. Two soldiers from the truck in front restrained the terrified guard while the general calmly removed a cellphone from the guard's trembling hands. Koglu walked back to the car and leant into the window. 'Formalities, gentlemen. Please forgive the delay. Security, nothing more. Please be comfortable.'

Ashe pointed through the rear window. 'Look!' Fless and Beck turned to see lines of Turkish Special Forces in black combat suits emerging from cover to surround the facility. 'They've been waiting for Koglu's signal!'

'Sure about that, Ashe?'

Before Ashe had time to answer Beck's troubling question, the party caught sight of a group of tired-looking troops in green fatigues slinking out from behind the barrack-block, their hands on their heads. Right on cue, Special Forces from the truck in front jumped out to form a cordon for the disarmed men. At the end of the line, each man was body-searched, handcuffed and shackled.

Koglu directed with oily ease, returning again to the limousine.

'These captured men have abused their position in the Special Forces. They are very extreme. Very extreme views. Fanatical types exploiting the requirements of the state in this troubled area.'

Ashe looked at Fless and raised his eyebrows. The two men knew well enough that, in the past, extreme rightists had proved useful enough to the dirty conflict that had been waged against Kurdish terrorists in the eastern provinces.

Koglu poked his head through the front window again, smiling. 'I trust you will inform your superiors that Turkey always tidies up its own mess. We do not need to be told. See for yourselves!'

The captured men were herded miserably into the troop-carrier which then manoeuvred round and trundled off as fast as it could down the approach track. Koglu got back in the limousine.

Ashe looked at him pointedly: 'The purpose of this facility, General?'

'Yes, this has been an... interrogation centre, a centre for Special Forces. Fortunately, as a result of successfully dealing with PKK activity within our country, it has functioned chiefly as a supply and rest centre.'

'It hasn't been used as a spearhead base for sending forces into Iraq then, General?'

Koglu laughed. 'You know as well as I do, Dr Ashe, that the Turkish army does not undertake such activities. Our government forbade helping the invasion of Iraq from across our borders. This, however, did not deter the invaders.

'But, as Mr Beck is fully aware, the Turkish state is fully committed to the global war on terror. And to prove the strength of that commitment, we are bringing you here today: a special privilege. Here, gentlemen, you will see for yourselves the very weapons of mass destruction developed under the protection of Saddam Hussein that the Americans, the Israelis and the British failed to find. You are witnesses to the professionalism of Turkey's military forces that have rendered this prize to the forces of justice without endangering the life of a single civilian.'

Fless looked at Beck and shook his head. If Fless had only been permitted to do his work...

Ashe was intrigued. Turkey would get both the credit and the weapon. Had he not been in such mixed and febrile company, he would have laughed his socks off. Turkey: ever a wild card, not to be underestimated.

Beck was having none of it. Scoring cheap points off the USA's high-risk anti-terror and pro-democracy agenda was intolerable. 'With respect, General, just ask the question: who's providing the greater part of security for the Free World? Is it you?'

Koglu turned and looked Beck in the eye. 'At this particular moment in your life, Mr Beck, it is. And I trust, on reflection, you'll thank God for your ally.'

110

The limousine drew to a halt by the entrance. The chauffeur opened the doors, saluted the general and returned to the driver's seat for a cigarette.

The party was shown through the front door to a comfortable mess-room at the front of the main block, with soft black sofas, a widescreen TV, a bar, fine carpets on the walls, and a large desk. Behind the desk, in a green combat jacket and jeans, sat Colonel Mahmut Aslan. Aslan slowly rose to salute the general.

'Please come out from behind your desk, Colonel. I regret I must relieve you of your command, as I have relieved your men of their weapons. Your associate is under guard in what looks suspiciously like an unauthorised laboratory. If al-Qasr attempts to move, he will be shot. Before we take you away, I have undertaken to our allies that they will have an opportunity to acquire information for their enquiries. Not something I personally approve of, but I have been overridden in this matter.'

Aslan looked Koglu up and down. 'You know, General, there is a spiritual purity about this place you can't quite find anywhere else in Turkey.'

'You're a criminal, Aslan! The only question my superiors have is why you should obtain this terrible weapon and keep it to yourself. We presume you're trying to sell it to the highest bidder.'

Aslan shook his head. 'Sorry to disappoint you, General. There *is* no weapon of mass destruction here. Or at least... not quite the kind of destruction you dream of. '

Koglu rubbed his boot heels in frustration. 'You should have been a novelist, Colonel. Always weaving tales.'

'I thought you liked fiction, General.'

Koglu sensed a loss of control. 'You're bluffing of course.'

'No.'

Aslan's 'honest' look incensed the general. 'Are you saying, Colonel, you no longer possess the DNA weapon?'

'Can Professor al-Qasr join this discussion?'

'No discussion. You're under arrest.'

'But you do want *something*. You can use the intercom link with the laboratory. It's here, General, here on my desk.'

The general inspected the intercom speaker housing.

'Where do I switch it on?'

'Press "Laboratory".'

Al-Qasr sat in the dark, wrapped tightly in sealing tape. A hard-faced guard watched him, his Uzi submachine gun trained at the professor's head.

The buzzer went on the intercom. The guard raised the butt of his weapon. The buzzing continued. The guard warily approached the intercom. As his right finger caressed the Uzi's trigger-guard, his left hand glided over the possible buttons.

'Try "Mess-room".'

The guard pressed the button.

Al-Qasr leant towards the microphone. 'Let me speak to Aslan.'

In the mess-room, Koglu nodded Aslan to answer.

'Sami, listen to me. Our only chance is to explain the operation to General Koglu. Tell him straight, Sami. Don't fuck this up.'

Al-Qasr smiled weakly at the guard, cold as stone by the door, then addressed his audience. 'I want it to be known that I am, and always have been, a scientist, dedicated to truths that will help the human race in its evolution. I always wanted the world to know what I've achieved. This reward I have sacrificed.'

'Noble bastard,' muttered Ashe.

Aslan was irritated. 'Just explain the plan, Sami.'

Koglu pushed Aslan away from the desk. 'Come to the point, al-Qasr!'

Al-Qasr laughed maniacally. 'Everyone wanted my weapon. Saddam wanted it. The Pentagon wanted it. Al-Qaeda... Everyone! Now you come to me with insults!'

Koglu interjected. 'Keep making speeches, and your last chance will become your last words!'

'Humility befits those standing on the holy threshold of genius, General. I have made the most devastating weapon to the nations of the world—'

Koglu erupted. 'Bring al-Qasr here! Guard! Drag him to the main block!'

111

The guard shoved al-Qasr into the mess-room on the end of his Uzi. Still bound with tape, the professor shuffled forwards.

'Well…' Koglu licked his lips. 'Al-Qasr is finally under control – something the British, Americans and Israelis failed to achieve. Sit here, Professor, and answer my questions.'

'Ask yourself some questions, General. What is the nature of deterrence?'

'You tell me!'

'I will. And you will thank me.'

'What is the nature of deterrence, Professor?'

'One side has a mighty bomb. The other side also has it. In the old days, that was enough. There was some reason, if not honour, among the thieves. But now we see men in charge of nations so inspired by dreamworlds they risk the annihilation of their countrymen.'

Aslan winced at al-Qasr's rhetoric. 'Just tell them about the weapon, Sami!'

'The leaders have bunkers of course, for themselves, their friends and their families. Above all, they have their beliefs. In these they hide. How can we reach them?'

'Tell us!'

'With bunker-busting shells? No! I put it to you that the only deterrent that is going to work is the one that hits the beliefs of the enemy *where it hurts most*.'

Intrigued, Koglu's eyebrows rose. 'And how do we do this?'

'I don't refer to religious beliefs, General, or political beliefs. These are acquired as people grow up.'

'What beliefs?'

'I mean the most basic beliefs we are born with. Instincts. Things so deep that we take them for granted. Beliefs without which no nation or people could ever be shaped.'

'What are you saying?'

'Are you a patriot, General?'

'I am ready to fight and die for my country.'

'I believe you. Patriotism – or nationalism – is not only the last refuge of the scoundrel, as English scoundrels are always saying. It is also the first refuge of the threatened nation. And the nation is based not only on beliefs, but facts. The fact of reproduction. Commonality. The fact of things shared.'

Ashe spoke up. 'You mean *race*, Professor. Just say so.'

'Race, family, culture – deep and vital assumptions about the future. How could a dictator rule a nation where there was no nation?'

'But there have always been nations, tribes...'

'Not necessarily, General. Our mythology preserves knowledge that once it was different.'

'Mythology!'

'Yes. First there was the myth of ancient Troy. Then Schliemann discovered it – and he discovered it with science! Look at the myth of the Tower of Babel! In that myth, division into races is seen as a punishment, a punishment sent by a jealous God for man's relying on his own knowledge and building to the skies. But, today, the sky is not the limit. *Now* we see division into races as genetic mutation, occurring over many thousands of years. Primordial genetic mutation has resulted in the principal races and sub-races of the world. Was this a tragedy? Or an opportunity?'

'I don't know, and I doubt if I care, Professor. What have you discovered?'

'I have discovered a lost truth, General. As a result of the ancient practice of endogamy—'

'En... *what*?'

'Marriage confined strictly to a family or clan, General.'

'Thank you, Colonel. Go on, Professor.'

'Thanks to endogamy practised over millennia, I have discovered a genome template that takes us beyond Babel into a totally new era. My scientific manipulation of this genetic material unleashes extraordinary power. I present to you a retroviral weapon to change humanity, permanently!'

Al-Qasr's speech held nothing new for Ashe. His attention wandered, not out of frustration, but because something was shifting his awareness away from the depressing scenario conjured up by al-Qasr's apocalyptic, visionary science. As though pulled up magnetically into Ashe's consciousness, an image was struggling to surface. It was there; then it was gone. Then it was there! The image was clear: the weird man, the camouflaged figure who'd stopped him on the road to ODDBALLS that terrible morning, nearly nine months before. The charcoal-written sheet thrust at him by the green prophet... What had it said? *The Tower of Babel is being rebuilt and must be destroyed.*

Was there to be a catastrophic new division of the human race?

'And so, General, we come to the weapon. Imagine, General, imagine all of you, if your son and his wife are expecting a child, and when it is born, it looks nothing like its parents, or brothers, sisters or cousins. Imagine if the child is simply *of another race*. Mutated beyond any control of the parents.'

Koglu looked nonplussed.

'A few crazy idealists might think "How nice!" But think again. Imagine if, after the retrovirus takes hold, with every replacement of fresh cells in the individual, personal characteristics begin to change. Not only in the child, but in the parent as well. Think about it! Depending on how the weapon is targeted, the Arab gives birth to the Jew, the Jew to the Arab, the Chinese to the Japanese, the Japanese to the Korean, the Indian to the African. And even these isolated race-types will change beyond recognition – different mentalities, unfamiliar identities. And so on, and on, and on. And on. In less than a generation, there will be no nation to govern.

467

No commonality to appeal to. Brother would not recognise sister. Children would feel divorced from parents, teachers, each other. There will be nothing left to defend! No idea of home!

'The nation that succumbed to this weapon, General, would be cast into the most profound and permanent identity crisis conceivable. After a short period, the long-term effects would become entirely unpredictable. More than this, I can target this weapon to affect one family, any family I choose, or one individual, at any time.

'No group of people who knew that something like this existed would ever allow their rulers to risk exposure to its cataclysmic psychological power. And remember, General, this weapon causes no obvious death or destruction. You could even say it is *harmless*. Indeed, physically speaking, it is the world's first completely harmless weapon. But when its potential is fully grasped, is this not the most devastating weapon against human culture imaginable, a hair's breadth short of annihilation of a species? A weapon of destruction of the masses! Think about it!'

Ashe got up. 'I *have* thought about it. And what we have here is something incredible, marvellous. Almost beyond imagining.'

Beck was incredulous. 'The destruction of human culture – *marvellous?*'

Ashe sensed something strange happening outside of the compound. He walked towards the window, took a closer look into the distance. He turned to al-Qasr. 'Tell us, Professor, what distinguishes the genetic material on which the weapon is based?'

'Technical secrets must be reserved. I can only say that the distinction lies in the pre-mutational character of the material.'

'We get that already. Give an example.' Ashe was sure there was movement at the compound perimeter.

Al-Qasr thought for a second. 'Pineal gland function...'

'Do you refer to the production of dimethyltryptamine?'

'What?'

Ashe turned to Koglu. 'DMT for short, General. It's like the brain's own spirit-and-vision drug, produced, according to recent research, in the pineal gland. That's the tiny gland between the brain's hemispheres. DMT affects perception experience. Isolated, it can induce "spiritual experiences", infinity beyond reason... maybe even... *God*.'

Koglu banged the desk. 'What's he on about, al-Qasr?'

'Genetic mutations found in the rest of our species are absent from the test material.'

'What is this "test material"?'

Ashe answered. 'The professor extracted DNA from a specific line of Yezidis.'

'*Kurds?* Damn Kurds! This is insane! Genius belongs to the Turks! Atatürk was surely right about this!'

'Well, General. You can *believe* you are a superior race, but the genes hold the truth.'

'*Truth*, Dr Ashe? Truth! This is all theory!'

Al-Qasr shook his head, wriggling under his burden of sealing tape. 'No, General. Not theory. My weapon is fact!'

'How can this be fact?'

'Because our inherited genetic mutations have reduced the pineal gland's capacity to produce the type, quality and quantity of DMT you find as a potential in my ancient genetic profile.'

'So the Yezidis are freaks. So what?'

'General Koglu, you are an ignorant man!'

Koglu gave Ashe a murderous stare. Beck and Fless backed Ashe up. 'He's right! Why don't you listen?'

Ashe addressed al-Qasr. 'Don't you see, Professor, if you would only cease thinking in terms of weapons, what you have here is a discovery that could positively transform the whole human race.'

'Don't you mean human *races*, Dr Ashe?'

'That's the point, General. How can I put this? What if al-Qasr's discoveries give us the opportunity to *undo* the Babel story – the division of the races and loss of spiritual vision? Rather than threatening the end of one nation, could we not envision a return to humankind as one supremely gifted race?'

'I had no idea British intelligence had become a recruitment ground for New Age fantasists!'

Aslan laughed out loud. 'General Koglu! You surprise me! I thought you had a commercial brain. Can you not see the potential – for Turkey?'

'I gotta say, General...'

'Yes, Mr Beck?'

'Well, from what I'm hearing here, I reckon the world's just about ready for some kind of evolutionary leap. I'd be dishonest if I... well... I guess we'd all like to buy into this thing.'

Koglu rubbed his chin. 'I'm not stupid, Colonel Aslan. I can see that if Mr Beck is interested, there will be more in line behind him. Do I take it now that you wish to be a benefactor, rather than a traitor, to your country?'

'I have never been a traitor, General. Turkey is my religion! And I want our nation to enjoy all aspects of this discovery. The weapons potential will free Turkey politically. The innovative science and technology – this we can sell. Tell *that* to your friends in Ankara!'

'Have I misjudged you, Colonel?'

Fless broke the silence. 'And just who's going to be the new Atatürk, General? You? Or the colonel?'

Koglu became agitated. 'Colonel, it is clear we have the makings of a deal. But what are we to do with our... foreign visitors?'

Koglu stared at the three defenceless agents.

Al-Qasr spoke up. 'Kill them. And get me out of this! And call your guard off. He gives me the creeps.'

Through the window, silhouetted against the setting sun, Aslan observed a personnel carrier approaching. It skidded into the forecourt. Thinking it one of his own, Koglu drew his pistol and aimed it at Fless, Ashe and Beck.

Ashe spoke up. 'Aslan's men have come for you, General. Look!'

Koglu looked out of the window, sniffed, then turned abruptly, pointing his gun at Aslan.

112

Two stun grenades shattered the mess window. Struck in the head, the force blew al-Qasr and his chair into the wall. Massive flashes blinded everyone save Aslan. As Koglu lurched, disoriented, from side to side, gripping his ears in pain, Aslan, who had bided his time, pushed the desk sharply into Koglu's legs. The general fell moaning to the ground. Seizing the general's gun, Aslan put it to Koglu's mouth, and fired.

Outside, the general's special forces let rip on Aslan's relief force. Amid desperate shouting, a shower of mortar shells scoured the darkening skies, then scorched the horizon. The barrack house exploded, shooting blast debris in all directions.

Al-Qasr, blinded, wriggled on the floor. With blood pouring out of his head and over his burning eyes, his bound legs kicked the guard. Coming to his senses, the guard panicked. Seeing al-Qasr screaming at him, he flicked the Uzi's safety-catch and squeezed the trigger. Two bursts of live rounds rent through al-Qasr's writhing body. As the blasted corpse vibrated and rippled against the wall, the guard turned on Aslan. Aslan stepped back, tripping on Koglu's body as the guard let rip.

Gambolling out of a line of fire that sent splinters and sparks shooting across the mess, Aslan lost grip on the pistol. Seizing the moment, Ashe leapt forwards, straining for the gun. As the guard tried to refocus, Ashe fired. The guard reeled backwards as the demented Uzi punctured the tattered ceiling with aimless rounds.

Beneath a storm-shower of plaster, al-Qasr came to, desperate to prop his crumbling body against the wall, but his time, and his life, had run out. With blood flooding from his face, al-Qasr slumped, rigid, to the floor.

Aslan leapt onto the dazed guard, grabbed the Uzi and struck the guard hard in the neck, knocking him out cold. Reaching for a spare magazine from the guard's blood-soaked belt, he reloaded. He stared at Ashe. *What did that stare mean?* Ashe's capacity to react stuck like a heavy boot in a dune. Fearing he was next, Ashe tried to raise his gun at the colonel. Aslan smiled. 'Don't bother, Tobbi. Save yourself. Under this carpet is a trapdoor. Meant for me. It leads to the hillside. God be with you!'

Though Aslan had suspected Koglu was intent on humiliating him, and had made precise preparations, he hadn't reckoned on al-Qasr's death. Standing tall in the scattered chaos, Aslan gazed for one last moment at what was left of Sami al-Qasr: 'Goodbye, Sami!' Then he turned quickly to Beck and Fless, gesturing with the gun. 'Follow *him*!' Aslan saluted Ashe, smashed the rest of the glass with the Uzi's butt, and, gun blazing, launched himself into the crossfire outside. Smoke soon enveloped him.

The battle stormed on until both sides realised there was no one giving orders. By then, the facility was engulfed in flames. Every scrap of authentic DNA material from the Baba Sheykh went up in the conflagration that lit the skies until dawn. Aslan's body was presumed destroyed in the furnace that overwhelmed the laboratory.

In the morning, it was reported in the press that resistance in Fallujah was stiffening, but futile. Ashe's experience did not find a place in the annals of history, for are we not told that it is the winners who write history? And in this case, the question remained – and would always remain – who had won and who had lost?

113

Lalish in late November has something of a child's Advent feel about it: an air of expectation and immanent holiness. All of the buildings are spotless. The paths are spotless. The stones are like leaves of vellum. The shrines are clean, and Lalish, the Yezidis' reflection of heaven, is pure and peaceful.

Accompanied by Karla Lindars, Ashe arrived in Lalish early. They were to witness the final ceremonies of Rozeh and Sinàn's week-long wedding. Here at last was an opportunity for Ashe to show his secretary why he was so entranced by the place and the people to whom it was sacred. For Karla, it was a chance to take a fresh look at the man she admired and who never failed to irritate her slightly. It was also an opportunity to acquire a new, oriental wardrobe. Karla looked dazzling in her drifting turquoise and sky-blue abbaya. Ashe was only concerned that with her golden-blond hair, let down for the occasion, she might appear to upstage the princess.

Princess Laila had been attending to Rozeh. Rozeh's wedding rituals had begun at her new home in Bashiqa over a week before Ashe's arrival. There, following a hot bath, Rozeh's friends had adorned her hands with henna. Having donned a red veil, Rozeh had then fastened a belt about her virgin waist with a special, large buckle, brought to her by Princess Laila, her Sister of the Hereafter. Rozeh had then been set on a horse that carried her from Bashiqa to Lalish, to the groom's temporary apartment above the Sanctuary Guesthouse. The apartment had been lent for the occasion by Sinàn's relative, the Mir – or Prince – of the Yezidis who was away on urgent business in Germany. Himself pondering whether or not to leave the country, Sinàn had not yet found the right place to set up a household.

Rozeh had arrived on horseback at Lalish's Sanctuary Guesthouse carrying some *berat*: earth from a holy shrine, rolled with the spittle of the Sheykh of the Adani clan into a ball. The Adani Sheykh, who presided over the nuptial agreement, had given her this prized token in exchange for gifts to himself and Rozeh's *Pir*, or spiritual guide. Having helped Rozeh dismount, Laila had handed Rozeh a jar of sweetmeats, a role normally reserved for the bride's future mother-in-law. Alas, Sinàn's mother had not lived to see the happy day. Rozeh had then smashed the sweetmeats against the threshold of her 'new home'. As Rozeh had entered the house, a sheep was slaughtered. Rozeh had then been led into the aromatic bridal chamber, veiled by an Adani Sheykh and by her Pir.

Later that night, Sinàn had been brought to the bridal chamber by his Brother of the Hereafter. The 'Brother' and two friends had guarded the door while the marriage was consummated. Afterwards, the friends had been invited in to share some food. Following the consummation, Rozeh had begun a seven-day period of silent seclusion in the bridal chamber.

Throughout the week that followed, Lalish had joyed in sporadic dancing, as relatives and friends toasted the couple and invited the blessings of God and His Angels upon them. Now on this, the seventh day of the seclusion, the bride would leave the room for a final, simple ceremony. To this ceremony, the English visitors had been invited.

Ashe joined Sinàn for a short walk among the mulberry bushes and oak trees on the slopes of Mount Erefat above the Sanctuary of Sheykh Adi.

'You look splendid, Sinàn.'

'Traditional clothes. I borrowed the silk jacket and trousers from the Mir. The jewellery comes from… many years ago. Strange how things turn out, Dr Ashe.'

'Destiny, Sinàn, that's all. *Kismet.*'

'I was thinking… Had Laila succeeded in getting Rozeh on to your plane at Mosul all those months ago, my bride and I would never have met.'

'Rozeh wanted to be a doctor. It was important to her.'

'I will help.'

'Don't you want your wife at home, like those who wore your clothes before you?'

'What Rozeh believes is right, is right for me. I want to thank you again for honouring your word and bringing the Baba Sheykh back to us.'

'I'm sorry it didn't work out.'

'No! What happened was the unbreakable will of the sheykh. It is a sin against God to stop the true will of another.

'Also, you should know, the sheykh was very ill. Baba was dying, even when we were in Germany. His heart. He gave too much of it to his people. Tell me, Toby Ashe, will you see his speech is published?'

'I'll do my best.'

'You are a friend of the Yezidi people.' Sinàn bowed to Ashe.

'A great honour, Sinàn.'

Ashe gazed down to the conical *qubbe* that dominated the roof of the sanctuary below them. 'I only wish I'd been born a Yezidi.'

Sinàn laughed. 'Forgive me, but that is very foolish! I must go now and prepare myself. And, look, here is your beautiful secretary lady! And, Dr Ashe, remember – you are not married!'

Sinàn made his way back down the slopes, pausing to bow before Karla on his way down. Ashe called after him. 'No, Sinàn, but *she* is!'

'What were you shouting down the hill, Toby?'

'Oh, nothing. Just good luck.'

'What a charming young man the doctor is! I'm sure you could learn something from him.'

'Listen to that, Karla! Listen! In the valley. The *daff* and *shebab*.'

'The what?'

'Tambour and flute. The *qewwals* are singing again. And they're lighting the shrines. See, the *feqirs* use olive oil from the mountains. They slap the oil on the sides of walls. Quite magical.'

Karla and Ashe sat down on the ground, Ashe's arm round Karla's shoulders.

'It's perfect. Even overcast as it is.'

'That's how I like it, Karla. Far away from the world and enclosed like a jewel, lit only by its inner fires.'

'Still a romantic, aren't you? Even after all you've seen.'

He was quiet for a moment. 'I wonder what Melissa would think of all this.'

'Why don't you ask her?'

Ashe gave Karla a hug, then got up and headed down into the flame-kissed valley. Karla shook her head in mock disgust, got up and patted her damp bottom, wondering if among the trees and the echoing music she might find herself a sheykh of her own.

114

'Come now, Tobbi. Come before the older guardians arrive. They will not permit outsiders to enter the sacred place.'

Princess Laila led Ashe to the left of the Shrine of Sheykh Hesen. He remembered his last visit: how he had stared at the little door, knowing he should go through it; knowing his life would be different if he did. He remembered how Major Richmond had urged him to leave well alone, not to offend his hosts.

Destiny. This was a special door. And now it was being opened to him. A few steps led down to a small cave, lit by tiny olive-oil flames. Laila and Ashe crouched down, easing their way through a narrow tunnel.

They emerged into a spacious cave.

From the northern, natural wall of the sanctuary, water gushed forth from the rock. This was the Zemzem, the sacred brook of Lalish, another miracle of the Sufi saint, Sheykh Adi. He had tapped the stone with a stick – like Moses in the wilderness. Except this was no wilderness; this was a place of miracles.

Laila, eager, wide-eyed, turned to Ashe. 'You can wash your hands in the stream and your sins will be forgiven.'

'Let's do it together.'

In the waters, each washed the other's hands. Their fingers found each other's fingers and they held hands and beheld each other's faces.

'Yezidis cannot marry outside of their people, can they, Laila?'

'Marriages are made in heaven, Tobbi.' She gripped his hand tightly. 'And is not Lalish heaven on earth?'

The waters splashed down onto the rock and, after a few metres, disappeared once more under the sanctuary walls, emerging on the other side in a narrow gunnel leading to the guesthouse. A group of Rozeh's young friends laughed and gossiped as they washed their pans and dishes in the sacred spring water.

Guests were gathering outside the Sanctuary Guesthouse. Ashe and Laila made their way over to Sinàn, waiting apprehensively for Rozeh to emerge from her seven days of silent seclusion.

'Ah, Toby! There is something I wanted to tell you this morning, but I could not bring myself to say it.'

Sinàn took Ashe's arm and walked him over to the pergola in the corner of the courtyard where the Baba Sheykh had last conversed with his people.

'I realised what you meant, when you said you wished you had been born a Yezidi. You meant that you wanted to be able to marry my sister.'

Ashe wished neither to give offence nor to reveal his feelings.

'Don't be ashamed, Toby Ashe. But it is the law. And we have special laws telling us whom we can marry. Have you not wondered how I, of the Chol royal family, can marry Rozeh, the daughter of a man and woman who ran a shop in Mosul?'

'The thought had occurred to me.'

'Then I tell you a secret that only you and my closest family know. Guard it forever with your life. It means you are the friend of the Yezidis, and the Yezidis are your friend. Do you want to know?'

'Yes.'

'The Baba Sheykh told me many things on our travels. Many wonderful stories. Some happy. Some sad. He told me how he lost a son – his only son – in the war with Iran. I could never tell him that this was the work of al-Qasr. It would have destroyed

Baba Sheykh completely. But he told me that when he knew his son was gone, he hardly knew himself. In the strange times that enveloped him, he had a little adventure. A romance with a lady. A lady from his clan. And she had a little girl. And the girl was given—'

'To the childless couple in Mosul!'

'This is my Rozeh, of the Fekhr el-Dîn branch of the Shemsani sheykhs!'

'The line goes on!'

'Let us hope so.'

Sinàn looked to the stairs in the corner of the guesthouse hall. 'Now she comes!'

Rozeh appeared, radiant and shy, from the shadows. Laila walked forwards out of the sanctuary with a large bowl of porridge made from seven types of grain. The princess led the procession down through the valley, accompanied by music, singing and dancing. The procession passed by the shrine of Sheykh Shems and continued up onto the slopes of Mount Meshet.

They arrived by the banks of the stream where the Baba Sheykh had hurled himself to his immortality. The banks were strewn with flowers. The bride and groom plunged their hands into the great bowl carried by Laila, throwing seven handfuls of the porridge into the waiting stream.

Sinàn and Rozeh then jumped over the stream, and everyone cheered. The bowl was handed over to the bride, who shared the contents with her friends while tambour, flute and song graced the mountainside.

Ashe heard a whisper in his ear: the deep voice of Laila, the Magdalene of his life who opened once more the jar of his heart.

'They say the stream flows under all of the Middle East, even unto Mecca. It is always there—'

'Even though men don't see it.'

115

A familiar figure stood on the other side of the well-wishing stream. A bony, gnarled, barefoot stick: Ranald Crayke was waiting.

'Will you cross the stream with me, Laila?'

'This one you must do alone.'

Ashe leapt over the stream and grabbed Crayke's sinewy arm.

'Fancy a walk, Ashe?'

Ashe nodded.

'Sorry I missed the dancing.'

'There's plenty to come, sir.'

'Indeed.'

The men made their way back into the valley.

'This has been quite an operation, Ashe. I have watched you grow with pride.'

'Thank you, sir. I only wish I could have brought things to a prettier conclusion.'

'Goodness me, no! You have served well.'

'Still something that puzzles me, sir.'

'Proceed.'

'The Tower bombing. Who did it?'

'I am here to enlighten, dear boy. Thanks to your memory returning of that fateful day, we were able to follow up your "green prophet" story.'

'And?'

'Prepare for a surprise, Ashe.'

'I'm prepared.'

'All done by an Englishman.'

Ashe's brain froze, then melted. '*The green prophet*—'

'Operates more prosaically under the name Colin Firman. Currently under psychiatric custody. Turns out Firman had been living rough in Broxbourne Woods for months. Ex-SAS. Had a grudge against the brigadier.'

'Some grudge!'

'His story will interest you. An explosives expert, Firman was badly wounded when undercover in Iraq before the first Gulf War. They have a code about getting bodies back wherever possible, but Firman's comrades never came to help him. What Firman didn't know was that his comrades were dead, their bodies disposed of... so he thought he had been abandoned. As if this wasn't bad enough, Firman was captured and subjected to medical experiments by—'

'Al-Qasr?'

'Right. Firman escaped during the 1992 bombing raid that destroyed the Baba Sheykh's son's remains. Found his way back to Britain and had himself committed into a psychiatric hospital, suffering from partial amnesia and severe psychological disorders. Poor chap's brain had been tampered with. Anyhow, he claimed to have developed spiritual powers of prophecy, listening to God and so on. Says he had this message from a higher power that the Tower of Babel was being rebuilt.

'After years of treatment, it finally looked as though Firman was responding positively to new medication. Coming out into what has been euphemistically called "care in the community", Firman found a home of sorts in Broxbourne Woods. One day he saw the Tower at Admiral Whitmore's house, and got strange ideas. What clinched the matter for him was seeing the brigadier and other senior military and naval figures there. The Tower became in his mind an affront to God, and Firman became the angel of vengeance.'

'And Reynolds?'

'The admiral's butler – something of a lost soul himself

– befriended Firman. Reynolds let Firman into the Tower to share food and drink, domestic supplies, and reminisce about service life. All against the rules, of course. After Firman's bomb went off, Reynolds immediately connected the explosion to Firman, whom he was fascinated by. Seems they'd discussed explosives and suchlike. Firman had asked him if he'd ever felt like blowing up his superior officers. Reynolds blamed himself for what happened and went to ground in Scotland. Forensics found his fingerprints on the sheets of paper used so threateningly by Firman. Once Special Branch tracked him down, Reynolds led us to Firman's woodland burrow: a remarkable underground complex.'

'A reflection of himself perhaps.'

'Quite.'

Ashe sighed. 'So the archdeacon was really another of al-Qasr's victims.'

'Indirectly, yes. Makes you think, doesn't it, Ashe?'

Ashe tried to see the funny side. 'Must have been something about the Tower that attracted Oddballs...'

'That's the ticket, Ashe! Cheer up! If you're sad, it's because you hoped for too much too soon. Forgive me for saying so, but I'd say you're still labouring under the impression that our work is about finding the truth.'

'That's one of the attractions, sir.'

'Wrong, Ashe. The greater part of our work is deception.'

'*Deception*? That's one word for it.'

'Listen, then forget. For quite a while there have been high-level attempts in Europe to counter those elements in the Turkish military that oppose entry into the EU and, where possible, to encourage progressive movements in Turkey. The Koglu and Aslan types are only two extreme aspects of resistance to progress.'

'*Progress?* Those men loved their country!'

'They loved an idea of it. And not a very nice idea when you get to know about it.'

'And what business is that of ours?'

'Ours is not to reason why, Ashe. Fortunately, we have the willing help of courageous people like Yildiz and Yazar, who also, if I may say so, love their country.'

'Yildiz and Yazar – working for you?'

Crayke smiled. 'Not exactly working for us, no. Common interests. In their hearts they work for Turkey's future, and their own. They got wind of curious goings-on concerning Colonel Aslan. They knew about his skills and the reputation he'd earned from his career with special forces in the eastern provinces. Aslan, in turn, being nothing less than brilliant, began to look into Yildiz and Yazar, suspecting they knew something about his activities on the Turkey–Iraq border. To Aslan, they were a threat, and as far as he was concerned, that made them a threat to Turkey.

'You, dear Ashe, served Aslan's purpose well. He manipulated the intelligence, and got you to pursue the two men through Iraq. This gave Aslan additional clout with the MIT, Turkey's National Intelligence Organisation, though Aslan's colleagues in Turkish security needed little encouragement to see Yildiz and Yazar as threatening to Turkey.

'Had Zappa located Yildiz and Yazar when you were first in Iraq, he was under instructions to protect them from MIT harassment.'

'So I was never going to be allowed to meet them?'

'Of course not. Aslan could have got hold of them through you. Unfortunately, MIT got closer to Yildiz and Yazar than you did. As MIT closed in, Zappa helped Yildiz and Yazar flee to Germany. And MIT in Iraq vented their frustration on poor Vincent Zappa, as you may recall. At this point, you'd used up most of your usefulness to Aslan, but not to me. Aslan eventually tracked Yildiz and Yazar back from Germany to Istanbul, where he had them arrested and interrogated. Now, thanks in part to your activities, they have been released, and in some respects we're back where we started.'

Ashe sat down outside the Sanctuary Guesthouse and stared at the ancient, human-sized relief of the black serpent that guarded the sanctuary door. Crayke observed Ashe's fascination. 'Beautiful isn't it?'

'Looks pretty damn black to me. In fact, everything does.'

'*Unenlightened*, Ashe! Until you see that black serpent as a radiant angel, you've seen nothing.'

'Then I've seen nothing.'

'Wrong again. Yours is the darkness before the dawn.'

'Is it always as black as this?'

'Look, Ashe, there are jobs we'd rather not do. Be in no doubt that your friend Aslan was a better man than those who gave me – and you – your orders.'

Ashe smiled. 'Yes… *Aslan*.' He gathered up some dirt from the courtyard stones, spat on it, and rolled it in his hands. 'It's a pity, really' – he flicked the unholy *berat* into the courtyard air –'that he's an Oddball.'

Crayke caught the ball of dirt and crumbled it between his fingers. 'Takes one to know one. Ready?'

Ashe nodded, pulled himself together, and left the Market of Mystical Knowledge for a more common market, and home.

Select Bibliography

Drower, E. S., *Peacock Angel, Being some Account of Votaries of a Secret Cult and their Sanctuaries* (John Murray, London, 1941)

Guest, John S., *The Yezidis – A Study in Survival* (Routledge & Kegan Paul, London, 1987)

Joseph, Isya, *Devil Worship: The Sacred Books and Traditions of the Yezidis* (Kessinger Reprints, 2005; originally published 1919)

Kreyenbroek, Philip G., *Yezidism – Its Background, Observances and Textual Tradition*, Texts and Studies in Religion, Vol. 62 (The Edwin Mellen Press, Lewiston, Queenston, Lampeter, 1995)

Robinson, James M. (ed.), *The Nag Hammadi Library* (E. J. Brill, Leiden, 1984)

Spät, Eszter, *The Yezidis* (Saqi Books, London, 2005)

Acknowledgements

I should like to thank the following for their authoritative assistance in researching the background to this novel: Simon Carpenter, Adrian Cassar, Tuvia Fogel and Flavio Barbiero.

Anthony Cheetham, Laura Palmer, Lucy Ridout and Tom Webber provided greatly appreciated, expert publishing and editorial commitment. My heartfelt thanks to all of you at Head of Zeus.

Details of the mythical Hemlock Club derive from *The Scrutinies of Simon Iff* by Aleister Crowley (Teitan Press), edited by Martin P. Starr.

I am grateful to Patricia Churton, Michael Embleton, Philip Wilkinson, and to my agent, Fiona Spencer Thomas, for checking the manuscript.